GUARDED

by Dominique Wolf

ISBN: 978-0-620996-13-6

Published by Dominique Wolf
Formatting by Bob Houston eBook Formatting
Editing by Four Aces Media
Assistant proofreader: Miguel Pregueiro
Cover design by Dominique Wolf (Picture supplied through Canva
    ProLicense by peeterv from Getty Images Signature)

*To all the women in my family that have taught me what it means to be strong and independent. If you're reading this, it's time to close the book now. If you don't, enter at your own risk, and we will **not** be talking about this at family gatherings.*

PLAYLIST:

- ♫ "I Wanna Be Your Slave" by Maneskin
- ♫ "Clandestina (feat. Emma Peters)" by Filv
- ♫ "23" by Maluma
- ♫ "That Way (feat. Jeremy Zucker)" by Tate McRae
- ♫ "Otra Noche Sin Ti" by J Balvin, Khalid
- ♫ "TKN" by Rosalía, Travis Scott
- ♫ "Talking Body" by Tove Love
- ♫ "Hola" by Miguel Pregueiro
- ♫ "Friends" by Chase Atlantic
- ♫ "Animals" by Maroon 5
- ♫ "Close" by Nick Jonas, Tove Love
- ♫ "Youngblood" by 5 Seconds of Summer
- ♫ "Hurts So Good" by Astrid S
- ♫ "Exile" by Taylor Swift, Bon Iver
- ♫ "Caught In A Lie" by The Hics
- ♫ "On Our Knees (feat R.O)" by Konoba
- ♫ "I'll Make You Love Me" by Kat Leon
- ♫ "Cold" by Lee Cole
- ♫ "Saturday Nights" by Khalid
- ♫ "Maps" by Maroon 5
- ♫ "I Can't Carry This Anymore" by Anson Seabra
- ♫ "Billie Bossa Nova" by Billie Eilish

PROLOGUE:

"*S*enhor Neves,*"* the arrogant man just shy of thirty said as he took a seat on the chair across from João Neves. "What seems to be the problem here?"

Unsettled, João cleared his throat, trying to regain his composure as a confident man who could stand his ground, even though the fear was eating at him from the inside out.

"Antonio, your father and I had an agreement," João said, leaning his hand on the back of his leather chair. He needed something to keep him balanced as the piercing black eyes of Antonio burned into him. He had expected to see Antonio's father, but Duarte Nazario never handled things like this. It was beneath him. He sat on his throne, barking orders at the men in his ranks as they handled his dirty work. From the years of being stuck in business with the Nazarios, João was well aware of how things operated within that family.

"We agreed that you could use the hotel as a front and go about your business but selling drugs from the hotel was never part of the original agreement," João said.

Antonio clasped his hands together, resting on his lap. A look of pure boredom had settled on his face as he looked over at the older man. Impulsive and apathetic - Antonio was often one of the most feared men in the rankings of the Nazario family. Being the eldest son, he seemed to have absorbed all the necessary traits needed from his father. He certainly didn't care for complaints such as this one. If they decided to change their original agreement, they would do it because who would stop them? No one had managed to even infiltrate their family in the slightest. They operated in the shadows, leaving nothing but headlines in their wake. Notorious for how they cemented themselves as the backbone of Portuguese society, the Nazarios had their fingers in every pie, and no one had dared to stand up to them. Not even when men were dropping like flies on their doorsteps. If someone got in their way, that earned them a target on their back, and the only way to get rid of it was when they hit the bullseye.

And they never missed.

"João, this hotel was agreed to be a front for our businesses. Let's just say that we have recently expanded, and this is now part of the agreement," Antonio explained.

João eyed the door of his office. The only way out was through there, and the last thing he wanted was to be trapped in here with someone as ruthless as Antonio. One wrong move, and he would put a bullet in your head.

"But your men are selling heroin and cocaine to my guests." João shook his head. "I can't in good faith stand by and let that happen."

"That's exactly what you're going to do." Antonio brought himself to his feet. "You're going to stand by and mind your own fucking business because if you don't, we can easily replace you."

"This is my hotel."

"And you owe my father how much money?" Antonio challenged.

João clenched his jaw, refusing to say anything further on the debt that had gotten him in this position in the first place. Inheriting the hotel from his father was his saving grace at the time. However, it was proving more and more difficult to get himself out of the corner he had been backed into, thanks to the looming amount owed to this notorious family.

"Two million?" Antonio continued. "Or was it three million euros?"

João remained silent.

"Unless you can give that money to me right now, I suggest you stay out of our way." Antonio reached for his gun and pulled it out from underneath his shirt. "Or we can sort this out right now."

He lifted the gun and pointed it at João, whose airways had since constricted his breathing as the fear of staring down the barrel of a firearm crawled across his skin.

He lifted his hands. "Antonio, I don't want any problems."

"And yet, you're continuously getting in my way," he snapped.

"*Desculpe,*" João surrendered. "But you have to understand tha-that this is dangerous." His mouth was dry as he continued. "There are young people - even children - that stay at this hotel. I have to protect their interests."

Antonio rolled his eyes and cocked his gun. "Doesn't sound to me like you're minding your own business. It sounds like you're trying to stop ours, and do you know what we do to people who get in our way?"

Tension hung thick in the air as João stared at the gun. He was paralyzed, thinking about all he had done to get himself into this position. He was looking out for his family. He was trying to save his daughter. That was all he had ever wanted. A dull ache pulsed in his chest as he thought of her and all they had lost. He refused to allow any more loss in the family. For years he had been pushed around as this debt hung over his head. He did questionable things and stood by while the most dangerous men in Portugal dictated what could and could not be done in his hotel. He was an accomplice to all they had done, and he had reached boiling point. While he expected the fear to continue as he stared at the gun, he was surprised by the deep anger that presented itself instead.

"You've been a thorn in my side, *Senhor Neves.*"

Without thinking, João walked around the desk, slowly and carefully watching Antonio's moves before he stopped in front of him. He was tired of being pushed around, but he knew this was a losing game.

"*Desculpe, Antonio,*" he repeated, extending his hand as a sign of surrender.

Antonio eyed his hand, a puzzled look in his eye as he tried to decode what João was truly doing. There was no trust between these two men, and there never would be.

"It's a shame that you borrowed all that money from my father, and you still couldn't even save your daughter," Antonio muttered.

João flicked his eyes to meet Antonio's, a deep rage burning in them as a chord was struck at the mention of his daughter. No one had dared stir up that conversation.

"If you're not careful, you might not be able to save your other one either."

Something snapped inside of João, and in a movement of swift bravery, he reached for the gun that Antonio still had pointed at him. Thankfully, he had caught him off guard, and nothing but rage fuelled João's movements as he had Antonio struggling for the gun.

"*Caralho!*" Antonio shouted as João kneed him in the stomach, causing him to double over and let go of his gun. João fumbled at it but used his other hand to steady the gun as he pointed it at Antonio. He was shaking, but there was no going back now. He had succumbed to his emotions and would later regret what happened next.

Antonio laughed. "And what do you think you're going to do, João? You going to shoot me? You'll be dead before you even have the chance to leave this office. And that bitch wife and daughter of yours will be next."

"*Calar a boca!*" João shouted. "Don't you dare speak of my family. You have no right!"

"You brought this on yourself," Antonio spat. "Your daughter is dead, and it's all your fault."

"*Eu disse para te calares!*" João shouted, his throat burning.

"You don't have the guts to do it." Antonio eyed the gun as he stepped forward, forcing it between his eyes. "You don't have the stomach for this, *cabrão*. You're too weak. You always have be-"

João Neves nestled a bullet between Antonio's eyes before he got a chance to finish his sentence. He dropped to the floor, blood spilling from his head.

Frozen in time, João replayed all that had gotten him to this point, and a deep regret settled inside of him, consuming every part.

"What have I done?"

CHAPTER 1:

24 HOURS EARLIER

Milena

"**M**ilena Neves, you march yourself upstairs right now and get changed," my mother ordered. "You are *not* wearing that dress!"

"Yes, I am," I retorted.

"You can't even call that piece of material a dress!" She huffed and turned to call for my father. "Please come and tell your daughter that she's dressed like a hooker."

I rolled my eyes and turned to examine my appearance in the large mirror we had downstairs. *What the hell was she going on about?* This is a perfectly normal cocktail dress. Sure, it was shorter than she may have expected as it sat more than halfway up my leg, but it was summer, for crying out loud. To be fair, if I didn't have so much *junk in my trunk,* the dress probably would have been longer, but I didn't care. The tight black material clung to the curves of my body, and I loved it. The dress was a halter neck that had some material cut out where my cleavage could be on perfect display. I would usually shy away from wearing something this daring around my family, but I was feeling extra slutty tonight at the expense of my mother.

"Where did you even get that dress?" my mother asked, her judgemental gaze hardening. "It's that London fashion isn't it? You went to the UK, and now you dress like a whore."

"Whoa *Mãe!*" I turned to face her. "I'm not dressed like a whore. And even if I was, what's the problem?"

"The problem, Milena, is that your father has many of his business partners coming to the party tonight. Older business partners, might I add, and it's inappropriate for him to have his daughter walking around like that." She flung her hands around, gesturing to my dress. "You need to cover up."

I glared at her. "I don't need to do anything. I am wearing a perfectly normal dress, and if that makes them uncomfortable, then they're the ones with the problem, not me."

We held each other's gaze, neither one of us backing down. It was like looking in a mirror - if the mirror showed what we would look like when we were older. We were told our entire life how we were the splitting image of our mother.

"You're the only one told now. There's no 'we' anymore." I heard my sister's voice in my mind again, and she was right. It had been years since we were a 'we'.

"You're right, Carina. Desculpa, irmã."

And before you start thinking I'm crazy, no, I'm not. I just casually believe that my dead twin sister speaks to me in my mind. Perfectly normal, right?

Anyway, back to what I was saying. My mother and I - copy and paste. From our golden tan skin to our thick, dark brown hair to the dimple we both had in our chin. We were the same height and carried more curves in our hips and butt like a lot of other Portuguese women. The only difference between us was our eyes. She was blessed with beautiful light blue eyes, and I was stuck with my father's dark ones. Shit-colored eyes. That's what Carina had always said. I tried to argue with her, but it's difficult to do that when she was right. To be fair, they weren't always so bad. In the right light, they became a lighter, more golden color, but those moments were very far and few.

Our looks were where our similarities stopped. Other than that, we were nothing alike, and that was often exhibited in something as simple as our choice of clothing. I suppose I couldn't blame her for the way she thought. She had been hard-wired that way. Her upbringing was deeply rooted in conservative ways of thinking. The ways that believe a woman was meant to take care of her man in the most traditional sense. The ways in which women should cover up - *'Don't show your shoulders!'*; *'How dare your knees be on display?'*; *'Is that an ankle showing?'* - Blah blah blah. I couldn't care for that one bit. No one would tell me what to do or what to wear - especially not when the reasoning was due to what men would think. I didn't give a fuck.

"Are you two ready?" My father rushed downstairs, rolling the sleeves of his white button-up shirt up to his elbows. When it came to the similarities between my father and me, the dark eyes and lack of height pretty much summed it up. I had always thought that he carried his age well, but over the years, one could notice how the stress had taken up residence in the form of the wrinkles on his face. His dark hair had since sprouted gray around his ears, poking out from underneath the glasses he wore. He stopped at the bottom, his eyes peering over his glasses as his gaze landed on me and looked to my mother for help.

"Don't even bother." She rolled her eyes. "I've already argued with her about that cloth she calls a dress."

"I don't have time for this. We're already running late," my father snapped. I had always associated my father with authority. He had this ever-intimidating demeanor that I had often feared but growing up, he showed a softer side to Carina and I. In front of others, he put up the front, but I knew the real him. At least I used to. I can't say much about our non-existent relationship now.

"Good thing we're all ready to go then." I turned to my mother with a smug look on my face.

Milena - one. Francisca Neves - zero.

I loved my parents.

Of course, I loved them but more in a *I-have-to-because-they-are-my-parents* kind of way. After we lost Carina, everything changed, including every part of who I was. The sweet, innocent young girl I once was, was replaced with a hard-headed, sharp-tongued, cold, witty, stubborn woman, and that was quite the shock to my parent's system. It took years before they even realized, though. Once Carina was gone, it was like I had lost them too. I was forced to become self-sufficient and deal with my grief all by myself. We all had our ways of dealing, and unfortunately, that isolated us all. Instead of coming together to process what had happened, it forced a wedge between us, and after all this time, it still remained.

I was a twenty-three-year-old, independent woman with a clear understanding of who I was now, and truth be told, I often found myself wondering if my parents even liked me.

You'll be back home in no time.

*H*ome.

London. Not Algarve, where my family's home was. Where I was right now for the summer, I hadn't grown up here. We had moved from Lisbon to Algarve shortly after Carina's death. My grandfather passed away just shy of six months after her and left his hotel to his only son - my dad. From being someone who had never experienced loss, it seemed to snowball after that, and instead of becoming used to it - I shut it off. It was the only way for me to cope, and now there was absolutely no way I was going to allow any of that in. In the beginning, it was possible that we could get through this emotional turmoil. We would be there for each other as a family and with people constantly around, reassuring you that she was in a better place now - you could almost believe them. But once all that disappears. Once everyone left and it was just my parents and I, the distance and loss started to settle in. I was left with nothing but my thoughts for company and the new void that lived inside of me. So I did what I had to, to survive.

I was well aware that it wasn't the healthiest way to deal with my grief, but it was the way I had become most accustomed to, so there was no going back.

When my father came to own the *Villa Hotel, Algarve, l*et's just say that running that hotel became the most important thing to my parents. I assumed it was their own way of deflecting from the loss we were all experiencing. I did all I could to distract myself from the pain, too, instead of allowing it in, and now it was far too late to even think of visiting it again. As soon as I graduated, I took my chance to get out of Portugal. It was tainted with the memories of the family I once knew, and I couldn't handle being suffocated by that on the daily. I was better on my own anyway.

"Let's try and enjoy ourselves tonight, *sim?*" My father reached for my hand and my mother's. "Milena is back for the first time in months. The hotel is hosting a big summer party today. The weather is great. We have more to be happy about than not." His enthusiasm oozed pretense, but instead of instigating in some way as I usually would, I simply nodded.

"*Sim, meu amor.*" *M*y mother reached out and cupped his face. "*Vamos.*"

"*I'*m certainly looking forward to tonight," I said as I reached for my clutch bag on our kitchen counter. "Who doesn't love an open bar?"

I turned towards our front door without waiting for a reaction from my parents.

I needed a drink. Now.

***

"I didn't even know you were coming back for the summer," Aurora said, flicking her hair over her shoulder. "I thought you'd be kicking it up with the lifestyle of the rich and famous."

I rolled my eyes and slowly ran my index finger over the rim of my wine glass. "And leave you here to party alone? That would be cruel."

"You did it last year," she pointed out, arching her eyebrow at me as she lifted her own glass to her lips. "I get it. Hell, if I was you, I'd want to stay in London too. You know how much I hate this heat."

Truth be told, I never used to like Aurora. We met out of convenience when her parents were invited over to our house for dinner a couple of years ago, and she came along with them. Her father, Christopher, was looking at going into business with my father just after he inherited the hotel. It didn't work out for them in the professional space, but over time, I started to see Aurora in a social space a lot more, and I had, surprisingly, come to enjoy her company. Don't get me wrong, she was a complete bitch, but she credited that to her general distaste for people. I couldn't exactly fault her on that. They were pretty shitty sometimes. Years later, we continued to keep our friendship alive whenever I came to visit home. It was a friendship of convenience thanks to being in the same place at the same time. Outside of this, we hardly spoke. I was thankful she was here tonight, though, as the crowd was all new to me. I hardly recognized anyone here, so I stuck with who I knew.

And what I knew - the *what* being the alcohol from the bar. I leaned against the bar, lifting my glass to my lips. The white wine spilled onto my tongue, and I kept it for a moment, giving my palate a taste for it.

The bartender wandered back over to our side and smirked at me. "You need anything else, sweetheart?"

I would usually feel offended by the use of that word, but with his thick

British accent, I was actually flattered. It happened a lot when I first moved to London. Those accents had me hanging on every word. I took a moment to assess him. He was cute in a boyish kind of way. Dirty blonde hair, dark brown eyes against his tanned skin. He looked more like he spent his time on a surfboard than he did pouring drinks behind the bar. He flashed his brilliant smile, and I assumed he had women falling at his feet when he did that. I didn't mind it - it was a pretty good smile, but I was still figuring out exactly what I wanted from the night.

I decided not to rule him out just yet and battered my eyelashes at him. "Nothing yet, but I'm sure I'll think of something."

His eyebrow lifted, and the interest flashed clearly in his eyes. He took the cloth that was in his hand and flicked it to rest over his shoulder. "What's your name?"

"Milena."

"Nice to meet you, Milena. I'm Xavier."

I extended my hand over the bar, and he lifted it to his lips. A tad archaic, but I was impressed by his chivalrous ways.

"And I'm Aurora, thanks for asking," Aurora jumped in, placing her empty glass in front of Xavier. "I think I could do with a top-up, though 'cause this glass is looking pretty empty."

Xavier chuckled and grabbed Aurora's empty glass. "Of course, miss."

"Miss?" she scoffed. "How old do I look to you, *boy?*"

"Don't answer that," I advised Xavier before gesturing to her glass. He snickered before disappearing to top her up.

"He's not even your type," Aurora said dryly.

"My tastes could change." I shrugged.

She snorted. "Not possible."

"Fine." I caved. "He's not typically my type, but I can acknowledge there is a certain attractiveness to him, and that could work in my favor for tonight."

Xavier returned with Aurora's glass and handed it over to her. She gave him a fake smile and nodded as a thank you. Although she had changed over the years, she still had bitchy tendencies - if it's a part of who you are, it's very difficult to try and change.

Xavier turned his attention back to me. "I'm off in about an hour or two; if you're still around, then maybe we can get a drink?"

Straight to the point. I like it.

"Look out for me," I said.

"Oh, I will," he said before disappearing to the rowdy customers on the other side of the bar. I brought my glass back up to my lips as Aurora continued to eye me.

"What?" I asked.

"Nothing." She sipped on her own drink. "Have you noticed the amount of security your father has here tonight?" She glanced around the beach. "Seriously? You could have sworn he was hosting royalty here."

I turned to scan the area. I hadn't really paid it any attention, but she was right. Scattered across the beach and the area leading up to the hotel was filled with men in black suits. They didn't look like guests at all. Their white earpieces totally gave them away, and they all stood the same as if they were constantly on alert. Shoulders pulled back and continuously scoured the area.

"Weird," I murmured but made a mental note to ask my parents about it. Aurora opened her mouth to say something, but her eyes darted past me, and she froze for a moment before shifting her gaze back to mine.

"Incoming," she warned, and I turned to follow her gaze, which landed on the familiar figure I hadn't seen in months.

"Milena." He stopped between Aurora and me, slipping his hands casually in the pockets of his pants.

"Fabiano," I said dryly.

Fabiano and I broke up months ago after a brief stint of a relationship. He was textbook toxic with major commitment issues, and truth be told, I didn't like being tied down. I had been planning to break up with him for a while before I actually did. After I caught him hooking up with one of the waitresses, it just made that a whole lot easier. Objectively, I could acknowledge he still looked good. His dark hair had grown out as well as his beard since I had last seen him. He looked much older and still held that same intensity in his light eyes. The black button-up shirt he had on was rolled up to his elbows and complimented his dark skin perfectly. He may be a looker, but he was trash, and I had put that out months ago.

"*Estás bonita, a*s always." He leaned forward to kiss both my cheeks in the typical greeting. "Nice to see you again. And you Aurora."

He turned to her, and she just glared at him before turning back to me.

"You'll find me anywhere else but here."

And with that, she was gone, disappearing into the crowd. I couldn't blame her. If she had stayed, she probably would have thrown her drink in his face again, and I know how much she hates to waste alcohol.

"Just as friendly I see," he commented, taking the spot in front of me where Aurora stood. "It's nice to see you again."

"Mh-mm." I lifted my glass for another sip. I was going to need all the help I could get right now to endure this conversation.

"I'm sure you've been thinking about me."

I scoffed. "Haven't even crossed my mind."

"Milena," he said in a low voice. The way he would say my name was something I used to be hung up on, but now it just made my skin crawl. "You don't need to lie to me," he continued. "You can admit that you miss me."

I laughed. A loud, obnoxious laugh that was fuelled by pure disbelief. His arrogance had yet to sway, and it was laughable.

"This guy is quite the piece of work. I can't believe you even dated him," Carina's voice said in my mind.

"Don't judge. I did what I wanted at the time."

"You mean you did who you wanted."

I ignored her and turned my focus back to Fabiano.

"Miss you? Please." I rolled my eyes. "You didn't make as much of an impact as you seem to think."

He stepped closer to me, closing the proximity between us, causing a flicker of irritation. He was so close that I could smell that overused cologne of his. The woody-incense-like aroma entered my nose, bringing back all the times when we were together. I often found that scent on my clothes, and while I used to welcome it, now I was not a fan.

"Well, I've been thinking of you," he said.

"Good for you."

"And now that you're here, what better way to start our summer?" He reached out and rested his hand on my arm.

"What the hell are you talking about?" I pulled my arm from his grip. "You're not even supposed to be at this party."

"It's an open party, Milena. Anyone is allowed to be here."

"Yeah, but *you* have no business being here." I crossed my arms. "So, what do you want, Fabiano?"

He opened his mouth to speak but closed it, stopping to think for a moment. I lifted an eyebrow at him, waiting to see what bullshit answer he would come up with now.

"Can you seriously tell me that you don't miss us at all?" His eyes were begging for the answer he wanted to hear, but I couldn't deliver.

"Yes," I answered without hesitation. "I don't want to be with you, which I thought was pretty clear when I broke up with you."

"Yeah b-"

I interrupted him. "And do you remember why I did that?" I stepped closer to him, refusing to stand down, "I think it might have had something to do with the way you fucked that waitress on the bar."

"Good one."

*H*is jaw tightened. I thought I would feel something when I saw him again. I almost wished I had because often, I found myself thinking how unusual it must be to feel no emotions. I wasn't affected by things that would usually bother others. I had become a master of my emotions, and I would always be in charge of them. Or at least I had convinced myself I had that kind of control. I hadn't felt a flicker of anything real for years.

"This was fun, but you're wasting my time." I reached for my wine glass and turned to leave, but his hand grabbed my wrist.

"I'm not done saying what I need to say," he said.

"I don't care what you have to say." I tried to pull my arm from his grip, but he tightened it around me. "Fabiano, let go of me."

"You won't even give me a chance to explain myself," he retorted.

"Explain yourself?" I scoffed. "God, Fabiano. Move on. We went out for a few months; I'd hardly call that an epic love story."

I didn't love Fabiano. It was often difficult to categorize what we had as a relationship, but he had technically asked me to be his girlfriend. I was so caught up in the tension between us that I ignored all the major red flags waving in front of me.

"You're a heartless bitch, you know that?" he snapped.

I tried to pull my hand from his grip again, but he wouldn't budge. Before I could move or say anything further, a figure stepped from behind me and grabbed Fabiano's forearm.

"You're going to let her go right now," a deep, raspy voice said.

"Who the fuck are you?" Fabiano shouted, causing a few heads to turn in our direction. This guy was a fucking embarrassment. I turned to the figure towering over Fabiano right now. He must be one of my father's security for the evening as he had the same black suit on and an earpiece sticking out. Up close, I noticed his side profile that displayed a dark black beard with his strong jawline on display beneath it. It was clenched, and I swear he was going to break a damn tooth.

"I'm going to give you three seconds to remove your hand, or I'm going to do it for you, and that's not going to end well," the stranger said, his voice full of warning.

I looked down at his hand on Fabiano's arm, littered with tattoos. *Nice one.* Fabiano released my wrist, and I stepped away from him quickly. I refused to run away, though. I would not stand down when he was the problem here.

"You should leave, Fabiano," I told him.

"I'm not going anywhere."

The stranger stepped in front of me, stopping between Fabiano and I. He was much larger than Fabiano and holy hell, was he intimidating. He had that aura to him.

"Out. Now," he instructed. "Don't make me ask twice."

Fabiano glared at him before darting his eyes to me. "What, Milena? You can't even fight your own battles now."

"Fabiano, if you want me to fuck you up, I'll gladly show you what I can do," I said through gritted teeth. I could handle anything on my own. I didn't need anyone to do anything for me, and he knew that. He had struck a nerve because he wanted a reaction. For a moment, we just stood staring at each other before he finally turned and took off in the opposite direction. I turned to say thank you to the stranger, but I didn't need his help, but he had already stalked off in the same direction without even a glance back at me.

"Seriously?" I mumbled.

I didn't even get his name. I didn't have the opportunity for anything before he disappeared. *What the fuck was up with that?* I turned back to my glass and tilted my head, downing the rest of it before setting it back on the bar. Xavier appeared in front of me as I brought my head forward. "You okay?"

I nodded. "I could use a top-up, though."

"After that, I think you could use something stronger than wine."

I let out a small laugh. "You're right. I'll trust your judgment on what I should have next."

"On it." He smiled at me. "Don't move, sweetheart. I'm not done with you just yet."

He turned to get my drink for me. I glanced down at my wrist, which had a faint red mark around it. *Fucking asshole. T*hat guy was a piece of shit, and he clearly hadn't changed.

Now that he was gone and I was about to get a new drink, I had a new focus for the night. Get fucked up kind of drunk.

"Mãe e Pai aren't going to be happy with you if you're drunk again," Carina said.

"What they don't know won't hurt them," I answered.

Carina had always been the more responsible one. She was the one who gave our parents fewer hassles. She was always covering for me or warning me against most of the decisions I had always wanted to make. Carina was better in every way, and even though she had been gone for over five years now, that still hung over me - haunting me every step of my life.

"Xavier," I shouted. "Could you add a tequila shot too, please?"

"Coming right up!"

CHAPTER 2:

Milena

Xavier's arm snaked around my waist, pulling me closer to him to help me stand up straight. I had passed my intoxication check-point about three shots ago and now, the world was spinning.

"Come on, beautiful," he said as we started to walk together. "Now you're going to have to direct me to your place because I have no idea where I'm going."

A giggle bubbled on my lips. "Yo-you're taking me home?"

"I'm going to try."

I glanced up at him and he was already looking down at me. I leaned my head against his shoulder as we walked along the beach. I had kicked my heels off a while ago and I had no idea where I had left them. I also had no idea where Aurora disappeared to but she was very good at that. She was always on her own mission and I would usually only hear from her the next day, letting me know she was at least alive.

"I was having fun with you," I told Xavier who smiled, revealing an ever so slight crease in his cheek. He was cute. Not usually my type as we had already established but there was an attractiveness there and with the amount of alcohol in my system, it had since escalated. I would take what I could get right now. Drunk Milena always ended up wildly aroused.

The waves crashed against the shore as we continued in the direction towards my parent's house. I took a deep breath in, filling my lungs with the fresh night time air. I could practically taste the ocean's salt water on my tongue. I loved the ocean. I loved that even though it was widely intimidating, it could also be so peaceful. Some things should only be admired from a distance.

"Do you like the ocean?" I asked, randomly saying whatever thoughts or questions that entered my mind.

"I love it," Xavier answered, his hand resting against my waist.

"You look like a surfer."

He chuckled. "Is it that obvious?"

I nodded with a smile on my face. "You've just got that *thing* going on. It's cute."

He glanced down, cocking an eyebrow at me. "You think I'm cute?"

I pretended to think for a moment as I glanced up at him. He squinted his eyes playfully as he waited for what I was going to say next. "I think you're more than cute."

I stopped in my tracks, causing him to stop with me. I turned into him, resting my hands against his chest. I could already tell he was well-built just by the way his white shirt sat on his body.

"You okay?" he asked, his eyes full of wonder and slight concern.

Even though I could feel the alcohol pulsing through my body, I was over-aware of every little thing around me. I could still hear the music blaring in the distance from the party at the hotel. There was indistinct chatter around me with the small groups of people scattered across the beach. The moon glistened against the water that looked like it was moving ever so slightly - except for the waves that crashed against the shore, causing the water to creep closer and closer to where we stood. My feet were deep in the sand now, and even though I hated how it had made its way between my toes, it was the only thing keeping me anchored right now.

I felt Xavier's hand on my bare arm this time, bringing me back to the present moment with him. A small rush of unexpected desire pooled deep inside my stomach. It had been a while since I've had someone give my body what it needed - someone other than me, of course. Feeling Xavier's hand slowly moving up and down my arm, that was all I could focus on right now.

"Milena?" he said my name softly but with the intoxication, nothing could have sounded sweeter. I flicked my eyes up to meet his. There was definite interest behind them - there was no way he could stop me from noticing the way his eyes slightly darted over down my body before flicking up to meet mine again.

"Xavier, you've been really sweet to me this evening," I murmured. "Is that all you can be though?"

"What do you mean?"

I stepped closer, closing the proximity between us. "What if I don't need sweet right now?"

I didn't know what I was doing but the aroused part of my brain had taken over. I could hardly even say it was my brain actually. My body had taken over and it had a mind of its own. His eyes fell to my lips and I could feel him reciprocating my own interest. I didn't care who was around us. I just focused on the clear tension that seeped its way between us.

"Whatever you want, Milena, I'd give it to you," he said in a low voice. "Bu-"

Before he could continue, I wrapped my arms around him and my lips found his. He was soft and careful at first, but I didn't want that. I was never one for the polite, sweet way of being. If I was going to be handled, I needed it to be rough. I used my tongue to part his lips and nipped softly at his bottom lip, causing a deep groan in his throat as he wrapped his arms around my waist, pulling me closer to him. Desire coursed through my veins as he deepened the kiss. I couldn't think of anything but the way his hands felt on my body and his lips against mine. I didn't care that we were on a crowded beach. I just didn't care about any-

"Milena?!" I heard my name being shouted, which caused Xavier and I to jump apart. I turned in the direction of the voice, and my mother stood on the wooden walkway along the beach, her arms crossed.

"What the hell do you think you're doing?" she huffed, eyeing between myself and Xavier.

I rolled my eyes. "I think it's pretty clear what I was doing," I answered dryly. Her eyes darted back to an awkward Xavier, who looked to me for help. A flicker of irritation presented itself over our interruption. I was enjoying myself, thank you very much.

"Your father doesn't need you to be acting like this at his party."

"*Meu Deus, Mãe,* I was kissing him - not fucking him." The words left my mouth before I could stop them.

Her jaw dropped slightly as she glared at me. "Your mouth is filthy. You need to sort that out." She turned to Xavier. "Who are you anyway?"

"Uh," he fumbled, trying to gather himself before stepping forward and extending his hand. "Xavier, ma'am. One of the bartenders from tonight's event."

She politely shook his hand, but her face made it very clear she was less than impressed by finding him making out with me. Before our interruption, I was pretty much ready to do much more with him, but a beach was hardly the place for that.

"Well, Xavier," she started. "I don't think you were hired to feel up my daughter."

"Mãe!" I shouted, the embarrassment of her words settling over me. I turned to apologize to him but my mother cut in again.

"I hate to cut your little interaction short but you need to get home, Milena. Now," she instructed.

"Xavier's walking me home," I argued.

"Not anymore, he's not." She glared at me. "I don't want some stranger at home with my daughter."

I opened my mouth to argue but she lifted her hand, cutting me off. "Jerome will take you home."

She turned to gesture to him as he stood outside the car. He had been my father's driver for a couple years now so he was well acquainted when it came to the adventures of drunk Milena who often came out to play whenever I came home to visit. He had driven me back home many times when my mother would put me in the car after she had reprimanded me for whatever it was that I had done at the time. There was always something. Cue the eye roll as I knew I was in for an earful from her tomorrow.

"Home, Milena," my mother instructed. *"Agora."*

She turned on her heels and headed in the direction back to the party. I hated being scolded like a fucking child. If I wasn't feeling the alcohol as much as I was, I would have gone against exactly what she wanted from me. I turned to invite Xavier back to my house but he beat me to the punch.

"I'm going to head home," he said, glancing back in the direction of my mother.

"She's not coming back," I said dryly. "You don't have to leave now."

"I do. As much as I'd love to come home with you or have you come home with me, you're drunk, Milena and I don't want to take advantage of you when you're not in the right state of mind."

"I know what I'm doing, Xavier." I tightened my jaw in irritation.

He reached out and rested his hand on my arm. "Look, it's not that I don't want to because trust me, I do." His eyes darted down my body before flicking up to mine again. "But not like this."

I didn't want to head home alone, not with this annoying amount of arousal that had seeped into every part of my body. He was being a good guy, I knew that but fuck, that's not what I needed right now. I heard a whistle from Jerome's direction as he tried to get my attention. I rolled my eyes before turning back to Xavier.

"Well, it was fun while it lasted." I reached up and cupped his cheek. "You take care, Xavier."

"You too, sweetheart."

We said our final goodbyes and he turned in the direction back to the hotel. He was obviously only headed in this direction because of me. I sighed and turned back in Jerome's direction as he continued to gesture for me to come to the car. *Geez, calm down.* I took a deep breath in, the world now starting to spin again as I moved. I stepped onto the wooden walkway before stepping onto the gravel road of the parking lot, leading to where he stood.

"Jerome," I mumbled as he opened the door for me.

"Senhorita, Neves. Como está?" he asked as I stumbled to the car seat. *"Cuidado, Milena."*

I felt him come closer to me but I shooed him away. *"Estou bem, Jerome."*

*M*y body could no longer hold me up and next thing I knew, I was lying on the backseat. My right arm draped over my eyes as I waited for the world to stop spinning. The alcohol was unsettled inside of me now and I could feel it slowly working its way back to the surface. The car was moving now and I prayed that I could hold it together until I got home. Last thing I needed was my mother on my case about throwing up in Jerome's car - again.

"Do you need me to get you anything?" I heard Jerome ask.

I mumbled what I thought was a question about stopping to get food, but when he had to ask me to repeat myself, I had realized I wasn't going to be much help to myself right now.

"Nada. Just get me home, *por favor,"* I managed to get out before closing my eyes again, welcoming the darkness.

CHAPTER 3:

Vincenzo

I was not a morning person.

I never have been and I definitely wasn't going to be in a good mood when the way I was being woken up was due to my cell phone ringing with the incessant annoying ringtone. I jolted awake as the ringing pierced through me, causing a rise of irritation inside. I reached for it, not once lifting my head and my muscle memory of my screen allowed me to answer my phone and bring it to my ear without checking who it was.

"What?" I muttered, not caring who was on the other end of the line.

"Enzo, it's me," Carlos' voice came through the phone. "We have a situation."

"You're going to need to give me more information than that." I rolled over, still keeping my eyes closed as I needed some time to adjust to the light coming through my room.

"Dead body. One of the *Nazario* men."

The mention of the *Nazarios* caused me to sit up abruptly, giving myself no time to adjust to the morning. That name was not one you took lightly to hearing. How could you when they were one of the most infamous organized crime families in Portugal?

"What happened?" I asked.

"João Neves - we worked his party last night at the hotel, he needs us now for personal protection for him, his wife and his daughter."

"Who is responsible for the dead body?"

"João is. Drug dealing gone wrong - I don't know, some shit like that.

I'm still waiting to get the full story, but I'm on the way to get them now. They aren't all together. The daughter is at their family home."

"What do you need me to do?" I flicked the bed covers off me, turning to rest my feet on the floor next to the bed. Once I switched into work mode, I was ready to go.

"The daughter. You're responsible for her. You need to get her out of the house and come meet us. I will text you the address."

"On it." And with that, I disconnected the call.

I had worked a couple of jobs with Carlos in Italy when we were both hired as part of the protection of the minister of defense. Even though personal relationships weren't something that were advised within the unit, Carlos and I had an understanding and I had him to thank for the job I now had in Algarve. Once his contract was up, he came back to his home country and when I got a call from him a few days ago with a new opportunity, the timing couldn't have been better. I had been released from my own contract once a new minister was elected and truth be told, there was nothing left for me in Italy. Nothing except my grandmother, who hasn't recognised me for years now. Deciding to get her the care she needed wasn't an impulse decision. I tried my best, for the longest time, I tried but in the end, it was what was best for her. I lived paycheck-to-paycheck to ensure she continued to get the best care. She was all I had left. Even if she didn't know it herself. I was left with nothing but the memories of all that I had lost.

I had taken my first job in personal security for a famous actress in Romania and whenever opportunities would arise, I would often sway towards the ones outside of my home country. *Thanks Nonna for the Romanian-language lessons. M*y grandparents raised me and my grandmother taught me languages as her way of distracting me from dealing with the loss of my parents. Their mixed heritages helped me learn Italian, Portuguese, Romanian, English, and a tad bit of Spanish. In the long run, I was thankful for the additional language skills. It allowed me the opportunity to seek jobs outside of Italy. I loved the country - it was beautiful but it reminded me of all that I had lost since my parents were taken from me.

My phone buzzed with the address from Carlos as well as a link to more information on the daughter. The more you knew about the person you were hired to protect, the better. That way it avoided any surprises and allowed one to do the best job possible. I clicked the link and the first thing I noticed when her picture loaded was that I had met her last night. Well, met was a bit of a stretch. I helped her get rid of that piece of shit that was harassing her by the bar. I hadn't put two-and-two together since all the pictures that were given to us previously of the Neves family, including Milena Neves, were youthful, innocent looking ones, and that was the furthest thing from how she looked last night. Objectively, I could acknowledge that she was a breathtaking beauty. Subjectively though, there was no place for that in this line of work. Number one rule was to never develop personal relationships. The goal was pretty simple - protect her. Nothing more, nothing less.

Within minutes, I had managed to pack up what I needed and get dressed, ready to go and find Milena Neves.

CHAPTER 4:

Milena

I am never drinking again.

That was the only thought that entered my mind when I woke up with a throbbing headache behind my eyes that reminded me it was alcohol-induced.

And completely self-inflicted.

I groaned as I slowly rolled over, careful to open my eyes as slowly as possible to avoid the bombarding light seeping into my room. The sun was shining bright, reminding me that it was one of the things I needed to avoid today if I didn't want to keep feeling like absolute shit. No bright lights. No loud sounds. I needed to stay in my hole of darkness until this hangover had punished me enough.

But what a time I had last night.

I smiled to myself as my eyes slowly fluttered open, adjusting to the light around me. Last night's party had been a surprisingly great way to be welcomed home (minus the Fabiano part) and I couldn't stay mad at myself for the amount of alcohol I had consumed. I remembered partying on the dancefloor with Aurora before she disappeared. I remembered Xavier and the countless amount of shots he and I consumed together. I remembered our kiss. I also remembered my mother completely cock-blocking me and the fact that I was probably in for quite the lecture today for my behavior last night. I reached for my phone and squinted to see the time.

Seven-thirty.

I had half-expected to sleep the day away, but my internal alarm clock would never allow me to sleep past eight. I placed my phone back down and closed my eyes, focusing on nothing but the constant throbbing. There was a lingering nausea hovering over me, just waiting for the perfect moment to strike. I compartmentalized my plan.

Step one - get out of bed without falling over.

Step two - make it downstairs without throwing up.

Step three - find headache tablets.

I slowly swung my legs over the side of my bed and brought my body up, still keeping my eyes closed. I took a deep breath in and opened them, this time adjusting to the light much quicker than before. My feet touched the wooden floors of my room as I stood up. I glanced down and noticed I was in nothing but my underwear from the night before. A quick scan of the room revealed my dress on the floor in the corner. I didn't even remember coming home last night. The last thing I remembered was getting into Jerome's car, but I had always been surprisingly good at making it to my bed in one-piece, no matter the amount of alcohol I had consumed. I made my way over to my set of drawers against the wall and yanked open the top one, reaching for an oversized shirt. I pulled it over my body and closed the drawer.

Step one was successful. Now on to step two.

I opened the door of my room, it scraped against the floor the way it always did as I strolled outside. The house was silent. I wasn't even sure if my parents were home but it certainly didn't sound like there was anyone else here but me. I rested my hand against the railing as I made my way downstairs, slowly and one step at a time. I counted step two as a mini-victory as I strolled into the kitchen. Surprised to see that not even our housekeeper, Cecilia, was here this morning.

Strange.

I can't remember the last time the house had ever been this empty.

"Cecilia?" I shouted, immediately regretting it as the headache throbbed again.

"Fuck, okay - no shouting then," I muttered to myself as I walked over to the cupboard where we kept all our medicine. I ruffled through it until I pulled out a box of headache tablets.

"Bingo." I popped two in my hand and grabbed a glass before heading to the fridge to fill it with some cold water. I washed the tablets down and turned to lean against the kitchen counter. A piece of white paper caught my eye. I leaned over and reached for it, glancing down at my mother's handwriting.

Your father and I have some business to sort out in Lisbon. We will be in touch. Try not to burn the house down while we're gone.

I rolled my eyes at my parent's lack of faith. You set a fire once and suddenly they treat you like a serial arsonist. Whenever my parent's referenced what happened that night, there was no way to stop the guilt that washed over me. I had never meant to do it but it happened and nothing had been the same since then. I refused to give into where my mind was headed so instead, I went back to ignoring it. I left the note on the counter and made my way back upstairs. The headache tablets would, hopefully, start working their way through me soon and after a nice, hot shower I was convinced I would be as good as new. While I was aware that a cold shower would be more effective, I was not insane and needed the heat, no matter the weather. I strolled into my en-suite bathroom and went to turn the shower on. Stopping in front of the large mirror I had in front of my basin, I saw my appearance for the first time and came to the conclusion that I looked like death. I leaned forward, looking at how my makeup from the night before was still on my face but not at all where it was supposed to be. My eyeliner had smudged, and I would definitely be compared to a raccoon of some sort.

"Milena, this is not your best look," I said to myself before turning away from my reflection.

I pulled my shirt over my head, my underwear following as the steam surrounded the bathroom. I stepped into the shower, closing the door behind me, and allowed the hot water to hit my body. I took a deep breath in, soaking in the feeling. I leaned my head back, allowing the water to work its way through my hair. For those few moments, I was calm. I reveled in it. I reached for my face wash and made sure to get rid of the monstrosity that was last night's look. I took some shampoo and conditioner through my hair next. As I leaned my head back to wash out the excess product in my hair, I heard it.

A loud crashing sound from downstairs made me jerk my head forward. I froze for a moment, trying to focus my attention on the sound but all I could make out was the water hitting against the floor. I turned the tap off and reached for the towel, wrapping it around my body as I stepped outside.

Tiptoeing through my room, I heard movement downstairs and a sudden, unexpected, fear washed over me, warning me that something felt wrong. I slowly reached for my door handle but before I could yank it open, my door was already pushed towards me and a large figure stepped inside.

"What th-" my sentence was cut off as large arms grabbed me, a hand covering my mouth as he pulled me further into my room, kicking the door closed before doing so. I attempted to scream, but all that came out was a muffled sound against his hand. The fear settled over me, and I felt my throat tighten. I couldn't think straight so I did the only thing I could - I bit the hand.

"Fuck!" A familiar deep, raspy voice muttered as he pulled his hand away. My back was up against his body, and I couldn't make out who he was but as I tried to escape from his grip, he tightened it around my waist. He was strong - much stronger than me and the fear continued through me as I started to realize I had no chance of escaping his hold.

"Did you seriously just bite me?" I heard a flicker of annoyance before his hand came over my mouth again. I tried to scream once more. I tried to wiggle out of his touch but I couldn't. He had me in a hold that wouldn't budge.

"Milena," my name rolled off his tongue in a way I had never heard before, a hint of an accent, but I couldn't quite place which one. "Your father sent me. I need you to stay calm."

I froze in his grip as he pushed through my closet doors, pulling us both inside. I had always found my closet to be large but being forced inside it with some strange man, I was now aware of just how tiny it could be. I was terrified. He pulled us to the far corner behind my winter coats.

"You need to do exactly as I say," he instructed, keeping his voice low in my ear. *Where did I recognize that voice from?* "I'm going to let go of you now but you have to be quiet. We need to stay hidden until they leave."

What the fuck was going on?

My breathing had since picked up, and I tried to remain calm but every part of me was consumed by fear. He slowly removed his hand and turned me around to face him. The only light coming through was from the wood slates in the design of my door. I couldn't even make out any of his features.

"Milena, stay hidden until I say otherwise," he whispered.

Without hesitation, I dropped down. I tightened my grip on my towel and at that moment I couldn't move. I was paralyzed with fear. I felt him drop down next to me.

"Don't move." His voice was barely audible.

Suddenly, I heard them in my room. Heavy footsteps against my wooden floor. There had to be about two or three of them. I couldn't be sure. I heard metal sliding as one of them cocked their gun.

"Oh my God, Milena. They have guns," Carina's voice echoed.

I swallowed in an attempt to control my fear, but I was just a moment away from completely losing it. I felt his hand on my back, reminding me that I wasn't alone. Here I was stuck in my closet with a man I didn't know. *My father sent him - sent him for what?* My mind was running wild. I had never been more confused or terrified in my life.

A figure stepped in front of my closet, stopping the light from coming through. I held my breath as I waited for them to find us. I expected it but when I heard someone shouting from downstairs, the figure turned, allowing the light back inside and we heard the footsteps become faint as they left my room.

"We're not in the clear," he whispered close to my ear. "Stay put."

I hated being told what to do. I was incapable of following instructions but with the warning in his voice, I went against my nature and stayed exactly where I was. Time moved so slowly. I felt like I had been stuck in that cupboard forever before I felt his hand against my back again, bringing me back to reality.

"Stand up."

No, *"you're fine now"*. Or *"please"*. Just another order. I was losing track of how many instructions this stranger had given me but the flicker of irritation inside of me warned that I wasn't about to endure this for much longer. I needed answers.

I slowly stood up. He pushed his body past me as he reached for my closet door. He was so close now, I couldn't help but breathe him in. He smelled faintly of cigarettes, a musky cologne, and a fresh smell I couldn't quite place. But I kind of liked it.

Creaking open the door, we were greeted by nothing but the sunlight. For the first time, I was able to identify his features. He was tall - significantly taller than me and he was large. His shoulders were broad and the muscles on his arms were clear through the black shirt he was wearing. He wasn't unusually large - he had the kind of build that you couldn't help but admire because it was clear he put in the work. Tattoos lined up and down his dark skin. I watched as he lifted the back of his shirt and reached for a gun.

Oh my fuck.

A gun.

He lifted it up as he slowly stalked towards my door. I couldn't move. I stood frozen watching this unfold. He stuck his head through the door and glanced to either side. After a few more moments of scanning the area, he dropped his arms and relaxed his shoulders. He turned to me and my breath caught in my throat.

He was hot.

"Now is not the time to be admiring the stranger in your room, Lena," Carina said.

She was right but his attractiveness caught me completely off-guard. A dark beard sat against his strong jawline, the color matching the darkness of his hair. It was kind of curly on top which softened his appearance in some way, but his deep brown eyes had a hardness to them that quickly made that disappear. My eyes fell to the tattoo on his hand and I suddenly remembered where I had seen him.

"Hey, you're the guy from last night," I pointed out. "You helped me."

"I work for your father."

That much was clear. He had been at the event last night and he was the same man who made sure Fabiano left me alone last night. Now he was here, barking orders at me while people had just broken into my house. I was beside myself with confusion right now.

"What the fuck is going on?" I asked, my voice barely recognizable.

"Quite the mouth you've got there," he commented.

I snapped my gaze up to meet his. "Who the fuck are you?"

"Vincenzo De Rossi."

"Okay, Vincenzo De Rossi, what the fuck are you doing in my house and who the fuck were those people?"

His facial expression remained hard and unchanged. "Do you always swear like this?"

"How about you answer my questions first?" I tossed back.

"Your father sent me."

"You already said that."

He ignored me and continued. "I need you to get dressed and come with me."

"Like hell, I'm going anywhere with you," I retorted.

"Milena, pack what you need but we need to leave now." His voice was full of warning. "I'm going to step out so you can get some clothes on." His eyes wandered over my body, suddenly making me aware of the fact I was just in a towel. "Call your father and he will explain. We need to be out of here in two minutes."

He didn't wait for me to respond before stepping out of my room, closing the door behind him.

I rushed over to my bedside table, frantically dialing my father's number. After the second ring, he picked up.

"Milena?"

"*Pai*, what the hell is going on?" I couldn't control the emotion in my voice.

"Milena, I need you to listen to me okay?" He tried to hide it, but the fear in his voice was clear as day. "Is Vincenzo there?"

"Yes. There were people in the house."

"I need you to go with him. Do exactly what he tells you. He's going to protect you."

"But what is happening?" I asked, swallowing to try to keep the fear at bay. "I don't understa-"

"There's no time to explain now, *querida*." I couldn't remember the last time my father had used that endearing name for me, which was how I knew that something must have gone terribly wrong. "I promise that I will but I need you to get out of that house."

"But I don't want to leave you and *Mãe*."

"You're not. We're going to see you soon. He's going to bring you to meet us. I promise all will be explained but, Milena, this is serious and I need you to get out. Now." His voice was hard but full of trepidation.

"Okay," I said softly.

We disconnected the call and my body moved before my mind could register what I was doing. I couldn't think straight as I reached for my clothes, pulling another oversized shirt over my body. I slipped on a pair of underwear, a pair of shorts following. A knock at the door made me stop until I heard Vincenzo's voice. "Milena? I'm coming in."

He pushed my door open and stepped inside. "You ready?"

"No, I'm not ready! What am I supposed to pack?" I huffed, panic rising in my chest.

"Essentials. Whatever you need that we can't get on the road."

"How long are we going for? Where are we going?" I asked, the questions spilling from me.

He ignored me as he walked over to the window, looking down at our driveway. "Fuck. They're back. We need to go. *Now!*"

I frantically reached for whatever I could, shoving it in one of the bags I grabbed from my closet. I couldn't even think straight and I had no idea what I was actually grabbing. I pulled my sneakers on and pulled my charger from my nightstand. Vincenzo took the bag from me. I was never the kind of person who felt fear. Besides the fear I once felt of the possibility of losing Carina when she first got sick, this was the most terrified I had ever been. It felt as if the world around me was starting to crumble and I had no idea how to stop it. I stopped by my door frame, needing a moment to get my breathing under control but Vincenzo's hand wrapped around my wrist, pulling me with him.

"I can walk just fine without you grabbing me!" I squirmed.

He rolled his eyes, never once removing his hand around my wrist as he guided me downstairs. "Follow me."

He was constantly looking around which didn't help my anxiety one bit. There was shattered glass across the floor in the kitchen. I didn't know if they found what they were looking for but they sure made a hell of a mess.

"Who were those people?" I asked as he pushed through the back door. He ignored my questions and our walk quickly turned into a run as we made it to the garage at the back of the house. My father never used it. At least I had never seen him use it. Vincenzo opened the door to reveal a shiny black SUV that had clearly been sitting there for a while, given the amount of dust on it. *Was this a getaway car?* Why would we have one of those? Clearly something had been going on for a lot longer than I had realized.

"Get in." He released my grip and yanked the back door open, tossing my bag onto the seat. I rushed over to the passenger side as he jumped into the driver's seat. He didn't even bother waiting till I had my seatbelt on before pulling out of the driveway and turning down the street.

"God, do you always drive like a crazy person?" I shouted, pulling the seatbelt across my chest.

"Only when I'm trying to save someone's life."

"At this rate, you're going to be the one to kill me," I muttered.

Earlier my biggest problem was surviving my hangover and now it was just about surviving. Just as we turned the street, a swarm of bullets came around us causing a high pitched scream to leave my throat.

"Fuck!" I heard Vincenzo mutter as he pulled his gun out. "Milena, down!"

Bullets hit the car, causing the panic inside of me to vocalize as I slid down my chair, ducking out of the way. Bullets hit our windows, ricocheting right off. *How the hell?* Clearly this car was well-equipped for an attack like this. Vincenzo cocked his gun and I watched as he stuck his head out the window, one hand on the steering wheel and the other was pulling the trigger as the shots left his gun. In one quick motion, he turned down the nearest street leaving the stray bullets in our wake.

"What the fuck is going on?" I shouted, frantically glancing around as I sat up straight again. The adrenaline coursed through my veins.

He remained silent as he changed lanes, stepping on the accelerator as he started to approach the highway. He was going well over the speed limit but I didn't care - not when I was just being shot at. It was clear that he had the skill needed behind the wheel. The whole shooting while driving thing really cemented my sudden faith in his driving skills. He kept his eyes ahead of him. "Your father will explain."

"I'm not waiting to hear from him. I want to know now."

He ignored me and that only fuelled my irritation more. He wouldn't budge, no matter how many times I asked him. Here I was in the car with a complete stranger allowing him to take me away from my home and no one was giving me any indication of what was really going on. I should be terrified right now. I was terrified but, surprisingly, not of him.

"Pass me your phone," he ordered.

"Why?"

"Do you ever do what you're told without argument?" he asked dryly.

"No, so it's best you learn that now."

"Milena, your phone." He opened his hand, waiting for me to do as I was told.

"Lena, do it," Carina said.

*M*y true nature was begging me not to do what he was asking but I reluctantly handed it over, the severity of the situation hovering over me enough to give in. He pressed the button that opened the window by his door and before I could comprehend what he was doing, he tossed my phone outside the car. He kicked the car into a new gear, speeding up.

"Are you fucking kidding me?!" I shrieked, turning back. "Why the hell did you do that?"

He shrugged. "Protocol."

"I need my phone," I argued.

"You'll get a new one."

"Stop the car!" I shouted.

He ignored me again. I watched as he tightened his grip on the steering wheel, constantly stealing glances around us. My eyes fell to the tattoos on his hand again. *It was a butterfly?* No, a bird with open wings. I shook my head and focused my attention back to the task at hand.

"Stop the car, Vinnie!" My voice was rising with emotion now. For a split second, I couldn't remember his name, but I had clearly gotten it wrong given the glare I had earned from him.

"It's Vincenzo," he clarified through gritted teeth. *Okay, so calling him Vinnie was a mistake originally but it seemed to piss him off which was good to know. Might have to keep doing that.*

"I don't give a fuck," I snapped. "Stop the car now."

"No."

The sheer audacity of this man. He was insufferable. I reached for the handle on my door but he quickly locked the door before I could get there in time.

He eyed me from the side. "What exactly do you think you're going to do? Jump out of a moving car to get your phone?"

"I'd much rather jump out of this car than be in it with you. I don't even know who you are," I reminded him.

"I told you, I'm Vincenzo De Rossi and your father sent me to protect you." He repeated like a robot that had been programmed to say the same phrase over and over again.

"I don't need protection," I snapped.

He scoffed and shook his head as he turned his attention back to the road. He didn't slow down as he zipped through traffic, often approaching other cars at a speed that made me believe we would crash at any moment.

"You won't even tell me what's going on so for all I know you're kidnapping me," I pointed out.

"You came with me willingly."

I shook my head. "Wrong. You practically dragged me out of my house and you still won't tell me why."

"People are after you and your family," he said.

I tried to stay calm as I asked, "And how do you know that?"

"I think my first clue was when your house was being broken into and then the whole being shot at made it pretty clear," he said dryly.

Okay, that may have been a dumb question, but I rolled my eyes at his sarcasm. Witty and infuriating. What a combination.

"They were looking for you," he explained.

"You don't know that," I retorted.

"Yes, I do. That's why I was sent to find you."

"Are you taking me to my parents?"

"Yes. They are headed to a safe house just outside of Lisbon and we will meet them there."

There was a brief moment of relief in knowing I was going to my parents. I didn't feel like being alone with some stranger while our lives seemed to be falling apart. They would know what to do and how to handle this. They had to know how to get us out of this mess, right?

Vincenzo zipped through traffic, continuing to display his skill behind the wheel. He didn't stop if he could avoid it and had no problem breaking any speeding laws as to put enough distance between the people who had shot at us and where we were headed.

"And what exactly is going to happen when we get to this so-called 'safe house'?" I asked.

"Well, given its name, I would say that you're going to stay there so you can be 'safe'." The sarcasm rolled effortlessly off his tongue which caused me to roll my eyes again.

"Do you ever answer without a sarcastic response?"

He ignored my question but his lips twitched in amusement before going back to its default setting. He was all serious and brooding. If this were any other situation, I would have probably been drawn to him. He definitely had everything I found attractive but he was a clear asshole who barked orders at me and I didn't like it one bit. I didn't care that people were clearly trying to kill me. I still didn't like being told what to do - especially when no one was explaining to me what was really going on. I was left in the dark right now and I hated it.

We were on the highway, well on our way to the north when his phone started to ring. He answered it and brought it up to his ear, clearly not wanting me to hear the conversation but that didn't stop me from leaning closer, trying to pick up what I could.

"Yes?" he answered, listening intently. I tried to pick up what the voice was saying but they were speaking a language I couldn't quite place. Spanish? I understood a bit of that thanks to my Portuguese so I ruled that out. Maybe it was Italia-

My thoughts were interrupted by Vincenzo. "Understood."

And with that, he ended the call. I opened my mouth to ask him what was going on but before I could, he gripped the steering wheel and abruptly slammed his foot on the brakes before turning us in the direction of the nearest off-ramp, making us turn back to where we just came from.

"What the hell are you doing?" I shouted, leaning my hand against my door to try to keep my body from knocking against it as he continued his reckless way of driving.

"Change of plans." He stepped on the accelerator, zipping back down the highway towards Algarve again.

"Why are we going back? I thought we were going to Lisbon!" I shouted.

"Can't. They found your parents," he said.

My breath caught in my throat. "Th-they what?"

"The safe house has been compromised. Don't worry, they got out of there in time but I can't take you there now."

I huffed and flung my hands around, exasperated. "So what? We're just going to drive around aimlessly?"

"No. I'm going to go with plan B. We are going to stop just an hour out of Algarve to swap cars and then we are headed for Sevilla."

"We're leaving Portugal?" I didn't hide the shock or concern in my voice. My parents were in the north and now we were putting even more distance between us.

He nodded.

"For how long?"

"Indefinitely."

I tried to process his words and a sudden rush of nausea came over me as I processed everything that just happened. I was sick to my stomach with worry over my parents. Were they going to be fine? How were they found? Who the hell is after us? I had just been shot at - *oh my God*. I had just been shot at. The reality started to settle in and there were now white spots in my vision now as I leaned my head back against the headrest, trying to stop the world from spinning.

"Milena?" I heard his voice in the distance."Milena, stay with me."

"Milena!" Carina's voice shouted. "Keep your eyes open!"

But I couldn't, and instead slipped into darkness.

CHAPTER 5:

Milena

"**M**ilena?" I felt a hand on my cheek, the touch burning against me. "Can you hear me?"

My eyes slowly fluttered open, landing on the face of Vincenzo De Rossi who was leaning close to me. Too close. *Ever heard of personal space, Vinnie?*

"Thank God," he muttered and dropped his hand. "You scared the shit out of me."

I sat upright in my seat as he leaned back against my passenger door that was now open. I glanced around and noticed he had pulled over on the side of a deserted road. I didn't know where we were or how long I had been out. The pressure in my chest increased suddenly as my mind was bombarded with all that had happened.

"Whe- where are we?" I managed to get out.

"Just outside of *Huelva.*"

I looked around again and noticed that I wasn't in the same car I was in before. I turned to the back and my bag was sitting on the seat.

"Did we change cars?" I asked.

"Yes."

I turned back to him. "Did you carry me?"

He shrugged and nodded. "You weren't waking up so I had no choice. I was just glad you had a pulse."

"So why'd you stop now?"

"We're getting closer to the apartment and I need you awake," he said dryly.

I leaned my head back against the headrest, closing my eyes and my headache reminded me of its presence through the insistent throbbing. "I need to speak to my parents."

"Easy fix," he said, causing me to open my eyes again. He pointed to the glove compartment. I pulled it open and a small black phone lay in it. I reached for it.

"Told you that you'd get a new one," he commented.

"Too bad it's not from this century." I turned it over. "No camera. No apps. Nothing."

"I'm sure you can live without posting on Instagram for a while if it means you'll stay alive."

I rolled my eyes at his very obvious, way-off assumption. "What makes you think I care about that shit anyway? You don't even know me."

He said nothing and instead closed my door and made his way back to the driver's seat. He closed his door and leaned to the back, pulling two caps to the front. He handed me one.

"Put it on."

It was a dusty old gray cap. I eyed it in his hand. "Why would I do that?"

He sighed. "We need whatever disguise we can manage right now."

"You think some shitty old cap is suddenly going to make me look like a whole new person?" I scoffed. "You're obviously not very good at this."

"Wait till I make you cut and dye your hair, then we'll be heading in the right direction."

My hand reached up to my hair, "I'm not doing that."

"We'll see." He dropped the cap on my lap before pulling his own over his head. "You can wear those sunglasses too. It's not the best but it's all we have right now."

Reluctantly, I grabbed the hat and shoved my dark long hair underneath it before placing the sunglasses over my eyes. The sun was shining brightly through the windscreen, directly in my eye line, so I was thankful for them but I would never admit that to Vincenzo. The pounding in my head had yet to falter but I couldn't just blame the alcohol for that now.

He turned the car on, the engine roaring to life before pulling back onto the road.

"So what exactly is going to happen when we get to *Sevilla?*" I asked.

"There's a small apartment in the city center waiting for us."

"Isn't that too obvious?"

"You'll be hidden in plain sight. And once we get to the apartment, we'll stay there until told otherwise."

"Seriously? You think I'm going to stay locked up in some apartment with you for God-knows how long?"

He remained silent, keeping his eyes on the road.

I shook my head. "Nope. That's not happening. You can't do that."

"It's my job."

"I don't care. I'm not some damsel in distress that needs to be locked away in a tower," I snapped.

He rolled his eyes and I could have sworn I saw a brief flash of a smile on his face. Was this seriously amusing to him?

"You seem to not care for your life at all," he pointed out.

"Well, considering I have no idea what's going on, I'm not about to take your word for it that something bad is going on here."

"You were just shot at and you're acting like that wasn't enough of a clue that something is wrong?" He clicked his tongue in irritation and just as I was about to respond, he interrupted me. "Your father pissed off the wrong people, okay?" he muttered. "A man was killed at the hotel this morning.."

My breath caught in my throat and I swallowed, attempting to control the rising emotion. No way. Someone was killed? *What the fuck.*

"You're lying."

He turned to me. "Why would I li-,"

"My father is a hotel owner, not some criminal." My stomach dropped as I allowed what he said to truly settle in. He was quiet as I repeated it over and over again in my mind. The extra security at the party last night, the getaway car. Was he expecting something to happen? Had he been preparing for this? I didn't want to believe it but I couldn't ignore what was right in front of me. "Someone was really killed?"

He nodded before turning back to the road.

"Who was it?" I asked.

"Can't say."

"What does my father have to do with this?"

"Can't say."

"Seriously? What can you say, Vincenzo?" I asked, exasperated.

"Nothing further."

I huffed and crossed my arms, turning to face outside my window.

"It's not my place to tell you what's going on, Milena," he said softly. "I'm just here to protect you."

"My father isn't a bad man. I don't believe he would be involved in something like this."

"Sometimes good people get caught up in things they shouldn't have."

"What the hell does that mean?" I snapped.

"Nothing. Look, it would save both of us our energy if you stopped asking me so many questions. I am not here to answer them for you. Phone your father and ask him. Your parents have the other burner phone now."

I rolled my eyes and reached for the phone on my lap. There was only one number programmed in it. I dialed it and lifted the phone to my ear. My leg was bouncing up and down against the car floor. It was my nervous twitch - I couldn't help it, especially in highly emotional situations.

I tried to focus on my breathing and getting that under control. My world was slipping further and further from the one I once knew and the fact that all I could hear was the ringing in my ear wasn't helping my stress levels one bit. It rang and rang until it eventually disconnected.

"Fuck," I muttered and dropped the phone onto my lap.

"You swear a lot," he commented.

I rolled my eyes as I allowed the sarcasm to drip off my tongue. "You're perceptive."

There it was again - a slight pull of amusement on his lips before being replaced by his ever-hard demeanor. Was this guy even able to crack a smile? I would put money on that not being possible.

"Are my parents joining me in *Sevilla?*" I asked.

"I don't think so. When I spoke to Carlos they were headed North."

"Who is Carlos?"

"Your parent's bodyguard."

Never heard of him before. Had they always had a bodyguard or was this all recent changes in their lifestyle? The more I was learning, the more I was starting to realize that I didn't know my parents at all.

"Is that what you are?" I eyed him. "My new personal bodyguard?"

"Technically, yes."

"And how did they find my parents in Lisbon?"

"We don't know yet."

"The note, Milena." Carina whispered. I sat up right, remembering the note I found this morning on the kitchen counter. That note told them where to start looking.

"Merda," I muttered. "The note back at home."

"What note?" He eyed me.

"The note my parents left for me this morning telling me they were heading to Lisbon. That probably gave them away."

"We don't know for sure but it could have pointed them in the right direction." Vincenzo thought for a moment. "Was there anything else on that note that we should know about?"

I shook my head. "They just said they had business to sort out in Lisbon."

Should I have thrown the note away? Was it my fault that they were found? But how could I have possibly known that people were going to break into my house to look for me? Fuck, this was all too much.

"Lena, breathe."

I took a deep breath in and crossed my arms again, bringing my feet up to rest on the dashboard in front of me.

"Take your feet off the dashboard," he instructed.

I ignored him and rested my one ankle on the other. "I'm pretty sure *bodyguard* does not mean you get to tell me what to do."

"On the contrary, that's exactly what I have to do."

I scoffed. "You're going to have a hard time doing your job because I don't like being ordered around. I have a bit of a problem with authority.

"Clearly." I watched as he rolled his eyes at me.

"I don't want to go to *Sevilla.* I want to go to my parents. If they're caught up in some shit then I don't want to be away from them," I admitted, my voice cracking with emotion unexpectedly. *Now is not the time to allow yourself to become a victim of your emotions, Milena.* I reprimanded myself for my moment of weakness.

"I can't do that, Milena," he said softly, my name rolling off his tongue causing an unexpected stir inside of me. *What the hell was that?* I've heard my name a million times before but there was something about the way he said it that breathed new life to it.

"Why not?" I probed.

"There's not enough time to get you to where your parents are headed. Their previous house was compromised and that doesn't look good. They are trying to deal with this internally and they want you to be somewhere safe while they handle all of this. They don't want to put you in harm's way."

I didn't like that one bit. I didn't like being isolated, even if it was for my own good. This all seemed too surreal to be happening right now. I didn't want to believe it. I was ready to wake up from this nightmare any moment now, please.

"A hit has been ordered on you and your family," he explained. "Do you understand the severity of the situation now? People have been ordered to kill you, Milena. They were in your house. They shot at you now - they shot at us. This isn't a game."

I swallowed, tears now forming in my eyes. I turned away from him, forcing my gaze outside my window as I focused on the rows of trees passing us. I refused to cry in front of him. I refused to give him any indication that I couldn't handle this, no matter how much I was actually falling apart inside. I would never show weakness and would rather allow the burning in my throat to continue than to allow those tears to escape.

"Who did my father get on the wrong side of?" I asked softly, trying my luck again.

"You're not going to stop asking me until I tell you, are you?" He eyed me.

"Nope, so you might as well just get it over with."

He sighed and turned to me. "I don't know the exact details of what went down but sounded like a drug deal gone wrong which ended up in the death of one of the *Nazario* men."

Nazario.

I had heard that name before. Anyone who lived in Portugal had heard that name. The Nazario crime family operated in the shadows across the entire country and had been for years. I had heard whisperings about them growing up but never really believed the stories. No one had seen them before, we were only taught to fear them. Some spoke of their dealings with them before and the way they would ruthlessly get rid of anyone that was in their way. It sounded like fiction to me until now. Now, I was pulled right into the middle of it and I wasn't sure how to process that information.

"My father doesn't deal drugs," I defended.

"I'm just telling you what I know."

I refused to believe it. There has got to be some kind of misunderstanding here. My father had his faults and there was no denying that he and I bumped heads many times, but he was not a criminal. He was not a bad man. He was my dad. *Pai. papa. C*ould it be that I never really knew him at all?

I didn't want to keep talking to Vincenzo about this. I was angry and confused and being stuck in a car with him was the last thing I thought I would be doing today. I turned my attention outside again as we passed a sign that read *"Bienvenido a Sevilla!"*

I had been to plenty of places in Spain and *Sevilla* was on my list of destinations I wanted to visit, but I never thought it would be like this. Traveling hadn't really been a priority for my family after we lost Carina. I hadn't even managed the two-hour trip from Algarve to *Sevilla* until now.

"Your shoes, Milena. Take them off the dashboard," he instructed again, but I ignored him.

I lifted the burner phone still on my lap. "Is this shitty little thing really my new phone?"

"We can't have anything that can track your location."

"What about my laptop?" I asked, glancing over the rim of my glasses.

"Not allowed."

I turned to gape at him, removing the glasses. "You've got to be kidding me! Am I seriously supposed to just be locked up with you in some random apartment without even the ability to watch Netflix to pass the time?"

"I didn't say there would be no laptop at all. I said you can't use the one you have. You think they're not already trying to find you again?" He turned to me. "They were in your house, Milena. I doubt they have forgotten to try to track your devices. That's child play to them."

How was this happening right now?

He tapped my leg this time, his hand against my bare skin causing an unexpected amount of electricity to course at just his touch. *What the fuck was happening?* First I was hung up on the way he said my name and now this?

Was I attracted to this stubborn, bossy man? No way.

"Are you seriously going to leave them up there?"

"I don't understand why they're bothering you," I argued.

"What if we crash? Do you know how many broken bones you'll have sitting like that?"

"Then you better focus on the road, old man." I clicked my fingers to indicate he should draw his attention forward again.

He shook his head and turned his eyes forward again. "Old man," he scoffed. "How old do you think I am?"

"At least forty," I said it but didn't mean it. He had to be bordering thirty. I had the sudden urge to push his buttons. He was far too controlling for my liking.

He rolled his eyes. "And let me guess, you're about nineteen now, little girl?"

Did he ju-?

I whipped my head to the side to face him. "Little girl? I'm twenty-three and I certainly don't think you were hired to insult me."

"If you keep acting like a little girl then I'll treat you like one."

My blood was boiling and I had just about enough of Vincenzo De Rossi. We had started to approach the city and found ourselves in some traffic. The car came to a stop at the traffic light and before I could be stopped, I jerked the handle of the car door and opened it, slipping outside.

"Milena!" His voice boomed but I ignored him and kept going, moving further and further away from him. I crossed the road and took off down the street.

CHAPTER 6:

Vincenzo

I had never met anyone who cared less for their own safety than Milena Neves.

The light turned green on the traffic light and I immediately pulled into the nearest opening spot along the curb, narrowly missing the car in my blind spot.

"Seriously?" I huffed and pulled up the handbrake. She jumped out of the car. Her life was in danger and she took off running down the street. I was meant to be protecting her and somehow, her brain did not seem to register the severity of the situation. I yanked my door open and slammed it closed behind me before locking it. Shoving my keys in my pocket, I took off down the street in the direction she ran off in. The anger was pulsing inside of me at her sheer stupidity.

Pulling my phone from my pocket, I dialed Carlos' number. After the second ring, he picked up. *"Ciao, Vincenzo, come va?"*

"Why did you stick me with the daughter?" I muttered, glancing around the street as I picked up my pace.

He chuckled. "What happened?"

"She jumped out of the car and took off down the street."

"I heard she was a bit of a loose cannon," he commented casually.

"Thanks for the warning," I replied dryly. "Can you track that burner phone, please? She has it with her."

"I don't know how you lost her already." This time he couldn't hold back his laughter.

"I didn't lose her. She's a piece of work," I huffed.

My phone buzzed and I brought it forward, the tracking location of the phone coming through on my screen.

"Grazie."

"Please let me know when you have her safely at the apartment," he said. "We're still on the road but headed towards Porto now."

"What's the plan?" I asked.

"We're going to decide once we get there but all I know is they can't go back home and with the Lisbon house compromised. I wouldn't put it past them to know about the others. We need to take extra precautions now. Their house was ransacked again after you left with Milena. The Nazarios aren't fucking around, but what do you expect when their eldest son was killed?"

"Fuck. They took out the son?" This just went from bad to worse.

"Yup. Antonio Nazario. I still need to get the full story from *Senhor Neves* but I'll get Afonso to send over what we have at the moment." He stopped and said something to someone in Italian before returning to our conversation. "Listen, Enzo, I gotta go. Find Milena and keep her in that apartment. I wouldn't put it past the Nazarios to have connections in Spain."

"Got it."

I disconnected the call and glanced down at my phone, following the pulsing red dot on my screen that gave away Milena's location. Thankfully, almost everything of ours had a tracker - it was certainly helpful in moments like this. I took off down the street, picking up my pace as I zipped through the crowds of people. She was infuriating. I was trying to do my job and keep her safe and here she was running around the streets of Sevilla as if she didn't have a hit on her back. *Stubborn, stubborn woman.*

I watched as the red dot turned down a street. I noticed an open alleyway close to where she was headed and turned to make my way through it, the crowds disappearing as I entered. It was old and narrow. There was no one except me walking through it now and I was careful to keep my movements as quiet as possible. She was set to turn around the next corner that would pass this alleyway any minute now and I needed to grab her before she took off again. I didn't expect a twenty-three-year-old to be this much work. I was hired to protect her - not to be her fucking babysitter.

Stalking closer and closer to the opening in the alleyway, the red dot was approaching. I took a deep breath in and as she turned and I noticed her body come into view. I wrapped my arm around her waist and pulled her into the alley, my hand covering her mouth as she tried to scream.

"Don't you dare bite me again," I warned in her ear.

She didn't bite me but she did elbow me in the stomach and even though it pained me to keep my composure, I didn't even flinch. I had experienced much worse. I turned her around and pinned her up against the wall. Her dark brown eyes peered up at me with nothing but rage behind them.

"Milena." I didn't bother hiding the contempt in my voice. "I am going to remove my hand but if you so much as breathe too loudly, I will duct tape your mouth shut. Got it?"

Her jaw tightened but her gaze never left mine. I didn't trust her but I was pretty sure if someone had to see us now, I would end up in jail.

I slowly pulled my hand away from her mouth, surprised that she had followed my instruction.

"See, was that so hard?" I muttered.

"How did you find me?" she huffed.

"I have my ways. Just remember that when you try some shit like this again. I will always find you."

She pushed me against my chest, creating distance between the two of us. "I don't trust you."

"You don't have to. Your parents hired me to protect you and that's what I'm going to do so you better get used to it. I'm not going anywhere."

People started to cross the alleyway, some turning in our direction. I lifted my hand and leaned it against the wall, trapping her body between mine.

"Don't move," I warned. "You've already brought enough attention to yourself by running away the way you did."

"I'm impressed you were able to find me so quickly."

"It's my job."

"You're not very good at it considering I already managed to escape from you."

I rolled my eyes and dropped my arm. "You're acting like I'm the bad guy here."

She crossed her arms. "I don't know that you're not."

Enough now. I was tired of her bratty back and forth. I had a job to do and I was not about to let her childish antics stop me. I grabbed her wrist and started to pull her down the alleyway in the direction of the car.

"Let go of me!" She tried to wiggle out of my grip but I tightened it.

"Stop making this harder than it needs to be," I warned, stopping to pull her closer to me. "We are close to the apartment and then we can get a hold of your parents and you can hear it from them. I am not your babysitter but I sure as hell will not let you stop me from doing my job. I am not leaving your side, you got that?"

She flicked her eyes to meet mine and it was the first time I noticed the close proximity between us. She was so close I could smell the coconut shampoo in her hair. It was kind of nice.

Seriously? I didn't even like coconut. Or maybe I did...

I stopped the thoughts before they went any further. She was a loose-cannon and I needed to get her under control before she got us both killed.

"I'm going to hold your hand now," I explained. "Wouldn't want anyone to think you're with me against your will."

She scoffed but said nothing further. I slipped my hand into hers, tightening my grip around her hand. She had small hands - fitting perfectly in mine. Her skin was softer than I expected. *Why do you care how soft her skin is, Vincenzo?* I reprimanded myself to keep focused. It was just skin. Perfectly normal hand skin. *Okay, you need to stop now.*

I turned us down the street and walked her back over to where I had parked, making sure to scan the perimeter as we approached the car. I walked her back to her passenger side and unlocked the door, opening it for her. I was not about to give her an opportunity to sneak away.

"Look at you pretending to be a gentleman," she snickered sarcastically.

"Trust me, I am no gentleman." I shut the door as she got inside and walked over to the driver's seat. After pulling my own door closed and turning the car back on, we were back on track. I dialed Carlos through the hands-free kit in the car.

"*Sì, Enzo?*" he answered.

"*L'ho trovata,*" *I* said in Italian, telling him that I found her. I didn't need her to listen to my conversations so I switched to my mother tongue.

"*Bene, ci sentiamo dopo.*" And with that, he ended the call.

"You're Italian?" she asked.

"Yes."

"What are you doing working in Portugal?"

"I don't have to answer your questions."

I noticed her roll her eyes. "Of course not. You'd rather we sit in silence."

"Correct. I'm not here to be your friend, Milena," I said. My sentence coming out a lot harsher than I intended it

"Right," she mumbled. "You're just here to bark orders at me."

"I'm here to protect you," I clarified.

"Whatever," she muttered and turned to face outside her window.

I sighed. She infuriated me. I had only been with her for a handful of hours now and I could already tell this was going to be my toughest job yet. She had this innate ability to get under my skin in a way no one has ever done before. *Vincenzo, this is your job. I* had to remind myself to remain professional and went against my nature as I turned to her and apologized.

"I think we got off on the wrong foot here, Milena." I turned into the underground parking lot of the apartment building we were staying in. "I'm not here to make your life miserable. I need you to work with me here. I'm here to keep you alive."

She turned to me, a flicker of emotion in her deep brown eyes. For a moment I could see her vulnerability and I felt a little bad. I didn't stop to think about how this must have been affecting her. Empathy - or even sympathy - weren't exactly traits I had at my disposal. I had shut off a long time ago.

I parked the car, killing the engine. "Let's start over." I turned to her and extended my hand. "Truce?"

She eyed my hand suspiciously before flicking up to meet my eyes. "I don't like you."

"You don't have to. You just have to let me do my job and not jump out the car like you did."

She held my gaze for a moment, the thoughts mulling over in her mind.

"Fine." She muttered and shook my hand. "I won't jump out of the car again."

We had come to an impasse, but I didn't trust her. Milena was a ticking time bomb just waiting to explode.

CHAPTER 7:

Milena

The first thing I noticed when we stepped into the apartment on the third floor of the building was the smell.

Dust.

There was nothing but the smell of dust that surrounded us, clogging my airways causing me to sneeze. Once I got that under control, the next thing I noticed was just how small the place was. A one-bedroom, one-bathroom apartment with a kitchen and living room that was small enough to fit into my bedroom back at home. I didn't want to sound like a brat - it wasn't the size of the place that was an issue for me, it was the fact I had to share it with this overbearing man that didn't have me jumping for joy.

I jumped as Vincenzo shut the door behind us. I was on edge now and there was a growing suffocating feeling in my chest, making its way to my throat that was terrifying me.

"Breathe, Lena," my sister's voice murmured.

It should be second nature, but right now I was so overly aware of the air coming through my nose and out my mouth. No matter how deep I tried to breathe in, not enough was filling my lungs.

Vincenzo dropped our bags by the old couch before walking over to the small balcony, opening up the door to allow some fresh air in. Judging by the way the place was, it was clear that no one had been here in years. The paint was chipping off the walls and the furniture was easily decades old. Except for the small flat screen TV against the wall. That was definitely new. I had been so distracted by everything that happened that I hadn't even had a moment to appreciate the beauty that was Sevilla and unfortunately, now was not the time. There would be no time to play tourist.

"You take the bedroom. I'll take the couch," Vincenzo said, bringing me back to reality.

I eyed the old leather couch again. Besides how dusty and worn out it was, I noticed the size of it. I flicked my gaze back to Vincenzo, deducing that there was no way he would fit comfortably there but quite frankly, I didn't care.

"That couch is half your size," I commented.

"Don't worry about me."

"Trust me, I'm not." I rolled my eyes. "You could sleep on the floor for all I care."

He ignored me and walked over to the small kitchen counter. It had two single bar stools in front of it and he pulled one out before pulling himself onto it. His phone buzzed in his pocket and I watched him pull it out, glancing down at the screen before looking up at me.

"Phone your parents again."

I wanted to ignore his new order but I couldn't deny that I wanted to speak to them. I was sick to my stomach with worry over them so instead of arguing, I reached for the burner phone in my pocket and dialed their number before walking over to the balcony. I could do with any other view than Vincenzo right now.

By the third ring, I heard my mother on the other side.

"Milena?" she asked, her voice full of fear. "You there?"

"Olá Mãe." The tears unexpectedly built in my eyes.

"Estás bem? They said you arrived at the apartment."

"Yes, I'm here but you're not."

"Eu sei," my mother's voice cracked. "Your father, he's got himself in a bad space, Milena."

I brought my hand up rubbing across my forehead, trying to contain my emotions. "I don't understand what's happening *Mãe.* Vincenzo said they found a dead body,"

I heard her sigh through the phone. "He wasn't supposed to tell you that."

"I wouldn't stop asking," I defended quickly. I don't know why I defended him but it was the truth. "And you can't keep the truth from me. I deserve to know what's going on."

"I know. You do but I can't explain it all right now. Your father and I, we are going to plan what to do next and then we will let you know.

"*But Mãe..*" I started but she interrupted.

"Please, Milena. I need you to trust us right now. We need to keep you safe." I could hear her trying to hold back the tears. "I can't lose another child."

I shut my eyes, trying to keep my own tears at bay as I allowed my mind to briefly wander back to my sister. Everything was better when she was still here. Our entire family was one completely different than the one I had become accustomed to over these last few years. My relationship with my parents was the perfect example of how tarnished everything became as we all became consumed by her loss. This wasn't helping my overwhelming emotions. I slammed on the brakes, stopping these thoughts from going any further before the all-consuming grief washed over me again.

"When am I going to see you again?" My bottom lip trembled.

"I don't know bu-,"

Her voice disappeared as my breathing, suddenly, became short and the world started to spin again. I had to lean against the wall to keep from falling over and before I knew it, I felt Vincenzo's arm around my waist.

"Milena, hey," he murmured and guided me to the couch. "I think you should sit down."

"Milena?" My mother's voice came frantically through the phone but I couldn't respond. I felt Vincenzo sit me down before taking the phone from my hand. I dropped my head in my hands as the shock settled over me.

"*Senhora Neves,* it's Vincenzo," I heard him say. "She's fine. I think she's just in shock."

I tried to form the words to let them know I was okay. I tried to say anything but nothing came. I was nauseous and I could do nothing but close my eyes and attempt to focus on my breathing.

I couldn't hear what my mother said but Vincenzo continued. "Yes. I'll do that. She'll be fine."

He said his goodbyes quickly after that, and I heard his footsteps against the floor as he walked to the kitchen. I didn't move. I kept my eyes shut until a few moments later, I felt his presence in front of me. He rested his hand on my knee and I focused on his touch. It was warm against my bare leg and I didn't expect the brief way my breath got caught in my throat. *It's the shock.* I brushed that out of my mind before taking another deep breath in, filling my lungs with as much air as I could manage.

"You need to drink this." I opened my eyes as he handed me a glass of water that was almost white. I eyed it suspiciously.

"Sugar water," he explained. "I'm not trying to poison you. It'll help with the shock."

He was in front of me on his haunches as I took the glass from him and slowly brought it to my lips, sipping on it. It wasn't great but it wasn't bad either. I took a few more sips before handing the glass back to him. He placed it on the coffee table behind him, bringing himself to sit on the edge before turning back to me.

"Milena," he said softly. "Are you alright?"

An unexpected giggle formed on my lips. It wasn't funny. Nothing about this was funny but here I was, laughing at the ridiculousness of the situation. I dropped my hands and my gaze landed on his face in front of me.

"Am I alright?" I repeated, between my laughter. "Let's see. This morning I woke up and my biggest issue was nursing my hangover. Now I'm in Sevilla with some stranger who is trying to keep me alive because people want to kill me."

A new wave of laughter bubbled over. "And I don't even know why. 'Cause my father angered some people? Seriously? And you're asking me if I'm alright?"

He opened his mouth to speak but I continued.

"No, I'm not, Vincenzo." The laughter quickly slipped away and I had to tug on my bottom lip to keep from crying. "None of this is okay."

He rubbed his thumb against my leg. "I know."

There was nothing he could say to make me feel better. I didn't even know what would help me right now but I knew I was one moment away from a complete breakdown. I refused to give in to that so instead, I stood up and walked past him. "You said it was one of the *Nazario* men that were found dead. Did my father kill him?"

The silence that hung thick in the air following my question spoke wonders. I turned to face him as he sat on the couch now, looking up at me. I tried to read him - I tried to get some kind of emotional indication from his eyes but there was nothing. He held himself together and gave nothing away.

"Vincenzo," I started slowly. "Is my father the reason that man is dead?"

"Milena, I-,"

"Yes or no," I said through gritted teeth.

He sighed, his hardened gaze faltering momentarily. "Yes."

And with that one word, the world I once knew came crashing down around me. I leaned against the nearest wall, internally begging for the world to stop spinning. There was no way my father was a killer. He and I had our differences and he was never the same since Carina died but he was a good man. I didn't believe he would be capable of something like this. There was just no way. Denial started to creep up on me.

"Your father owed a lot of money to the Nazario family," Vincenzo started to explain. As much as I wanted to know more, it was also becoming painful to hear. "He made a deal with them years ago."

"My father wouldn't get involved with criminals."

"There is so much you don't know."

I ignored that comment. "So why don't you tell me?"

He sighed. "Stop asking me that. I will tell you only what you need to know. Unless I am instructed otherwise, these details are none of your business."

"None of my business?" I laughed but there was no humor behind it, only shock. "My life has been completely turned upside down and you think this is none of my business?"

I started to pace up and down the room, the thoughts running around in my mind. "I have a target on my back now because of what happened and no one wants to fucking tell me the truth. How is that fair?"

He remained silent which only fueled my anger more.

"I can't stay here forever. I have a life to get back to in London."

"That's not going to happen anytime soon." He shrugged and leaned back against the couch.

"I'll be safe there."

He rolled his eyes. "You think that's not one of the first places they'll look for you? You don't seem to understand who we're dealing with here."

I narrowed my eyes at him. "You can't keep me here forever."

"I will do what I get told to do."

"I'm telling you that you can-,"

He interrupted me. "I don't work for you, Milena."

He held my gaze and neither one of us was ready to look away. I wanted him to know that I wasn't going to take any of this lying down. I would not be a damsel in distress. I would not allow myself to be a target in a war that had nothing to do with me. This is not the life I wanted. I could feel the emotion rising in my chest again and I refused to show weakness in front of him. I would keep the pretense up in front of him. I walked back over and reached for my bag before heading into the bedroom. "I'm going to shower."

"I'll organize some food."

"I'm not hungry," I shouted from the room before slamming the door closed. I dropped the bag by the bed before sitting on the edge, finally allowing the tears to overwhelm me. My hand covered my mouth in an attempt to control the sound coming from my throat. I didn't want to be consoled. For the first time in years I longed for the place that had caused me to feel like an outsider. I longed to be back home.

CHAPTER 8:

Milena

For the next couple of days, I lived disconnected from my reality. I hovered between my denial and overall shock from the situation. Between the constant nausea and tightness in my chest, I felt as if I was going to disappear into myself. When I came home for the summer, the last thing I ever would have thought would happen would be locked up in some old, rundown apartment with a man I didn't even know two days ago.

I heard the front door open and shut again. I slowly sat upright in bed. It was surprisingly comfortable which is one of the reasons why I had chosen to stay in for as long as possible. I didn't want to face what was out there waiting for me. I brought my legs over the side of the bed to rest against the tiled floors. The curtains were still drawn closed but I knew it was well into the day already. The sun was fighting to push through the dark curtains. I sighed and dragged myself towards the door, slowly opening it up. I peeked outside and Vincenzo was nowhere in sight.

"Vincenzo?" I shouted but was greeted by nothing but silence. I opened the door entirely and walked into the kitchen in search of something I could fill my stomach with. I wasn't sure if the nausea was from the shock or from the lack of food in my system. Unsurprisingly, I had no appetite. I couldn't stomach anything. I scanned through the cupboards and instead of pulling out something to eat, I decided on making a cup of coffee instead. Bringing the kettle to a boil, I leaned against the counter, facing the rest of the living room. A laptop stood open on the small coffee table in front of the couch where Vincenzo had taken up residence. I looked around, making extra sure he was nowhere in sight before I slowly tiptoed towards it. I glanced at the screen that had a window open with an on-going chat on. I shouldn't be snooping but I didn't care. Everyone seemed to want to keep me in the dark and I refused to allow that to happen. I would find out for myself what was really going on. I sat down in front of the laptop and pulled it closer to me. I scanned across the open chat, my breath getting stuck in my throat as it landed on a picture of a dead body, blood scattered across the floor.

I was going to be sick.

And yet, I couldn't look away. There was a single bullet wound in the middle of his forehead and the blood spilled onto the floor beneath where he lay. There was no way my father was capable of something like this. I should have stopped then and there but my body seemed to move without consulting my brain. I continued to scroll down, trying to find any English in the chat that was otherwise filled with Italian. My eyes stopped at the word *'figlio'*. I recognized that. It meant son. I opened a new tab and translated the entire sentence:

It was the Nazarios eldest son, Antonio Nazario, that was killed.

"Oh God." My hand went up to cover my mouth as I processed the new information. My father had killed their eldest son. That made this incredibly personal to them and I wasn't surprised at all by their retaliation. *What happens now?* I can't stay locked up in here forever. That was no long-term, viable solution to this. I ran my fingers through my hair and leaned forward, eyeing the yellow folders on the table. I glanced at the door once more, making sure that Vincenzo wasn't about to barge through the door. The coast was clear for now so I pulled the files closer to me, flipping the first one open. Pages and pages of headlines were piled up in the folder. I flicked through them, each of them highlighting a horror story that was said to be linked to the Nazarios.

"Man found dead on his doorstep - alleged criminal activity with the Nazarios."

"Three dead in an alleged hit. Believed to be the work of Duarte Nazario."

"Eight killed in a fire at a factory in Galegos. A case of arson being investigated."

"Family of four found dead in their car...."

I was going to be sick. The articles continued, detailing the horrific crimes of the Nazario *family*. Never once has anyone in the higher ranks been arrested - that was one thing about that family. They had a knack for evading law enforcement and they had done a pretty good job up till now. They had infiltrated every part of Portuguese society that I was pretty sure they had more people on their payroll than anyone realized. And now they were after my family.

My father killed their son.

Over and over again, I continued to repeat that there was no way this was real. This had to be some terribly, sick nightmare I was in. I turned back to the laptop to see what else I could find out.

Before I could focus on the conversation in front of me, the handle of the door opened and Vincenzo stepped inside before I could cover my tracks.

"What the hell do you think you're doing?" He shouted, crossing the room to shut his laptop in front of me. I knew I was in the wrong but I refused to allow him to know that.

I stood up, crossing my arms. "Finding out the things you refuse to tell me."

"You have no right to go through my stuff, Milena." He was angry now.

"And you have no right to keep things from me," I shot back. "Why didn't you tell me my father killed their son?"

"I don't owe you any explanation. That's not my job."

"No, but your job is to protect me and don't you think that would work out better if you actually let me in on what was going on here?"

His jaw tightened and he kept his hard gaze on mine. His eyes were so dark that they almost looked black. He had an intimidating demeanor to him but I refused to crumble in his presence. That was not my style.

"My father killed one of their sons, didn't he?" I repeated.

"Yes," he muttered.

"And that's why they're after me? An eye for an eye?"

"That's what we think."

I took a deep breath in. "Wonderful."

I pushed past him to go and finish making myself a cup of coffee. You would think that hearing this would have made me feel worse but at that point, I had gone numb. I felt nothing. I reached for a mug from the cupboard, going about my business.

"They're not going to stop until they kill me," I said, no flicker of emotion in my voice.

"That's not going to happen."

I glanced back. "You think you're that good at your job that you can stop a father from avenging his son?"

He remained silent.

"That's what I thought," I muttered.

"You don't know what I'm capable of, Milena." His voice was low and thick with warning. There was so much weight in that statement that sparked a brief intrigue in the subtext behind it.

"Have you spoken to my parents?" I asked.

He shook his head. "They are with Carlos just outside of *Guimarães*. There is nothing new to report but your parents will be in touch when they can. They are trying to limit contact as to avoid any kind of interception."

"But they're okay, right?"

"Yes, they're fine."

For now. I swallowed, keeping my emotions at bay. They were hovering in the back and I was using every ounce of energy I had to keep them away. They would completely destroy me if I thought too long about how lonely I was now. I hated being alone. Most of my life, Carina and I had been attached at the hip. I had never felt true loneliness until she left and I had spent years trying to fill that void - never once finding anything that quite made me feel whole again.

"Milena, don't go there. You're going to be fine," Carina reassured me *even though I didn't believe it myself.*

I filled my cup with hot water and stirred, turning the water black. "So what now?"

"Now, you get comfortable and stay put until we're told otherwise."

"We've already been here for days."

"And we're going to be here for much longer so get used to it," he answered dryly.

"Doesn't seem like much of a plan. Seems like we're putting off the inevitable here."

"They don't know where you are so we'd like to keep it that way. We have men back in Algarve taking care of the situation,"

I leaned against the counter, wrapping my hand around the warm cup of coffee. "And what does that mean? Are you guys going to take out every single one of the Nazario men?"

"If we have to then we will."

I scoffed. "Seems unlikely." I did a quick scan of the few wooden cupboards and pantry as I searched for a snack. "I see you went shopping without me."

"Well, we needed to stock up now didn't we?"

"Mm-hmm." I stopped on a packet of rice cakes. "And your idea of stocking up was to buy this?" I eyed him. "You should have just gotten cardboard instead; it's pretty much the same thing."

I saw him roll his eyes as he took a seat in front of his laptop, opening it back up again.

After scanning all the cupboards and the fridge, I noticed there was one very important thing missing here. "You didn't buy any alcohol," I pointed out.

"And why would I do that?" he flicked his eyes past his laptop.

"It would certainly help pass the time," I mused.

"No alcohol."

This time I rolled my eyes. "God, Vincenzo, you really are a bore."

He ignored me and looked back at his laptop. I tapped my foot anxiously against the floor. I hated the idea of being cooped up here. I was claustrophobic and not only in the physical sense - in the mental sense too. If I was trapped in my own mind for too long, it never ended well.

"What if I need certain things?" I asked. "I wasn't able to pack everything."

"Then you tell me and I'll get it."

"Okay, well I forgot my vibrator so do you think you could organize me one of those?" I kept my face as unchanged as I could manage as he paused and looked up at me, searching to see if I was being serious. I casually lifted my mug to my lips, never breaking eye contact as I waited to see what reaction that would earn me. There wasn't much for me to do here so pushing Vincenzo's buttons was going to be the most entertaining activity available.

"There's a detachable shower head in the bathroom; I'm sure you can sort yourself out," he answered, keeping his voice monotone.

Well played.

That had caught my attention. It was the first time I was remotely intrigued by Vincenzo De Rossi. I tugged at my bottom lip to keep from smiling. "I mean that's not ideal but that'll do for now I guess."

"Then it looks like you're sorted."

This man was insufferable. I hated that he gave me exactly what I was dishing out. I had yet to find anyone that ever challenged me this way. I refused to allow him that kind of power so I would keep up the front. "So let me get this straight, there is no phone," I started to list.

"You have a phone," he pointed out.

Ignoring him, I corrected my statement. "So, there is no phone from *this* century. No laptop since you took it from my bag - thanks for that by the way - no alcohol, no sex." He didn't even bother looking up at me as I continued. He was getting on my nerves. Sitting there on the couch in his tight black shirt that sat perfectly around his arms. I had a weakness for lean arms with tattoos and he just happened to have both. Too bad he was a pain in my ass so I refused to acknowledge anything attractive about this man.

"You at least going to organize us some weed?"

"My God, Milena!" he said, exasperated. "Are you seriously incapable of keeping yourself occupied without needing something to assist you?"

"Yes!" I shouted. "Because you've completely fucked up my plans."

"I did not fuck up anything." I was surprised by his choice to curse but it was kind of... sexy? *Stop Milena, there is nothing sexy about this man.*

Not even that dark beard of his or the tattoos that lined his hands.

"I am not the reason you're here," he reminded me. "I'm just the product of the reason."

I wanted to argue. I wanted to scream and shout at him but he was right, he wasn't the one to blame. I was already starting to go fucking crazy and I had no idea how to stop that from happening.

I took one last sip of my coffee and placed the empty cup in the sink before turning back to him.

"A Kindle," I said.

"What?"

"I would like a Kindle, please. If I'm going to be locked up here, I might as well catch up on some reading."

He held my gaze for a moment before nodding. "Fine. I can do that for you."

"Great," I muttered before turning towards the room. "You know where to find me."

CHAPTER 9:

Vincenzo

Milena spent the rest of the day locked in the room. I couldn't blame her. If I was in her situation, I probably would have done the same but I did feel kind of bad. She was infuriating and continued to provoke me which was already driving me fucking insane but I could admit that she was in a situation that no one deserved to be in. She didn't choose this but unfortunately, we were both stuck now.

I didn't like that she had seen the picture of Antonio. That wasn't the kind of visual she should have been exposed to but I should have known better than to leave my stuff lying around for her to find. She was tenacious - like a dog with a bone.

And then to ask me to get her a vibrator. *Holy fucking shit.* She was shameless and I don't know how I managed to keep it together when deep inside, I was actually intrigued by what she had asked for. I shouldn't be thinking of her that way but when the words left her mouth, there was no stopping the heat that rushed to my groin.

You're crossing a line.

You are here to protect her. Not fuck her.

Not even if she caused a stir inside of me that had been dormant for the longest time. I refused to acknowledge it. This never happened to me. Professionalism was key and not getting involved with your subject was the most important rule. No strings attached. No feelings. No fucking. This was nothing I couldn't handle.

I was working hard to convince myself that there was nothing attractive about Milena Neves. Not even the sexy curves of her body that she hid underneath that oversized shirt of hers, peaking out in stolen moments when she reached up for something or sat down and the shirt hiked up her thigh. There was so much that I could grab and squeeze if I had my wa-...

Seriously, Vincenzo. Get your shit together.

I shut the laptop and stood up, pushing that out of my mind. Clearly being cooped up here with her was already getting to me. So I needed a break. She wanted a Kindle so I would get her one. I walked over to the bedroom door and tapped lightly. "Milena?"

I heard shuffling from inside before she yanked it open, standing there in nothing but a towel wrapped around her body.

"What?" she asked.

"Uh-," I coughed, regaining my composure. "I am going to get your Kindle and some other supplies. Do you need anything else while I'm gone?"

"You're leaving me alone again?"

"I don't have a choice considering it's just you and I here and there are things that we need if we're going to be staying here." She rolled her eyes at my statement but I continued, "I need you to work with me here, Milena."

Her only reply was the glare that she shot my way.

"I'm going to ask again, do you need anything else?"

"How about a cloak of invisibility?"

I stood there, dumbfounded and she gawked at me. "Seriously? Have you never watched Harry Potter?"

"No," I replied dryly.

She rolled her eyes. "Of course you haven't. Let me guess, all you watch is probably some boring-ass documentaries about World War II or something,"

I lifted an eyebrow at her. "Sounds like someone is making assumptions."

"That's all I can do since you're a blank piece of wood who gives me nothing," she muttered.

A blank piece of wood? I almost laughed. She was creative, I'd give her that. I refused to engage with her though - even when I found her amusing.

I ignored her comment. "So just the Kindle then."

"And a box of cigarettes," she said.

"Smoking is bad for you," I pointed out.

"You smoke," she tossed back.

"How do you know that?" I arched an eyebrow.

"I could smell it on you."

She's smelling me now?

I ignored that and continued. "Smoking is bad for *you* - I didn't say anything about it being bad for me."

She rolled her eyes. "Well thanks for the tip, *senhor,* but my health is none of your concern."

She was right, but I wanted nothing more than to tell her no. God, she was an infuriating little thing and there was a deep arousal inside of me that wanted to make her bow down to my every order. *Senhor. T*he things I could do if she submitted herself to me. I shifted uncomfortably as my mind wandered to where it shouldn't.

"Fine," I muttered and turned towards the front door.

What the fuck was happening to me?

***

Turns out some fresh air was good for me to start thinking clearly again. Those thoughts were a momentary lapse in judgment. I couldn't help that she was a sharp-tongued, bitchy little thing. I couldn't help that a part of me was actually attracted to that about her but the bit of time away from the apartment put everything back into perspective. I was here to keep her alive. So whatever attraction there was, that was about to be locked away in my mind and would be left untouched. The focus was simple - keep her alive, return her to her parents and be on my way. Nothing more, nothing less.

I eventually ended up finding her a Kindle. It was the least I could do for her at this point since she wasn't even allowed to enjoy this great summer day. I leaned my head back, soaking in the heat before snapping back into work mode. I had to work quickly to get whatever other supplies we were going to need for now. Being the only one from the team in the city, I had no choice but to leave her alone. I was counting on her being mature enough to work with me here and not do anything stupid while I was gone.

After finally shaking off all unnecessary thoughts, I was back in business. There were various aspects of this job that eventually became part of my natural way of being. You were trained to be aware of your surroundings. You were expected to make eye contact with every person you passed on the streets, as a precaution, mentally taking in anything memorable about them. Long hair, piercings, facial structure, eye color… anything that would need to be recalled in a necessary moment. You needed to be alert and ready for any attack and with the Nazario's searching for Milena, there was no time to take chances. I made sure to analyze my surroundings as I approached our apartment building on the corner. The street outside of it was fairly busy but that's what we wanted. We didn't want to draw attention and what better way to do that than to be hidden in plain sight. I yanked the glass door open and stepped inside, headed for the elevator. It was so old. Even the buttons were faulty which didn't reaffirm any confidence in the building itself. I made it to the third floor and pulled the keys out of my pocket, unlocking the door.

I stepped inside. "Milena? I'm back."

I closed the door behind me and placed the brown paper bag I had on the kitchen counter. I had stopped to opt for something more for her than rice cakes. Microwave popcorn and a box of chocolate chip biscuits. I didn't even know if she liked that but if she didn't then more for me. I also grabbed a few boxes of cigarettes. The universe knew I was going to need them.

"Milena?" I shouted again, my senses now on full alert. I instinctively reached for the gun hidden underneath my shirt and brought it up, pointing it as I did a scan of the area. I reached her door and knocked lightly, hoping for a response but there was nothing. I pushed it open and scanned her room but was greeted by nothing but silence. I rushed over to the bathroom, pulling the shower curtain open but she wasn't there.

"*Cazzo!*" I shouted.

I ran my fingers through my hair, feeling like an idiot for having left her alone. I did a deeper inspection of the apartment but there was no indication of any struggle. Everything was as it was. In her bedroom, her wet towel lay on the bed and her bag sat on the floor.

Where the fuck is she?

I pulled my phone from my pocket and sent a little prayer to the universe that she had the burner phone on her. I wouldn't consider myself religious but if there's something out there, I could do with their assistance right now. I hadn't been gone that long but it was plenty of time for something to have gone terribly wrong.

I slammed the cupboard door shut out of frustration. I opened up the tracker on my phone that was connected to the burner she had. Thankfully, I could see the pulsing red dot on the screen. I dragged my fingers across the screen, zooming out to get a better look at the perimeter.

Okay, she was close. *Thank fuck.*

"Where did you go, Milena?" I muttered to myself and zoomed into the map again, getting a better view of where she was. Just a few roads up from here. Before I knew it, I was out the door again and headed down the stairs. Pushing through the front entrance, I pulled my cap lower and stalked off in her direction. She better hope that she was taken because if I find out she left the apartment after she was told not to, I was going to lose my fucking shit. Was she so incapable of following the rules? They were to keep her alive, dammit!

"Questa donna sarà la mia fine!" I muttered to myself.

I picked up my pace as I stalked towards the red dot that had now stopped in one spot. Turning the corner, the location showed her in what looked like a hair salon. *Seriously?* I stopped in front of it, glancing down at the phone to make sure before looking up again.

Opening the door, I stepped inside just as she had turned to leave.

"Lo siento," she said before looking up and realizing it was me. *"Foda-se,"* she switched to her mother tongue.

I grabbed her wrist. "Are you fucking kidding me, Milena?"

She tried to pull her arm from my grip, but I tightened it.

"Vincenzo, you're making a scene," she said calmly, glancing around to see if anyone was watching us. A couple of women had stopped to glance over which caused me to drop her arm. I pushed the door open and stepped back, waiting for her to leave first. She left the salon and I followed closely behind her, grabbing her elbow this time.

"You had one job," I muttered close to her ear. "Stay in the fucking apartment."

"Look who's the one swearing now," she snapped.

"Don't test me, Milena."

"I needed a few things," she said casually. "And look, I have your dumb cap and sunglasses on since you thought these would help make a brilliant disguise, so what's the issue?"

Her sarcasm has yet to falter. "The issue is that they're just a dumb cap and sunglasses. Not your blanket of invisibility,"

"Cloak," she corrected, judgment passing on her face.

I glared at her. She pulled her arm from my grip and lifted a brown paper bag up. "A better disguise is in here. I was not about to cut and dye my hair like you ordered so I went with the next best thing,"

"And what is that?" I asked, guiding her down the street back towards the apartment.

"Wigs," she announced with a smile. "And multiple ones. That way I can decide which Milena I want to be,"

Her nonchalant attitude about the fact that people were out there trying to kill her exasperated me. She continued with this blasé attitude as if she didn't care if she died or not.

"Do you think this is a game?" I stopped her, forcing her to look at me. She narrowed her eyes at me, her dark brown pupils hidden beneath her long eyelashes.

"I know it's not a game, Vincenzo," she said, a flicker of irritation in her voice. "I'm trying to make the best of a fucked up situation because I refuse to have this derail my life."

"If you keep fucking around like this, you're not going to have a life to derail," I said through my teeth.

She jerked her head back as if she physically felt my words. Her jaw tightened and she took a deep breath in before replying. "Did you get my cigarettes?"

That's what she was concerned about?

"They're at the apartment."

"Great," she muttered and took off in its direction. I took a deep breath in, trying to shake my irritation. *This woman.* I shook my head and followed her. We made it back upstairs and I locked the door behind us.

"Am I going to have to tie you to your bed?" I asked her.

She whipped her head around, arching her eyebrow at me. "You think I have a problem being tied up?"

There she did it again. Her fucking sexual innuendos sent the heat pulsing through my veins reaching my groin that jumped to life at her words. The corners of her lips pulled in amusement.

"What's the matter, Vincenzo? Changing your mind now?" she probed, taking a step closer to me.

"Don't tempt me, Milena." Her lips parted and her gaze held mine. A sudden tension had seeped into the air surrounding us, probing us to give into it. She infuriated me in the worst way and yet, I couldn't seem to pull my gaze away from her. She ran her tongue across her bottom lip as her gaze dropped to my lips. God, what I'd have those lips do.

Vincenzo, stop this right now.

"Don't try that shit again," I warned and walked past her back to the couch. I had never been this affected by anyone before. She was suffocating me and as much as I could do with another break from this unspoken tension between us, the last thing I was going to do was give her an opportunity to pull that shit again.

"Looks like I'll need to use that shower head after all," she said before disappearing into her room.

Did she ju-? God, now I am going to need a cold shower.

CHAPTER 10:

Milena

"No," I shook my head. "This isn't happening - please tell me this isn't true." The tears streamed down my face as reality started to settle over me. I stood up, rushing through the hospital corridors. People around me shouted my name, wanting me to stop but my body carried me closer and closer to her room. She wasn't gone. She couldn't be. I pushed through the double doors and was greeted by her lifeless body. The sound of the flatline increased in volume and mixed with the deep cry I let out.

"Carina!" I screamed. "Come back!"

My body jolted up as the tainted memory released me from the nightmare it had turned into. Tears stained my cheeks and a pulsing ache deepened within my chest. Whenever I thought of Carina, the grief presented itself. While it used to be unbearable, over time it had cemented itself around my heart and I had almost gotten used to the pain. I ran my fingers through my hair, sweat staining my hairline. I took a deep breath in, trying to calm my emotions down. Carina haunted every part of my life but the day I found out that she had died, that was the worst nightmare of all. I knew that my dreams had become an altered version of reality - often causing more pain at the sight of her lifeless body. I never saw that and thank goodness for that. I would never have been able to survive having that image permanently burned into my brain. Up until Carina's death, I had never experienced loss before. I had never lost a family member, a friend or even a pet. Loss was something I had never encountered. The day I did, I went into shock. I didn't know how to handle the deep grief that settled over me at the deep hollowness that was taking up residence inside of me.

I tried to stop it but my mind couldn't help but replay the true events of that day…

The doctor's words echoed in my mind, disconnecting me from reality.

I wanted to cry. I wanted to scream. But instead, I remained silent as I stared down the empty hospital hallway in front of me. The same hallway I had become accustomed to over the last year. The potent smell of disinfectant was no longer overwhelming as I had breathed it in everyday we came here to visit her. It was a difficult adjustment at first but the longer she was here, the more well-adjusted we all became to our new version of what was normal. This place became our second home and I had always believed that the day would come where we got to take her back to the home we both knew and loved.

Turns out I couldn't have been more wrong.

"Milena?" I heard someone say my name but it was more of a faint echo in the distance. I couldn't move. The tears began to pool in my eyes as the pain constricted my airways, causing an ache in my throat as I tried to hold them back.

There was no way she was dead.

She had been suffering for so long but she was going to get better. She had her entire life ahead of her - there is just no way that the world would be this cruel. I had already accepted that this was just a small bump in the road that we were going to get through as a family. She was going to get better. She deserved to get better. She deserved to live the life that should have been meant for her. Not this. She didn't deserve to go through this.

But I quickly learned that as much as you think you're in charge of your life, you don't get to decide what you deserve. It decides for you.

"I'm sorry for your loss, Milena," Nurse Sabrina had said, extending her arm to rest her hand on my shoulder in an attempt to soften the blow. She had taken care of Carina over the last few months and we had all welcomed her as a recurring presence in our lives. "We can take comfort in knowing that she's no longer suffering."

Now it was my turn to suffer in the deep grief and denial that was now going to be a permanent part of who I was. It felt as if someone had just ripped away a part of my soul with no way of getting it back. I tried to grasp it in the darkness but it was to no avail.

I shook my head. "Sh-she's not dead," I said, my voice barely recognizable. "No. No way."

"Milena..." I felt my mother's presence beside me, forcing my gaze to break from the fluorescent lights I kept my focus on. My head slowly turned, landing on her grief-stricken face. The tears stained her eyes as she reached for me, burying her head in my shoulder. She couldn't hold back the wailing that now escaped from her throat.

"This can't be happening," I whispered, my voice cracking with emotion as the tears started to spill over. She tightened her grip on me as she cried and cried. Everything was a blur to me from that moment onwards. I could only focus on the all-consuming sadness inside of me.

My twin sister was dead and there was nothing I could do about it.

I reached up and wiped away the stray tears that had managed to escape. Growing up, I had always been the one to protect Carina. She was the more reserved one, she was never a rule-breaker and she definitely wasn't one for confrontation. She was soft-hearted and people often took advantage of that. Enter me. I was her protector. Anyone tried something with my sister, I would make them sorry that they ever dared to look her way. The first fight I ever got into was back in fourth grade when some little bitch had pushed my sister in the mud. There was no reason except for their cruel enjoyment but I quickly rectified that situation by socking her in the face. One punch and her nose was broken. I was suspended and told to apologize but I refused - she had been terrorizing Carina for months and after that day, she didn't even dare stepping a foot in her direction. I would always protect her and the worst part about her getting sick was not being able to do that at all. There was no one to punch and no one to blame. I had to watch as my sister withered away to her illness.

The same suffocating pain that I had become accustomed to was making a painful appearance tonight, and I couldn't allow myself to acknowledge it. I shook my head and wiped my tears. I sat up straight and took a deep breath in. My body was on high alert now and I knew I wasn't going to manage to sleep anytime soon. Instead, I pushed the blanket off me and reached for a pair of material shorts, pulling them over my underwear. I hated to sleep in anything other than my underwear but with Vincenzo in the other room, I couldn't exactly walk around like that.

Vincenzo.

Fuck, that man aggravated me in ways I had never been aggravated before. I hated that he could dictate what I could and couldn't do. This was my life and I deserved to decide how to handle this situation. Not some imperious Italian man. My only source of entertainment was continuously learning what it was that pushed his buttons. With the two of us cooped up in this place, there was nothing for me to do but poke the bear, and what better way to do that than to flirt with him. It's what I was good at. I had quickly learned all the ways in which I could reel a man in and get what I wanted from him. Since I had become disconnected from my true emotions, I took on a more primal approach to life. I used men for nothing but sex when I needed it. It filled that void inside of me, even if it was just for a moment. My only ever attempt at a relationship was that sad excuse for one with that asshole, Fabiano and look how well that turned out. I had accepted a long time ago that I wasn't wired to be in a relationship. No companionship. No vulnerability. Nothing that suggested the interference of emotions.

I slowly opened my door, careful not to make any noise. I glanced inside and Vincenzo lay facing the wall with his back to me. He wasn't wearing a shirt and I was caught off guard by the amount of tattoos spread across his entire back. My mouth went dry and a flicker of attraction stirred inside of me. So, Vincenzo had a great back? *Who cares, Milena?* I didn't use the shower head earlier but with this rush of fascination towards Vincenzo, I was toying around with the idea.

I shook my head and walked over to the kitchen counter to grab a box of cigarettes and a lighter. I wasn't a big smoker. It was quite the slap in the face to my sister who died of cancer but that was the irony - she had never even touched a cigarette. She had done nothing that could have put her in that situation in the first place and yet, it happened. You can do everything right in this world and it can still fuck you. I usually did it in social settings but given the situation, this was about as social as it was going to get. I tiptoed across the room to the balcony door and slowly opened it with enough space to step outside before shutting it behind me. I took a deep breath in, allowing the cool nighttime air to fill my lungs. My gaze landed on the river in front of me. We were situated in an apartment building that had a view of the *Guadalquivir* river. The moonlight glistened against the water and I welcomed the calming view.

I leaned against the wall and pulled a cigarette out, putting it between my lips as I lit it. I pulled the smoke into my lungs and dropped my hand, exhaling before settling my gaze back in the distance. Sevilla was beautiful. It was a city that was meant to be explored. I had never imagined that I would have ended up here due to these circumstances. The ache in my chest reminded me of the hollowness that now resided inside of me. I never thought I would say this, but I missed my home. I missed my parents. I missed my life. It wasn't what it had once been, but I would trade anything to go back to that over what had become of my life now. For the most part, I had been left in the dark. Just a couple of updates here and there from Vincenzo but other than that, I was isolated. I had no one to turn to and nowhere else to go. I hated it. I used to be very good at dealing with my emotions, but after Carina died, I switched off entirely. I refused to give in to them in any way and over the years. I became cold. I refused to show emotion in any form and instead, I hid behind my sharp comments and witty responses. I hid behind humor and any other defense mechanism I could cling to. I would use anything I could to avoid dealing with the sadness and anger I felt inside of me.

Tears brimmed my eyes, forcing them to shut as I swallowed, trying to stop the pain that was now forming in my throat from holding back. I brought the cigarette back to my lips, the bottom one quivering as it focused on nothing but the pulling of the smoke into my lungs.

What good would crying do?

I wanted to cry over everything that was out of my control. My father was a killer and I had a target on my back. How was I supposed to begin to process that information? My brain wanted to implode at just the mere thought of it all. I didn't want to believe my father was capable of something like this but when the flashes of the dead body entered my mind, a rush of nausea came over me. There was just no way he could have done that. Not my father. The sweet man I had grown up with. The loving father I had once known. The same father that would sit with me while I completed crossword puzzles. For hours, we would do them together. Carina would join every now and then, but that was our thing. That was my fondest memory of my father. Nestled against his chest with the book rested on my legs as my feet dug into his leg. He never complained and engaged with me with such enthusiasm every time I would find a word. As I got older, we still continued our tradition but more sporadically and I had since become way too big to fit comfortably on his lap. After Carina died, that stopped all together along with any other form of bonding between my parents and I. I lost them all.

A tear escaped my eye and that opened up the floodgates for the rest of them. I lifted my hand to my eyes, trying to stop the tears now streaming down my face but it was no use. My emotions had gotten the better of me and I could do nothing but allow them to consume me. My lip trembled against the cigarette as I pulled another drag, the taste of nicotine now on my tongue. I leaned forward, my arms against the iron barrier as I flicked the butt of my cigarette onto the deserted street in front of me.

The sound of the door opening behind me caught my attention, forcing me to quickly wipe away the tears before I turned to meet Vincenzo's sleepy eyes. His hair was disheveled and he had changed into a gray shirt.

"Milena, you okay?" he asked.

I nodded and turned my attention back to the street, not wanting him to see me cry. I felt his presence next to me as he leaned against the barrier.

"I'm fine. I figured this is probably the safest time for me to be outside," I attempted to joke.

I noticed his smile out of the corner of my eye before bringing a cigarette to rest between his lips. I glanced at him, careful to not stare too long, but I couldn't pull my eyes away from the way his muscles tightened as he lifted the lighter closer to him. He dropped his arm as he pulled a drag, releasing the smoke into the air. He leaned forward, tightening his jaw which gave way for his jawline to make a brief appearance underneath his dark beard. I noticed a deep scar just underneath his jawline and down his neck just below his ear.

"What happened there?" I pointed to the scar as he glanced at me.

"Knife fight," he answered casually.

"Yes, 'cause every person ends up in a fight with knives at least once in their lives," I mumbled sarcastically.

A small smile played on his lips, and I actually celebrated that as a small victory. Vincenzo De Rossi smiling? The world seems to have gone mad.

"Only the lucky ones." He eyed me playfully.

My own lips pulled up in amusement. It was a lot more difficult to deny his attractiveness when he was calmer. And when he showed he could smile. It was a great one. The hard demeanor he carried around had been put to bed for the time being it seemed.

"Having trouble sleeping?" he asked.

I glanced towards the river again. "Something like that."

"Do you need me to give you a sleeping tablet?" he offered.

"Oh, so you do have drugs?" I turned back to face him just in time to catch him chuckle. A full-on breath of laughter escaped his lips and I was hung up on that sound.

"Technically, you just asked for weed, not drugs in general," he pointed out.

"Next time, I'll be less specific and just ask for whatever you got," I said playfully before returning back to his question. "I'm fine, though. I'm sure I'll fall asleep eventually. It's not like I have anywhere to be tomorrow."

He brought the cigarette back to his lips for another drag before removing it, keeping it between his index finger and thumb. "If it's any consolation, I am sorry that you're stuck here."

I didn't know if it was the nighttime air that had gotten to his head but late-night Vincenzo was a different person to the autocratic man who barked orders and reprimanded me the whole day.

"Well, you're stuck here with me so I can't imagine this is fun for you, either."

"It certainly has its challenges."

I rolled my eyes knowing very well I was the only challenge. I couldn't help it. He got on my nerves in a way no one had ever done before. It unnerved me the way he made me feel.

"If you get me some alcohol, I promise I'll be nicer to you."

"Bribery, huh?" he smirked, inhaling another drag.

"Choice is yours," I shrugged, "And maybe if you're nice enough, I'll even share some with you."

"How generous of you," he said dryly. "Too bad I don't drink."

"At all?"

He shook his head. "Nope."

"Any particular reason for that?" I gently pried, wondering how much he would be willing to share with me.

"It's really bad for your health," he said with a straight face as he brought the cigarette to his mouth again. A glimmer of humor in his eye revealed his playful irony at the slow-killer between his lips. I couldn't help but laugh.

"I didn't know you had a sense of humor." I glared at him playfully.

"You don't exactly give me many opportunities to present it now, do you?"

I rolled my eyes and glanced forward again, a small smile on my lips. "You're right. I'm too busy playing hide-and-seek with you when I run away."

"That was never my favorite game growing up and I certainly don't enjoy it now."

"Too bad."

I was surprised at the comfortability I felt with him. He was enough of a distraction to have calmed down my, otherwise, previous emotions that had reached the surface. I found myself relaxing - even if it was only slightly.

"What did you do back in London?" he changed the subject as he inhaled another drag.

"I was studying."

"What's your major?"

"Fashion," I answered. "But I also did a side course in marketing, specifically digital marketing."

He nodded, stretching his back before leaning against the balcony, this time moving closer to me. Did he do that on purpose? Should I even be thinking about that? We were inches from each other and I was over-aware of just how close his arm was to mine.

"I was heading into my final year," I continued, adamant to distract my mind. "But I don't think the Nazarios are going to care about that."

"We don't know what's going to happen. You could still go back," he said softly.

"You don't really believe that, do you?" I looked over at him. "You're just trying to be nice."

He remained silent and flicked what was left of his cigarette onto the street.

"Don't be nice. It's out of character," I teased, nudging him playfully. I hadn't planned to do it but it happened before I could stop it. My arm brushed his and I felt the electricity in my veins at such a simple touch. He glanced at our arms before glancing back at me and I could have sworn he noticed it, too.

I turned away from him. "Is my father going to go to jail?" I asked, changing the subject in an attempt to ignore the sudden tension in the air.

"I don't think the Nazarios are the type to get law enforcement involved."

"Oh right," I mumbled. "They just take matters into their own hands."

I thought I could handle talking about it, but when the pressure in my chest started to reappear, I needed an escape. I needed out of the thoughts bombarding my mind, displaying every fear I now had.

"Don't your family miss you?" I asked.

"Uh-" He was clearly caught off-guard by my change in subject again but just went along with it. "I don't have much family. My grandmother lives back in *Palermo,* where I grew up."

"And your parents?"

"Both dead," he said. There wasn't a harshness to the way he said it, but there was also no flicker of emotion. He didn't strike me as the kind of man to allow his emotions in so I didn't hold it against him.

"I'm sorry," I said softly.

"Don't be. It happens."

"Are you going to bond over death now?" Carina said, her dry humor almost forcing me to smile.

I watched his hand briefly tighten around the iron rod of the balcony and that told me more about the internal battle he was facing. I didn't believe that he was as alright with that as he may have wanted me to believe, but I didn't push him. I recognized that same internal battle as I had the same problem.

"I'm sure your girlfriend misses you." The words left my mouth before I could stop them. I don't know where it came from but it earned me a snicker from Vincenzo and for the first time, I noticed his slight dimple. A small dent in the right side of his cheek. He turned and leaned against the balcony, this time facing me.

"I don't have a girlfriend."

"It's probably 'cause you're all domineering."

"Some women like that," he pointed out.

"It's only fun if it's in the bedroom."

There I went again, running my mouth. *Seriously, Milena?* This time he smirked and he couldn't stop the flicker of curiosity in his eyes.

"Oh? There's clearly more than meets the eye with you, Milena."

"I didn't say I liked it," I said quickly, lying through my teeth to try and save face.

He lifted an eyebrow and gave me a look that clearly showed he didn't believe me. "I think you do."

I swallowed, trying to get a handle on the rush of arousal that stirred inside of me but with the way his eyes wandered down over my body, there was just no way. He flicked his eyes to meet mine again, and I swear he was feeling the tension, too. I could almost taste it.

I wonder what he tastes like.

"I think I should head back to bed," he said, breaking us both out of the trance we had been sucked into. His eyes betrayed him, though. There was more behind them. "*Boa noite, M*ilena."

"*Boa noite,* Vincenzo."

CHAPTER 11:

Milena

After my interaction with Vincenzo last night, I was wide awake for other reasons. There was more to that brooding man than meets the eye and I couldn't help but be continuously drawn to him. While my entire life was falling apart around me, he was the only constant right now and I was learning more about him. I *wanted to* learn more about him. I wanted to know more about the man behind that officious front.

Sleep eventually found me but when I woke with a sudden jolt this morning from another nightmare, I was too scared to close my eyes again. This time, the visuals of my parents' lifeless bodies flashed before me and the fear had returned. I wiped the sweat off my forehead and swung my legs over the side of the bed, thankful that the tiles were cold against my feet. It was hot in here. Summer was relentless. I walked over to the curtain and pulled it open, reaching for the windows and opening them up allowing whatever cold air it could manage. I was disappointed by the warm air that rushed into the room instead.

"That's not going to help," I muttered to myself.

I pulled my shirt over my head and dropped it on the bed, reaching for a gray vest from my bag along with a sports bra. I pulled that on first, securing my boobs in place. They were so big and I often found it uncomfortable to go without a bra. Pulling the vest over next, it sat against the bra but I was pleasantly surprised by how good my cleavage looked. It wasn't intentional but hell, sometimes my boobs did what they needed to do. Too bad there was no one here to enjoy that view. Grabbing my material shorts, I brought them up over me as they rested just above my belly button. Anyone who preferred low-rise bottoms in any way was seriously deranged.

Or probably genetically blessed.

I opened the door and stepped into the living room, noticing that Vincenzo's couch was empty. I walked over and opened the balcony door and window, needing some fresh air in this stuffy place. I walked over to the TV and turned it on, welcoming whatever voices were coming from the news. Vincenzo wasn't here and between the deafening silence and the hovering overthinking in my mind, I needed something else to focus on. When I didn't, I easily got consumed by the black hole in my mind. The news reporter spoke in Spanish but I was just happy that I didn't feel entirely alone.

I grabbed my burner phone on the counter and dialed my parent's number. I hadn't spoken to them in days and I was anxious to hear from them again. All this waiting around was torture. I tapped my foot against the floor as I listened to the ringing on the other end. It rang and rang. I didn't want to give up so when it went to voicemail, I ended the call and tried again. I leaned against the kitchen counter and allowed my eyes to settle on the TV. Flashes of a burning building were shown on the screen and when they showed the entrance, I froze.

That's my father's hotel.

His hotel was on fire.

I rushed over to grab the remote off the coffee table and turned the volume up, trying to focus on what they were saying.

"We can confirm that a bomb was set off on the tenth floor of the hotel in the early hours of the morning," the reporter shared.

"Oh my God." I breathed, my hand covering my mouth.

"It is unclear at this point who is behind this attack but law enforcement is on the scene…"

I dropped onto the couch, feeling the weight of the situation hanging over me. The door flung open and Vincenzo stepped inside, stealing my attention for a moment.

"Milena? What's wr-," his sentence got caught as his eyes landed on the TV.

"*Cazzo,* they're already reporting on it." He dropped the bag he had in his hand by the counter and rushed over to grab his laptop.

"When did this happen?"

"A few hours ago." He walked past me to sit by the kitchen counter, pulling the barstool out for him to sit on.

"Uh-," I scrambled to find the words I needed. "Was anyone hurt?"

"There are about eight civilians that were taken to hospital. No deaths at this stage but two are in critical condition."

God, I was going to be sick. This was my family's fault. People were about to be collateral damage in a feud they had no part of.

"You don't have to worry, Milena. This just proves that they still think you are somewhere in Algarve. They have no idea you're in Sevilla."

"That's not what I'm worried about," I answered softly. "This is their way of sending a message, isn't it?"

"It's possible. We think that they're trying to draw your father back home by attacking his properties."

"I should go back."

He lifted his head to meet my gaze just past his laptop. "You're not going anywhere."

"Innocent people are being attacked now because of what my father did." My voice cracked as the emotion worked its way into my throat. "There has got to be a better way to fix this situation."

"We are working on it but we can't have you rushing back home to play martyr," he snapped.

Okay, so moody and domineering Vincenzo was back.

"I'm not playing anything," I snapped, not bothering to hold back my irritation. "But this is my father's fault. He is the reason we are in this situation and look at the damage that's being done. They bombed our fucking hotel - what are they going to target next? I need to go back home," I repeated.

He opened his mouth to say something further but quickly closed it and glanced at his laptop. He clearly had more to share.

"What, Vincenzo?" I snapped. "Spit it out."

"There's nothing left for you in Algarve," he said, his voice devoid of emotion again.

"My whole life is there," I argued. "That's my home."

"The hotel wasn't the first place they targeted."

"What does that mean?" I huffed.

"They got to your house first," he explained. "They tore it apart before setting it on fire."

My breath got stuck in my throat and my mouth went dry. *My home was set on fire?* I couldn't process what he was telling me. I refused to believe it.

I shook my head. "No."

"Milena..." he started but I interrupted him.

"You're lying."

"No, I'm not." He sighed and stood up, walking over to me. "You said yesterday that I should let you know what's happening so that's what I'm doing. I don't want to lie to you - your parents are worried you wouldn't be able to handle everything that's happening but they're wrong. You're stronger than they give you credit for."

"He's right." Carina agreed.

Was he? Was I really strong enough to handle this because I certainly didn't feel like I was?

"I don't think watching the news is something you should be doing right now though," he said.

"It's not like I expected to see that," I retorted. "I just can't sit in silence. It drives me fucking crazy."

My chest started to rise and fall at a quicker pace as my breathing picked up. I could feel the world starting to spin again but I refused to give into it. I needed to get my shit together. I stood still and focused on the small hole in the wall in front of me. I felt his hand on my arm, forcing my attention to his touch.

"I tried to call my parents," I said, keeping my eyes on his hand on my arm. "There was no answer. I don't even know if they're okay. Have you heard from them?"

He shook his head. My bottom lip trembled and I caught it between my teeth to stop it as the tears pooled in my eyes.

"Hey," he murmured and pulled me into his arms. It caught me by surprise but there was something comforting about being held by him. I couldn't move. I just allowed myself to be held as I used all my strength to hold back my tears.

"My father is a murderer," I muttered. "My house is gone. The home I once knew along with the family I once had. Everything has changed now and

I can't - I don't know - how is this going to get better?" I couldn't gather my thoughts to form a coherent sentence. I had no fucking clue how to make it out of this. He said nothing, instead, he just lifted his hand to cup the back of my head as he held me close to him. I couldn't help but breathe him in - his usual cologne infused with a cigarette smell surrounding me. It was starting to become a smell I welcomed. In his arms, I had managed to get a handle on my emotions and immediately cursed myself for showing my weakness. As a knee-jerk reaction, I pulled away from him and took a deep breath in as the tears brimmed my eyes.

"Sorry. Don't worry about me," I muttered. "I'm fine now."

"No, you're not."

I avoided his gaze but I couldn't help but look his way when he reached for my hand again. I couldn't think straight when he touched me. It was all fuzzy in my brain. What the hell was happening to me? I walked past him, forcing his hand to fall from mine.

"Is this my life now? Constantly hiding, running away and hiding in the shadows?" I shook my head, already knowing the answer to my question. "Doesn't sound like much of a life."

I walked past him towards the kitchen counter, reaching for the box of cigarettes. "I can't do that, Vincenzo. You don't know me but I can't live a life in hiding. I can't stay stuck in one place for too long. I'm not built that way." My hand was shaking as I brought the lighter to the cigarette between my lips, lighting it up before I pulled a drag. Releasing the smoke into the air, I watched as it floated through the apartment. "I need excitement. I need adventure. That's who I am. This-," I gestured towards the apartment. "This doesn't work for me. I'm already sick of this place."

The air around me started to become thin and I was trying my hardest to ignore the aching pressure in my chest. I was claustrophobic and it felt as if the walls were closing in on me. I didn't want this. God, I wanted nothing more than to go back to London and stay there. I shouldn't have come home. Last summer I had decided to stay in London so I could spend time doing what I wanted to do. I didn't think it would bother my parents considering they were always working but when they asked if I would come home this year, I felt bad saying no. Now that didn't even matter because I was spending my summer apart from them anyway.

"I hate being alone," I admitted.

"Milena," Vincenzo said, stepping closer to me. "You're not alone."

"You're only here because you've been hired to do so." I flicked my eyes to his, pulling another drag of my cigarette before resting it between my fingers.

He ignored my comment. "I'm going to get you out of this. My job is to protect you and nothing is going to stop me from doing that. I can promise you that."

He spoke with such surety and confidence that I almost believed him.

"You don't know me, Milena, but I don't make a promise unless I'm sure I can keep them."

His dark eyes held mine with such an intensity that I half-expected my legs to buckle beneath me. The tension I had felt last night had resurfaced again. I was drawn to his determination and confidence. I knew he wasn't untouchable but at that moment, I believed he could be.

I was thankful for his phone ringing, breaking me out of my trance. He pulled it from his back pocket and brought it to his ear. *"Si?"* he waited. *"Gracias."*

*H*e dropped his arm and walked back over to the open laptop on the counter.

"How many languages do you speak?" I asked. Up till now I had heard him speak quite a few.

"Four or five," he said casually. "Italian, Portuguese, Romanian, English and enough Spanish to get me by."

Impressive. I had only managed to master two. Spanish wasn't too hard for me to follow thanks to the Portuguese but other than that, I didn't feel like I had the brain capacity to learn anything further.

"But Italian is your first language right?"

*"Sì bellezza, l'italiano è la mia prima lingua." H*e switched and my jaw dropped slightly, hanging on his every word. While I couldn't be exactly sure, I managed to deduce that he confirmed it was his first language. I was also pretty sure he had thrown a compliment in there. *Bellezza? D*id he just call me beautiful?

Pull yourself together, Milena.

"What made you learn the others?" I asked.

"My grandparents - mainly my grandmother - thought it would be a good distraction."

Distraction? Before I had time to ask a follow-up question, he continued as he clicked through his laptop.

"She's Italian-Romanian so she switched between the two and had learned Portuguese for work years ago. Guess she wanted me to learn as many languages as possible."

"Impressive skill-set you have there. Must have been a nice way to bond with her." I was prying, I knew that but it was easier to speak about someone else's family since mine was in shambles.

"Yeah…" he paused for a moment and a flicker of nostalgia was present in his eyes, "It was."

He glanced back down at the screen, snapping back to the present. "Ah finally!"

I walked over to where he stood and my eyes fell on the screen that was separated into four rectangles on the screen, clearly displaying a live feed of the streets outside. Every few seconds they would change, showing our apartment building from a different angle.

"Cameras?" I asked

He nodded. "We had them installed around the entrance as a precaution. Can never be too careful."

An older man stepped into frame, looking around as he spoke on his phone. The angle changed again and revealed a couple walking along the curb across the road.

"And the building management just let you do that?"

"What they don't know, won't hurt them." He shrugged casually.

I leaned over the counter to press what was left of my cigarette into the ashtray, killing it. My eyes glanced over to the brown paper bag next to his laptop. I walked to the other side of him, peeping into the bag. I was surprised to see a small box of famous Portuguese custard tarts, *Pastel de nata,* peeking out from behind the clear plastic square on the front of the box.

"Where did you get these?" I pulled the box out, my eyes lighting up at them. They were my absolute favorite.

"There's a small Portuguese bakery around the corner and I figured you might enjoy these."

I didn't buy that. I narrowed my eyes at him. "Out of all the options available, you just happened to decide on these?"

He eyed me. "I have great intuition."

I rolled my eyes. "I think you just have great intel." I popped the lid open, bringing one of the custard tarts to my lips. I had never been so happy to have something as simple as this. The sweet custard delighted my taste buds and I immediately felt better. Who says food can't make you happy? I call bullshit.

"Do you have a file on me?" I asked casually.

He leaned against the counter, propping an elbow up before leaning his head against it as he turned to face me. A few stray strands of his hair fell forward and I had to physically fight the urge to reach out and move it back.

"Maybe," he answered.

"Can I see it?"

"Nope."

"But it's about me," I argued.

"Yes but it's *for* me," he retorted.

I took another bite. "If you want to know something about me, just ask."

"I'll take that into consideration."

I was enjoying every last bit of my pastry. It reminded me of home. It reminded me of when my father would bring some back whenever he went out past *Belém. He* knew how much Carina and I enjoyed these. "No one does these quite like *Pastéis de Belém.* They made the first one more than one hundred years ago," I explained, not knowing why I felt the need to give him a history lesson.

"Never had one," he said.

I gaped at him. "Are you serious? You don't even realize what you're missing out on."

He leaned over to try to grab one from my box but I slapped his hand away. This time he gaped at me.

"Oh? Didn't your file tell you I hate to share?" I pulled the box closer to me, arching an eyebrow playfully at him.

His lips pulled in amusement briefly. "I guess the file doesn't know everything."

I pushed the box back to where it was, allowing him to finally grab one. His dark arms were lined with tattoos - not a single part was left clear. I noticed the bird tattoo he had on his hand, but I also noticed the protruding veins. It was kind of... attractive?

"How many tattoos do you have?" I asked.

"I lost count a long time ago."

I watched as he peeled the paper off the pastry and brought it to his lips. There shouldn't be anything seductive about the way someone eats a freaking custard tart but damn, what I would give to be that pastry right now. To have his lips wrapped ar-

"It's good," he said, breaking me out of dirty thoughts. My cheeks flushed and I averted my eyes away from him as he continued to eat. I was losing it. I focused back on his tattoos as I grabbed a bottle of water from the fridge.

"What tattoos do you have on your back?"

He looked confused. "How do you know I have any on my back?"

I swallowed some of the cold water as I sipped. "Uh... I saw it last night when I came to get a cigarette. You.. uh- you were facing the wall and you didn't have a shirt on." *Why the hell was my mouth dry?* I was drinking water and my mouth was dry - what the fuck? So I saw him without a shirt, what's the issue here? I couldn't stop the small amount of heat from spreading across my cheeks.

"It was too hot to sleep with one," he said casually. "And it's a lion."

"Any significance to it?"

"I could lie and say that it's a symbol of courage and bravery but the truth is, I just like getting tattoos."

I smiled at his honesty. "Must have been painful."

He shrugged. "Nothing I can't handle."

He turned back to his laptop and for a moment, we sat in comfortable silence. He had managed to distract me enough that I no longer felt overwhelmed by my emotions. My breathing had returned to its normal pace and although the aching pressure in my chest was still there, it wasn't suffocating me anymore.

"So, what's the big plan for the day, Vinnie?"

"Don't call me that," he warned.

Second time he's been bothered by that nickname. I wondered if there was a reason behind that or he just didn't like that.

"What should I call you?"

"Vincenzo."

"Boring."

He arched an eyebrow. "My name is boring?"

I shrugged and leaned against the counter, my hair falling forward against my chest.

"What about Mr. De Rossi?" I suggested. "Or we could go with the good ol' fashion '*sir*'?"

He shifted in his chair. *Did he like that?* Now, I was intrigued. He was my main source of entertainment and since my biggest flaw in life was not knowing when to shut up, I knew that was exactly what was happening here. I didn't care though. A part of me was curious to see how far I could push him.

"Vincenzo will do," he repeated, a quick flick of his eyes to mine revealed his own curiosity.

"What about Enzo?" I suggested.

He thought for a moment. "Definitely better than Vinnie."

"Enzo it is then!" I announced. "So what's the big plan for the day, Enzo?"

"I hooked up the wifi for you so you can use the spare laptop to watch Netflix." He slipped off the barstool and walked over to his stuff, grabbing the laptop he had there.

That was sweet of him.

"Maybe I should use this time to educate you on movies such as Harry Potter," I said.

"Or maybe I should educate you on something other than that."

I rolled my eyes. "I don't think I want to be roommates with someone who hates on Harry Potter. Doesn't say much about your taste," I teased.

"Trust me, my taste is great." He stopped in front of me and handed the laptop to me. "You go and enjoy. I have some things I have to sort out first."

"Fine." I took the laptop from him. "But tonight then? If you're nice enough, I'll consider letting you choose the movie."

He smirked. "Fine. Tonight. I'll get us some pizza."

"This is starting to sound like my kind of date." The words left my mouth before I could stop them. *Again.*

"If this were a real date, we wouldn't even get through the movie."

My lips parted as my desire flicked deep inside of my stomach. *Oh, Vincenzo was sexy. He* flashed me a small smile before making his way back to his own laptop by the counter. He was so nonchalant with what he said and here I was, cheeks all flushed and with a deeper arousal that wasn't present before.

"Shout if you need anything," I said as casually as I could manage before rushing back into my room.

CHAPTER 12:

Vincenzo

My eyes opened and landed on the rolling credits from the movie we had decided on. There was no other way to decide fairly on who gets to choose a movie other than three rounds of rock, paper, scissors. Milena managed to win every round and was not shy about boasting about her underrated guessing skills. That's all it was, a guessing game but truthfully, it was nice to see her smile. It was way better than having her scold me which was pretty much what she had done most of the time since being here. We had set the laptop up on the coffee table since we didn't have a cable to connect it to the TV and sat on either side of the couch to watch. I glanced over and she had fallen asleep against the armrest of the chair. All I could hear was her soft breaths as I watched her chest slowly rise and fall. Stray strands of her hair had fallen over her face and for a moment, I just wanted to reach out and touch her. There was something about her that made me want to know more. Who was the woman behind the walls she had so clearly built around herself? I was well-aware that the many thoughts I was having about her would be deemed inappropriate but I couldn't stop it. Being cooped up here with her clouded my judgment. The best I could do was pretend it wasn't there which is proving to be a trying task.

I stood up and grabbed the box of cigarettes on the table next to the laptop. I pulled one out and was just about to head to the balcony when I heard her start to murmur. I turned to face her, making sure that I hadn't heard wrong. She was quiet for a moment but as I turned towards the door again, she started shouting.

"No, no, no!" Her eyes were still closed but I watched as her face twisted in pain. "Carina!"

I rushed over to her. "Milena!"

"Carina! I'm sorry!" Her voice was strained and I could hear the pain in her screams. I grabbed her shoulders, trying to shake her awake. She was so deep in her nightmare that it had manifested into tears that now stained her eyes.

"Milena!" I raised my voice. "Hey, wake up."

I shook her and suddenly her eyes flung open, landing on me. There was so much behind those dark brown eyes right now. A deep hollowness that I had noticed previously but she did a pretty good job at hiding when she was conscious. Tears continued to escape from her eyes but when she realized that was happening, she quickly tried to compose herself.

"Vincenzo?" Her voice was hoarse as she sat up abruptly, pulling away from my touch. "What happened?"

"You were having a nightmare," I said softly. Before I could stop myself I reached out and cupped her cheek, small sweat droplets now against my hand but I didn't care. With the dark look in her eyes, I could see that she was in no position to be alone right now. I had never considered myself to be empathetic in the slightest but there was something about those eyes of hers that were drawing me in. The eyes are the windows to the soul they say.

"Sorry, I'm fine," she said but her tone was less than convincing. I dropped my hand and she wiped the sweat off her forehead with the back of her hand. "God, it's hot in here." She jumped up and walked over to the door leading to the balcony, opening it up to allow the night time air inside. I hadn't known her very long but I already gathered that she was not one to show her emotions if she could avoid it. She hid behind this hard, cold demeanor but I suspected that her emotions controlled her way more than she was letting on. I recognized those traits as a reflection of my own.

"What time is it?" She asked as she reached for a bottle of water from the fridge.

I glanced down at my watch. "Just after one."

She sipped on the water, her gaze staring off into the distance. I could tell she was still holding onto the nightmare that she had. When I was given the assignment, I scanned through the information that was given to me so I already knew that Carina was her twin sister that had died. I hadn't gone into depth about what happened to her and instead of reading about it in her file, I decided to do what she asked of me. She said if I wanted to know anything that I should ask her. If we were going to practically live together for God-knows how long then it only makes sense to get to know each other better. Especially if nightmares like this was a recurring thing she had to go through.

"Milena?" I stood up and walked over to the kitchen counter, stopping to lean against it. "Do you have nightmares often?"

She kept her gaze on the water bottle in her hand, her knuckles white from holding onto it so hard. She carried all this tension and I figured she was trying to hold her emotions back. Another thing I did too.

"It happens most nights," she admitted.

"You were calling for your sister."

Her head lifted abruptly, a hard look settling across her face. "How do you know about her?"

She had gone straight to defensive mode. I had to be careful about how I had this conversation with her. She was a flight risk and I was learning everyday how to handle her. She was not like anyone I had ever encountered.

"Let me guess," she carried on before I could reply. "That folder you have probably told you everything."

"It mentioned her but I don't know the details," I explained. "You said I should ask you if I wanted to know something."

"So, is this you asking?"

I nodded. "What happened to your sister?"

She swallowed and averted her eyes but I had already seen the pain washing over her. She placed the water bottle on the counter and walked over to grab herself a cigarette. I watched as she lit it up, her back to me as she faced the balcony. I was almost sure she wasn't going to say anything further but then she exhaled and her soft voice filled the room.

"Carina was my twin sister." She took a deep breath in. "And she died when I was seventeen."

Her voice held the same hollowness to it that her eyes emitted and now I knew the reason for it. I didn't move. I stayed leaning against the counter as I watched her, waiting for her to continue. Her long wavy hair hung down her back, settling just above the waistband of her shorts. I averted my eyes -

gawking at her body was not what she needed right now.

"When I was sixteen, I accidently set fire to our room at the boarding school we attended." She continued with her back turned to me so I didn't have to hide the very obvious surprise on my face when hearing this. Arson was definitely not something I expected from her.

"You started a fire?"

She turned halfway back to me, her side profile on display, "It was an accident. I left my candles way too close to the curtains and the wind was blowing and before I knew it, we were all being rushed out of the building. Carina and I had to be taken to the hospital due to the smoke inhalation and that was when the doctor's found it."

She pulled another drag of her cigarette, letting the smoke out into the air as she ran her fingers through her hair. She turned around to face me. "They found the growths on her lungs." Pausing to take another drag, she shook her head. "Cancer. Imagine that. Sixteen years old. And she had never even touched a cigarette before."

She leaned down, the cigarette now resting between her two fingers. "My parents tried everything to save her. Any treatment, any doctor - they were desperate." The more she spoke about it, the further I watched her go into her own mind. I wanted to tell her to stop. I wanted to tell her that she didn't have to say more but I couldn't form the words. I just stared at her.

"They sold everything they could to get the money they needed. Cancer is no cheap disease." She laughed but there was no flicker of humor. It was the kind of laugh that came from not being able to process the unfairness of what happened. I stood up and walked over, stopping in front of her. She didn't move. Her gaze was stuck ahead of her as she got trapped in her own memories.

"Milena," I murmured. "You don't have to say anything more."

"Carina died." Her voice was hollow now. "I had to bury my twin sister. Do you have any idea what that feels like?" I knew the question was rhetorical so I stayed quiet. "It's like burying a piece of your soul."

I reached out and rested my hand on hers on the counter. She glanced down to face it before looking up at me as if I had broken her out of the trance she was stuck in. Tears filled her eyes but she didn't allow them to spill over. She took a deep breath in, shut her eyes for a moment before letting her breath out and composing herself.

"Carina should be here right now, not me."

"Don't say th-,"

She killed the cigarette in the ashtray on the counter, moving her hand away from mine. "She didn't smoke. She didn't do anything that could have caused what happened to her. Me on the other hand?" She chuckled but there was no humor behind it. "I did it all. Look at me now - look at this." She lifted the cigarette bud before tossing it down, shaking her head.

"Mil-,"

"I don't want to talk about this anymore," she muttered and walked past me. Her abrupt change in attitude caught me by surprise but I didn't want to push her. Her emotions were getting the better of her and she was fighting to stop that from happening. She walked into her room and shut the door behind her, leaving me with nothing but the silence for company.

**

She stayed locked up in her room for days. She would only come out to ask if I had heard anything from her parents to which I was met with the same disappointed look when I told her I hadn't. I hadn't heard from anyone. Last I knew was that Carlos was taking them into hiding after the safe houses were compromised. The apartment we were staying in was a last minute plan that I had devised myself. This old apartment was one that my father had mentioned years ago during an assignment he had. When he died, it was left to me but I hadn't bothered coming here until now. When I heard the Nazarios were involved, I knew this was not a situation to be taken lightly and my fight or flight impulse kicked in. The plan was clear - keep them alive. That's what we were all getting paid for. I hated being so out of touch with the rest of the team that was on the ground back in Algarve. My instruction was clear though - protect Milena Neves. No matter what, I had to keep her alive but I was watching how being locked up here was starting to slowly destroy her inside.

By the time the weekend rolled around, I had to step out to get some food that needed to be restocked. I was on my way out of the elevator when I first heard the loud music blaring from our apartment. There was no one else currently living on our floor but that didn't stop the concern that kicked in. She was meant to be staying hidden - not bringing attention to herself. I quickened my pace and as I approached the door, I heard her. Singing *Careless Whisper by George Michael* at the stop of her lungs.

I slowly opened the door, pushing it open as her singing continued.

"Tonight the music seems so loud, I wish that we could lose this crowd," she sang - and not well, might I add. She was standing on the couch with her back turned to me. With the volume of the music and her own voice, she clearly hadn't heard me come back. I should be telling her to stop but I couldn't help the amusement that bubbled on my lips for a slight moment. She was carefree and it was a good look on her. Another good look was the shorts and sports bra she was wearing. I couldn't pull my eyes from the curves of her body. Usually they were hidden under oversized shirts but my God, Milena had nothing to hide. As I shut the door, she jumped and turned around, her cheeks immediately becoming flushed.

"Vincenzo!" She exclaimed. "How long have you been standing there?"

"Long enough for the free show," I shouted over the music before walking over to grab the remote that was now in her hand. She was still standing on the couch which gave her enough height to now be eye to eye with me. I reached for the remote but she pulled it back, a playful look on her face.

"Turn it down," I instructed.

"Nope," she popped the 'p' and tugged at her lip. "You-" she pointed at me. "Don't tell meeeeee," she dragged the word out a bit too long that it made me suspicious. "What to do!"

I eyed her suspiciously. Something was up but I couldn't quite put my finger on it. I tried to reach for the remote again but she dodged me, clearly enjoying this little game of hers. Instead of going for the remote, I grabbed her arm and pulled her closer to me.

And that was when I smelled the alcohol on her.

"Have you been drinking?" I gaped.

She giggled like a little school girl and shook her head, even though her eyes had already given her away. I walked over to the TV and turned it off before turning back to her. "Where the hell did you get alcohol?" I asked, not bothering to hide my anger at her blatant defiance. "I specifically didn't get it for this very reason."

She rolled her eyes and jumped off the couch. "What reason, Enzo?

Because you didn't want me to have fun?"

"You're bringing attention to yourself, Milena."

"Bringing attention to myself?" She repeated, this time laughing as she jumped off the couch and walked over to the kitchen counter. "Who is here to see me, Vincenzo?" She glanced around the room, flinging her arms around. "There's no one but you and me here. Just like always. Just like it's going to be for God-knows how long."

She reached for a plastic glass on the counter, bringing it up to her lips. I walked over to her and grabbed the drink from her hand. "Hey!" She shouted and tried to reach for it. I brought it up to my nose, the smell of vodka entering my airways. "Where did you get this?" I asked her again.

"A shop."

"And when did you go to a shop when you were supposed to stay put?" I cocked an eyebrow at her, irritation flickering inside of me. "How many times have you left the apartment?"

She rolled her eyes. "I'm not answering your questions."

"Oh, yes, you are."

"No, I'm not." She stepped closer to me, challenging me. She was so close to me now that I couldn't help but breathe her in, the smell of her coconut shampoo surrounding me. There was something else behind her eyes now - curiosity? attraction? She was difficult to read but there was more now which caused an unexpected amount of tension to surround us. It was harder to ignore my attraction to her when she was looking at me like that.

"Milena." I breathed, trying to find the words needed but they escaped me. She took the opportunity to grab the cup from my hand.

"You can have some too." She leaned the cup over to me. "You don't have to punish yourself by not joining in on the fun."

"Getting drunk with you is hardly on my job description."

"Is that going against the rules?" She eyed me, an amused smile playing on her lips.

I nodded.

"What else is against the rules, Vincenzo?" Her eyebrow lifted ever so slightly with interest. She quickly regained her composure but it was too late. I had already seen it and a rush of arousal was now pulsing through my veins.

"You know it's just you and me here," she murmured. "There's no one else that will know what goes on in this apartment."

I swallowed, trying to keep the heat from rushing straight to my groin but was unsuccessful. I was begging for freedom now from the button of my jeans that kept me in place. Being attracted to Milena was something I had never anticipated. I was here to do a job for fuck sakes but she was making it more difficult for me to remember that when she, now, had the ability to make my dick hard.

She placed the cup down on the counter and stepped even closer to me, our bodies inches from touching. I could already feel the heat radiating off her and everything around me dissipated. All common sense - out the window.

"Vincenzo." She breathed name and I knew that if I didn't stop this right now, I was going to fuck her into oblivion. Her eyes dropped to my lips and for a moment, I thought about all the things I could do to her. I thought about the way it would sound to have her moaning my name for the world to hear. I thought about her wrapped around my body while I fu…

Vincenzo, stop.

I managed to snap out of the trance she had sucked me into and took a step back from her. She seemed surprised by my reaction and to be fair, I was surprised I had managed to stop this before it went any further. Milena was becoming a temptress and I had almost fallen into her trap.

"Milena, what are you doing?" I asked.

"What?" She pretended to be innocent but she was well-aware of the thin ice she was walking on. "You know I'm right. No one would ever have to know. It could be our little secret."

"Nothing is going to happen here," I said, knowing very well I was trying to convince myself of this. "I am here to keep you safe."

"And satisfied," she quipped.

"No." I shook my head. "Just safe. And alive. I am here to protect you."

"By keeping me locked up here for the rest of my life?" She rolled her eyes. "I'd rather be dead."

I was taken aback by her words. "Don't say that. Your parents need you alive."

She reached for the cup on the counter again and downed what was left of her drink, "We haven't heard from them in weeks. For all I know they could be dead in a ditch somewhere."

"Milen-," she interrupted me.

"As far as I'm concerned, I'm on my own now. My father fucking killed someone and now I'm in this mess. I don't hear from them. I don't know what the next step is. I'm fucking stuck here."

She shook her head, the humorless laughter bubbling on her lips again. "We're stuck here, Vincenzo, but that doesn't mean this needs to be a prison."

The proximity between us closed again as she stepped forward, this time resting her hand against my chest. I could feel her touch through my shirt, igniting every part of me with arousal. My dick twitched, begging to be buried deep inside of her. Now was not the time to be thinking with that head.

"I could think of many things you and I could do to pass the time," she said in a low voice. Without thinking, I stepped forward, turning her as to trap her between me and the kitchen counter. I leaned my hands on either side of her and we were inches from each other. Her breath caught in her throat and she was looking up at me with those big brown eyes of hers. *God, why did they have such an effect on me?*

"This is never going to happen," I murmured, my eyes dropping to her lips. "I'm not here to fuck you, Milena."

She didn't even flinch at my words. Instead, she lifted her eyebrow, a curious look settling across her face. "Then I might need to find someone that will."

"You're not leaving this apartment," I warned.

"Try and stop me," she challenged. Before I could react, she ducked underneath my arm and took off towards the door. I turned to run after her as she yanked the door open and sprinted to the elevator.

"Milena!" I shouted. "Stop!"

She ignored me and pushed the button to the elevator, turning back to me as she pushed it over and over again, hoping it would come quicker. As I reached her the doors opened and she jumped inside. I was hot on her tail and stepped into the elevator just before the doors shut.

"Foda-se!" She shouted, reaching for the buttons. She pressed multiple ones while I pressed the number back to our floor.

"Milena, fuck, stop this right now!" My voice raised as my anger escalated. Was she fucking crazy? She ignored me and reached for the button for the ground floor. I pressed the third floor button again and the elevator suddenly jolted to an abrupt stop. Both of us stood looking at each other as we just realized what happened.

"Now, look at what you've done!" I shouted.

"Me?" she snapped and whipped her head to face me. "You're the one who was fucking pressing all the buttons,"

"No - I was stopping you from doing that," I retorted. "You are supposed to be staying in that apartment and now we're stuck in the fucking elevator. What is wrong with you?"

She rolled her eyes and pushed past me, stopping in front of the buttons. She pressed the emergency button and it rang. She let go of the button and the ringing stopped so she tried again but there was no answer.

"Where's your phone?" she asked.

"On the counter."

"Well that's not very helpful now is it?" she scoffed.

"If you had just stayed in the apartment, none of this would have happened."

"You can't keep me locked up in there!"

I stepped closer to her. "Yes, I can, and I will."

CHAPTER 13:

Milena

He was so close to me now, I could smell the nicotine on him mixed with that cologne he wore. It was an intoxicating smell and with the alcohol pulsing through me, it was opening up my every sense, causing a flicker of desire inside of me.

"Even if I have to tie you to that damn bed of yours," he said, finishing his thought. My eyes flicked up to meet his and a thick tension surrounded us, suddenly making this elevator feel smaller than it was. He noticed it too because I watched as his eyes fell down to my lips, causing my breath to get caught in my throat. I was dying to taste him. He looked like the kind of man who knew his way around a woman's body.

"Seems like it has a pretty steady headboard," I murmured.

"Milena." He breathed, his voice sounding as if I had said something that pained him, "You're making this so difficult for me."

"What's so difficult, Vincenzo?" I probed, my curiosity getting the better of me.

"I… We can't."

"Why not?"

He shook his head and took a step away from me, running his fingers through his hair. He couldn't hide the exasperation he was feeling and I was dying to know the true reason behind it. He had to be feeling the tension too - it was practically suffocating us at this point. He wanted me as much as I wanted him - right?

"I am not touching you, Milena, so get that out of your head right now."

He popped the fantasy bubble in my head with his words. This time I flinched at the hardness in his voice. It was the first time I felt as if the tension I was feeling might have been one-sided. The alcohol still pulsed through me but the sudden embarrassment over what I had just done was overpowering that. *What was wrong with me?* Why wouldn't I do what I was told? I refused to allow it to affect me in front of him so I turned to my defense mechanism.

I rolled my eyes and sighed. "Fine. You're not my type anyway. You would have just been convenient."

He looked less than impressed but he said nothing further. Instead, he turned to the buttons and pressed the emergency one again. I needed to get out of here. I had made enough of a mess and knowing that Vincenzo wasn't going to give me what I wanted, there was nothing else for me to do except start accepting my new life. Cooped up in some apartment until I was told otherwise. I wanted to keep fighting it but I was tired. I was starting to give up - what was the point anyway? Vincenzo had made it pretty clear he was never going to let me out of his sight so there was no way I could escape him. And what if I did? Where would I go? Who would I call? I was truly alone now.

Time creeped slowly as we stood in silence. It felt like forever before the elevator finally moved again and started to head up. I didn't say anything as we reached the third floor again. I had never been more thankful for an elevator working. The doors opened and I stepped outside, dragging myself back to the apartment. Disappointment hung heavy on my shoulders and without a further word to Vincenzo, I walked into my room and shut the door behind me. I didn't want to face him. I didn't want to speak about what happened. I just wanted to move on and deal with my humiliation without his company.

CHAPTER 14:

Vincenzo

I gave her a couple hours to herself but I had a better solution for her to deal with everything so here I was, banging on her door. "Milena! Open up!"

There was no response. I sighed and took a moment to compose myself. I was still reeling from the anger and frustration she had caused me earlier - both normal frustration and sexual. I was one bad decision from fucking her on the kitchen counter before I came to my senses. She continuously went against everything I said, clearly not having a healthy outlet for her own frustrations. I wasn't going to just sit back and do nothing about it.

"Milena!" I raised my voice this time and just as I was about to bring my knuckles against the door again, she yanked it open.

"What?" she snapped. Her eyes were dark and droopy - she had been crying again. I handed her the boxing gloves I had sitting underneath my arm. After she slammed the door behind her, I needed to compose myself and fresh air seemed to do just that. I saw these in the window of some random sports store and the idea popped into my head. She eyed them before turning her gaze back on me, narrowing her eyes.

"And what exactly would you like me to do with these?"

"You're going to hit me."

She scoffed, but I remained unresponsive. She lifted the gloves in front of her. "You're being serious."

"Dead serious."

"Vincenzo, I'm pretty sure I'm about to have a fucking hangover." She tried to hand the gloves back to me but I shook my head. "I'm not doing this." she said.

"Oh, yes you are," I argued and took one glove from her, pulling the velcro apart to open it up for her to slip her hand in.

She crossed her arms.

"Milena…" My voice was full of warning, begging her not to test me on this. "You've been complaining about being stuck here with no outlet for your frustration. I'm giving you one."

"I had something else in mind."

Again with the sexual innuendos. This woman would be the death of me. I had never needed to show such restraint before. I swear I deserved some kind of reward for that.

"I thought you'd jump at the opportunity to hit me," I challenged.

"It's definitely crossed my mind more than once since being here."

"So then?" I gestured to the glove I was still holding open for her. "Unless you don't think you'll be able to do it."

She rolled her eyes. "I could easily hit you."

"Then prove it."

I was starting to realize that the only way to get Milena to do anything was to challenge her to prove you wrong. She was stubborn and way too proud. She even went as far as to yank the glove from me and put it on herself. I had no idea if she ever had any experience with boxing gloves but the way she slipped them on and tightened them with ease showed me that this wasn't her first rodeo. I walked backwards into the living area that I had already cleared before knocking on her door.

"I'm going to need you to fight back," she said, lifting her arms up to have her fists shielding her face. "I don't want you going easy on me."

"Of course I'm going to go easy on y-" She didn't even wait for me to finish my sentence before extending her arm in a quick motion in front of her. My reflexes were way ahead of me and I used my forearm to block her hit. I eyed her - almost impressed at her attempt to catch me off guard.

"You didn't wait for your opponent to get ready," I pointed out.

She replied by extending another swing at me. This time extending her right arm first and then her left trialing directly after. I blocked them with ease which earned me a glare from her.

"Surely as a bodyguard you should always be ready for any attack." She turned her body and took a swing at me from the side, causing me to lift my hand and catch her fist just in time.

"Good thing I always am." I kept her fist in my hand and we were inches from each other. I could hear her breathing and I couldn't help but drop my eyes to her lips. They were slightly parted, her shoulders heaving slightly already. I wanted her. I wanted to feel those lips and see what she was capable of with them. She clearly noticed my moment of distraction and took advantage of that, using the moment to push against my chest, causing me to take a step back from her.

"I don't need you in my personal space. I need you to leave me alone, Vincenzo."

I ignored her and lifted my hands up, opening my palms for her to use as a punching bag. "Hit me."

Her right fist connected with my left hand.

"Again."

She repeated the action, this time adding more intensity behind her movement,

"Again." Her right fist slammed against my left palm and her left fist followed shortly after that against my right palm.

"Come on, Milena. You can do better than that," I challenged her. "I told you to hit me."

"I am hitting you," she said through gritted teeth as her fists slammed against my palms repeatedly before she brought her arms to rest just above her chin.

"You're just trying to punish me for drinking earlier," she muttered and took a swing at me, causing me to lean to the side as her fist swiped past my face. She was getting angrier now. *Good.* She needed to let it all out. And I wasn't just talking about the emotion she had gathered since being stuck here - it was clear that she had been holding plenty more in for years now.

"I don't need you to punish me," she said, her voice raising as she continued to throw punches at me, me dodging every one of them.

"Fuck!" she shouted and took a step back, dropping her arms. "Stop dodging every punch!"

I chuckled which earned me a dark glare from her.

"Is this funny to you?"

"Yes."

"I'm just a joke to you."

"That's not what I said," I clarified. "But I'm certainly not going to allow you to really hit me. You'd never be able to do that."

"Oh?" Her nostrils flared in anger. "You think I won't punch that pretty little face of yours?"

Here we go.

She stepped forward and lifted her arms up, trying to throw a punch but her fist got caught in my grip.

"I should be flattered that you think I'm pretty."

"Not the adjective I would use to describe you," she threw back.

"Hate to break it to you sweetheart but you already did."

"Do not call me sweetheart." She took another swing at me. "It's patronizing."

I released her from my hand with more force than I intended and she stumbled back. Her jaw tightened and she stepped forward, throwing punches at me from both directions, meeting my open palms. The sound of her heavy breathing, grunting and slapping of the glove against my hands surrounded us and I could see the frustration in her eyes.

"I hate that I'm stuck here with you," she shouted. "You're obnoxious. Domineering."

"Go on."

"Stubborn."

"You're one to talk."

"A fucking pain in my ass," she said through her teeth as she stalked forward, putting more force behind her latest punch. "You love telling me what to do."

"That's my job," I argued.

"No." She shook her head. "Your job is to keep me alive."

"And how can I do that if I don't tell you what to do?"

She threw another punch. "Easily. You allow me to decide what I want to do. This is my fucking life."

"Yes and your life is in danger - surely, I don't have to remind you of that?"

"You remind me every second of every day." Another two punches against my palms.

"And I obviously have to keep doing that because you don't seem to grasp the concept."

"I grasp the concept just fine," she spat at me.

"No, you don't," I stepped forward, catching her off guard as she stepped back. "*You're* stubborn. Defiant. Infuriating." I stepped closer to her, forcing her to move backwards until her back was against the wall. "You think you know better and you have no problem challenging my authority."

"I don't give a shit about your authority," she challenged, lifting her chin so she could hold my gaze.

We were so close that I could feel her breath on me, landing against my skin and causing a stir inside of me more powerful than the last one. Sweat droplets sat against her hairline and her eyes were drowning in so many different emotions. Anger. Slight fear and I swear there was something resembling intrigue in her eyes.

"I'm in charge here," I said. "So get used to it."

"Never."

She pushed against my chest, causing me to step back away from her. She may have created space between us but that didn't remove the very clear tension that hung in the air. I wanted nothing more than to pin her up against that wall and show her all the ways I could make her bow down to me. Her body would be at my mercy and I had plenty of ways to show her what I was capable of if she gave me half the chance.

"I'm done playing this game with you," she muttered, reaching for her one glove but I stepped closer.

"We're done when I say we're done."

She glared at me. "Are you on a power trip or something? I'm not doing this anymore."

"Milen-" I tried to reach for her but she side-stepped me, tossing the one glove to the ground as she reached for the next. I grabbed her wrist before she was able to do so.

"You're angry," I said as calmly as I could manage.

"And you're perceptive," she said dryly.

"I'm just trying to help you. Why can't you see that?"

"Don't you get it?" she asked, shaking her head. "I don't want your help."

She tried to reach for her glove again but I stopped her and before we both realized what was happening, she swung her arm without the glove towards my face, slightly clocking the bottom of my jaw. My face jerked in the direction of the punch and I was stunned.

"Vincenzo, fuck -," Milena started as I stepped away from her, my hand resting against my jaw where she hit. It stung but I was more shocked than anything else. "I'm sorry - you kept pushing at me and..."

I turned back to her with a slight smile that caused her to stop, clearly confused.

"Why are you smiling?"

"Not bad," I commented and walked past her towards the fridge to grab a bottle of water. "I didn't think you had it in you."

"This is a lesson to not underestimate me then."

She looked exhausted but the sadness in her eyes was no longer the most prominent emotion. She was calmer and that was worth getting punched for.

CHAPTER 15:

Milena

After Vincenzo's brilliant idea (which I would never say out loud to him) of handing me boxing gloves, I needed to get some food in my system. I felt bad for having punched him so I decided to make us some food as a semi-apology. He didn't say anything about getting hit by me except for "not bad". He was impressed when he said that which actually made me feel pretty good. Who would have thought that punching him in the face would help so much?

The chicken pasta I made soaked up what was left of the alcohol in my system and all I was left with now was the sinking feeling in my stomach at the realization of my new reality. After everything that happened today and all the days before this, I could no longer fight the denial. This was my life now.

"Where did you learn to cook?" he asked as he picked up a forkful of the chicken pesto pasta I had made. After giving him a list of the exact spices I needed for the chicken, I tried my best to recreate one of the recipes I recalled from my memory of what my mother would make. It wasn't as good as hers but it was a close second. We were seated at the kitchen counter and had barely said anything to each other in the last hour or so while I cooked. He was back and forth on the phone, speaking in Italian so I had no idea who was on the other line, I just focused on the meal and truth be told, it came out pretty good.

"I used to watch my mother in the kitchen when I was much younger. Carina was actually the one who got involved and tried things for herself while I just observed. My mother would cook and then after we ate, I would help her with the dishes," I explained between my bites. "When I got into high school then I would try to make a few things myself but it wasn't as often and after Carina..." I let my sentence trail off knowing that he knew what I was referring to. "We never did it again."

I held a lot of resentment towards my parents after Carina's death. I wasn't supposed to lose them as well and that was almost worst. Losing someone that's still right in front of you - that was a different kind of loss.

"Anyway," I shrugged and continued. "Back at the house in Algarve, we had a lady that pretty much ran the household. Her name was Cecilia and since my parents were always busy with work, she was the one who taught me more meals to make. She knew I enjoyed it but I also knew it was her way of keeping me distracted I guess."

"From what happened to your sister?"

My eyes were on the food in my bowl and I slowly played around with it at the end of my fork. I just nodded and filled my fork with some food, bringing it up to meet my mouth. He didn't say anything further and I was thankful for that. I didn't feel like bringing up Carina again. I was already angry at myself that the conversation came up at all but my nightmares betrayed me.

"Can you cook?" I asked, lifting my head to look over at him. He had his forearms leaning against the counter now as he placed his fork into the now empty bowl.

"Enough to get by."

I nodded and turned back to my food. As much as I wanted to push for conversation to distract from the silence that hung in the air, I just didn't have it on me to scramble for a topic.

"Why haven't we heard from my parents?" I asked.

"Carlos has them in hiding."

"And how long are they going to stay in hiding?"

"It's difficult to say. We have men on the ground in Algarve right now trying to evaluate the situation."

"And what have they found?"

He paused for a moment, eyeing me carefully before giving in. "Right now, there's no way you guys can go back to Algarve. There's nothing there for you and there are men looking for you guys everywhere."

"So, are we supposed to be on the run for the rest of our lives?"

That didn't seem like much of a life but right now, I was numb to everything that the idea didn't even cause a flicker of emotion inside of me.

"Either that or you'll need to start over somewhere. New place. New identities, New life."

I looked up at him and he was being dead serious. A new identity? No more Milena Neves? How could I just leave my life behind like that?

"Or," Vincenzo continues. "All the Nazario men in Algarve are taken out."

"Seems unlikely," I said dryly. "The Nazarios have infiltrated pretty much all of Algarve. It would be a massacre."

"Or if you just take out the guys at the top, that'll also put a kink in their continuation." He eyed me. "How much do you know about them?"

I shrugged. "As much as the next person I guess. I've heard the name a few times along with some stories about their crimes and the way they operate but honestly, I thought it was all bullshit. I mean an organized crime family in Portugal? When has anyone ever heard of that?" The question was rhetorical but it still stood. You don't think too much about these things when it doesn't affect you.

"Does this mean I have to drop out?" I asked, knowing I was probably already well-aware of the answer.

"Too soon to tell."

"I have to go back in September," I explained. "If I go back."

I was starting to accept the reality of what was happening more and more. I used to be so sure of my future - I had it all figured out but now, nothing had ever been more unclear. And I hated it. Since Carina died, I had felt so lost in the world. Lost and alone. She was the part of my soul that made it whole and I had never been the same since. Moving to London helped. At least there I could start over and be whoever I wanted. My past didn't follow me there and I enjoyed the freedom of deciding what I wanted out of my life.

Now, that had all slipped through my fingers and it was gone.

I reached over and grabbed his empty bowl, picking it up along with mine and placed it in the sink behind me. This pasta dish was the first proper meal I had in weeks and my body was thanking me for that.

"I know that I'm meant to be locked up here like a prisoner but I'm starting to go crazy," I admitted. "Is there no way I could be let out just to go for a walk or something?" *God, I sounded like a fucking dog.* "If the Nazarios don't kill me then my own mind might," I attempted to add some humor to that phrase but my delivery was anything but hilarious. I was actually being dead serious.

"It's too dangerous."

"But you can come with me." I walked over to where Vincenzo sat. "Please, just for a few minutes. I need to feel normal again."

His eyes met mine and I could see the reluctance in them but there was something more. It was almost as if he wanted to give me what I wanted - he felt bad enough about being stuck here but he was clearly designed to follow instructions that this was difficult for him.

"I'll wear one of those wigs I bought," I suggested. "And your dusty old cap."

"If you cleaned it, it wouldn't be dusty anymore," he pointed out.

"But then it loses its character."

He smiled. A small little pull of his lips in amusement that made me feel surprisingly warm inside to see. I liked this part of him.

He leaned his elbow against the table. "And how do I know you won't run away again? I'm not sure I trust you."

I shrugged. "I have nowhere else to go. I'm alone now."

He reached out and rested his hand on my own that sat against the kitchen counter. His touch was soft and warm against me. I was surprised at how comfortable that felt.

"You'll never be alone, Milena. Not as long as I'm here."

I didn't want to read too much into that. I had to remind myself that Vincenzo was being paid to be here - this wasn't a choice that he made and he had made it pretty clear earlier that whatever was happening between us was one-sided. I didn't say anything further to him and instead, I started to clean up around us. I emptied the rest of the brown paper bag and at the bottom sat a flier. I pulled it out and glanced across it, noticing that it was an advert for a street party that was going to take place tomorrow night.

I turned it around to show Vincenzo. "Where did you get this?"

He looked up from his phone and his gaze landed on the paper in my hand. He reached for it. "They were handing them out a couple streets away.

I didn't even see what it was."

I pulled it back from him and pointed at the theme. "It's a masquerade street party."

"I can read," he said dryly.

I rolled my eyes. "This is perfect."

He eyed me, suddenly realizing what I was suggesting. He started to shake his head. "Not happening."

"Why not?"

He looked at me, dumbfounded. "I'm not taking you to a party, Milena."

Why did my name have to sound so sweet coming from him? "But it's a masquerade party. It's literally about being anonymous - what better party is there for us to attend? No one would even know we were there."

"It's not happening."

"Why not?" I repeated, sliding the flier across the counter back to him. "It's right on the street. We can stick to ourselves and we'll have masks on the whole time. You can't tell me this isn't the perfect opportunity for me to get some fresh air."

"You want some fresh air? Stand on the balcony."

"You know that's not what I mean."

He pushed himself off the bar stool and walked over to the fridge, grabbing a bottle of water from inside. He twisted the cap open and brought it to his lips.

"I'll even wear one of the wigs I have. Double disguise - a mask and a wig." I was actually feeling a flicker of hope inside at the prospect of being allowed outside. I was starting to lose myself in my own mind and I was dying for an escape - even if it was just for a few hours. I needed something to save me from the way I was drowning.

"It's not happening." He leaned against the counter. "Forget it."

I grabbed the flier and put it in front of him. "It's a fucking masquerade party, Vincenzo. No one is going to know who I am."

He grabbed the paper from me and tore it up. "I can't take that chance with you."

"Can't or won't?"

"It's the same thing."

"No it isn't," I retorted. "You act like you're this big, fancy bodyguard who can protect anyone-"

"I've never said that," he interrupted but I continued.

"And yet, you're too afraid to take me to a masked party. On the street. That's freedom and no one will even know who I am. You're obviously not as sure of your skills as you think you are."

He cocked an eyebrow. "Are you challenging me?"

I stood my ground and shrugged. "Just seems like you're all talk and no do."

"I will not be manipulated by you." He stepped closer to me. "The answer is no - end of discussion."

The anger crawled across my skin as he reprimanded me. I refused to accept his answer. I was going crazy inside and I would not stay put when the perfect opportunity had presented itself. I didn't need to go for hours - just enough to feel normal again. What was the point of life if this was how it was going to be?

"Listen to him, Milena," Carina said.

Of course, she would agree with him. She used to be the one who steered me away from potentially bad decisions but she wasn't here right now to stop me. And I wasn't going to let Vincenzo do that either.

"Good luck trying to stop me," I muttered and pushed past him. "You're either going to come with me to protect me or you're going to spend the night trying to find me. The choice is yours."

He grabbed my arm, stopping me in my tracks. "You don't even have a mask."

I turned to face him. "Then I guess you better go get us some."

CHAPTER 16:

Vincenzo

I was starting to think that Milena had a death wish.

She disregarded her safety as if it meant nothing to her which only made my job of keeping her alive that much harder. I refused to be manipulated by her but I had also learned to take her threats seriously and if she was going to be running around at some party, the best chance I had of protecting her was to go with her. Even if it went against my better judgment.

But here we were, getting ready to go to a street party and I couldn't shake the feeling that this was a bad idea. Carlos would fucking kill me if he knew I was doing this but as Milena liked to remind me, there was no one here but us. No one knew what would go on here and I certainly wasn't going to tell him. I wasn't a fucking idiot.

"Thanks for agreeing to this," she shouted from the bathroom.

I rolled my eyes. "You didn't exactly give me much of a choice now did you?"

She stepped outside and flashed me a smug smile. She finished tying the back of her black eye mask over her now blonde wig that she had decided on for tonight. The hair sat just above her shoulders and I didn't like this look on her.

"Don't ever cut your natural hair," I commented.

"You don't like it short?"

I shook my head and leaned my arm against the back of the couch. "Longer is better."

"More to grab right?"

There she went again, running her mouth with her sexual innuendos like she always did. I knew she was doing it on purpose to get a reaction out of me but it was starting to become more and more difficult to remain unphased. Especially not when she had on the same tight, black dress that she wore the first night I met her. My dick throbbed against my jeans and I was thankful I was sitting down - I was going to need a moment or two to calm that down. That dress was the sexiest thing I had ever seen and the way it hugged the curves of her body was making it more and more difficult to pull my eyes from her.

"How the hell did you manage to pack that dress?" I eyed her. "That's not exactly the kind of thing you pack when you go into hiding."

"I didn't know what I was packing. You didn't exactly give me a lot of time so I grabbed whatever was around me." She shrugged. "This was on the floor. Clearly a part of me knew I was going to need it."

"For someone with a target on her back, you sure don't act like it."

"Maybe that's 'cause I'm not afraid of dying," she shot back.

That was something I had come to learn about her. If I didn't know better, I would say that Milena didn't care for her life at all. She wouldn't care if anything happened to her and a part of me was bothered by that. A woman like that had more to offer this world than she clearly realized.

"You should be."

She ran her hands over her dress before clamping them together. "Okay, I'm ready."

I could already hear the music in the distance. The party was taking place along the main road right outside our building and would go on for miles. Apparently, this was an annual thing that took place in this area - there was no way I would have known that considering I knew nothing about this place before coming here.

I stood up and walked over to her. "Some ground rules. You do not leave my side. You do not engage with anyone. You do not drink-"

"Nope. Not following that rule."

"Milena," I hissed. "Those are the rules."

"How about this?" she interrupted, taking over from what I was trying to say. "I won't leave your side. I won't engage with anyone and I'll let you order me drinks."

"I'm not doing that."

She narrowed her eyes at me. "I think you are. If you don't want me to engage with anyone then I can't be the one to order my own drinks so it looks like you're the chosen one."

"We shouldn't even be doing this," I reminded her, which earned me a classic eye roll.

"Well, we are so you need to get over it." She walked over and stopped in front of me. "It'll be fun - you'll see."

She smiled before walking Milena past me towards the front door and I followed her lead. This was definitely one way to guarantee I was going to get fired.

CHAPTER 17:

Milena

I loved crowds. That was usually unusual for a lot of people but I hated being alone. I needed people around me and I loved being amongst the buzz of an event like this. It was like getting another hit of a drug I had been deprived of for so long as we stepped into the crowd along the street. Bodies flooded the streets as the music boomed through the speakers around us. Most businesses in the area had offered their premises as bars for the party and the attendance for tonight was unlike anything I had experienced. I made a point of attending as many music festivals as possible while living in London but none of them felt as good as this one. This one felt like freedom and I was soaking in every moment. I couldn't make out anyone around me as masks sat on every single person passing by. It was the perfect disguise and I was more than happy to be out tonight.

Vincenzo was less than impressed but I hadn't given him much of a choice.

We stood by the bar waiting for the drink that he had ordered for me. He was not going to be the one to drink and since I wasn't meant to talk to anyone, he was the only way I could get it. And boy did I need it. I didn't want to think of the fuck up that was my life right now so instead, I focused on the music seeping through me. I slowly moved my body to the afro-beat as I lost myself in the rhythm. I had helped myself to what was left of my vodka at home - Vincenzo had no idea but it was the perfect way to ensure I had some alcohol in my system. He was constantly scanning the area, his gaze landing on the same spot in the far left of the area causing me to turn.

"What are you looking at?" I asked.

He pulled his gaze away and looked down at me. "Nothing."

The bartender placed my drink on the bar and before Vincenzo could pay, I broke his rule and ordered a shot of tequila for myself. The bartender nodded and was off before Vincenzo could turn around and glare at me.

"Are you seriously incapable of following a simple rule?" he shouted over the music.

"You would never have ordered me a shot," I pointed out.

"Because I'm not here to get you drunk. You're here to enjoy some fresh air for about an hour or so and then I am getting you back to that apartment."

"Then I better use my time wisely."

My shot was placed in front of me and I wasted no time taking it, allowing the alcohol to burn down my throat. It was awful but it was what I needed. The intoxication started to creep up on me and I welcomed it as I helped myself to my drink.

"*Vamos.*" Vincenzo grabbed my hand and pulled me through the crowd. He glanced in that direction again and started to pull me in the opposite one. I tried to see what or who he was looking at through the crowd but there were just too many people around. I continued to sip on my drink, but I also couldn't ignore the pulsing electricity coursing up my arm from his touch. I had come to accept that I was attracted to him. I mean, how could I not be? But the worst part was he didn't even try. Even right now, all he was wearing was a slim fitted black t-shirt with black jeans. Nothing special and yet, I couldn't pull my eyes away from how the material clung to the muscles of his arms. And the tattoos that lined his skin had me in a trance. I flicked my eyes up to his face that was partially covered by his plain black eye mask.

"*God, Milena. Do you want to stare at this poor guy any more?*" Carina's voice echoed.

"*Can you blame me? Look at him.*"

"*It's never going to happen,*" she shot back.

"*We'll see.*"

I pulled my attention from my own thoughts and brought my drink up to my lips, allowing the bitter vodka taste to spread across my tongue. We were pushing through the crowds of people but as soon as a new *beat* came through the speakers, I stopped dead in my tracks. Whoever the DJ was for tonight, he knew what he was doing.

"Oh my God, I love this song!" I shouted, causing Vincenzo to stop and turn to me. A few people around us turned to me which earned me a stern glare from him.

"Thanks for announcing that to everyone," he muttered, leaning closer to me. "But it's time to keep moving."

I shook my head before taking another big sip. "One dance."

"Not happening."

"Just like coming to this party was 'not happening'?" I probed.

His jaw tightened. "Milena, do you have to make this so difficult?"

I rolled my eyes and took one more big sip, finishing off my drink. That had to be finished in record time but there was no one to confirm that victory. I placed my empty glass on the nearest low wall that was lined with people sitting on it. All around us, people had stopped to dance and with the alcohol working its way through me, I wanted to be one of them.

I grabbed his hand. "One dance, please?"

He stopped for a moment, clearly trying to think of another way to reject me but instead he sighed and pulled me closer to him.

"One dance," he repeated.

CHAPTER 18:

Vincenzo

I had already fucked up in more ways than one with Milena so there was no stopping me from agreeing to one dance with her. Selfishly, I wanted an excuse to feel her close to me. I wanted to see if there was really something between us or if it was just the fact that we had been cooped up in the apartment. I pulled her body closer to mine, my chest pressed up against hers as my one hand rested on her waist. The other hand held hers and we started to move. The music seeped through us, allowing our bodies to move as one.

She was so close to me. Her height forced her to reach just below my chin but she was close enough that I could breathe in that coconut smell of hers. It was one I had started to welcome. At that moment, I forgot about everything. I forgot that we were on the run and my only job was to protect her. I forgot that I was hired to be here and that the tension surrounding us right now was wrong. This wasn't allowed. Being attracted to her the way I am was going against everything I knew. *What was it about her?*

Her gaze lifted to mine and confirmed that she was feeling it too. Desire swam in her eyes and I was slipping further and further from control. There was so much I wanted to say and do to her. If this were any other scenario, I would have had my way with her a long time ago. I would have happily ripped that dress off of her before she was even allowed to step outside of the apartment. I noticed the wandered gazes from the men around her - none of them subtle about it which only made me want to rip their eyes out. I had never felt a possessiveness like this before and I wasn't sure how to begin to deal with that. She wasn't mine. She was mine to protect. But that fucking dress…

Instead of giving into the salacious thoughts bombarding my mind, I forced my gaze away from her and scanned the area. We continued to move to the music but that same man caught my eye in the distance. I had noticed him throughout the night and there was something familiar about him. I swear I had seen him before but I couldn't quite place him. *Did he live in this area and I just happened to see him around?* I couldn't ignore the fact that my gut was telling me that he meant trouble. He kept creeping closer throughout the crowd and was the only person not wearing a mask. He attempted a disguise beneath his shitty old cap. A mask would have made more sense but this man didn't strike me as one with much of a brain. He turned towards us again. Pulling Milena closer to me, I turned her around, forcing her in the direction of his eye line. I needed to see something.

"Milena, follow my lead," I murmured close to her ear and she stiffened against me, "No, carry on."

"What's going on?" she asked.

We continued to sway to the music. "There's a guy in the far right corner. The only one without a mask, do you see him?"

"Yes," she answered. "He keeps looking over here."

"I thought so," I muttered.

"Was that who you were looking at over at the bar?"

"I was looking at everyone," I pointed out. "But he keeps showing up."

"He looks familiar."

I looked down at her. "What do you mean?"

"I swear I've seen him on the cameras a few times. I never really paid attention but he's got that same cap on that I've seen before."

She's right. The pieces fell into place as she confirmed how I knew this man. He had lurked outside of the apartment building a few times which only meant one thing - he was after her. I turned the two of us around again so I was in his eyeline. He averted his gaze as soon as I made eye contact and my intuition forced me on high alert. We continued to move as casually as we could manage but when I turned us around again, he was gone.

"Where did he go?" she asked, glancing around the crowd.

I lifted my hand to cup her face, forcing her gaze on mine. "Don't look for him. Keep your eyes on me."

I didn't need anyone to notice the sudden worry that settled over her face. Even though she wore an eye mask, there was no mistaking it. I was on high alert now and I needed to get Milena back home safely. I slowly trailed my fingertips against her back, reminding her that I had her. I would never let anything happen to her.

"Do you know him?" she asked.

I shook my head.

"We should draw him out," she suggested.

"What do you mean?"

"I mean we should try and see if he would follow me. He could just be a random passerby but if he is a threat, he would follow me."

"You want to be the bait?" I gaped at her.

She shrugged. "You got a better idea?"

"Any idea is better than that," I muttered. "I'm not taking that risk with you."

The song started to change and we stopped moving. Her body was still up against mine but we were no longer dancing. Now, we just stood and I was overly aware of the fact her hand was still in mine. The tension was suffocating me and even though there was a looming threat right now, all I could do was drop my gaze to her lips as I wondered what she tasted like.

"Vincenzo." She breathed my name with a sense of longing before her gaze flicked past me. "Stay close."

Before I could stop her, she turned and took off in the opposite direction.

"Milena!" I shouted but she had slipped past the people around us. I took off after her, pushing through the crowd as I kept my eye on her. New revelation - Milena was fucking crazy. I had made it very clear that she would not be the bait but she was not one to be told what to do as she repeatedly showed me. She was on her own mission and I was angry at myself that I had allowed my own desire to distract me from doing my job. She was headed towards a deserted alley and to my surprise, her idea had worked. Stalking closely behind her was that same man I had seen earlier.

Confirmed. He was definitely after her.

She disappeared down the alleyway and shortly after that, he followed. I picked up my pace and kept my hand firmly on my gun that was hidden beneath my shirt. As soon as I was out of the crowd and stalking down the dark alleyway, I pulled it out and held it up. Nothing but big trash bins lined the walls and the dead end ahead of us.

Milena had reached the brick wall at the end and slowly turned around and he stood right in front of her.

"There you are," he said before I cocked my gun, forcing him to freeze.

He looked around before turning to meet the barrel of my gun. Milena didn't move and he slowly lifted his hands up.

"You looking for something?" I asked.

He shook his head. "I already found it, thanks."

Cocky. Wrong move. I reached for him, taking a fistful of his shirt in my hand before shoving him up against the nearest wall. I held the gun to his temple, my protective instincts had taken over and there was no going back.

"Who sent you?" I demanded.

He chuckled. "You and I both know the answer to that question. Everyone is out looking for her." He cocked his head in the direction of Milena who stood behind me.

I tightened my grip on him. "How many people know where she is?"

"Enough. Anyone who wants to get in the good books of *Senhor Nazario* is out looking for Milena Neves."

I slammed his head against the wall.

"Vincenzo!" Milena shouted, stepping closer to me as the man in my hands flinched in pain. I felt her hand on my shoulder but I shrugged her off and positioned my gun against his temple again.

"How did you find her?" I shouted.

He remained silent. I was thankful that there was hardly any light in this alleyway. It was going to make it much easier to dispose of him without any witnesses. The music was blaring through the area which means I wouldn't have to worry about the sound of the gunshot. The silencer I had on the gun and the music would mask it all. I had it all figured out and I would do what I needed to.

I let go of his shirt and wrapped my hand around his throat. "I asked you a question so I suggest you fucking answer it."

"Vincenzo," Milena repeated. "Stop!"

I turned to her, "Milena, this is not a fucking game. This is kill or be killed - the choice is yours."

She quickly shut her mouth and took a step back, a flicker of fear flashing across her eyes. I didn't want her to fear me but I needed her to understand the severity of the situation. People knew where she was now which means we needed to leave. Her safety had been compromised.

"How. Did. You. Find. Her?" I repeated slowly through gritted teeth as I turned back to him.

"The traffic cameras," he managed to choke out before I released my grip on his throat enough to hear what else he had to say. "The Nazarios have men working for them with access to that shit. They caught you entering Sevilla."

"*Merda!*" I muttered, letting go of him. He dropped to the floor, his hand immediately going up to his throat. I pulled him up by his shirt again. "What's your name?"

"Benjamin."

"Well, Benjamin, you picked the wrong side," I said before turning to Milena. "You're not going to want to see this."

"No! Wait, please!" Benjamin begged.

I ignored him as Milena shook her head. "You're not going to kill him."

"Milena," my voice was full of warning. "Turn around."

She stepped closer to me. "Vincenzo, please. You can't kill him."

"Please don't!" Benjamin cried out, forcing my attention back to him. "I owe him money. *Senhor Nazario* - I was just trying to settle my debt."

"Does it look like I fucking give a shit?" I muttered. "You're a threat to her."

He shook his head frantically. "Please, I won't tell anyone I saw her. I'll leave her alone."

Milena stepped between us, facing me as she rested her hand against my chest. "Let him go, Vincenzo."

"He was ready to sign your death sentence." I glared at her. "And you just want to let him go? How do you know he won't come after you?"

The sound of the celebrations from the crowd momentarily broke us out of the situation we were in. I glanced back down the alleyway but there was no one watching us. I had positioned ourselves behind some of the larger bins - I wasn't a rookie and if I was going to get rid of him, I would make sure no one knew I was.

"I won't come after her," Benjamin begged. "Please."

If this was my first rodeo, I probably would have believed him but I had enough experience to know that you could never trust anyone. I reached for Milena's hand and pushed her behind me before settling the gun between his eyes. He cowered down, the tears running down his face. I used my other hand to support the bottom of the gun as Milena tried to pull me away.

"Don't do this, Vincenzo!" she cried.

"I will not take chances with your life, Milena," I shouted. "You can either watch me kill him or you're going to turn the fuck around but when I count to three, he's dead."

"Vinc-"

"One," I started counting, ignoring her pleas for me to stop. Benjamin had his eyes closed and his arms up, surrendering. Unfortunately, his fate was sealed the moment he decided to come after her. My job was to protect her and that meant getting rid of anyone who was a threat. There was no space for negotiation.

"Two."

"Please don't do this," Milena cried out. I glanced back at her and she was shaking her head, tears brimming her eyes. How could she even think of giving him another chance? He was working for the men that wanted her dead.

"Turn around, Milena," I said, this time softening my tone.

She shut her eyes, shaking her head but she slowly started to turn around. "Three." As soon as she had her back to me, I didn't wait a moment longer before pulling the trigger. With the silencer on, the only sound was the suppressed click that went off as the bullet settled between his eyes. Benjamin dropped to the floor and I didn't wait around to admire my work. I reached for Milena's hand and we took off running back into the crowd. I shoved my gun back underneath my shirt and pulled her in the opposite direction of the apartment.

"You didn't have to do that!" she cried out. "We could have let him go!"

"Let him go? Are you hearing yourself right now?"

"I can't believe you did that!" she shrieked. "How could you ju-just? You fucking ki-," she stopped in her tracks. "Oh my God, he didn't have to be ki-," I stopped and pulled her closer to me, interrupting her sentence before she said what she was going to say.

"Yes he did," I hissed. "Milena, wake the fuck up. People want you dead. If I don't get rid of them then they are going to get rid of you. What are you not understanding?"

The tears brimmed her eyes, just waiting for a release. She caught her bottom lip between her teeth as it trembled. She was about to break down and I needed to get her as far away from here as possible. I hated to see her like this but I did what I had to do. She needed to understand that. I slipped her hand in mine again and started to pull her through the crowd.

"You're going the wrong way," she shouted. "The apartment is back there."

"We're not going back there."

"What?"

"Our location has been compromised. We're leaving Sevilla."

CHAPTER 19:

Milena

I had experienced my own fair share of loss but I had never experienced being the reason behind someone losing their life. Until today. And I didn't know how to begin to process that information.

"We're getting off at the next stop," Vincenzo said softly to me, pulling my attention back to reality. Everything that happened after Vincenzo killed Benjamin was a blur. He had money, burner phones and our passports stashed away in a safe for if our location was compromised. He had thought of it all. Now we were on a bus headed outside of Sevilla and for the first time, I felt as if all hope was lost. I had gotten rid of the awful blonde wig and now had my hair shoved underneath a different old cap that he had. Pulled over my dress was a checkered button up shirt that Vincenzo had in the bag. We had nothing but the clothes on our back and whatever resources he had hidden inside that bag of his. Thankfully I had chosen the kind of dress that one could wear sneakers with because they turned out to be pretty practical when being on the run. As soon as we were on the bus, he dialed someone's number and spoke another one of his many languages through the phone. As much as I wanted to know what he was saying, I also wished that I could escape all of this.

Vincenzo killed a man. A man who was trying to get me killed for the sake of settling his own debt. I had a target on my back now and there was nothing I could do to get rid of it except run. The phone on Vincenzo's lap rang and he lifted it to his ear. I didn't even bother attempting to listen to that conversation either and turned to stare outside the window. I focused my attention on the dark sky, trying to count the amount of stars I could see. One, two, three… Eight, nine, ten… Fiftee-

"Milena, your father is on the phone," Vincenzo said, handing me the phone. I stared at it in his hand before turning my attention back outside.

"Milena," Vincenzo said in a low voice. "He wants to speak to you."

"I don't want to speak to him," I muttered.

"You need to sp-"

I whipped my head around, glaring at him. "I don't need to do anything. All I need to do right now is find a way to stay alive because people want me fucking dead. What I don't need to do is speak to the man responsible for this."

Vincenzo glanced around, making sure that no one had heard what I had just said but thankfully, there weren't too many people around us. I was too numb to care. I heard a muffled voice through the phone which forced Vincenzo to bring it back to his ear.

"Yes *senhor,* she doesn't wan-" he stopped. "Alright. We will let you know when we get there." Another moment passed. "I will. *Adeus.*"

He disconnected the call and I could feel his gaze on me but I did not falter. I kept my eyes on the moving objects of the night as I leaned my head against the window. The last thing I wanted to do was speak to my father. I blamed him for this and after what happened tonight, I was going to need some time to adjust to my new life. The new life I was stuck with because he killed someone. Just like Vincenzo had.

God, I felt sick to my stomach.

Was everyone around me a killer? Was I supposed to become accustomed to that and accept it? People were losing their lives at the hands of others and I was struggling to come to terms with that. I knew that there was good and bad in the world but I never realized just how many blurred lines there were too.

The bus came to a gradual stop and Vincenzo's hand tapped my leg. "Let's go."

I turned and followed his lead as we made our way off the bus. I stepped onto the curb and as soon as the bus took off down the road, there was nothing but silence around us. I couldn't make out anything in the distance and the only light came from the faulty street lights.

"Where the hell are we?" I asked, glancing around at the nothingness that stood around us.

"Just outside of *Badajoz.*" He turned to the left and signaled for me to follow. "This way."

"There's nothing here. Where are we going to stay?"

"There's an old motel a couple roads up. This is the closest stop to it so we have to walk the rest of the way."

"Wonderful," I mumbled.

We had only managed a few steps along the dirt road before Vincenzo killed the silence that had settled between us.

"Why didn't you want to speak to your father?" he asked.

"Because I didn't feel like it."

"Bullshit. You've been wanting to speak to your parents for weeks and now you had the chance and you turned it down," he probed.

"Well after the events of tonight, I didn't quite feel like speaking to the man responsible for this in the first place," I snapped, the sarcasm dripping off my tongue.

"This isn't your fath-"

I stopped and whipped around to face him. "Don't you dare say that this isn't his fault. We're in this mess because of him so it's one hundred percent his fault."

He sighed. "Your father didn't mean for this to happen, Milena."

"I don't want to talk about this," I snapped and quickened my pace to walk past him.

"You're walking awfully fast for someone who doesn't know where they're going," he commented.

"And you're being awfully calm for someone who just murdered a man," I shot back.

"You mean I'm being awfully calm for someone who just did his job and protected you."

"Call it what you want. You killed a man."

"Milena," he called for me but I ignored him, not even bothering to look back at him. He called for me again and I knew he had stopped. After a few moments, I heard his footsteps pick up again before he gripped my arm, forcing me to stop.

"I did what I had to do to protect you," he defended his actions. "I'm not going to apologize for that."

"You didn't have to kill him!" I retorted.

"Trust me when I say that I did. Do you think I enjoyed doing that, huh?" he asked, a flicker of emotion in his voice. "I don't. That's the worst part of the job but that's exactly what it is - it's part of the job. He was going to hand you over to the Nazarios on a silver platter and I was not going to let that happen. I'm not going to let anything happen to you."

He was so close that I could feel his breath on me. I wanted to be angry at him. I wanted to fear him but I couldn't. He was putting his life on the line for me and the unexpected warmth that spread inside of me over that made me feel so guilty. Here I was, almost happy that he would go as far as to kill someone to protect me - how fucked up is that? This was his job. His job was to protect me so why was I so moved by that? I didn't want to admit it but a part of me was hoping that there was more to his reasoning. There was some unspoken connection between us and as much as I tried to ignore what was happening between us, I couldn't. I had never been drawn to someone like this. I had been attracted to men before but with Vincenzo, it was deeper than that. The attraction seeped to the deepest parts of my body and I wanted to get lost in him. I *wanted* him. His eyes dropped down to my lips, forcing my breath to get stuck in my throat. He slowly brought his eyes back to meet mine and there was something different in them. I would dare say it resembled a sense of longing but that's what it seemed like.

"Do you trust me?" he asked in a low voice.

Without hesitation, I slowly nodded. A sense of relief washed over him and he let go of my arm. "Good."

He said nothing further and continued towards our destination. We were walking next to the worn out road that was starting to become nothing but a dusty, dirt road. My body was aching and the exhaustion started to take its toll. I took a deep breath in, filling my lungs with the cool night time air as the moon shone down on us. I wanted to stay in this moment of calm. I didn't want to face this new reality that was forced on me. We continued in silence for who knows how long before a dim, warm light in the distance caught my attention. It was a small establishment but it was so far from civilization that I welcomed it. The adrenaline had left nothing but the longing for calm in its wake and for the first time, I was happy to be away from people.

Vincenzo went a few steps ahead of me as we started to approach the short cobblestone walkway to reception. The sign hanging on the wall just outside read, *Cape Rojo* but I could only tell the closer we got. The lights lighting up the *e* and the *j* weren't working so the name from a distance was *Cap Roo*.

"You'll be safe here,"Carina said.

"You don't know that."

*S*he was always the optimist and I, the pessimist. Everything I had was left behind and I couldn't see light at the end of this tunnel. I was starting to become consumed by the hovering anger and sadness that I had been putting off for weeks.

I stood by the entrance as Vincenzo went to talk to the older receptionist that was peering at him from behind the desk. She was gesturing some directions to him as she handed him a white key card. The clock on the wall behind her revealed the time to be just after midnight and I was surprised there was even someone awake to welcome us. They probably got a lot of random stop-ins throughout the night.

Vincenzo thanked her and made his way back to me. "We go this way."

I said nothing but followed him back out the main entrance. He turned right and headed towards the lined doors of the rooms that stood side-by-side. We stopped at the furthest door from reception and he swiped the card, unlocking the door. He pushed it open and waited for me to step inside before closing the door behind us. He found the light switch against the wall and the light flooded the room, revealing one double bed in the middle. If I thought the place in Sevilla was small, boy was I wrong. This was one room with one adjoining bathroom. There was no kitchen. Only a mini-fridge on the one side of the bed that acted as a bedside table and a microwave on a small table in the far corner. There was no TV, no couch - there was practically nothing here.

"They don't have any rooms with single beds," Vincenzo said, forcing me out of my own thoughts. He walked past me and turned the lamp on by the other bedside table. "But I don't mind taking the floor."

I shook my head. "We can share a bed, Vincenzo."

"You sure?"

"You said you were never going to touch me," I shrugged. "So sleeping in the same bed should be no problem."

He opened his mouth as if he wanted to say something more but quite frankly, I didn't want to hear it. "Do you happen to have any other clothes in that bag of yours? I don't want to sleep in this dress."

He shook his head. "I've just got that shirt you're wearing. Do you want my t-shirt?" he offered.

"The one you're wearing?"

He nodded. I was tempted to say yes but I would make do so instead I shook my head. "That's fine, I'll just button this one up."

I watched as he walked over to the bathroom, flicking the light on as he peered inside. "You want to go first? There's a towel hanging on the rack."

I didn't move. I couldn't. I couldn't even begin to process everything that had happened and I could feel I was going into shock again.

"Milena?" I heard his voice but I couldn't acknowledge him. All I could do was allow the tears that had built up to finally find their escape as they spilled over, running down my cheeks.

"Hey," he murmured, stepping in front of me. "Milena, it's okay."

I shook my head. "No it's not. This is all my fault."

"No, Mil-"

"It is!" I retorted. "It was my idea to go out. You warned me and I refused to listen and now someone is dead because of it."

"Benjamin made his choice."

"So did I." I caught my trembling bottom lip between my teeth. "I'm scared, Vincenzo."

I hadn't said that out loud and I wasn't sure why I decided to do that now. I often thought I didn't care for my life but that wasn't entirely true. I didn't want this target on my back. I didn't want any of this.

His hands cupped either side of my face, his touch burning against my skin. He forced my gaze up to meet his deep brown eyes that, for the first time, were swimming with his own emotion.

"Milena, you don't have to worry. You're safe now," he reassured me.

"For how long?" I choked. "You said so yourself, my death sentence has been signed. That's the only way out of this."

His thumb caressed my cheek and leaned closer to me, forcing my eyes up to meet his. "I *will* protect you. You're going to make it out of this."

I shook my head, the tears stopping against his fingers. "How? What kind of life can I have now?"

And that was when the cries that I had been holding back for weeks finally found their way to the surface. He brought my head against his chest and he let me cry, slowly running his hands over my hair as he attempted to console me. I couldn't stop crying and that only angered me. I was supposed to be better than this. I was supposed to be stronger than this. But I just didn't have it in me any longer.

"Milena," he murmured and slowly pulled away, his hands making their way back to cup my face. "Listen to me, everything is going to be fine. You're going to be fine."

He slowly wiped my tears off my cheeks and I couldn't stop the way that warmed my heart. He was so delicate with his touch. I didn't know if it was because of everything I was feeling but the sudden longing and desire I had felt towards Vincenzo also came rushing to the surface. I could think of nothing but his touch. It was so comforting to have it right now. I wanted more. I *needed* more.

My eyes dropped to his lips as I ran my tongue over my bottom lip in a quick motion, slightly tugging it between my teeth as the desire coursed through my veins. The tension resurfaced between us, begging for a release. I lifted my gaze to meet his and I could see his desire mirrored my own. I wanted to kiss him. I wanted to do so much more. I wanted to feel something other than all this pain.

"Vinc-"

He shook his head and dropped his hands. "We can't."

"Why not?" I probed as he stepped away from my touch. He looked as if he had just realized what he had been doing and I watched as he retreated into his mind again. "You can't pretend there isn't something between us." I stepped closer to him again. "I know you feel it, too."

"No." He shook his head.

"You're lying."

His eyes were begging for me to stop but I couldn't. He could deny it all he wanted but it would be a pointless thing to do. The tension between us was one kiss away from completely consuming us. After everything that had happened tonight, I needed something more. I needed him. I waited for him to tell me he was feeling it too. I was practically begging him to but he didn't. Instead, he just stood there, looking at me but no words formed on his lips. I didn't want to feel as hurt as I was feeling but I couldn't stop the disappointment that entered my chest.

"Fine," I muttered, regaining my composure. "You're right. There's nothing between us."

I turned to head towards the bathroom but I felt his hand on my wrist, causing me to turn back to face him. He was at a loss for words, I could see it in his eyes. He stopped me and yet he couldn't tell me why.

"Tell me what you want and I'll stay right here," I told him. "But if you let go of me then I'm going to shower and I will never bring this up again."

I hoped he would pull me closer to him. I waited for him to tell me what I knew we were both feeling. I was practically crying out for him to give me what I needed but instead, he let go of my hand and I had my answer. I held back further tears and the pain contracted in my throat. I tightened my jaw and nodded.

"Message received."

I stepped inside the bathroom and shut the door behind me.

CHAPTER 20:

Vincenzo

As I stared up at the ceiling, I could do nothing but replay over and over what happened between Milena and I. She was ready to cross a line that I just couldn't bring myself to step over - no matter how I wanted to. I wanted her, more than I have ever wanted anything in my life. I had never felt an all-consuming desire like this before but Milena wasn't like anyone I had ever met. There was so much more to her than meets the eye. She showed me true vulnerability that I knew she kept hidden from the rest of the world. I knew because I did the same. She was stubborn, feisty and adamant to prove to everyone that she didn't need anyone but beneath that was so much more. She was empathetic, even in moments when she shouldn't be. She tried to save the man that was ready to have her killed to suit his own personal interests. It angered me but she was a good person, even if she didn't believe it herself. I wanted to comfort her. I wanted to take away all her pain. She was the first person to ever jolt some kind of emotional reaction inside of me and it terrified me. I was always so good at being in control but not with her. She, unknowingly, had me relinquish control to her and I was so close to giving in. I wanted to admit to her that this wasn't one sided but I couldn't. This wasn't part of the job. Being attracted to Milena was never supposed to happen but it was getting harder and harder to deny it.

Especially right now when she was sleeping next to me. Her body inches away from mine. I had to fight the urge to roll over and pull her body close to mine. I couldn't shake the thoughts of wanting to take her in every way I could. I couldn't shake the deep desire begging me to give in. I was standing on a ledge, just about ready to give it all up for one night with her. That's all I needed to do. I needed to fuck her out of my system and then everything would go back to the way it was. I had obviously waited too long to fuck someone. I had a few women that were in a mutually beneficial arrangement with me for exactly what I needed. Unfortunately, I couldn't stop thinking about what it would be like to have Milena in that way.

She took a deep breath in and rolled over, the shirt she had on lifting enough to expose her bare backside. The thin material of her thong sat against her body and the heat flooded straight to my groin at just the sight of her skin. I had never fought harder than I was in that moment to stop from reaching out. The things I would do to her if I had half the chance.

Get up, Vincenzo.

I reprimanded myself and sat up, turning to rest my feet against the carpet on the floor. I ran my fingers through my hair, trying to get a handle on the lascivious thoughts bombarding me.

Air. I needed some fresh air.

My body was moving before my mind could register. I slowly unlocked the door and stepped outside. I was in nothing but my jeans, sitting on my waist. It was still dark but the cold air reminded me that it was the early hours of the morning. Milena didn't say anything further to me after she went to shower. When she was done, it was my turn and by the time I came back, she was already asleep. I was itching for a cigarette but I hadn't bothered packing that in my bag of essentials. I added that to the mental list of all the things we needed. After we bought our bus tickets, I got a hold of Carlos and we implemented the plan we had in place in case our location was compromised. He managed to wipe all my devices that were left back at the apartment. The last thing we needed was sensitive information landing in the hands of the enemy.

I remembered the vending machine I noticed by reception that had all you would need which included boxes of cigarettes. Half-way to reception, I realized I had no money on me so I turned to make my way back to the room to grab some cash. As I went to open the door, it was yanked open. A disheveled, half-asleep Milena stood there, her breathing was faster than normal and there was clear worry in her eyes.

"What's wrong?" I asked, stepping closer to her.

She ran her fingers through her hair. "I couldn't find you. I- I thought something had happened."

Without thinking, I reached out for her and slipped my fingers into her hair as I cupped her face. "I'm right here."

I shouldn't be doing this. I shouldn't be touching her but she just looked so terrified and I wanted to take it all away. I wanted to take away her fear and her sadness. My greatest achievement would be finding what could make Milena Neves smile. It had appeared a handful of times in the past - while they were few and hard to come by, I clung to the memory of what she looked like in a brief moment of happiness.

She slowly lifted her hands to rest against my arms. Her touch was like a shock to my system, lighting up every part of me that it could manage. It was short lived as she dropped them, realizing what she was doing before turning to walk back over to bed - not another word left her mouth. I stared at her, surprised by her abrupt change but I also couldn't blame her. I had practically left her out to dry earlier and even I could acknowledge how harsh that must have been. I felt guilty for that. I felt guilty for lying to her but what was I supposed to do? Could I really give into what I wanted? It would go against the ethics code of this job.

But when I looked at her, I forgot all about the fact that this was a job. I could think about nothing but her and I knew now that my reason for wanting to protect her was because of more than just what was expected of me. I *needed* to protect her.

God, get a grip.

She sat with her back towards me, facing the wall of the room. The only light came from light in the passage outside of the open door next to me. I should just grab my money and go get my cigarettes. That's what I needed. A cigarette or two.

I reached for some cash and closed the door behind me.

CHAPTER 21:

Milena

Rejection was a bitter pill to swallow and I had stupidly allowed myself to experience it twice in one night. Vincenzo closed the door without another word to me. He was the one who reached out and touched me. I didn't ask him to but he did it.

"He's got a thing for you."

"He obviously doesn't if he keeps rejecting me."

"Can you blame him?" Carina's voice asked. "He was hired to protect you and now he wants to do way more than that."

"No, he doesn't."

"We'll see."

I shook my head at my clear delusion. There was nothing between Vincenzo and I. The overwhelming emotions inside of me had clearly become so entangled that it couldn't tell the difference between them anymore. I was desperate to cling to anything other than my reality and what I was truly feeling. I needed something else to focus on but there was nothing. My foot was tapping against the floor anxiously as I waited for him to get back. Not because I wanted anything from him - I just wanted to make sure he was okay. After all, who would protect me if he's gone?

"Sure, that's the only reason," Carina said.

It was. Vincenzo being around meant that I stayed alive and apparently, deep down inside that was what I actually wanted. Just when I thought I was ready to die, the deepest parts of me betrayed my true feelings. That wasn't what I wanted at all. When it came down to my life and Benjamin's, I selfishly chose my own. I sounded like such an awful person even saying that. How could I possibly think my life is worth more than his? I used to believe I was a good person but maybe I was wrong. A good person doesn't choose not to visit their family when they have a chance. A good person doesn't make things difficult for their parents. A good person doesn't smoke when their sister died of lung cancer. I made Vincenzo's life difficult by constantly defying him. I chose my own life over anothers.

I was not a good person.

Before I could be sucked in by my own self-loathing, the door opened causing me to jump up only to find Vincenzo stepping back inside the room. The room was dark again but I leaned over to my bedside table and turned the lamp on.

"Thanks," he murmured and dropped the boxes of cigarettes on top of the mini fridge on his side of the bed. He was shirtless which forced me to swallow as I focused on ignoring the deep warmth that flickered inside my stomach. My eyes wandered over his arms as I watched him, lifting a cigarette to his lips. His muscles flexed as he lit a match and brought it closer to him, lighting the cigarette before he killed the flame and pulled the smoke into his lungs. I should be disgusted by such a bad habit but I was the furthest thing from that. I had never seen anything more sexy. The desire coursing through my body had even managed to make my mouth dry.

"C-could I please get a bottle of water?" I asked, sitting back down on the bed. One leg against the bed and the other dangling over the side. He placed the cigarette between his lips again before leaning down to grab a bottle for me. He handed it to me and I twisted the cap open, bringing the bottle to my lips to allow the liquid to seep into my mouth.

"Did I wake you?" he asked.

I swallowed the water as I shook my head. I didn't even feel him getting off the bed but my eyes were suddenly forced open and then I realized he wasn't next to me. After everything that had happened, I was terrified of what was still to come. He walked over to the door and opened it slightly, allowing the smoke that had gathered to leave the room. He leaned against the wall as he continued to finish his cigarette. I could have stared at him for hours, soaking in every curve of his muscles or tracing the ink against his skin but somehow I managed to pull my gaze from him.

I placed the water bottle on my side. "Good night, Vincenzo." I said and lay back down, my head resting against the pillow as my back faced him. I reached over and turned the lamp off.

"Good night, Milena."

I closed my eyes, wanting more than anything for sleep to find me but my mind was far too awake for that. My eyes opened again as I stared ahead of me even when I heard Vincenzo lock up the door after finishing his cigarette. I heard his light footsteps against the ground. There was no other sound than his movements. I suddenly felt the weight of his body against the bed as he lay back down. We were so close to each other - I could almost feel the heat radiating off his body. I shut my eyes. *You just need to sleep this off.* Tomorrow will be a new day. I even tried to count sheep, attempting all I could to find sleep. After what felt like an eternity, I huffed and rolled onto my back, my gaze landing on the darkness ahead of me.

"Can't sleep?" I heard his soft voice ask.

"Nope."

"Me neither."

The silence settled around us for a few moments. I waited to see where this conversation would go. There was so much I wanted to say but I also wanted to say nothing further. I didn't know how to be around him now.

"Did you grow up in Algarve?" He asked, surprising me with his choice of topic. I was thankful for the darkness around us. It made it a lot easier to engage with him without having to look at him. That turned my insides to jelly. *God, I sounded like such a child now.*

"No. We lived in Lisbon for most of my life. We only moved to Algarve after my grandfather passed away," I explained. "He left the hotel to my father so once that happened, we relocated."

"Did you like it there?"

"It was beautiful but it never felt like home to me. We had lost my sister then my grandfather - it felt almost selfish to enjoy something as fickle as moving to a new place. None of that matters anyway."

If he was looking at me with those intense eyes of his, I would have said none of this. Maybe I was overtired - or just over everything but my filter had officially slipped away.

He was silent for a moment but before I could give him an opportunity to say anything, I decided to ask him a question. "How did your parents pass away?"

I had turned my head slightly, looking over at his side profile. His lips parted as if he was about to say something but he slowly shut them, looking as if he was contemplating whether to answer my question or not. I almost felt guilty for overstepping before he finally answered.

"Car accident."

"How old were you?"

"Eight."

I tried to picture eight year old Vincenzo and what that might have been like for him. It broke my heart to think about and instinctively, I slid my hand across the bed until I found his. I slowly reached for it and squeezed. I waited for him to pull away from me but instead, he slipped his fingers in mine. I didn't expect him to share more - a part of me was hoping for it but Vincenzo was as guarded as I was.

"My grandparents took me in," he started to explain. "My father's parents. They pretty much raised me but a couple years after my parents died, we lost my grandfather after he suffered an aneurysm."

My heart ached for him and all the loss he experienced so young. I wanted to say something to comfort him but he continued.

"After that, it was just me and *nonna.*" He spoke with such vulnerability in his voice that I hadn't expected.

"Is this the same grandmother that taught you all those languages?" I asked.

"The very same one. Guess it was her way of distracting me - us, actually - from all the loss. I was never a talkative child but learning languages changed that."

It was endearing to hear how he spoke of his grandmother - and the tone in which he spoke about her. It was kinder, calmer - nothing like his usual emotionless tone that I had become accustomed to. There was so much more to this man.

"Does she know what you do for a living?" I asked.

"She doesn't know much anymore to be honest. She doesn't even remember who I am." His voice was now hollow and devoid of emotion in a different way which only made my heart reach out to him. "She has dementia.

Over the years it started to get worse but when I came home one day and she attacked me thinking I was breaking in, that was when I knew she was too far gone."

"Vincenzo," I murmured and squeezed his hand again. "I'm so sorry."

"Don't be," he said but I could hear the pain in his voice. "These things happen but the least I could do was get her the help she deserved. That's part of why I take any job I can get - to make sure she continues to get the best care."

He was opening up to me which only made me want to do the same. He was allowing himself to show vulnerability which was something I wasn't even sure he was capable of. But he was and it was beautiful to see. He was doing what he could to help her and that just made me feel something deeper for him. A new found respect had formed. His true vulnerability reminded me that although sharing my own wasn't something I had been able to do for years, there was something about how comfortable he made me. I wanted to share the parts of me that I hid from the world.

"You asked me earlier why I didn't want to speak to my father," I said softly. "The truth is I am having a hard time with all of this. You said he's responsible for the Nazarios son's death. What happened?"

He was silent for a few moments before I heard him sigh. He kept his hand in mine, caressing it with his thumb as he spoke. "Milena, I don't believe it's my place to explain what your father did to get you to this point. That should be something you should hear from your parents."

"They don't tell me anything," I retorted.

"After what happened tonight, they have to tell you. You can't decide on the next step unless you have the full story."

"And what exactly is the next step?" I asked.

"Going on the run. It's clear that they aren't going to stop until they find Milena Neves so we need to make sure that she doesn't exist anymore."

I shut my eyes, feeling overwhelmed by what he was saying. I knew he was right. The only way to get out of this now is for me to disappear - for good.

"Where am I supposed to go?" I whispered.

"Anywhere you want - the world is waiting for you to decide," He said in such a way that it almost sounded like an adventure to be excited about.

"Isn't there a place you've always wanted to go, but haven't had the opportunity yet?"

"There's a few. Mexico. Colombia, South Africa," I answered. "My sister and I spoke often of all the places we'd want to explore."

Carina always spoke about wanting to visit South Africa - Cape Town, specifically. She showed me pictures of it and truthfully, it was breathtaking. We would always speak about our plans to travel once we finished school. For the longest time I had believed it was a sure thing but after losing her, it felt wrong to even think about doing any of it without her.

"Are you an only child?" I asked him, wondering if he would have mentioned his siblings by now if he had them.

"Yes. Just me."

Thought so.

"That's lonely."

He let out a breath of amusement. "I don't mind being on my own. It's all I've ever known."

"I hear my sister's voice in my head sometimes," I admitted, surprising myself that I finally said that out loud.

"You do?" He kept his voice neutral - no flicker of judgment or concern behind it like I had expected.

"Yes. And trust me, I know how crazy that sounds. I know that it's not really her but when she died, I felt as if I had lost a piece of who I was." I couldn't believe I was talking about Carina right now but there was no stopping the words that were flowing out of me. "I didn't want to go on without her. I couldn't handle the grief and I even went as far as questioning whether life was worth living."

I felt his thumb slowly caress my skin again, reminding me he was here. My thoughts manifested themselves in the form of my sister's voice as an unwilling coping mechanism that had cemented itself in my life over the years now.

"Carina and I were attached at the hip. I had never been without her until she started having to stay at the hospital. She suffered for so long that I knew it was better for her when she died but it wasn't better for me." The emotion forced its way into my thoughts, turning into tears that were now spilling over onto my cheek again. "I didn't want to live without my sister and the one night

I started questioning what I could do about that was when I heard her in my mind for the first time."

He remained silent and I suddenly felt like an idiot for oversharing like that. He let go of my hand but I felt him shift closer to me.

"You probably think I'm crazy," I said, trying to hide behind an attempt at a joke.

"Come here." Was all he said before reaching for me. He pulled me closer to him and my head found his hard chest as my arm draped across his torso. He rested his hand against my hair and slowly caressed it. It was exactly what I needed. I needed to feel safe. I needed to feel heard and understood and in that moment, Vincenzo gave me all of that.

"I don't think you're crazy. I can only imagine what it must have been like to lose your sister," he murmured softly.

"You've suffered your own fair share of loss," I reminded him.

"I know, but I was so young. I felt like it just became part of who I was."

I was surprised at how comfortable I felt in his arms. We spent all this time denying whatever was happening between us but during these early hours, it was almost as if we weren't capable of staying apart. I slowly started to draw circles against his chest with my finger. "What made you become a bodyguard?" I asked.

"My father was a detective back in *Palermo* and I had always admired him. He lived to protect other people and I would always hear these stories of how much of a hero he was," Vincenzo explained. "I wanted to be just like him. Strong. Protective. Good. I always believed he was invincible - until he wasn't."

His voice twisted with emotion and I half-expected him to stop but he kept going.

"A car accident. Seriously? He gave so much of himself to the world - my mother too. They were good people and still they were taken from this world in a way that was completely out of their control."

I slid my hand up along his chest to rest just under his jaw, slipping my fingers into his hair. It was my way of reminding him that I was here before he got lost to his memories.

"I quickly learned that the world owed us nothing. Before my parents died, I was always that quiet child in any group. I used to think there was something wrong with me but my mother would always say, *'There's nothing wrong with you, Vinnie. You're just an observer more than a talker.'"* He let out a soft laugh at his memory.

"Vinnie?" I repeated. "Is that what your mother used to call you?"

He nodded and I suddenly understood why he didn't like it when I called him that. It wasn't to be rude - it was just a constant reminder of her. A pang of guilt presented itself inside of me.

"So, that's why you didn't like it when I called you that," I said softly.

"It was difficult to hear in the beginning - I know that may sound stupid b-"

I shook my head, interrupting his sentence. "No, I completely understand."

"You didn't let me finish," he said playfully, eyeing me in a way that made my insides turn to jelly.

"It was difficult to hear in the beginning but things are different now - with us," he murmured, alluding to the elephant in the room that there was something between us. I was comforted by his shift and sharing something as personal as what he just did. I couldn't help but smile.

"Little Vinnie would be happy to see how far you have come from that quiet kid you speak about," I said softly.

"I think so too. I just never liked to bring attention to myself in any way but after the accident, it was almost as if I wasn't afraid of anything anymore. There was this little asshole that I went to school with who went around bullying others - including myself," he continued to caress my hair as he spoke. "I became fearless. Nothing could be worse than what I was feeling at the time so one day, he was bothering one of my other classmates and I had just had enough. I stood up to him. Got into my first physical fight."

"At eight years old?" I lifted my head to gape at him.

He shrugged. "Listen, he had been asking for a beating so I'm surprised no one had done it sooner. I got a free pass 'cause the teachers knew what had happened to my parents but no one ever messed with me again. I guess that kind of stayed with me all the way into my adult life. I've always felt the need to protect people - just like my father. Most people actually end up scared of me but I guess that's a good thing in this line of work."

"It's that demeanor of yours." I rested my head back against his chest.

"You're so..." I stopped to think of the correct word to describe him. Stand-offish? Mean?

"So?" he prompted.

"Intimidating."

"You didn't seem very intimidated the first time you met me," he pointed out. "In fact, I distinctly remember you biting my hand."

"To be fair, you grabbed me. I went into flight or fight mode."

My head lifted slightly as his chest did from the laughter he allowed to slip from his lips. I was obsessed with that sound. I could listen to his laughter all day. I lifted my head and rested my chin against his chest, looking up at him. He had a deep crease that resembled a dimple on the right side. It hardly made an appearance, but I wish it would. That would mean he would be smiling or laughing.

"See you don't look so intimidating when you smile," I commented.

He leaned his head down, glancing over at me. "That's not something I do much."

"Well, you should. It looks good on you."

His eyes lit up with surprise at my unexpected compliment. Vincenzo De Rossi kept himself sheltered from anything remotely resembling any emotions but he was starting to let his guard down. We were similar in that way. Both of us make sure to ignore any kind of human emotions. I was intrigued by him. He had piqued my interest and the underlying attraction had yet to falter. In fact, with each moment spent with him it started to become something deeper. An understanding. A relatability that I hadn't found with anyone else.

"And for the record, that wasn't the first time we met," I corrected.

"Oh?"

"We met the night before at the party you worked for my parents. You helped get rid of my ex."

"Ah yes - the asshole with a *punch me face.*"

This time I laughed. "He really does have a *punch me face,* now that I think about it."

"How long were you guys together?" he asked.

"A few months," I replied. "Honestly, it was barely even a relationship. It quickly ended when I caught him fucking a waitress on the bar."

"Oh fuck."

"Yup."

"Now I'm kind of wishing I had punched him."

I chuckled. "He wouldn't even be worth the energy it would take to do that."

He had moved his hand to rest against my back. Even through the material of the shirt, I could feel his touch burning against me. I was so over aware of his touch. Was he doing that on purpose? Did he know what he did to me when he touched me? I swallowed, trying to get a handle on my thoughts before they disappeared into a dark, lascivious place.

"And you?" I asked. "Any previous eventful relationship story you have to share?"

"That would require a relationship and since I've never really had one of those, it makes this conversation pretty null and void."

"You've never been in a relationship?" I lifted my head again, not being able to hide my general shock over that statement.

He shook his head.

I eyed him suspiciously. "Are you telling me you're a virgin?"

He threw his head back in laughter. "You don't need to be in a relationship to have sex, Milena."

I was thankful he couldn't see the heat that had definitely spread across my cheeks. I couldn't stop my mind from thinking about what it would be like to have sex with Vincenzo. It didn't take long for the deep desire in the pit of my stomach to reappear as I allowed my thoughts to wander.

"So not a virgin then," I repeated as casually as I could manage.

"Definitely not."

"Body count?" I asked.

"People I've had sex with or people I've killed?" he asked with such a nonchalant energy to him that it could have almost passed for a normal question.

"Uh…" I scrambled. "Both?"

He shook his head, his lips pulling up in amusement. "I'm not telling you that."

"Why not?"

"Because the people from my past aren't important."

The looming question still lingered around us. I hadn't thought of the fact that Benjamin might have not been the first person that Vincenzo had killed and I wasn't sure how that made me feel.

"What's your body count?" he asked, pulling me back to the conversation.

"Zero," I answered. "I've never killed anyone."

He rolled his eyes, letting out a breath of amusement as he did that. "With that temper it's hard to believe. I'm surprised I'm still here."

My jaw dropped slightly but I couldn't hold back an amused laugh at his comment. "First time for everything."

"You wouldn't do that."

"I mean I've thought about it. You definitely pushed my buttons enough with your constant need to bark orders at me."

He rolled his eyes. "You hardly even listened to me anyway."

"And I hate to break it to you, but I probably still won't." I teased.

"Oh, I expect nothing less. Anything else would be out of character."

I nudged him playfully. "I'm not that bad."

"I didn't say you were." He laughed. "But you are a handful."

This time I was the one rolling my eyes.

"I didn't say it was a problem though," he murmured. "I've never met anyone like you before."

"I don't know if that's a good thing," I admitted.

"It's a great thing,"

I tugged at my bottom lip, trying to hold back a smile as the heat spread across my cheeks again. I swear he was flirting with me. *Right? O*r was it in my head? Could very well be.

He yawned, bringing his hand up against my hair to caress it again. He moved so naturally with me, it was a feeling I was starting to welcome. Seeing him yawn brought on my own and I could feel the exhaustion hovering over me again.

"We should probably get some rest," he said softly.

"You're right."

He shifted ever so slightly to rest his head against his pillow comfortably while still keeping his arm around me. I figured that was probably my cue so I started to pull away but he pulled me back, turning his head to face me.

"Where are you going?"

"To sleep?" I answered, unsure of why he would ask me what seemed fairly obvious.

"Stay like this a little longer." His hand rested against my back again, allowing me to reposition myself like I was.

We were supposed to be going to sleep now but I couldn't contain the bubbling excitement inside of me at what just happened. He wanted to keep holding me. He wanted me to stay close to him. What the hell does all of that mean? All I knew was I was more than happy to stay like this in his arms.

"I never thanked you for protecting me," I murmured.

"You never have to thank me, Milena."

"You killed someone for me."

"And I'd do it again. No questions asked," he answered with so much surety it made my heart skip a beat.

I wish I had the words to explain what hearing that did to me. A deep warmth spread across my chest and a deep longing developed for him, terrifying me. Did I have feelings for Vincenzo De Rossi?

I shook my head. There's just no way.

I should have moved and fallen asleep on my side but I couldn't bring myself to do it. With my head still rested against his chest, I drifted off into a deep sleep.

CHAPTER 22:

Vincenzo

I hadn't slept that well in a long time. When I rolled over and found Milena sleeping peacefully next to me, I welcomed the sight of her. Opening up to each other the way we had wasn't something that either of us expected but once it happened, there was no going back. I never planned on holding her, but I couldn't stop myself. Especially when she was sharing things with me that she had never told anyone before. We were connecting on a deeper level now and I could feel myself slipping further into her. I didn't know how much longer I was going to be able to stop myself from giving into what I truly wanted.

After a few more moments of racking my brain for what to do next, I pulled myself out of bed, careful not to wake her. I reached for my t-shirt hanging in the bathroom and pulled it over me. Reaching for my wallet and cell phone, I quietly stepped outside. I was greeted by the dark clouds in the sky, hiding the sun from making an appearance. A storm was definitely brewing and it felt as if it was a direct reflection of the storm brewing in our lives right now. My moment of weakness allowed me to go against my better judgment when allowing Milena to go to that party. I knew taking her out would put her in harm's way and now a man was dead because of it. Did I feel guilty about killing Benjamin? No. It was what I had to do to protect her and I would do it again. Was I a bad person for killing someone? Probably but I had a good enough reason to do it.

It wasn't a part of the job that I welcomed. Thankfully, it wasn't something that happened every time. There were very few situations where I had to take someone's life but the first time it happened, I was consumed by guilt. It happened during an attempted break in for a private client I was working with years ago. Her husband was head of the *Mediobanca b*ack in Italy and with an increase in robberies and home invasions, they hired private security as a precaution. We had arrived back after their annual fundraiser just in time to interrupt the attempted break-in at their home. Shots were fired and as soon as I pulled the trigger, there was no going back. Multiple ones hit the one robbers chest and I couldn't pull my eyes away from the way he bled out on the floor in front of me. It had been years since I felt a flicker of anything inside but that night, I couldn't escape the guilt.

"Great job, Vincenzo," my partner at the time had said with a pat on the back. I was being congratulated for taking someone's life. I used to believe in right and wrong but there was so much more to that. I was doing a good thing by doing the wrong thing and killing him. It was wrong to kill but when it was protecting someone else? Was it justified then?

It was now.

Milena had done nothing to deserve the target on her back so I didn't even think twice before pulling the trigger to save her. I would do everything I could to keep her alive which now meant going on the run for good now. I needed to get her as far away from Portugal and Spain as possible. If they found her once, they would find her again and I wasn't about to give them another opportunity.

I dialed Carlos' number and on the second ring, he answered.

"Vincenzo, everything alright?"

"For now." I got straight to the point - we didn't have time for polite pleasantries. "But we need to keep moving. We don't know how many people knew she was in Sevilla. It's not safe for her here anymore."

"I know. We need to get them all out."

"What's the plan?" I asked as I leaned against the concrete pillar outside, kicking the loose stones in the sand.

"First things first - we need to get you a car again. I've already spoken to Afonso and he is organizing everything for you but you may have to spend another night or two there. It's not easy for them to get out of Algarve right now. It's like a warzone there." He explained.

I was thankful that we were far away from the eye of the storm. We could manage another day or two here but we definitely needed some supplies. Clothes, toothbrushes, toothpaste, food - my next mission was to find all of that.

"Tell Afonso to take it easy. We can manage here for the time being," I said.

"Once you have the car, we'll take it from there," Carlos continued. "Her parents are safe at the house outside of *Guimarães* but we're going to have to get them out of the country. There is just no way they can go back to Algarve - the situation is a fuck up."

"I know," I agreed. "We need to look at getting them new identities."

"Already on it. Listen, Milena's father really wants to speak to her. He was a mess after he heard what happened last night. What were you guys doing out anyway? She was supposed to stay at the apartment."

"Trust me, I know that but she wasn't making it easy."

I had avoided having this conversation with Carlos because when it came down to it, I was the one who allowed her to run about the streets of Sevilla, completely endangering her life. It went against the number one rule of my job and he knew it.

"You fucked up," he muttered.

"Carlo-"

He interrupted me. "Look, Enzo, I'm not going to lecture you. You know I trust you and your judgment but all I'm saying is you've never let your guard down like that before - don't start now."

I remained silent, unsure of what to say. He was completely right and there was no arguing about it.

"Get Milena to phone her father today," he switched the subject and I was thankful for it. "He needs it."

"You need to convince them to tell her the truth about what happened. She deserves to know."

"I'll be in touch."

He was about to hang up but I stopped him. "Carlos, can you do me a favor?"

"What do you need?"

"I need Afonso to get something else before he heads this way. I'll text you the details."

"Fine." Was all he said before he disconnected the call. I closed my eyes, leaning the phone against my forehead as I relived the conversation. I had fucked up. Milena hadn't given me much of a choice but the truth was, I had allowed my emotions to get the better of me. I shook those thoughts from my mind and focused on the plan at hand. I needed to get us supplies so I headed in the direction of reception. There was hardly any sound surrounding me except for the faint, elevator-style music playing from the small radio behind the counter as I approached. The older lady from last night was no longer present and instead, a young lady had taken her place. She didn't look older than sixteen or seventeen as she peered at me from behind her glasses, a flicker of irritation settling on her face as she looked up from the book she was reading.

"*¿Puedo ayudarte?* she asked.

"*¿Hablas inglés?*"

She nodded and switched to the neutral language between the two of us. "How can I help you?"

"I need a few things. Some clothes, toothbrushes, food - where can I get that?"

She glanced left and pointed to a set of doors at the end of the corridor. "Food there. Toothbrushes - there." She pointed to the vending machine. "Clothes - that you're going to have to travel a few roads up to find the nearest shop."

Well, that wasn't an option.

"Look, can you help me out?" I leaned against the counter. "My girlfriend and I-" I started to lie. "We left our bags on the bus on the way here so we have nothing but the clothes on our back. How much will it take for you to organize someone to get some clothes for us?"

She arched an eyebrow at me, clearly displaying her obvious suspicions of me. "You left your bags?"

I nodded.

"Well, that was pretty dumb."

I couldn't help but chuckle at her straight-shooter approach. It was a pretty fickle story but I was desperate and I couldn't afford to leave Milena alone for too long. It wasn't safe for her to be out just yet. I opened my wallet on the counter in front of her and grabbed two hundred euro bills. I positioned them between my index finger and my middle finger, leaning my hand over to offer it to her.

"Please?" I leaned over and noticed her name badge. "Sofia."

She narrowed her eyes at me, flicking her gaze between the money and me. "Add another hundred and we have a deal."

I grabbed another hundred and handed it over to her. "You can keep the one and use the other to get us the basics please. Clean underwear, a shirt, jeans - whatever."

"And what size does your girlfriend wear?"

"Uh- a medium?"

"You don't know your girlfriend's size?" She eyed me suspiciously again. "You sure she's your girlfriend?"

"Medium," I reaffirmed, even though it was a shot in the dark right now. "We're in room five."

She nodded and proceeded to dial the number for someone to come and cover for her. Either, I was going to get what I asked for from her, or she was going to keep the money for herself. Only time would tell. I headed over to the vending machine and started gathering things we needed. Toothbrushes, toothpaste, deodorant, headache tablets - I got what I could. Holding them in my hands, I walked back over to Sofia.

"Do you do room service?" I asked.

She looked around. "Does it look like the kind of place that could afford room service?"

"Your customer service could do with a bit of work you know," I pointed out. "You sure there isn't anything you can do to organize that for us?"

She rolled her eyes. "For another hundred, I'll organize all the room service you could need."

"Deal."

CHAPTER 23:

Milena

The sound of the door handle opening caused me to roll over, noticing Vincenzo slipping through with a whole lot of items in his hands. He kicked the door closed behind him before turning to notice me.

"You're awake," he said, walking over to the bed to drop what he was carrying against it.

I yawned and stretched my arms before propping an elbow up to lean my head against. "Someone went shopping."

"Just from the vending machine by reception." He sat down on the bed. "I just got some of the basics. Food is on its way."

"This doesn't seem like the kind of place with room service," I commented.

"Now it is since I paid the receptionist a hundred euros to do it."

An amused chuckle left my lips. "I really hope that includes coffee."

"Oh, I asked her for that - black right?"

I flicked my gaze up to meet his, surprised that he knew how I took my coffee. I nodded. "How'd you know that?"

"Just something I noticed at the other apartment."

"Look at him remembering the small things," Carina said. "Told you he has a thing for you."

"That thing is called doing his job."

I refused to allow my thoughts to head in the direction they were going. He had made himself pretty clear last night about where we stood. He was here to do a job and nothing more. Nevermind the fact that holding me was hardly part of the job description. He caressed my hair softly last night and I had fallen asleep in his arms. It had been weeks since I had slept as well as I did last night and I knew it was because I had him next to me. I wasn't afraid when he was close.

"Thanks." I forced a smile before turning my attention to the items on the bed. "We still need to get some clothes. I can't stay in this shirt forever."

"Already on it. We should have some items delivered later."

I eyed him. "Did you pay the receptionist to get us clothes too?"

"Yup." He couldn't hold back the small smile on his lips as if he was almost impressed with himself for being so resourceful. I ran my fingers through my hair and leaned back against the wooden headboard, trying to compartmentalize my thoughts. Last night was a rollercoaster and I was thankful for the small time out I found through my sleep. It was a dreamless night too - exactly what I needed.

"You need to speak to your father today," he said, bringing me back to reality.

"I don't want to."

"Don't you want to find out the real story about why you're in this mess in the first place?"

"He won't tell me," I argued.

"He will. Things have changed now and you deserve to know the full story."

I sighed. "And then what? What's our next step?"

"We go on the run," he said with a matter-of-fact tone in his voice.

"Together?" I arched an eyebrow.

"I'm here to protect you. Where you go, I go."

Even though it wasn't meant in the romantic way that he said it, I couldn't stop my heart from skipping a beat at those words. I refused to allow myself to even acknowledge the very clear flicker of feelings I had inside towards Vincenzo.

"Unless I'm told otherwise," he added, forcing a deep sense of disappointment inside of me over hearing that. I didn't want to think of him not being around. I also didn't want to think of these feelings constantly presenting themselves. Instead, I turned and got out of bed just as there was a knock at the door.

"That must be breakfast," he said, standing up as I walked past him to the bathroom.

"I'll be out now."

***

Vincenzo's pay-off had proved to be successful. We now both had a few more pieces of clothing than before which meant I was starting to feel a little normal after I showered and was now changing into the sweatpants and shirt she had gotten me. The size of the pants were guessed correctly but the t-shirt sat skin tight against my body - my boobs always needed a larger shirt if they wanted to breathe.

I peeked my head from behind the bathroom door. "Do you have a shirt for me?"

"What's wrong with the one she got you?" he asked.

"What's wrong is-" I stepped out from behind the door, revealing the skin tight shirt against my body. "That it's like a second skin. Seriously, did she shop in the children's section for this?"

His eyes dropped over my body and I watched his jaw tighten. He flicked his gaze back up and in a split second, there was something else behind his eyes. For a moment, I felt desired by him before he regained his composure and I was forced to ignore the tension that had settled in the air again. Maybe I should have kept the shirt on but I didn't have it in me to play with fire today.

"So, if you have a shirt for me, that would be great," I tried to say as casually as possible. He stood up and walked over to his backpack, pulling a gray shirt from it. He walked over and handed it to me but not before allowing himself to drop his gaze over my body once more. I slowly took the shirt from him and started to close the door, shutting off whatever was happening. As much as I wanted him to keep looking at me like that, it was a fruitless thing to want - he was never going to give me what I wanted. He wasn't feeling what I was feeling and the sooner I made peace with that, the easier things would be. I pulled the shirt off and replaced it with his before stepping from outside the bathroom. Vincenzo had his phone to his ear and turned to glance at me. "She's here." He handed the phone to me, gesturing for me to take it. "It's your father."

While there was still a burning resentment inside of me, I was in a calmer state than I was last night. I took the phone from him and took a deep breath in before bringing the phone up to my ear.

"*Olá, papa,*" I greeted.

"Milena, *graças a Deus!*" His voice was thick with relief. "*Como está?*"

I hadn't expected the emotions to rush over me the way they did just from hearing his voice. It reminded me of everything that had happened over these past few weeks and how I hadn't seen my parents. I was reminded of how much I missed them.

"I'm okay. What about you guys? How's *Mãe?*"

"She's okay, given the circumstances. We were so worried when we heard what happened last night," he said. "What were you doing out of the apartment? Vincenzo is supposed to be keeping you safe - not putting your life in dan-"

I cut him off. "He is protecting me but I haven't exactly made it easy for him. None of this has been easy."

"I kno-"

I jumped in again. "How did this happen, *papa?* You killed a man."

"Milena, there's so much more to the story than you know," he defended.

"Then tell me. You can't keep me in the dark any longer," I told him. "People are trying to kill me. I can't go back to the life I once knew because of this." I hadn't even realized that I was raising my voice until I felt Vincenzo taking a seat next to me on the bed, looking at me with concern. The tears were begging for a release but I refused to give into my emotions right now. I didn't care how much it pained me to hold them back.

"I never wanted this to happen," my father murmured. "I've always tried to do what was best for this family."

I shook my head to myself. "What family?" I snapped. "We haven't been a family since Carina died."

I didn't mean to say it but the words left my mouth before I could stop them. I was just so tired of holding back. When she died, I lost more than just my sister and best friend. I lost the family I once knew. I lost the parents that I had grown up with. I felt so completely alone. I had held back my true feelings and thoughts for years and I just didn't have it in me anymore to keep doing that. What was the point?

"Milena, you don't mean that." I could hear I had hurt him which only caused a deep bit of guilt to settle in my stomach. I leaned my elbow against my thigh and rested my head against my hand, looking down at the floor. "When your sister got sick, I did everything I could to save her." There was a hollowness that settled in his voice as he spoke of Carina. I caught my bottom lip between my teeth as it trembled, the tears forcing their way out now. I was never very good at holding them back whenever it came to Carina.

"Your mother and I weren't in the best place financially and the treatments, *meu deus,* they cost so much. I did what I had to do in order to get her what she needed. I...I borrowed the money and years later, they came to collect."

"You borrowed money from the Nazarios?" My voice was barely a whisper.

"I had no other choice. My daughter was dying. I was desperate."

I shook my head as the tears started to stream down my cheek. I didn't want to hear any more. All the anger I had towards my father was replaced with nothing but guilt. He and my mother had lost a child - I hoped to never know what that kind of pain felt like.

"I didn't mean to hurt anyone, Milena," he choked, only making me cry harder into my hand as I tried to hold it back. I felt Vincenzo's hand against my back but I kept my gaze firmly on the ground. The tears continued to drop onto it.

"I never meant for this to happen. They used the hotel as a front for their work. I let them do what they wanted, never getting in their way but then they started dealing drugs to the guests and it was getting dangerously out of hand. That was never part of the agreement - I was trying to explain that to him bu-" His voice trailed off as he shuddered, clearly crying through the phone. My heart shattered hearing my father's pain. I wanted nothing more than to be able to hug him right now.

"*Papa,* you don't have to say anything else," I cried. "I'm sorry. I don't need to know anymore."

My heart couldn't handle this. I thought I was strong enough but I was the furthest thing from it. I was made up of nothing but broken pieces, fighting to try and hold themselves together.

"I can't lose you too, Milena." He sniffed. "I need you to stay safe."

"I'm safe. You don't need to worry about me."

"You know I always do."

I took a deep breath in as I wiped my eyes. "When will I see you again?"

"Soon. I promise." He reassured me. "I have to go now but please just know how sorry I am for all of this. I never wanted this."

"You don't need to apologize."

"*Te amo*, Milena."

"*Amo-te também, papa.*"

We disconnected the call and I stared at the cell phone in my hand as I tried to get a handle on my emotions. I couldn't stomach hearing my father's pain. I blamed him for all of this, not knowing that this all started because he tried to save Carina. He did what any father would do and I felt sick to my stomach.

"Milena, hey," Vincenzo murmured, running his hand softly against my back. "It's okay."

I shook my head, tears running down my cheeks. "You were wrong when you said I was strong enough to handle this. I'm not."

His hand came around to cup my cheek, slowly forcing me to turn to look at him. "I'm never wrong. You are strong enough to handle anything. I know you are."

He leaned his forehead against mine, reminding me that I wasn't alone in this. I didn't feel strong at all. At that moment, I felt weak and without hope but there he was again, trying to pull me out of it. I wanted to take comfort in his touch but I couldn't allow myself to do that. My heart could only handle so much right now. I pulled away from his touch, standing up to pace up and down the room.

"I can't think straight when you do that," I confessed.

"Do what?"

I stopped and turned to face him. "Touch me. Hold me. Comfort me - any of it. I can't handle it."

"Mil-"

"And please don't say my name, I hate it when you do that."

He couldn't hide the very obvious surprise on his face at my reaction. I was trying so hard not to break but everything was pushing me further and further to the edge.

"What am I supposed to call you?" he asked.

"I don't know!" I huffed. "I've heard my name a million times but then you came along and it was like hearing it for the first time." I ran my fingers through my hair, exasperated. "And then you touch me and I lose my bearings. You held me last night, Vincenzo. Why did you do that?" I turned to face him, my breathing continuing to pick up pace as I deflected my frustration onto him. He remained silent, his eyes searching for the answers I was looking for.

"What am I supposed to think?" I asked. "You tell me there's nothing happening between us but then there you are again, holding me, touching me - telling me how strong I am, remember how I take my fucking coffee. It's driving me crazy!"

He stood up, walking over to me but I couldn't handle any more of this back and forth. I had reached my peak. I took a step back, holding my hand up to stop him. "Think about what you're doing. If this is just a job to you - if I am just a job to you then don't offer yourself to me like you've been doing. Don't comfort me. Don't tell me everything is going to be fine. Just do your job."

"Milena, I want... but I ca- fuck." He was fumbling now and I was surprised to see how unbalanced he seemed.

"You don't know what you want," I snapped.

"I can't have what I want."

"Why not?"

He ran his fingers through his hair, exasperated before stepping closer to me, trapping me between his body and the nearest wall. "Milena, I want nothing more than to take you right now and show you all the ways I want you." He slammed his hand against the wall next to me, causing me to flinch. "I want you so bad it hurts. It makes me fucking crazy. I want you more than I want to breathe right now and I don't know what to do about that because this can't happen."

I celebrated the small victory of being right about his feelings. I knew he was feeling it too. It was impossible to only be one-sided. He was right when he said this can't happen. This wasn't what was supposed to happen but my desire for him clouded my judgment and was begging me to give in. I was never very good at self-control and with the way I could feel his breath on my skin, making it dance with goosebumps up and down my arm, I couldn't hold back any longer.

So instead of saying anything more, I pulled into him.

His lips met mine and he froze against me. I was terrified that he was going to push me away. He was the responsible one. He was the professional one. He was the one to always do what was right but instead of doing what I expected him to do, I felt his arms encircle my waist as he pinned me hard up against the wall. His tongue parted my lips and oh my God, I already couldn't get enough of him. My legs tightened around him as his desperate kiss claimed me. My entire body had been set on fire and there was no fanning this flame. His teeth grazed my bottom lip causing a deep moan to fall from my lips.

"*Oh Dio*, I love that sound," he murmured against my lips before pulling at my bottom lip again. I couldn't hold back the moans as he nipped harder. *"Tesorina, ti farò urlare."*

I had absolutely no idea what he was saying but hearing his mother tongue falling from his lips caused the heat to pool between my legs, begging for his touch as the arousal crawled across my body. No part of me was left untouched by desire. He leaned his body into me and felt his erection hard against me. Shoving my hands in his hair, I gripped at it as I flicked my tongue over his. The tension that had been eating at us for weeks was finally getting what it wanted and I was dying for more. I needed more from him. I needed to *feel* more of him.

His lips left mine and he used his one hand to grab my chin, pushing it up to expose my neck to him. He started to work his way over my jaw and down my neck, stopping to suck on my skin. I was always so used to being the one in charge in the bedroom. All of my previous sexual encounters had me needing to guide them to show them exactly what I wanted. I was the one to usually call the shots but Vincenzo had me handing myself over to him to see what else he would do to me. He evoked feelings inside of me I had never experienced before - both sexual and otherwise.

"Ah - fuck, Vincenzo." I breathed, not being able to hold back. I was engrossed in the electrifying desire inside of me that was crying out for release. I was throbbing between my legs now and I needed him to touch me. I needed him *inside* of me.

"Please," I begged as his lips worked over my collarbone. "God, Vincenzo, please."

"What do you want, Milena?" he breathed against my lips. "I need to hear you say it."

"You. I want you," I moaned, my pulse fluttering as he looked at me with the deep intensity in his eyes that made me want to dissipate into thin air.

"Once we do this, there will be going on your back," he murmured.

"I don't care. You-" I gripped his hair. "I want you."

His eyebrow lifted slightly as his tongue ran over his bottom lip before pulling up into a sexy smirk that caused a rush of heat between my legs again. "You're going to take all of me, my sweet sweet, Milena."

His voice was laced with desire, but there was a thick challenge behind it too and I was ready for it. Whatever he would give me, I would take. I had never wanted anyone more. An animalistic desire rushed over him as he pulled me away from the wall, his strong arms carrying me to the bed. He tossed me down, making me gasp but I didn't have enough time to catch my breath before he grabbed my ankles, pulling me closer to the edge of the bed. His hands slipped underneath my shirt, burning against my skin as he pushed it up before I pulled it off, my bra joining it on the floor. He wasted no time feeling every part of me that he could. His hands were running up my arms then down my torso then his head was buried between my breasts - he was everywhere and I was consumed by him. He took my breast in his hand and he squeezed as his lips found my skin again. He moved with such urgency that I felt as if I was going to implode from the inside out. I reached for him, grabbing whatever part of his shirt I could. I needed it off. I needed to feel his body against me. He pulled away with enough space to pull his shirt over his head with one arm before tossing it across the room.

I groaned at just the sight of his body before my hands started to move over his chest and up his shoulder. I gripped at him. I dug my nails in his body. I was losing my fucking mind here as my senses started to overload. I ran my fingers over the markings along his chest. I wanted to spend my time going over each and every one of them. I wanted to show his body what I could do. I wanted to revel in the ecstasy of the orgasms I had caused him. I was selfishly narcissistic like that.

"I need to feel you." He breathed in my ear causing me to shudder beneath him as he mirrored my own thoughts. He wasted no time pulling at the string of my sweatpants to loosen them before pushing them down my legs and onto the floor. *Yes* - we were so close now. I was dying to feel him. I would welcome him very easily with the way I was feeling right now, my pussy pulsing with each passing moment without his touch. Suddenly, he cupped me, causing my breath to get stuck in my throat.

"God, Milena, you're so wet." He ran a single finger over the outside of my thin underwear. "I fucking love it."

He didn't wait a moment longer before slipping his hand underneath, the feeling of his hand bare against me already had me rolling my eyes back. He pulled my underwear off, giving him enough space. He teased me, slowly running a finger up and down my opening that was wet in anticipation. I was pretty sure I was going to stop breathing at any moment now. He stopped at my clit and slowly used his thumb to circle it, causing my body to jerk forward into his touch. I was so sensitive right now. My hand cupped the back of his neck and I dug my nails into his skin.

"Sii paziente, tesorina," his deep, raspy voice brushed against my skin. I loved hearing him speak Italian. It was the sexiest fucking thing I had ever heard and my body could have come undone from just that.

Without warning, he slipped a finger inside of me.

"Ahh…" I breathed, my head falling back against the bed and I soaked in the feeling. I could already feel myself tighten as he started to move, picking up the pace. My eyes rolled back and I was engrossed in his rhythm as he moved, knowing exactly the spot he needed to hit. While most men seemed to need a map and a fucking instruction manual, Vincenzo would be the man to write it.

"Fuck, Milena." He breathed. "You're going to feel so good wrapped around my cock."

Oh, yes. That was exactly the kind of thing I wanted to hear. I wanted him to whisper filthy nothings in my ear. I wanted him to tell me all the dirty thoughts taking up residence inside of his mind right now. I could think of nothing but having him buried deep inside of me. I was growing impatient. I lifted my head to meet his gaze. He was tugging at his bottom lip as he watched me, his eyes burning with his own desire.

"Pl-please, Vincenzo," I managed to get out between the rhythm of his finger inside of me. "Oh yes," I dropped my head back against the bed. Just when I needed a moment to catch my breath, Vincenzo was there to take it away.

His thumb circled my clit as he slipped a second finger inside of me. I was throbbing against him as a deep sound escaped him in reaction to his name falling from my lips in the form of a deep moan.

"Fuck me," I managed to get out as a strangled breath. "Vin-" the rest of his name was lost to the pulsing pleasure working its way through my veins as he found my clit again.

"God, I love hearing you talk like that," he groaned. "I'm going to make you come first then I promise you, Milena, I'm going to fuck you so hard, you won't be able to walk without being reminded of me."

Oh. My. God.

He picked up his pace, and between his attention to detail against my clit and the way he moved inside of me. I was gripping the bed covers as I cried out. I couldn't stop the moans leaving my lips and I didn't care who was in the room next to us - they were going to hear the euphoria I was in. My orgasm crawled closer and closer to its climax.

"Don't stop - oh God, Vincenzo, faster."

He gave me exactly what I wanted and my body surrendered itself to him as I released myself against his fingers that were still working their way inside of me. I cried out in pleasure, white dots in my vision as I allowed my orgasm to consume me. He removed his fingers and I watched as he brought them up to his mouth, licking my release off of them.

"Tastes as good as it looks, baby." He tugged at his bottom lip, looking down at me as if he was going to rip into me at any moment. I was still reeling from my orgasm but I wanted to feel him. I wanted him inside of me. I wanted Vincenzo De Rossi to fuck me into tomorrow but I also wanted the chance to explore him. To work myself over his body and over his cock, showing him what I was capable of. I propped up onto my elbows, trying to calm my breathing as he shifted his weight over my body, his lips hovering close to mine.

"My turn," I murmured, holding his intense eye contact.

He smirked and shook his head. "Who says I was done with you?"

With a look of challenge in his eyes, I was deeply intrigued about what else he could possibly do to me. My body had handed itself over to him on a silver platter and he showed me that he was no rookie when it came to handing out orgasms.

He leaned closer to me. "I need to taste more of you." Without warning, he leaned into me, slipping his tongue between my lips to allow me to taste myself. The eroticism of that act in itself had me moaning against his lips, nipping at his bottom one before he pulled away.

Without warning, he grabbed my hands and pinned them above my head, his one hand gripping both wrists as his lips found my neck again. "This is all about you, Milena." My name fell from his lips with a deep sense of longing laced with seduction."I've been wanting to do this for so long." I wanted to fight him. I wanted to fall back into old habits and take control but I was learning that Vincenzo was perfectly capable of giving me everything I didn't know I was missing.

He was sucking hard on my skin now, branding me in the most intimate way. I hadn't even had a chance to recover from my climax and he was already awakening my senses once more. With his fingers still wrapped around my wrists, he brought his face close to mine again. We were inches from each other. "You think you can stay still?"

I nodded.

"Let's test that out, shall we?" His tongue skimmed my bottom lip before he removed his hands from my wrists and moved down to position himself between my legs. My clit was begging for his touch again and with every moment without it, it continued to throb.

"I think you and I should play a game," he murmured.

"A game?" I lifted an eyebrow at him. "What kind of game?"

"You're used to being in control, aren't you?"

It was rhetorical as he was well-aware of what the answer was. He knew me. He knew what I was like. He didn't wait for me to give him an answer before he continued his thought. "If you can stay still and keep your hands where I have placed them until I am done with you, then you get to be in control." His hot breath against my skin caused a rush of chills over my body. I tried to squeeze my thighs together in an attempt to alleviate the pressure which earned me a hard grip on both thighs as Vincenzo flicked his eyes up to mine. "Milena-" His voice was full of seductive warning as he hooked his arms around my legs, pulling me closer to him.

"And what if I move?" I breathed.

"Do you trust me?" Was all he asked.

I answered without hesitation, "With my life."

"Then let me take care of you, *tesorina.*" *He* leaned closer between my legs, never once breaking eye contact which caused a deep stir inside of me. I had never experienced such an intense burst of desire. I wanted to believe that's all it was, but I would be foolish to think there wasn't something more. He leaned closer between my legs and anticipation pulsated through me. He wasted no time before leaning forward, allowing his tongue to flick up my opening, causing my body to surrender itself to him from the sensitivity.

"Stay still," he said, his breath hitting my skin. He brought himself closer to me again, allowing his greedy tongue to explore all the parts of me available to him. I was in a trance filled with nothing but pleasure. My body had never experienced such heightened senses and every touch, every lick, every suck against me had me begging for another release. Slipping a finger back inside of me, his tongue took care of my clit and what a combination that was. He was so attentive, always flicking his gaze up to meet mine, making sure he was getting the reaction he deserved. I was dying to reach out and touch him. To pull on his hair as I rocked my hips against him, allowing him to explore more of me with that tongue of his.

"Vincenzo," I groaned his name with a sense of desperation.

"I can't get enough of you," he said before plunging his tongue deep inside of me. With the way he ate me out, I couldn't comprehend how I had managed to make it this far without experiencing this. It was addictive. *He* was addictive. He had me high on the ecstasy he was giving me and I was greedy. The more I got, the more I wanted.

I lifted my hips, welcoming his tongue deeper as my hands slipped into his hair. I threw my head back, my moans filling the room. Everyone needed to know that Vincenzo De Rossi knew exactly how to take care of a woman's body. I wanted more - God, I needed mo-

Without warning, he pulled away, leaving my aching clit begging for more. He gripped my wrists, tightening his hold on me as he brought his face back to mine. "I was hoping you'd do that."

"Please, Vincenzo," I managed to get out between my heavy breathing. "I need to feel you inside of me." Pulling my one hand free from his grasp, I reached out and cupped his erection against my hand watching as he leaned his head back, the veins on his neck protruding. I could feel the wetness running down my legs, reminding me how easy it would be for me to welcome him where I've been dying to have him. He removed my hand, pinning it over my head again. I felt him lean his erection against me. "I can't wait any longer, Milena," he said, a deep longing in his voice for what we were both truly craving. He leaned across the bed and grabbed my sweatpants from the floor. "What are yo-" I started to ask before I saw him pull the string out of them. "Hey!" I objected. "I still need to wear those."

A soft chuckle fell from his lips displaying that God-given smile of his. I swear that was enough to make me stop breathing. It was beautiful. He leaned over me, grabbing my wrists and pulled me closer to the headboard. He wasn't delicate with his touch and I was thankful. I've never been a fan of that. I wanted it rough. I wanted pure, animalistic fucking. What I hadn't anticipated with him was the rush of unexpected emotions that had been hovering, now threatening to break-free with each passing moment together.

"You lost," he reminded me. "I'm in control now."

I felt him wrap the thick string around my wrists, binding them together. I stared at him in bewilderment as he managed to hook it around the one wooden pole of the headboard.

"I've thought about doing this since Sevilla," he murmured, running his finger down my cheek and then along my jaw. "To have you at my mercy."

He was creating an invisible thread down my neck and between my breasts. I held my breath in anticipation as I watched him soak in my body. He looked at me with such intensity - the kind that made me think he was ready to fuck me but also like he thought I was going to disappear. There was so much behind those dark eyes of his. He leaned closer to me again but his finger slipped between my legs. "You're nothing like I expected, Milena." Slipping between his domineering energy was this sudden vulnerability I didn't expect. "You're a fucking goddess."

My heart was suddenly added to the mix and an overwhelming warmth spread throughout - something way more than pleasure and desire. Something deeper. Something I had never experienced before. I tried to get a word out but with the way in which he picked up his pace with his fingers and added his tongue to the mix, I was lost to him. His tongue explored my opening on the way back to my clit where he attended to it until he had me screaming out as I came against him. He licked me up, soaking in my taste while I relished in my orgasm that was pulsing through me. I should have been finished then and there but I was still tied up and completely at his mercy.

And I wouldn't have it any other way.

He stood up and I watched as he unbuttoned his jeans, pulling his zip down. There was a dark look in his eyes and I held my breath. He pulled his underwear down, finally revealing himself to me.

Oh, this was going to hurt.

Good thing I loved the pain.

"I don't have a condom," he admitted. "But if I don't get inside of you right now, I swear to God Milena, I might die."

I shook my head. "I don't care."

"You and me both, baby."

I had lost all sense of responsibility and common sense. I just didn't care. All I wanted was him and I'd be damned if I didn't get what I wanted. He climbed over me, using his knees to part my legs as he positioned himself between me. He leaned down, his arms resting on either side of me. He balanced on one as he shifted closer to me, gently sliding himself up and down the creases of my opening.

"Ohhh…" I breathed, my eyes already rolling back.

He started to push slowly inside, stretching me out with his size that had me biting down on my lip to stop from crying out. He was ripping me as he moved inside but oh my, he felt incredible. Without warning, he pushed deep inside of me and both of us let out a sigh of relief. Skin to skin, we burned against each other and I didn't want this moment to end.

He started to move, slow at first as he thrust in and out of me. I tightened around him, the deep pleasure already pulsing through my veins. I was dying to run my fingers over his body but handing myself over to him like this was exhilarating. I lifted my hips, wrapping my legs around his body to welcome him deeper. His right hand gripped my hip, digging into my skin.

"Fuck, Milena, you feel so good," he said, leaning his head back as he soaked up being inside of me. The sight of him above me was the sexiest thing I had ever seen and it would forever be ingrained in mind. Watching the way his jaw tightened and the veins on his neck made an appearance was adding to the pleasure building inside of me.

"Am I hurting you?" he asked, bringing his gaze to meet mine.

I shook my head.

"Well, I'm about to, so if you want me to stop, you just say the word, understood?"

I nodded, my breathing getting caught in my throat in anticipation. He shifted us further up the bed and reached up, gripping the headboard. He slowly pulled out of me, teasing me as just the tip of him was inside before he thrust so hard inside of me that I cried out. And then he repeated that, each movement getting faster and faster until he was fucking me so hard that I had to shift my, still bounded, hands above my head to keep from hitting the headboard.

But, holy fuck did it feel good.

I had never felt anything like it before. I couldn't hold back my moans as I shouted his name to the world. "Yes, yes yes - oh my - Vincenzo." My eyes rolled back in my head as I felt his finger against my clit as he continued to move inside of me. I was ready to explode with pleasure. He held nothing back as he continued, his own moans slipping from his lips. I loved hearing that. My hands moved against the restraint, wanting to reach out to feel him. To feel his body. To run my hands over every part of him that I could manage.

"Vincenzo, please," I groaned, pulling my wrists against the restraints as he thrusted hard into me, hitting the back of my wall. Without stopping, he lifted one arm and grabbed the string, ripping it off of the headboard and off my wrists as it split into two.

I reached up and pulled him to me with a new sense of urgency. His lips crashed against mine and we devoured each other. I groaned against him as I parted his lips with my tongue, earning a deep moan from inside his throat which assisted with another orgasm that rolled through me as he pushed deep inside of me, each thrust harder than the one before.

"Yesssss!" I cried out as I dug my nails into his arms. I tightened around him as my climax crept over every part of me but he didn't stop. He couldn't.

"I-I'm close," he managed to get out as he thrusted harder inside of me, my legs already shaking from the lingering orgasm. With one hard thrust, he came inside of me. He dropped against my body, both of us trying to get our breathing under control. I didn't want this moment to end. I wanted him to stay inside of me and to do all of that again.

He slowly lifted his head to meet my gaze. I reached out and softly ran my fingers through his hair, my nails scratching his scalp. He leaned into my touch, his eyes closing but a small smile formed on his lips. It was a softer side to him which made my heart skip a beat unexpectedly.

He pulled out of me, leaving me with nothing but the lingering memory of him and the dripping liquid between my legs. He fell next to me, his back against the bed as he looked up at the ceiling. For a few moments, we didn't say anything. We just lay in comfortable silence as we waited for our breathing to calm down.

"We probably shouldn't have done that." I leaned over to look at him.

"We definitely shouldn't have done that."

I was silent for a moment. "But we're going to do that again, right?"

He leaned his head to the side, his gaze finding mine. *"Tesorina,* you're not ready for all I'm going to do to you."

Bring it on.

CHAPTER 24:

Vincenzo

I had fucked up.

I would usually pride myself on my professionalism. I had never overstepped or broken any of the rules. I stuck to what I had to do - nothing ever swayed me until I met her. I tried to rack my brain, trying to figure out what it was about Milena that had me so under her spell that I just caved like that but I couldn't put my finger on it. There were so many reasons that I found myself completely enraptured by her. She was the first person to remind me that inside my chest wasn't just a hollow shell like I had come to believe - I had a heart and right now, it had been awakened by her in every way.

She lay on her stomach with her hands hooked underneath her pillow. She was facing me but her eyes were closed and I watched as her body moved ever so slightly as she breathed. If you had to ask anyone what the most beautiful thing in the world was to them, you would probably get the cliché answers of the view of the ocean, the sky during a storm, sunrises and sunsets - most of the time, anything connected to nature would be considered the most beautiful but I would strongly disagree. If they could see Milena the way I was seeing her right now, in a deep peaceful slumber, they would realize that no beauty could ever compare. My voice of reason was shouting at me to stop this, to pretend this didn't happen - to get a grip before this turned into something it wasn't meant to be but it was far too late for that. I had fallen down the rabbit hole with her.

We spent the rest of the night lost in each other's bodies. Fucking over and over again until exhaustion washed over us. I wanted to be angry at myself. I should have at least felt guilty for what I had done but I couldn't feel anything but a deep feeling for Milena that closely resembled compassion. Or maybe even like. I liked her, right? I certainly liked fucking her - scratch that, I loved fucking her - but there was so much more to it. I had the strong urge to protect her, more than what was expected of me. I wanted to protect her from the looming danger but I was also interested in protecting her heart. I didn't expect to be so affected by seeing her in tears earlier but I was and that was when it dawned on me that I was too far gone.

I wanted Milena in ways I had never wanted anyone before.

I leaned my elbow against the bed and dropped my head into my hand as I looked over at her. Stray strands fell over her eyes and I reached over, careful to keep my movements as light as possible as to not wake her. I slowly pushed it back but I couldn't bring myself to move my hand just yet. I slowly trailed my fingers against her soft skin. I tried to find the right words to explain to her what she was. An unexpected breath of fresh air after I had been drowning. Rain against your skin after the beating sun threatened to leave a burn.

She was a relief.

It relieved me that after all this time, I could finally be introduced to the beauty this world had to offer.

We had completely devoured each other for hours, never fully being able to get enough. I thought I could fuck her out of my system and I would be able to move past that but I had never been more wrong. The more I had of her, the more I needed and there was no getting rid of her now. Every touch, every taste of her sweet lips, every part of her that she gave me only made me need her more. The rush she gave me was exhilarating and I was already in too deep with her.

"You've never let your guard down like this before."

Carlos' words repeated over and over in my mind, snapping me back to reality. I pulled away from her and slowly got off the bed. She was in a deep sleep and quite frankly, I needed some fresh air. She consumed me. I felt her in every part of me and I knew it was wrong. No personal relationships with the people you're protecting - that was standard procedure. I didn't need to be told twice. But now that I had finally gotten a taste of her, there was no way I could keep going with another hit.

I pulled my jeans back on before grabbing a box of cigarettes off the mini-fridge and stepped outside, careful to keep my movements as quiet as possible as I closed the door behind me. I walked over to the curb right outside our door and leaned against the concrete pillar. The sound of thunder boomed in the distance, pulling my attention to the sky. It was dark - not even the moon had made an appearance tonight. Shuffling came from the distance to my left, forcing me to turn towards the corridor where I saw an older gentleman walking towards me with a bag over his shoulder. It was the first person I had seen staying here and it looks as if he was just checking in. He nodded to me and stopped two doors down from ours. I politely nodded back in response before he made his way into his room.

I turned my attention back to the box in my hand. I pulled one out and rested it between my lips. I brought my lighter up to light the cigarette before letting the smoke out into the air as I leaned my head back.

This entire day I was focused on nothing but Milena and now that I stood outside, a free moment to myself, I started to feel the guilt that was waiting for me. Fuck, I should not have slept with her. *What the hell were you thinking?* The rational voice in my head repeated over and over, trying to find a reason that was good enough for breaking the rules. I wish I had one but selfishly, I wanted her - that was all it came down to. Even though I knew how this was going to end.

And that was the truth, it was going to end. This wasn't a long term thing - it couldn't be.

I was used to keeping myself sheltered from any relationships with anyone. It was a subconscious thing that happened when my parents died. I isolated myself in an attempt to deal with my grief which to an eight year old was a foreign feeling. It became a part of who I was and it became easier to avoid getting too close to anyone. Twenty-two years later, I hadn't even bothered trying a relationship with anyone. I had my casual hook-ups - all involved were willing and understood the nature of our arrangement but nothing ever went further than the physical. Until Milena. Her witty tongue and pure defiance had become intriguing to me. That intrigue turned to pure attraction and now there was something more.

But I refused to allow myself to even acknowledge that. I was here to protect her and make sure she got to her parents so they could start their lives over. That was the plan now and nowhere in that arrangement was there space for us.

Us. God, I was even referring to the two of us as one entity.

What the hell was happening to me?

I brought the cigarette back up to my lips and shook the rest of those thoughts out of my head. I pulled another drag as I heard the door creak open behind me.

"Vincenzo?" She murmured with a sleepy voice.

I turned to face her. The door was slightly ajar and she stood in the t-shirt that I was previously wearing. Her disheveled hair hung past her shoulders and when she lifted her hand to cover a yawn, I noticed she had nothing but her thong underneath.

This didn't stop her from stepping outside though and walking over to me. She extended her hand, gesturing for the cigarette in my hand. I handed it over to her and watched as she brought it up to her lips. She leaned against the pillar opposite to me and crossed her arms, staring out into the night.

We stood in silence. For the first time in my life, I was scrambling for conversation and I didn't know how to handle it. She completely had me off-balance now.

"You're awfully quiet," she commented, handing the cigarette back to me.

"Guess I'm just lost in thought." I took it from her.

She nodded, turning so her back was against the wall. She placed her hands behind her back and lifted her one leg up to lean against the wall. "And what is it that you're so deep in thought about?"

You. Always you.

"Nothing in particular."

"Liar."

I leaned my head to the side, looking over at her.

"You regret it, don't you?" she asked.

I was surprised by her assumption. "And what makes you think that?"

She shrugged. "You're good at your job. You obviously enjoy it - maybe even love it - but you don't strike me as the kind of guy who enjoys going against the rules, which is exactly what you did."

I turned my gaze forward, staring into the dark distance ahead of me as

I flicked what was left of my cigarette onto the floor. She was right. I wasn't that kind of guy - not when it came to this job at least. Back in school, I didn't give a fuck. I did what I wanted. I used to have a problem with authority when it was based on fickle rules and regulations. This job was not that. I quite literally had the lives of others in my hands and I took that very seriously. Maybe even too seriously sometimes.

"Am I wrong?" she asked.

No you're not wrong. I feel guilty that I allowed this to happen.

I should have said that but instead I said, "Yes, you're wrong."

"So you don't regret it?" A flicker of hope could be heard in her voice.

I sighed. "I probably should. We both know it shouldn't have happened but I don't think I can stop myself from touching you again, Milena."

CHAPTER 25:

Milena

S *tay calm.*

I mean sure, he only said something romantic which practically made my knees want to buckle from under me but that wasn't something I was going to let him know. I was going to attempt to remain as calm and collected as I had presented myself to be up till now.

"Good," was all I managed to say before turning to face the darkness ahead. I could feel his gaze on me but I didn't move. Not even when the air became thick with tension like it usually did when we were around each other.

"But -"

No buts.

"I don't think it's a good idea for us to let it happen again." He stepped forward, pulling my attention to him. I was facing his strong, chiseled chest that already sent a rush of desire between my legs. His body was so fucking hot. Dark tattoos lined his skin, making me want to reach out and run my fingers over each marking, hearing the stories behind them all. I wanted that kind of intimacy with him and it fucking terrified me.

"You're right," I said, knowing I was trying to convince myself here.

"It would be bad."

"So bad."

He leaned his arm next to me, trapping my body between him and the cold wall I was now up against. He was so close, the palpable tension between us lingering against my skin now. Heat pooled deep inside of my stomach, stirring up my desire again. I couldn't believe how ready my body was for him again. His eyes fell down to my lips. "Milena, you should stop me."

My tongue grazed over my bottom lip as my mouth went dry. That's the last thing I wanted.

"You know I'm not good at being told what to do."

Before I knew it, his hands were cupping my face and getting tangled in my hair as his lips found mine. I gasped as he held me up against the wall, finally allowing us to give into the tension that surrounded us since I stepped outside. He used his tongue to part my lips, flicking across mine as he leaned his body against mine. I could already feel his erection against me which only made the arousal shoot through my veins, seeping into every part of me. He didn't waste any time before moving his lips to my jaw and down my neck, using his hand to push my head up, exposing my neck to him so he could do what he needed. I already felt as if I was going to explode. The feeling of his lips against my neck had me being unable to control the soft moans that left my lips. I needed to feel all of him again. My body was ready.

"Vincenzo." I breathed, which earned me a soft groan from him. He brought his face up to mine, we were inches away from each other and I could feel his breath on my skin.

"Say that again," he murmured.

"Vincenzo," I repeated.

"Now get ready to scream it," he said before reaching for me, lifting me up so my legs wrapped around his waist as he pushed me up against the wall, his lips finding mine again. I could feel the cool air against my bare skin that was now exposed. The shirt I was wearing had lifted but I just didn't care. I didn't care about anything but Vincenzo and all I wanted him to do to my body. I was at his mercy.

Suddenly, someone cleared their throat which caused us to abruptly break our kiss. Vincenzo turned his head and I followed his gaze that landed on a man who was standing in the corridor. I froze, unsure of whether he was a threat or not but the lack of urgency from Vincenzo told me what I needed to know.

"Don't stop on my account." A thick Spanish accent came from the man standing in front of us. He arched a judgemental eyebrow as he locked eyes with Vincenzo. Even from here I could notice the way in which his jaw clenched, matching the judgment he didn't bother to hide in his gaze.

Vincenzo turned back to me for a split-second and I could see the guilt in his eyes. I unwrapped my legs from his body as he set me back on the ground. I had never seen this man before but there was clear familiarity between the two of them. He looked around Vincenzo's age and carried himself with the same intimidating demeanor. On his arms, he had dark markings running up and down his brown complexion and while he wasn't as tall or broad as Vincenzo, I still wouldn't pick a fight with him.

"Afonso," Vincenzo finally said, turning to face him. "Wasn't expecting you until tomorrow."

"That's because you didn't read any of my messages. Looks like you were a bit preoccupied." His eyes darted towards me. "You must be Milena."

"Uh yes, hi," I said awkwardly from behind Vincenzo.

Afonso nodded and turned his attention back to Vincenzo. There was so much unspoken between these two that I almost felt as if I was interrupting something.

"Milena, go inside and get changed," Vincenzo ordered.

My body moved before my mind could register what he said but I turned and slipped back into the room. I leaned against the door as I closed it and let out the breath that had gotten stuck in my throat.

"Okay, don't panic." Carina's voice attempted to comfort me.

"Don't panic? We were just caught by someone from his team."

"So? What's the worst that could come from that?"

I wanted to answer that but I actually had no idea. I knew what we were doing went against the rules of his job but we didn't exactly discuss the consequences. What if they assign him to someone else? My stomach dropped at just the thought of him leaving. I didn't want that. I wanted him to stay with me.

Shit, I was already in too deep here.

CHAPTER 26:

Vincenzo

We waited for Milena to close the door behind her before starting the inevitable reprimanding I was about to receive. Afonso turned his attention towards me again, crossing his arms across his chest.

"*¿Que mierda?! Estas loco?*" Afonso said, not bothering to hide his clear judgment. The fact he was speaking his mother tongue right now instead of English to me just proved he was angry. I couldn't blame him. This was hardly on the job description and to get caught outside like we were wasn't boasting well for my protection skills.

"I'm not crazy, Afon-..."

"You're fucking her?" He shook his head. "How could you let that happen?"

I sighed. "It's not like that."

"So you're not fucking her? 'Cause the way the two of you were going at it against that wall said otherwise."

His words cut through me, forcing a wave of irritation to form inside of me. *Mind your own fucking business.* That was really what I wanted to tell him but I knew I couldn't. I had fucked up by sleeping with Milena and Afonso knew it.

"Put an end to it."

I shook my head. "I don't think I can."

He walked over to me. "You can and you will."

"Afo-"

"If you don't then Carlos is going to reassign you."

He was right. If Carlos even got a whiff of what was happening between Milena and I, he would reassign me faster than he could say the word. Protect her. That was all I was supposed to do but I had never thought I would have developed any kind of affection towards her. I refused to allow her safety to be put in the hands of anyone but me.

"I didn't expect this," I admitted to Afonso.

He looked as if he almost felt bad for me. "Look, I'm not going to say anything to Carlos but Vincenzo, you have to end this. You're going to have to take her to meet her parents and then they're out of here. Their new identities are almost ready to go and there are no plans for any one of us to accompany them. You're never going to see her again."

A deep disappointment revealed itself along with something else I couldn't quite put my finger on. Hearing Afonso's reality check made me feel like shit. I was in way too deep with Milena and I didn't know how I was going to get out of it.

He handed me a single car key and gestured towards reception. "The car is out back there. Mauro is waiting for me in the other vehicle. We've packed as much as we could manage but whatever else you need, get on the road. Also, that thing you asked for, it's all in the glove compartment. You need anything else?"

Even if I did, I couldn't think straight right now so I just shook my head. "All good, thanks."

"Then I'll be going."

He said nothing more before turning and making his way towards the exit. His footsteps got softer as he walked away and I was now left with nothing but silence surrounding me. He was right. I had to stop this before it went any further. I was angry at myself for allowing any of this to happen in the first place.

How could I be so stupid?

I wanted to be angry at myself - truly angry but I knew I had no say in what transpired between Milena and I. I was driven by something deeper. I could fall for her - I knew I could but that wasn't an option. The only option here was to protect her. Nothing more, nothing less.

I took a deep breath in and turned to make my way back inside. I opened the door, stepped inside and closed it behind me. I turned to find Milena waiting on the bed, this time she had pulled her sweatpants back on and her hair sat in a messy bun on her head. Her eyes were full of trepidation and my first instinct was to hold her. I wanted to hold her but I couldn't.

"Who was that?" she asked.

"Afonso." I fiddled with the car key in my hand. "He brought us a new car and some supplies."

"That's good."

An awkward silence hung in the air as I walked over the spot where my shirt lay on the floor. I picked it up and pulled it over me, using every inch of self-control I had not to look in her direction.

"We need to get going," I said.

"Vincenzo," she murmured but I didn't stop. I started to gather what I could - I grabbed my gun, putting it into the back of my jeans. I lifted my cell phone off the mini-fridge and saw that there were tons of missed calls and messages from him and Carlos. *Fuck.*

"Vincenzo," she repeated my name and I felt her close to me now. Her hand rested on my arm, "Hey, what's going on?"

"What's going on Milena is that we need to get out of here," I muttered.

She stepped in front of me, forcing me to look down at her. "You know that's not what I'm asking."

"We shouldn't have done what we did." My tone was a lot harsher than initially intended but if I was going to stop this, I needed her to be angry at me. Or maybe even hurt. Even though just the thought of doing that to her was ripping me apart inside, I knew I had no other choice.

"You said you didn't regret it," she said softly.

"Well, I was wrong. I do." I stepped closer to her. "This is never going to happen again. You need to pack your stuff up and we're leaving."

I could see on her face that she was taken aback by my sudden change. Her jaw tightened and she was now glaring at me. "Not even five minutes ago you were ready to fuck me up against that wall and now you're just going cold on me? No. I don't buy it."

"There's nothing to buy. This is the way it's going to be now."

"Because Afonso saw us? Seriously? One guy sees us and that's enough for you to cut this whole thing off?"

I couldn't handle her glaring at me so I walked past her, reaching for my wallet. "This should never have happened," I repeated.

"You're lying to yourself."

"Milena, please." I sighed, already exasperated from this conversation. She forced herself in front of me again, the anger radiating now off her.

"What is so bad about what we're doing?" She asked, a flicker of real emotion in her voice. I hated to hear it. Guilt twisted inside of me over my tactics to push her away.

I ignored her question. "This never would have happened if we weren't forced together. There is no real world example of you and I ever even being in the same room if it weren't for what happened."

"No shit," she muttered sarcastically. "But guess what? It did happen. This is my life now and you and I are here right now - together." She stepped closer to me, resting her hand on my arm. "I don't care how we got here, I'm just glad that we did."

"Milena- " It almost pained me to have to say her name. She was making this so difficult for me. I need to put an end to this but I was fighting myself too.

"Don't act like you don't feel anything for me." She peered up at me with those big brown eyes of hers. "Don't act like you just fucked me, Vincenzo. There was more to it."

I didn't want to say what I said next but I had to. The only way to stop this was to hurt her. Even if it killed me inside to do it.

"No, Milena, there wasn't." My gaze hardened as I looked down at her. "I fucked you. That's all it was. Fucking. You were here and you were convenient but now, that's done. So you're going to pack your shit up, get in that car and I'm going to take you to where you need to go. Whatever this was - it's over now."

Her jaw clenched and I hadn't noticed the hand that crossed my face until the stinging started to spread.

"Fuck you, Vincenzo." She pushed past me and headed for the door. I whipped around and grabbed her wrist.

"Where the hell do you think you're going?"

"Anywhere but here!"

I pulled her back. "You can't go out there by yourself. There's still a target on your back."

"I'll take my chances." She pulled her wrist from my grip and yanked the door open.

"Milena - wait!" I shouted, trying to scramble to grab everything of ours that was still in the room. I grabbed the key card for the room and followed closely behind her as she stormed down the corridor. I've done it now. She slapped me and quite frankly, I deserved a lot more than that but it did what it needed. There was no way this would have worked out between her and I anyway. What was I hoping for? A relationship? To live happily ever after? That wasn't something I believed in. I had seen enough of the world to know how cruel it could be and it would be foolish to expect anything different.

I sped up my walk and stopped her as we got to reception. "Milena. Stop. I have to check us out."

"That seems like a you problem," she shot back.

"Do not move from here," I warned. "I'm not fucking around. You're not a child so stop acting like one."

She was glaring at me, her eyes practically throwing daggers my way. Behind the anger was a flicker of pain and I was the cause of it. There was no going back now.

"I want to leave," she said in a hushed tone.

"We're going to leave now." I turned towards reception and handed back our key card. The older lady who first helped us when we arrived sat behind the counter this time. She smiled up at me.

"Gracias, señor." She took the card from me. *"Esperamos que gustaron su estancia."*

"Gracias." I turned and made my way back to Milena who, reluctantly, waited for me by the entrance.

"Time to go."

CHAPTER 27:

Milena

Vincenzo De Rossi was an asshole.

Whatever I once thought of him, I was clearly mistaken. One minute he was ready to devour me up against the wall, and the next, he was throwing me to the curb. And I was so angry at myself for being upset about it. Upset and disappointed with a slight touch of embarrassment. Quite the combination to make me feel suffocated enough as we sat in a car together. We had been on the road for a few hours now, nothing but silence between the two of us. I kept my arms crossed and my gaze firmly outside my window. I refused to even look his way. I couldn't bring myself to do it. When I did, I was reminded of the hurt that sat inside my chest. I hated that I even felt anything towards him but I did.

"We're going to meet your parents in the north," he said, finally breaking the silence between us.

"Good."

"So you'll at least get to see them again."

"Yup."

I kept my responses as short as I could manage. I didn't feel like idle chit chat between us. We weren't friends - we were nothing but strangers actually. No matter what was shared between us that made me feel as if there was a deeper connection here, it was fickle and short lived. I needed to take those interactions for what they were - a simple way to pass the time.

"They were more than that, Lena," Carina said.

"Please don't say that."

"You know I'm right."

I refused to give any further attention to that back and forth in my mind. I was so angry with him but I was also angry at myself for having been in this situation in the first place. I had enough to deal with - I should never have added any complicated feelings to the mix.

"Once we're there, we'll be taking you to the nearest airport."

I swallowed and tightened my jaw, trying to ignore the pulsing fear and disappointment over hearing that. "And then what?" I asked.

"Then we'll get you guys out and you'll have to start over. Your parents will explain the next step in the plan when you're with them."

I was silent for a moment but I couldn't stop myself. "And what about you?"

"What about me?"

"Will you be going with us?"

"No."

I had already known that was what he would say but it didn't hurt any less to hear. Earlier he said he would go wherever I went but clearly that was nothing but a lie. I refused to acknowledge that I was disappointed over hearing that. I refused to acknowledge the truth.

"Good."

I heard him sigh, causing me to turn to look at him. He had his eyes firmly on the road ahead of us with one hand on the steering wheel and the other resting on the gear stick.

"What?" I asked.

"Nothing," he muttered.

I rolled my eyes and turned my attention back outside my window. The sun was slowly starting to scatter the light across the sky. It was early hours of the morning now and even though I had hardly gotten any sleep, I was far too awake to even think of that.

"Are we seriously going to sit in silence all the way there?" he finally asked.

"Yes."

"Milena..." There my name went again, rolling off his tongue and sending my stomach into a frenzy at that sound.

"I told you not to do that," I muttered.

"Do what? Say your name?"

"Yes. I hate it."

"What the hell am I supposed to call you then?"

I whipped my head in his direction. "Don't call me anything. I don't think you and I have anything further we need to speak about. You're here to do a job - so do it."

"I am doing my job. Part of that is to address you, in case you didn't realize." The sarcasm dripped from his tongue only infuriating me more. *He was the worst.*

"Please stop," I said.

He turned to face me. "Stop what?"

"Talking. Just stop talking, please. I just -" I was fumbling now but the frustration was reaching its breaking point and I was struggling to hold myself together. "I need you to stop talking. That's it."

He remained silent and glanced around the deserted road. We hadn't seen a car for miles and I was just itching for a break. The amount of tension and all that was unspoken between us was fucking suffocating me. I hated that I had allowed him to make me weak. But he did. He allowed me the opportunity to open up to him and share things I would never share. He made me feel safe enough to feel what was eating at me inside. He comforted me in ways I had never been comforted before. He allowed me to be weak because I knew he would be strong for both of us.

I turned my attention back outside the window.

"Breathe, Lena," Carina comforted.

I focused on my breathing - in through the nose, out through the mouth. I closed my eyes and leaned against the window. Nothing could be heard for miles and I welcomed it. It allowed me a moment of peace in what has been the rollercoaster ride of my life. I just wanted it to stop. All of it.

Abruptly, he turned to pull the car on the side of the road. My eyes flung open and I looked over at him. "What are you doing?"

"Taking a time out," he said. "Get out the car."

I didn't move. I kept my arms across my chest, refusing to do what he told me to do. I swear, my stubbornness was my fatal flaw but I couldn't stop it. Suddenly, my door was yanked open and I could feel his presence. My body was so attuned to him that I knew he was standing close to me. I could smell him but I refused to breathe him in. It was an intoxicating smell that I would usually welcome but I couldn't anymore.

"Milena," he said softly. "What can I do?"

I shook my head, an unamused laugh escaping me. "Nothing, Vincenzo. There is nothing that you can do."

"Look, I understand you're mad," he started to say but I whipped my head in his direction, dumbfounded by that statement.

"Mad?" I laughed again. "You think I'm mad because you acted like a total asshat back there?"

"Asshat?" he repeated, this time a flicker of amusement in his voice.

"Asshole," I corrected, cursing my mind for failing me with that mistake. "I think you're an asshole, Vincenzo and the last thing I want to do is be stuck in a car with you."

He reached out and rested his hand on my knee. Was he being serious right now? I glanced down at his hand before stepping outside of the car, pushing past him.

"You don't get to touch me again," I shouted.

"Mil-"

I turned around to face him. "Don't, Vincenzo. You're driving me fucking crazy here. There are people out there who want me dead but I can't focus on anything except what's happened between us. You want me then you don't want me. You tell me I was just a fuck for you then you're asking me what you can do. God, Vincenz-"

He stepped closer to me but I put my hand up, stopping against his chest. Almost instantly, the tension was palpable in the air.

"Don't," I warned. "You said so yourself, whatever there was between us. That's over now. You decided that."

CHAPTER 28:

Vincenzo

What the fuck was wrong with me? A few hours ago I had no problem absolutely obliterating whatever there was between us and now I find myself trying to get it back. As we sat in the car, the silence ate at me. Over and over again I replayed what I said to her and the longer I thought about it, the worse I felt. She was right. I was an asshole. The biggest asshole ever. I just couldn't get what Afonso said out of my head and I did what was expected of me.

But now that it was just the two of us again, I couldn't think of anything but her.

"Please don't," she repeated. "You made yourself perfectly clear back there."

"Milena, I never expected this," I admitted. "I have never been in this situation before. I'm just trying to do my best here."

"You're just trying to do your job now," she corrected. "Which doesn't involve what happened between us but the fact is that it happened and we can't change that."

"I kn-"

"Don't worry. I also just needed a good fuck and you were conveninent," she snapped.

She was using my own words against me and they sounded even worse coming from her. I slowly lifted my head to meet her hard gaze. Now that I was on the receiving end, I was feeling the raw sting from that statement. I was such an asshole for that.

"I'll be out of your hair in no time, Vincenzo, and I'll find someone else who will be just as convenient," she muttered and pushed past me, stepping towards her seat again.

I grabbed her wrist and turned her around, forcing her back up against the car as I trapped her between my body. I didn't want to hear of her with anyone else. That riled me up more than I expected and she had noticed. Her eyebrow arched and a small smirk presented itself.

"Oh? You don't like that?" she asked in a low voice. "Does it bother you to think about someone else's hands on my body?"

I fucking hated it. I knew she was trying to get a reaction out of me but I hated to even think of what she was saying. I was protective of her now in more ways than one - it was almost possessive.

She leaned closer to me, arching her head up so her lips were inches from mine. I couldn't stop my gaze from dropping down to them.

"And what about someone else kissing me?" she murmured. "God, he's going to taste so good."

"Milena…" My voice was full of warning. I closed my fists, trying to stop the jealousy that was rearing its ugly head.

Without breaking eye contact, she said, "He's going to fuck me until I forget all about you."

Something snapped inside of me. Jealousy quickly turned to anger and I refused to give into it but I couldn't stop the words coming out my mouth now. "No one else is going to touch you."

"That's not up to you," she shot back. "I'll fuck whoever I want."

"Milena, I dare someone else to lay a hand on you - I'll cut them off."

Her lips parted ever so slightly as her eyebrow arched. She was intrigued by what I said. She wasn't taking my threat seriously.

"If you're not going to touch me again, I'll find someone who will."

She pushed against my chest again, forcing me to move back from her. She was challenging me, pushing my buttons and I knew she wanted a reaction. I didn't want to give into it. I was trying so hard but my fuck, it was proving to be a difficult task. Especially when I couldn't pull my gaze from her. She was still wearing my shirt and I celebrated a small victory in that - even if it meant nothing, it meant something to me. And now knowing what was hidden underneath that shirt just sent the heat rushing straight to my groin and I was losing the internal battle.

"You can keep standing there but I'm done having this conversation with you," she snapped.

Don't do it. Don't do it. Don't do it.

But I couldn't stop myself. I reached for her arm again and pulled her to me, my hands finding her hair as her lips met mine. The satisfaction of her lips against mine was euphoric. We stumbled towards the car again, her back finding the door as the intensity of the kiss increased. She moaned against my lips sending my arousal through the roof before she pulled away, her hand connecting with the side of my face again. I couldn't hide the surprise as I turned back to face her but now there was nothing but pure desire burning in her eyes.

This time she was the one who reached for me, her hands finding their way into my hair as I pushed her up against the door with my body. The intensity of what was happening between us had reached new heights. She fucking drove me crazy. I was angry at how she pushed my buttons. I was still reeling from the jealousy of her threats but I was also so widely turned on right now. I would do anything I could to have her. And she was feeling the same. I lifted her one leg up, hooking it around my waist as I leaned my erection against her. A small groan escaped from her.

"Tesorina," I breathed against her lips. "I need to keep hearing that sound."

"We shouldn't be doing this," she said but brought her lips to mine, her tongue flicking against mine. I took her bottom lip between my teeth which earned me that beautiful sound again. I needed more. I needed more of her.

My hands ran down her bare arm before slipping underneath her shirt, taking her breast in my hand. I squeezed and I wasn't gentle about it.

"Ahh." She breathed, breaking the kiss but my lips quickly moved down her neck. I was thankful for my jeans holding me in place because I was just about ready to burst. The arousal pulsed through my body and I had one objective here - Milena. I needed her. I needed her body again.

But before I could take this any further, she pulled away and pushed me away from her. She was shaking her head, running her fingers through her hair in exasperation.

"We can't keep doing this." A brief flash of defeat flashed in her eyes.

I was breathing heavy now, just as she was as we reeled from that kiss. "I know."

My eyes couldn't help but drop over her body. I couldn't fucking think straight. All I could think about was being buried deep inside of her again. It was the closest I would ever get to heaven.

I stepped closer and leaned my back against the car. There we stood, side by side, with nothing but the tension surrounding us. It consumed us and I was trying my hardest to fight it but it was fucking torture.

I turned to face her and she was already looking at me. I shook my head and pulled my gaze forward again. "I can't think straight when you look at me like that, Milena."

"Like what?"

"Like you want me to fuck you up against this car."

"And what if I do?" she murmured, forcing my gaze back towards her.

"You're angry at me," I pointed out.

"I can multitask. I can hate you and want you at the same time."

I sighed. "You should hate me."

She turned her body so we were face to face again, the heavy tension pushing us closer and closer to giving into what we want. Her desire was fuelled by her anger towards me and as much as I should force us back into this car and back on the road, I couldn't think of anything else but her. I needed her again.

"I do hate you," she said but her eyes betrayed her. She wanted to hate me but she couldn't. The same way I was supposed to stay away from her but I couldn't.

"Good," was all I said before I grabbed her again, wasting no time before my lips found hers. She didn't push me away. Instead, her hands went straight for the buttons on my jeans.

"You can hate me all you want but I'm going to fuck you now," I said against her lips. "Is that what you want?"

"Yes." She breathed. "Do it, Vincenzo."

That was all I needed to hear. She wanted me as much as I wanted her and I didn't care where we were right now. We were both consumed by the increasing passion that we couldn't deny. Our bodies called for each other.

Without breaking the kiss, I pulled us away from the car and jerked open the back door. I turned her towards the seat and pushed her down. She pulled herself further into the car making enough space for me to get into the backseat and close the door behind me. She wasted no time pulling herself onto me, straddling me as her legs were on either side. Her lips found mine and I used my tongue to part them, needing to taste every part of her. She rocked her hips against me and I was aching to be inside of her. I reached for my button and popped it open as she pulled away and pulled her one leg out of her pants, opening herself up to me. I freed myself and her gaze fell to my erection. Her tongue ran over her bottom lip and I wanted to take it between my teeth. She positioned herself above me before lowering herself onto me, both of us letting out a sigh of relief. No other feeling compared to being inside of her.

She started to bring herself up and then slowly lowered herself again, soaking in the moment. Her head fell back and my lips explored along her neck. I took her ass in my hands and squeezed, trying hard to keep it together but I wanted every part of her. My hands were running up her arms next and then they were on her waist before finding her hair and pulling her lips to meet mine again.

She moaned against me as she lowered herself again, flicking her hips forward. My God, she knew exactly how to ride me and my eyes rolled back as I allowed my head to lean against the headrest. Her hand gripped the back of my neck, digging her nails into my skin.

"Yes, Milena." I breathed. "Ride me, baby."

And she did. She moved her hips backwards and forwards finding a rhythm that had my orgasm already building inside of me. The pleasure pulsed through my veins because of her. She consumed me. Every part of me craved her, longed for her, felt for her. No matter how much I wasn't supposed to, I couldn't stop it anymore. She had infiltrated me in every way and it was delusional of me to think I could rid myself of her.

Her moans increased in volume the harder she went and I had never heard anything more beautiful. Knowing she was feeling this because I was deep inside of her was sending my own arousal into a frenzy.

"Vincenzo..." My name fell from her lips and I claimed them. My hands gripped the sides of her hips as I thrusted harder, meeting her movements.

"My name." I breathed. "Say it again."

"Vincenzo," she moaned, throwing her head back.

"You will never moan another name," I warned. "You understand me?"

She whimpered, biting down on her lip as she tried to hold back her moans. I grabbed a fistful of her hair and pulled her head back as I pulled her body to mine, my lips finding her ear.

"Do you understand me, Milena?"

"I understand." She breathed.

"No one else will touch you or I swear to God, I'll kill them."

"You wouldn't," she challenged.

"You know what I'm capable of, *tesorina.*"

She pushed hard against me as she screamed out in pleasure, finding her climax. I grabbed her hips and picked up my pace, pushing closer and closer to my own. She was a fucking goddess and I wanted nothing more than to spend my life inside of her. I claimed her. She was mine.

I pulled her lips to meet mine as I reached my climax, releasing myself deep inside of her. She was still breathing heavy against my body but she held on, not wanting to end this. I didn't want it to either. And not just this moment - I didn't want any of it to end. I didn't want her to leave the country without me. I was the only one who could protect her because suddenly the reason for wanting to keep her alive was so much more than just part of the job description.

I had fallen for her.

CHAPTER 29:

Milena

I shouldn't have done that.

Repeatedly, I reprimanded myself for allowing Vincenzo back inside. And not just inside my heart but quite literally inside of me. As much as I wanted to sit in my self-loathing, I couldn't deny how it made me feel to be this close to him again. I wanted him in a way I had never wanted anyone before. It was the kind of longing that was connected to the deepest parts of my heart and I was terrified. I had never allowed myself to get emotionally involved with anyone - it wasn't my style. I wasn't one for feelings or emotions. I refused to show any form of weakness and that's what they felt like to me.

But with Vincenzo it was different.

I had never felt safer. He protected me and whenever he was around, I didn't worry too much because I knew he had my back. He had already proven what he would do to keep me alive and he couldn't deny that the reason for that had become deeper than what was required of him. He looked at me with a new sense of vulnerability. It made my heart flutter in a child-like kind of way. Without realizing, he had managed to slowly chip away at the walls around my heart. I had subconsciously made a point of keeping myself guarded but I couldn't be like that around him. Not anymore.

For the first time, I believed I was experiencing what it felt like to fall for someone. The circumstances couldn't have been worse but this was the last thing I thought would ever happen. I didn't want to feel this way about him. I wanted to hate him. It would make all of this so much easier but I had a strong suspicion that heartbreak was waiting for me.

He reached out and slowly ran his fingers through my hair, bringing me back to reality. I leaned into his touch. We soaked in these moments a little longer before we knew everything was about to change. I allowed myself a few moments of weakness before lifting myself off of him. I immediately regretted it as the emptiness settled over me. I sat down next to him on the backseat, both of us dressing ourselves again.

"I didn't mean what I said back at the motel," he murmured. "I was trying to hurt you"

I leaned my head to the side, bringing my gaze forward to meet his. "Why would you want to hurt me, Vincenzo?" I sighed. "Do you hate me?"

An unexpected chuckle left his lips but the humor never reached his eyes. "All of this would be so much easier if I did hate you, Milena but I'm incapable of that."

There it was again. That warm, giddy feeling working its way over me, making me a prisoner to my feelings. I wanted to reach out and hold his hand. Something so small and, seemingly, insignificant but it would significantly impact the way my heart would react.

"It would be easier for both of us if we hated each other," he said. "It would be easier to stop this from going any further."

I rolled my eyes and turned to face forward again. "Why are you so set on pushing me away?"

I didn't want to look at him. It was only going to hurt more when he ripped my heart out again. I was a sucker for his punishment. Deep down I was well aware that this was going to end in only one way and still I continued to pursue what was happening between us. It was real. And raw. And the most exhilarating thing I had ever experienced before. He thrilled me in more ways than one and I was intrigued by him. I wanted to allow myself to explore what I was feeling but I was on the verge of losing it all.

"Milena, my job, it-"

I shook my head and interrupted his sentence. "Don't tell me it's because it breaks the rules of your job. Who fucking cares? You were sent to protect me and you did. You've done your job, Vincenzo and you can keep doing that but we can also have this."

I was desperate for him to realize this. I was clinging onto any hope that we could have it both ways. I was so terrified of losing him that just the looming possibility was sending my thoughts into a frenzy.

"You've fallen for him," Carina said.

"Not yet."

At least that's what I was convincing myself. If I believed that I was still in control here, I could slam on the brakes at any point. I could stop all of this.

So why couldn't I just do that?

I felt his gaze on me but I kept my eyes ahead of me, staring at the sun that was now peeping through the trees in the distance. I clenched my jaw, trying to keep it together but I was slowly slipping further and further into the truth and that was that Vincenzo de Rossi had invaded me in every way possible.

"Please don't make this harder than it already is," he said.

I turned to face him, "Let me in, Vincenzo." I reached up and rested my hand against his cheek, the feeling of his rough beard against my touch. "God, I wish you would just let me in."

He reached up and grabbed my hand, slowly moving it away from his cheek. "I'm sorry."

"No, I don't accept that," I snapped.

"Milena, please." He sighed and turned to open the door, stepping outside. I followed behind him. He stood staring out in the distance but I couldn't move further than where I stood by the open door.

"You feel something for me. I know you do," I said, raising my voice so he could hear me from where he stood. "Why won't you just admit it?"

He shook his head and turned, stepping towards me. "And then what, Milena? What do you see happening between us? A relationship? You think we could have a future?"

I opened my mouth but quickly shut it. I couldn't find the words that were needed because I hadn't thought of that.

"We're wasting our time here. This can never be anything more than what it already is."

No. I refused to believe that.

"You're too afraid to let anyone get too close to you. You push them away because you think it will protect you but what kind of life is that?" I needed to hear his admission. I just needed to hear that he was feeling the same for me. I stepped closer to him, closing the proximity between us. As much as I was sick to my stomach with nerves, I was standing my ground. I wanted to fight for this. Whatever it was.

"You won't let anyone love you. You won't even allow yourself to love and it's just sad." I said and the unexpected emotion caught in my throat as tears burned my eyes.

"I don't have it in me to lose anyone else," he admitted.

"If you keep pushing me away, you're going to lose me and it will be your fault." I reached for his hand and slipped it in mine. "Don't do it. Don't push me away."

I wanted to scold myself for the desperation that was in my voice but I couldn't stop it. I had succumbed to my emotions and I clung onto what was happening between us. Everything else in my life had completely fallen apart but he had been the one to help me get through it. Day by day, he reminded me that everything would be fine. He gave me hope that I could still have some kind of life - even if I had to sacrifice the one I already had. He even made it sound like an adventure at times. He had this innate way of calming me in a way no one had before. He pushed my buttons and challenged me and I loved it.

I love h...

Don't, Milena.

I could never admit that.

"Just tell me you feel something for me," I whispered.

I waited for the response I was so desperate for but instead, he let go of my hand and walked past me to the passenger seat. I turned and watched him. *What the hell was he doing?* He leaned forward and grabbed something from the glove compartment. He turned around to reveal a long black box in his hand.

CHAPTER 30:

Vincenzo

I t pained me to hear the desperation in her voice. I was running from my feelings. It was what I was good at. I refused to allow myself close to anyone because I couldn't handle feeling any loss again. Loss was inevitable - I knew that so I removed myself from situations where that would happen as best as possible. It was my only way of being in control. It was my default setting and I didn't know how to break through but my God, I wanted to. I wanted to give Milena whatever she wanted. I wanted to tell her exactly what I was feeling for her. I wanted her.

But I just couldn't.

I turned around with the long black box in my hand. I lowered myself to sit on the passenger seat, my legs resting outside the car as I gestured for her. She slowly stepped closer to me, a look of confusion on her face as she eyed the box in my hand. I reached for her and positioned her between my legs and handed it to her.

She eyed it before looking back at me. "What's this?"

I reached for the lid and pulled it off, revealing the silver chain with a small locket at the bottom. I had Afonso organize this for me. I refused to give a reason and he didn't ask too many questions. I figured he already knew something had happened between us before he even arrived. Then the intense kiss he witnessed back at the motel confirmed his suspicions.

"From me to you," I said. "I can't give you what you want. I'm not that kind of man but you have to know that my reason for wanting to protect you is no longer because it's my job. I need to protect you because I need you in the world, Milena."

I had never said anything like that before. Part of the reason I had gone into a profession like this was because I wasn't afraid of dying because I believed that I had nothing to live for. That wasn't true anymore. I wanted to live and I wanted to keep her alive. I wanted to allow myself to give into my feelings and for the first time in my life, I wanted more. I didn't think I was capable of feeling anything for anyone else but there was no one like her. Hidden behind that feisty, independent, defiant mask was a vulnerable woman who deserved to be loved. And I wanted more than anything to be the one to love her but that wasn't what was meant for us.

I picked the necklace up. "I need you to promise me that you'll always wear this. No matter what happens between us."

The tears had returned to her eyes and she nodded. "I promise."

She turned around and pulled her hair to the side, resting over her shoulder. Her neck was exposed to me and just the sight of her skin sent the heat rushing over me. I wanted to leave sweet, soft kisses along her neck. I wanted to worship her. I wanted her to know what I was really feeling for her but I couldn't give her what she deserved. I couldn't give her what I knew we both wanted. No matter how much it was going to kill me inside, I was going to have to let her go.

I reached over and placed the necklace gently around her neck, clasping it so it could rest against her chest. Her hand went up to the locket as she turned around to face me. Her vulnerability shone through her eyes.

"I want to say those words to you, Milena." I grabbed her hands and looked down at them in mine. "But you don't deserve to hear that just once. You deserve to hear it every day for the rest of your life."

I lifted my gaze to meet hers. "And I will only say that to you if I know I'll get to do it again."

She reached up and cupped my cheek, leaning down to bring her lips to meet mine. It was a sweet, gentle kiss - nothing like what we had experienced up till now but this had so much more weight to it. There were so many emotions behind it that it was the kind of kiss I wanted to get lost in with her.

A car zipped past us on the empty road, pulling our attention away from our moment. I whipped my head around, immediately stepping into defense mode but the car kept driving until it was eventually out of sight. Our moment had passed now and we had a reality to get back to. The one where I needed to keep her alive because the universe knows now that I wouldn't be able to live in a world without her.

"Come with me," she said, bringing my attention back to her.

"What?" I turned to face her.

"Come with me when I have to leave." There was a flicker of desperation in her eyes now. "You don't have to stay behind."

I wanted to say yes. Hell, I wanted to drive us to the airport right now and buy a one-way ticket out of here. I would protect her. I could give her a good life. I could love her the way she deserved - or at least I could try my best but that wasn't in the cards for us. I had a job to do here and as much as I wanted to be spontaneous and follow my true desires here, I had to be practical.

Her eyes dropped as I waited a little too long to reply. She nodded and let go of my hands. "We should get going," she said, changing the subject and averting her gaze.

"Milen-" I started but she shook her head and faked a small smile.

"It's fine, Vincenzo. I was being delusional anyway. We should go." She stepped back, making space for me to get out of her seat. I wanted to say something to make this better but there weren't any words that would. Nothing I could say would tell her what she wanted to hear and I could never give her any false hope. A dull ache of disappointment settled in my chest as I started to come to terms with the reality of what was going to happen here.

And that reality was nothing. Nothing was going to happen between Milena and I. We both knew that but neither wanted to accept it. I stepped out of the seat and allowed her to take up residence as I walked over to the driver's seat.

Snap out of it, Vincenzo.

I had never been run by emotions before and I didn't want to start now but it was proving to be a trying task. The weight of disappointment and longing rested over me as I started the engine and pulled back onto the road, heading into a reality that neither of us was truly prepared for.

CHAPTER 31:

Milena

I was drained.

After the emotional rollercoaster I just got off of with Vincenzo, my body was playing catch up to my mind and I felt exhausted. Mentally and physically. We had been driving for just over an hour and nothing further was shared between us. There was nothing else we could say. Nothing would change the circumstances and even though I had put it out there, I knew he wasn't going to come with me if I left. His silence spoke wonders and I didn't know how to convince him that this could be what we wanted when I couldn't even convince myself.

"I want to say those words to you, Milena."

*H*is words replayed over and over in my mind. He wanted to share his feelings. He wanted to tell me exactly what I wanted to hear but he didn't. And I was actually glad. I didn't think my heart would be able to handle it if he said those three words to me and we still didn't get the ending I wanted. It was fast approaching and I was terrified of what was going to happen next. I was always one moment away from my imminent death but this was what I was more concerned about. He caught me by surprise. The last thing I ever thought I would find in a situation like this was him but now that I had, I didn't know how I was going to let him go.

"You want the aircon on?" he asked, finally breaking the silence between us.

I shook my head. "I'm okay, thanks."

"Okay."

The silence was back. Suffocating us with all that was unspoken between us. I turned my attention outside the window again. The sun had started to greet us, the light scattering across the sky as morning fast approached. Dark clouds hovered in the distance and it looked as if a storm was on its way. We were still on a quiet road - no flicker of civilisation had presented itself again. There was just empty land for as far as I could see as we drove. It felt as if we were the only two people in the world and for a moment, I lived in that fantasy. I had never been one to think of a small-town life. I didn't care for it. I had always wanted the hustle and bustle of life. I needed a thriving city that could expand on opportunities for me. I needed people. I needed a vibrant life. At least that's what I had always believed but now? Now, I would be happy to stop this car on any of these open patches of grass and live in a small house away from anyone else. Away from anyone that could harm me. Now that I wanted to live, I realized I wanted something way simpler than I thought. All that other fickle, materialistic stuff was insignificant now.

"You're going to be fine, Lena," Carina reassured me. "You're going to get the life you deserve."

Maybe I would but what was that? What did I deserve? If going on the run has shown me anything, it's that I actually had no idea what I truly wanted out of my life. Did I deserve anything good? If I did, why was this my life now? Surely if I deserved good, having a hit on my back wasn't aiding that? Maybe I didn't deserve anything good. Maybe I was getting exactly what I deserved. Compared to Carina, I had always felt like a pretty shitty person. I didn't try as hard as her. I didn't care as much as she did. I was always just one step behind her in everything I did. I knew people preferred her. I wasn't oblivious to that and I had often allowed it to affect me. I wasn't sure I deserved anything.

"There's a stop coming up soon," Vincenzo said, causing me to turn to face him. "We should stop and get what we need. We're going to be on the road for a while."

I nodded.

"You can get some coffee, too."

"You're going to let me out of the car without a disguise?" I challenged playfully. "I don't have that shitty old cap of yours anymore."

A small smile played on his lips. "I'm going to have to get you another shitty old cap then."

I loved that smile. I wanted to see more of it. I reached up and grabbed the locket between my thumb and index finger. I fiddled with it and somehow just knowing I had this around my neck made me feel calmer. Safer almost. It came from Vincenzo and that was the same way he made me feel.

"I need you to promise me that you'll always wear this. No matter what happens between us."

He was adamant about that - almost a tad desperate and as much as I wanted to know the real reason behind that, I let it go. I wasn't planning on ever taking this off. This was the only reminder I would have of him when we finally went our separate ways. I would always have a piece of him with me and I clung to that.

"Thank you for the necklace," I said.

"You're welcome."

I grabbed the other side of the locket and tried to slip my nail in between it, trying to open it up to see what was inside but it wouldn't budge.

"That doesn't open," he said quickly, reaching for my hand and pulling it away from the necklace. "It's not that kind of locket."

"Oh," I replied. "It's still beautiful. I love it."

"I'm gla-"

His sentence was interrupted by the sudden skidding of tires against the tar, causing us to turn towards the bright lights that were headed our way. Before I knew it, the car crashed into the front of ours, sending it spinning across the road. I screamed for Vincenzo as the world spun. He slammed on brakes, bringing the car to a grinding halt. Both of us jerked forward, our necks snapping forward and back again as the car stopped, the sound of screeching tires leaving the smell of burnt rubber in our wake. My voice was hoarse from screaming and a deep fear creeped up on me as we watched men spill out of the car that just hit us.

"They found us," I said, my voice a mere whisper.

"Cazzo!" Vincenzo muttered to himself before turning to me. "Milena, I need you to listen to me. When I say it, you need to run. Run and hide wherever you can."

I shook my head. "I'm not leaving you."

He cupped my cheek. *"Tesorina,* I'll find you again. I told you, I'll always find you but you need to run. I'll take care of this."

My eyes darted past him as I watched men start to spill out of the car. Vincenzo reached for his gun and cocked it before turning back to me. His eyes were full of warning but also so much more that there wasn't time to say. He couldn't hide his own fear as he murmured, "Run."

He jerked his door open as I did the same and I turned to take off down the road. My legs carried me faster than I ever thought possible. Adrenaline and fear coursed through my veins, aiding my speed as I ran down the road. I didn't know where to go. There was nothing but empty land ahead of us. Panic sat in my throat, tightening my airways as my chest started to burn. I was never very fit and I had certainly never run this fast in my entire life. A small shed-like structure stood in the distance and I took off towards it.

The sound of a gunshot going off stopped me dead in my tracks. My throat tightened further in fear as I slowly turned around, terrified of what I was going to see. One of the men dropped to the floor and relief washed over me as I saw Vincenzo pointing the gun at him. I was frozen as I watched him trying to take out the other two. Punches were flying now as Vincenzo tried to fight them off. He ducked and I watched him grab one by the head, slamming their head against the car door before the other took a swing at him. He swung his gun around and a shot went off, hitting the other guy in the shoulder. I was almost proud watching him. It was impressive to watch how he handled them with such ease. I almost fell-

A sudden hand came over my mouth, stopping my thoughts in their tracks. I screamed as arms tightened around my chest.

"There you are," a deep voice said.

Fuck. Whatever fear I had felt before, it was nothing compared to what was working its way through me now. I was kicking and screaming, trying to wiggle my way out of his grip but he wouldn't budge. I bit at his hand, causing him to jerk it away for a split second.

"Vincenzo!" I screamed but the hand came back over me again, forcing my mouth closed. The copper taste of blood stained my tongue.

"You little bitch," he muttered and started dragging me backwards. I watched as Vincenzo turned towards me. He stopped in his tracks as his gaze landed on me. I tried to scream for him to turn around. He wasn't in the clear but he was frozen as I continued to be pulled further and further from him.

One of the men was headed straight for him and there was nothing I could do but watch as the man used his gun to knock Vincenzo on the back of his head. I watched in horror as he fell to his knees in defeat. The tears were streaming down my face, blurring my vision as I was being dragged further and further from him. Further from the man that held my heart.

Get up Vincenzo! Oh my God, I need you to get up. I continued to shout this in my mind, hoping that eventually it would reach the surface and vocalize itself loud enough for him to hear. I was paralyzed with fear but I couldn't pull my gaze away from what was happening. I tried to grip at the arms holding me. I was kicking at him, trying my best to move my arms that he had pinned up against him. I was desperate to break free of his hold. Vincenzo needed my help. I needed to help him.

"Say goodbye to your little bodyguard," the voice hissed in my ear.

Vincenzo got up and turned around but the man swung at him, his fist connecting with his jaw as he dropped back down to the ground. I had never experienced an intense fear quite like this before. It was blocking my airways and I was starting to see white dots in my vision. I pushed through it and watched as one of the other men picked him up by his shirt. This man was much larger than Vincenzo and I watched as he pushed him onto his knees. Another one stepped outside of the car and walked towards them, cocking his gun on the way there. My vision blurred again as my world started to spin.

"Stay awake, Milena!" Carina shouted.

I tried. My God, I tried to keep my eyes open but the tears wouldn't stop blurring my vision. The blood drained from my face and I felt limp in the man's arms. He turned us around, pulling my gaze away from what was happening.

"No! Vincenzo!" I screamed against his hand but the sound was nothing but muffled. I watched as he dragged me towards a black SUV. I tried to look back. I needed to see what was happening. I needed him to be okay. I threw my head back and managed to slightly knock the man in the chin, causing him to drop his hand briefly.

"I'm going to fucking kill you myself if you do that again." The man seethed but I ignored his threat. I couldn't focus on anything but Vincezo.

I screamed for him at the top of my lungs before another man jumped out and opened the back door as the sound of a gunshot echoed through the air.

Vincenzo.

Oh my God.

My body dropped against the man's grip as the fear consumed me. No part of me was left untouched by it and a deep pain formed inside my chest.

"Say goodbye to your little bodyguard."

There was just no way. I refused to believe it. Vincenzo wasn't dead. *Was he?*

I was tossed into the backseat and let out a blood-curdling cry from inside as I experienced a consuming suffering that had taken hold of my heart. I refused to believe this was happening. We had come so far - how could this be the end?

There's just no way he's dead.

But I had no way of knowing.

CHAPTER 32:

Vincenzo

My hand was shaking as my finger released the trigger. The man in front of me stumbled back as his shirt started to soak with the blood spilling from his new chest wound. It felt as if everything was moving in slow motion but I kicked into defense mode and my body carried me before my mind could catch up. Thank fuck I had the second gun underneath my shirt. They believed they had the upper hand and that was important. The more they think they're in charge of the situation, the more arrogant they become, which gave me the perfect opportunity to catch them off guard. I had been doing this long enough - I knew the type of men they were.

"You bastard!" One of them shouted, lunging himself at me, fist first. I swung myself in his direction just in time to block his punch and use my other hand to clock his jaw. He swore as he stumbled, reaching for his face. As quickly as I could, I managed to pull myself up and cock my gun. I shifted between the two men in front of me who had their own guns pointed at me.

"How do you think this is going to end, huh?" The one said. He was a sight for sore eyes but the arrogance shone rife in his eyes. He would probably be the easiest to catch by surprise.

"There's two of us and one of you," the other one said.

"Where did they take her?" I demanded.

The one chuckled. "And why do you think we would tell you that? It's not like you're going to have the opportunity to be her knight in shining armor."

"She'll be dead long before you can find her," the other one said as he laughed.

Something snapped inside of me and I reached for the man closest to me, catching him off guard. I managed to disarm him as I used my own gun to knock his out of his hand, sending it flying across the road. I pulled him closer to me and locked my arm around his neck, pushing against his throat as I leaned the gun against his temple. He was strong, I'd give him that but with the adrenaline coursing through my veins right now, I was untouchable.

"Shall we try that again?" I asked calmly, my gaze landing on the man in front of me. "Where did they take her?"

"You think I won't fucking shoot you right now?" he shouted, his gun shaking as he stepped closer to me.

"I think if you take another step forward I'll shoot his fucking head off and then I'll shoot yours," I spat.

The man struggled in my arms as he gasped for air. I was applying enough pressure to restrict his airways just enough for them to cooperate. I kept my eyes on the one in front of me, watching as his eyes darted around nervously as he scrambled for his next move.

"Where. Did. They. Take. Her?" I repeated slowly.

"Fuck you!" he shouted, tightening his grip on his gun. "I'll kill you right now!" He inched closer, underestimating my threat. Without a second thought, I pulled the trigger. The bullet went straight through the man's head, blowing blood and brains all around us, some of it landing on my clothing. I tossed his lifeless body to the floor as the other man froze, the shock settling over him. I could think of nothing else but getting to Milena. I was desperate to find her and I was not about to let these fucks get in the way of that. Nothing mattered but her. I didn't care how many bodies I left in my wake.

I stepped closer. "I told you that if you took another step closer that I would blow his head off. All done so maybe now you'll be more inclined to cooperate here?"

"I'm not telling you a fucking thing!" he shouted, rage burning his eyes.

I sighed, indifferent to his lack of cooperation. I cocked my gun and brought it up, pointing directly at him. There we stood, both of us unwilling to back down and one second away from a bullet going off.

"She deserves a bullet in her head," he muttered as he lifted his other hand to support his own gun. I eyed him as I clenched my jaw, trying to keep my deep rage at bay but my finger on the trigger made the decision before my brain could. The bullet left my gun and landed between his eyes, blood spilling out of it as he dropped to the ground.

"Shouldn't have said that," I muttered as I stepped over the body. It was a bloodbath on this road and I felt bad for the poor soul who was going to find these bodies. I didn't give a shit about cleaning up my mess. I had more important things to do. Now that I was in the clear, my emotions settled over me as the adrenaline was starting to work its way out of me. A bullet had scraped past my right arm and I only registered the throbbing of the wound now. My shirt was full of blood. Some of it was mine and some were theirs. There was no time to care about that. I needed to find her. Now.

I rushed back over to our car that was still running on the side of the road. They had managed to damage the front corner but with the engine still running, I was going to use it. I yanked my door open and scrambled to find my phone. I dialed Carlos' number as I pulled myself into the car, shutting my door behind me. I leaned over the passenger seat to close the door as the phone continued to ring on the other line.

"Come on, Carlos!" I muttered as I straightened in my seat, pushing the car into first gear as I stepped on the accelerator. The call went straight to voicemail and I dialed Afonso next. On the second ring, he answered.

"Afonso, thank fuck, they found us!" I said. "They have Milena."

"Fuck," Afonso muttered. "Have you told Carlos?"

"He's not answering. I'm going after her but I need you to tell her parents or someone needs to get here. Fuck, I don't know but we n-"

"Vincenzo, slow down." He stopped me. "You can't go after her alone. If the Nazarios have her then it's going to be a bloodbath."

"I don't give a shit about that. I need to get her!"

"You're not thinking this through. You're allowing your emotions to ge-"

"Fuck you. I'm doing my fucking job which is to keep her alive. I can't do that if I don't go after her."

"You're going to get yourself killed."

"Then so be it," I muttered. "Get a hold of Carlos. Right now I'm going to need you to do something other than act like a coward."

I disconnected the call. *Typical Afonso.* Always too afraid to get into the thick of things. He hides in the shadows, handling logistics because he has always allowed his fear to get the better of him. He's never been very good at this part of the job which is why Carlos never gives him the responsibilities he has given me. I don't give a shit about myself right now. I don't care if I lose my life if it means that I can save hers.

I stepped on the accelerator and sped up. "I'm coming for you, Milena."

CHAPTER 33:

Milena

"Milenaaa…" I heard in the distance. I didn't recognise the voice but it was a deep, male voice. One full of taunting. I felt someone lightly slap my cheek, pulling me back to reality. My eyes slowly fluttered open as I tried to adjust to my surroundings. A bright white light sat in the distance but it was in my direct eye line that I had to close my eyes again. My body hurt. Every part of me was aching as I tried to bring my hand up to rub my eyes but found they were bound together. I flung my eyes open this time as I tried to break free of the bindings around my wrist. My eyes landed on an older, well-dressed gentleman. A slim-fit navy suit sat against him with a white shirt that complemented his darker skin. His hair was slicked back but the flickers of gray aged him. He looked completely out of place in the dingy old warehouse we appeared to be in. He looked ready to step into a board meeting. It was dark in the distance and the only light spilling through the room was that one that was also blinding me. I closed my one eye and leaned my head down, trying to avoid the light.

The man leaned in front of me, resting his hands on his knees as he looked me dead in the eye. "Well, hello there, little lady."

I tried to speak but the duct tape on my mouth forced out nothing but a muffled response.

"Ah, how rude of me. *Espera,*" he said and reached for the corner of the tape, ripping it off my mouth leaving nothing but a stinging across my face. I clenched my jaw, refusing to flinch at the pain. I slowly turned back to face him and he smiled at me. It was unsettling. It wasn't a welcoming smile. It was a dark one that had so much to be feared behind it and I did. I wasn't even sure how I ended up here. The last thing I remembered was being shoved into the car as the sound of a gunshot went off.

Vincenzo.

My heart ached at just the thought of him. Was he alive? Was he killed? What happened?

The man in front of me clicked his fingers, bringing my attention back to him. He looked annoyed at my distraction. "Focus, Milena."

"You know my name."

"Of course I know your name." He stood up straight, looking down at me. "I've been trying to find you for weeks now."

My mouth went dry. He was a Nazario - I just didn't know which one but I knew I should fear him. I was afraid, there was no doubt but I also knew I was on death's doorstep. This was what Vincenzo had tried so hard to avoid. We had done so well up till now, where did we go wrong?

"And do you have a name? You haven't even bothered introducing yourself," I muttered.

"Surely, I need no introduction."

I narrowed my eyes. "You're not as important as you seem to think."

"What the hell are you doing, Milena?" Carina warned. "That's one sure way to find yourself dead."

She was right but I didn't care. If I was going to be killed, I would go out Milena style and that included not backing down to some piece of shit man who thinks he is above everyone.

"Not just a pretty face it seems." He chuckled. "Quite a mouth you've got there. I'm sure it's gotten you into a lot of trouble before."

"Nothing I can't handle."

He lifted an eyebrow. "And now? Doesn't look like you're handling this situation very well."

"I'll manage, thanks."

"Well, Milena, lucky for you there is nothing to manage here. I've been trying to find you for weeks and now I have so we can finally sort out this situation."

"You mean you can finally kill me."

He leaned forward again. "Precisely. Only fair considering your father killed my son."

It was his son? The sudden realization dawned on me that confirmed he was Duarte Nazario. The head of the entire organization.

"Duarte," I whispered.

"Ah, so you have heard of me! Fantastic news!"

Whatever hope I clung onto that I would be saved from this situation quickly dissipated as the reality settled in. Duarte was ruthless and had enough motive to get rid of me. It was what he had been trying to do this entire time. He turned to the man that stood against the nearest pillar and gestured towards the chair that was next to him. *"Trázer cadeira."* The man did as he was told and placed a crappy old plastic chair in front of me where Duarte sat down. He scraped it against the floor as he pulled himself closer, our knees almost touching. I watched him, waiting in trepidation at what he had planned. If he was going to kill me, why hadn't he done it already?

"Your father put you in quite the tough spot now didn't he, Milena?"

I remained silent but kept my gaze firmly on his.

"First your sister and now you." He shook his head and my protective instincts kicked in.

"Don't talk about Carina," I warned.

"Now why wouldn't I talk about her? She's part of the reason you're in this mess too. Your father came to me when he needed money to save her and what was the point? She's dead now anyway so al-"

Something snapped inside of me and I went into a blind rage. Without realizing what I was doing, I leaned forward closer to his face and I spat at him.

"I told you not to talk about her," I said through gritted teeth as his eyes widened ever so slightly at my actions.

I watched as Duarte clenched his jaw and the anger made its way into his eyes. I had poked the bear and there was no going back now. He glanced at his jacket pocket and pulled a handkerchief from it, using it to wipe off my spit from his face. He folded it and placed it back inside before turning to look at me again.

"I was hoping we could have a civil conversation, Milena, but you seem to have left your manners behind."

"Fuck you," I spat.

He pulled himself closer and gripped my face with his hand, squeezing on either side of my cheek. The abrupt movement caused me to gasp as he brought his face closer to mine, the anger burning rife in his dark eyes.

"Don't speak to me like that you little bitch," he muttered. "Clearly, you need to learn a lesson on respect."

"You don't deserve any respect," I retorted.

He swung and the back of his hand connected with the side of my face. I was too in shock to register what had happened until a deep stinging started to spread across my cheek. Now I had done it. My biggest problem was not knowing when to shut up and now I was feeling the repercussions.

"A defiant little thing just like your father." Duarte kicked the chair back as he stood up, turning to the man against the pillar. *"Quanto tempo mais?"*

"Eles estão quase aqui."

Duarte turned back to me. "Not long now, Milena."

"Who are you waiting for?" I asked.

"Your father, of course," he said as if I should already have known that. "No use killing you without the right audience."

I swallowed, trying to process his words. The countdown was on to my death and I was starting to panic. I didn't want to die. I wanted to live. I wanted Vincenzo to be alive and I wanted us to run away - together. I was foolish to even think that there would be another way out of this. My fate had already been sealed. And Duarte wanted my father to watch. How the hell did they even find him?

"Don't do that to him," I begged, "He's already watched one daughter die, you don't have to make him go through watching another. Just kill me, whatever - but don-don't make him watch." My lip trembled as a rush of emotion came over me. My throat tightened as I tried to hold back the tears. I wanted to keep it together but it was useless.

"Your father didn't think of that when he killed my son," he said, the anger in his voice was unmistakable and his eyes darkened, "I now know what it feels like to lose a child because your father took my son from me."

"Your son was hardly a model citizen," I threw back at him.

"Watch yourself, little girl," he seethed.

I should have shut my mouth then and there but I was tenacious. And clearly very stupid.

"And what about all the people your family has killed?" Duarte turned his back to me, "You've broken how many families because of your own actions? Your family has inflicted more pain on others than you can ever imagine and now you want to be the one crying because you got a taste of your own medicine?" I scoffed.

Duarte spun around to face me again but this time he had a gun pointed directly at me. My breath caught in my throat as I stared at it. I never thought that when it was finally my time that it would be like this.

"You're pretty, Milena but you're not very bright," he muttered. "I hold your life in my hands and you're not even trying to stay alive."

"You're going to kill me anyway so I better get my two cents in before I go."

Before Duarte could say anything further, the sound of a message tone went off. We both turned towards the man by the door as he looked up from his phone.

"Eles já chegaram," he announced.

Duarte turned back to me, a devilish grin sitting on his face. He brought his arm down, removing the gun from my eyeline.

"Show time."

CHAPTER 34:

Vincenzo

An abandoned warehouse stood in front of me with not a flicker of life around it. I glanced back down at the tracker and the red dot continued to pulse in this area. Call it paranoia or a general understanding for how this world worked but deciding to put a tracker on Milena was the smartest thing I had done. She just wasn't aware of it and now was not the time to dwell on what her reaction would be. I had to protect her and knowing her every move was the only way. It led me here to where they had her. I figured there were probably Nazario men close by so I leaned over, opening up the glove compartment to grab a second gun that I hid underneath my shirt.

I turned the car off and locked my phone, shoving it in my pocket. By some sheer miracle the car had managed to get me here after all that damage but I wasn't holding my breath on it being reliable after this. Time to ditch it. The sky had since darkened thanks to the large storm clouds that had presented itself. I made sure to keep a gun underneath my shirt and another one in my hand. I was going in blind here. Usually, I try to prepare as best as possible for situations like this but I was being guided by my feelings for Milena here. I needed to save her. I needed to protect her and I didn't care who I had to kill. If anyone was a threat to her, they were done.

I stepped outside the car and shut the door behind me, careful to be as quiet as possible. I glanced around the perimeter but there was nothing in sight. The silence was unexpected and it unsettled me. Shouldn't this place be crawling with men? I rushed over to the warehouse and started to make my way along the wall, following it to the corner. I took a deep breath in and peeked my head around the corner, a dark SUV coming into view. I pulled myself back behind the wall. It was the same SUV I had watched Milena be dragged into. I glanced along the wall for an alternative entrance but there was nothing in sight. I cocked the gun and slowly started making my way around the corner. Leaning against the hood of the car with his back towards me was one of the Nazario men. He was glancing down at what I assumed to be his phone as I slowly stalked closer and closer, my movements as quiet as possible. I continued to be on high alert, constantly glancing around to see if there was anyone else in sight but the coast was clear. The sound of a video was softly coming from the phone in the man's hand and he chuckled to himself. *Seriously?* This man was watching videos on the job? Not the sharpest tool in the shed. I stalked closer and managed to get close enough that I rested the gun against the back of his head.

"Put your hands up," I instructed. He froze and dropped the phone to the floor as he lifted his hands up on either side of him. I walked around to stand in front of him, keeping the gun on him. He was younger than I expected but that explained his clear lack of understanding of the severity of this situation.

"Who the fuck are you?" he asked.

"Your gun." I gestured with my head towards him. "Where is it?"

"I'm not giving you my gun."

I cocked mine and settled my finger on the trigger. "I think you're going to do exactly what I say or I'm going to kill you."

He scoffed. "Oh ple-." I pulled the trigger and his body dropped against the bonnet of the car before sliding to the floor. I placed my gun underneath my shirt, next to my second one and walked over to him, patting him down.

"Idiot," I muttered to myself as I pulled his gun that was in the back of his pants. I rolled his body over and continued to search him, finally finding the car keys. If I was going to have any getaway plan here, I was going to need a new car. I shoved them in my front pocket and continued to stalk towards the entrance of the warehouse. I noticed the doors were slightly ajar as I got closer. I hadn't quite figured out what I was going to do next but I prayed my instincts were going to carry me. I lifted my gun up, resting my one hand underneath as I stepped closer. I paused as someone stepped outside, closing the door behind him. I froze, waiting for his next move. He turned and

I dropped my gun.

"Carlos, oh thank God!" I let out a sigh of relief.

"Vincenzo," he said, his light eyes wide with surprise.

"How did you get here before me?" I asked, confused. "Afonso said he couldn't get a hold of you."

"You should leave."

"Leave?" I was taken aback. "Why the hell would I do that?"

He looked unsettled. In all the years I had seen Carlos, I had never seen him quite so off-balance. He was constantly glancing around and a guilty look rested on his face. Something was nagging at me in the pit of my stomach.

"Vincenzo, I need you to turn around and leave," he said, slight desperation in his voice.

"I'm not going anywhere except inside to get Milena."

Carlos sighed and reached for his gun, bringing it up to point at me. *What the fuck was going on here?* I didn't bother to hide my very obvious surprise but I didn't move, careful to try and assess the situation.

"Carlos," I started, the realization dawning on me. "What have you done?"

He shook his head. "I don't have to answer to you."

His hand was shaking as it rested underneath his gun. We had never been on opposing sides and I found myself wondering when he had switched over. He was supposed to be taking care of Milena's parents but I realized that wasn't what was happening here. How long had he been betraying us?

"You're the reason they found Milena, isn't it?" I asked, already knowing the answer.

"Vincenzo, please."

I shook my head. "I'm not going to keep quiet to attempt to alleviate your guilt about what you've done. You fucking betrayed them. You betrayed all of us." The emotion was rising inside of me as the bitter taste of betrayal continued to make itself known. "And for what?"

He remained silent.

"How much did they offer you?" I asked.

He shook his head but I could see in his eyes that money had everything to do with his decision. "I've given you a chance to walk away from this alive, Vincenzo. What good is it to always be on the losing side?"

Although Carlos and I worked closely on many occasions, it was suddenly made clear that I didn't know Carlos half as well as I thought I did. The reality of my clear mis-reading of our relationship angered me. I had always considered him to be a leader, despite his impulsive ways. I had seen it a few times. Pulling the trigger before thinking, barging into a situation without giving it a second thought - things like that. We balanced each other out. I took a moment to think things through while he often abandoned reason. I felt like an idiot. I should have known it would come to this but how could I have even thought that my oldest companion in this business would throw in his loyalty for a hefty paycheck? I tasted bitter betrayal on my tongue.

"We're supposed to protect people."

"I've been protecting others my whole life," he muttered. "And where has that gotten me? Shitty paycheck after paycheck. Living in fear. Always on the run." He shook his head. "They gave me a way out of this. You would have taken it too. The money you would make would solve all your problems. You wouldn't need to take any of these jobs just to pay for your grandmoth-"

"Don't fucking bring her into this," I said through gritted teeth. He had known why I would take any job he offered me but I refused to give in to his manipulation tactics. There was nothing he could say that would make me understand why he would have done this. There was no reason good enough.

"You know I'm right. It's easier to be selfish in this fucked up world." he shrugged, suggesting it was the only way to survive what this world offered us. "I'm sick of protecting these rich, stuck-up motherfuckers who think throwing money around will solve all their problems."

"And what do you call what Duarte is doing to you?" I shouted. "He threw money at you and you caved with no regard for what your actions are doing to others."

I hadn't realized the resentment that Carlos had been wielding this entire time for the work we did. Yes, we worked with a lot of rich people who got themselves in dirty messes that were left for us to clean up but did he not know the real reason behind the *Neves* family and what got them into this situation in the first place? Or maybe he did but he just didn't care. I figured it was the latter.

"João killed his son. Don't act like he's innocent."

"Carlos, listen to what you're saying," I said, shocked at his apathy to the family he was supposed to be protecting. "You should know better than to pass judgment like that. You sacrificing an entire family for your own personal gain is hardly the act of a saint."

"I've never claimed to be a saint."

"You sure seem to be condemning a man as if you're Mr. high and mighty." I shook my head, the disbelief settling over me. "You've signed Milena's death sentence, Carlos. You might as well have pulled the trigger."

"I'm not the reason they're in this mess," he shot back.

"No, but your job was to help them out of it. It's what we've always done - for how many years now? And now you've gone and thrown that away?"

"There's no defeating the Nazarios, Vincenzo," he said. "You and I both know we were just putting off the inevitable here."

I shook my head. "Put your gun down, Carlos. You still have a chance to make this right."

"No. What's done is done. Milena is in there with her dad right now and there's nothing you can do about it."

"The fact that you believe I'd walk away from this just proves to me that you don't know me at all."

I didn't wait for his response as I brought my hand around, using the element of surprise to knock the gun out of his hand. It hit the ground and he stumbled back from the impact. He bent down to reach for it but I pulled my gun up and pointed it at him.

"Leave the gun," I ordered.

He lifted his hands on either side of him. "Come on, Vincenzo. You're not going to kill me."

"You underestimate me, Carlos."

"Afonso told me what happened between you and Milena,"

Fucking asshole. I stood my ground and kept my gaze on his, careful to anticipate what he was going to try next.

"You wouldn't go barging in there right now if you didn't have feelings for her." He shook his head. "You fell for her. How could you be so stupid?"

"You're in no position to talk to me about what's stupid, you fucking piece of shit." I said through my teeth. "And whatever happened between Milena and I is none of your fucking business."

"You're going to lose her, Vincenzo. Duarte is in there right now about to finish them both off and you're wasting your time out here with me."

I swallowed and clenched my jaw, refusing to allow him to know that his words were eating at me the way they were. *Enough of this shit.* Milena needed me and I was done entertaining this conversation.

"It didn't have to be this way, Carlos," I said. "You were on the right side."

"If you believe that then you're an even bigger idiot than I thought."

My emotions got the best of me as I pulled the trigger, the bullet landing in his chest. He stumbled back from the impact, his eyes widened in shock as he looked down at his wound before looking back at me. The look on his face confirmed what I already thought - he didn't think I would do it.

"You shot m-..." That was all he managed to get out before he fell to his knees. The blood continued to soak his shirt as he fell backwards, his body hitting the floor. I didn't have time to process that I had taken the life of the person who was the closest thing I had to a partner. None of that mattered until I had Milena safe again.

I leaned against the door and slowly pushed it open, my gun lifted as I walked straight into the unknown. A man in a navy suit had his back to me but slowly turned around as the door scraped against the floor. *Fuck.* Duarte Nazario stared right at me.

"And who do we have joining us now?" He asked, stepping to the side to reveal Milena tied up to the chair. Her hair had fallen forward but she revealed her injuries as she lifted her eyes to meet mine. Even from where I stood, I could see she had been crying and the blood that stained her cheeks revealed why.

"Oh my God," she cried. "Vincenzo, you're alive!"

Instinct caused me to rush over to her, but I was stopped in my tracks as a larger man stepped in front of me, blocking her from my view.

"Thank you, Eduardo," Duarte said. "Why don't you bring our uninvited guest over here?"

Eduardo pulled my gun from me quicker than I could register. I could usually rely on my reflexes but I had never been so off-balance before either. The sight of Milena tied up like that was just about destroying me from the inside out. The large man - Duarte's bitch, it seemed - took a step next to me and shoved my shoulder, forcing me to stumble forward.

"No, Duarte, leave him out of this," Milena begged. "He doesn't have anyth-"

"Milena, don't," I warned. Her eyes locked with me and for the first time in my life, my heart was calling out for someone else. There was this magnetic pull between us that I had never experienced and I just wanted to hold her. I wanted to comfort her and take away all her pain. I wanted to get her out of this situation. I would put my own life on the line to ensure that she got to live hers.

"Vincenzo, you shouldn't be here," she cried, the tears spilling over down her cheeks.

"I told you that I'd always find you."

Duarte cleared his throat and slipped his hands into his pockets. "Are you two done?"

I glared at him before he turned to the side where João Neves stood, being held by another one of their men. He looked terrified as he glanced at his daughter. Carlos had betrayed him by bringing him here and now he was facing his reckoning.

"*Senhor Neves,* do you know this man?" he asked casually.

João nodded. "He's my daughter's bodyguard."

"Is it?" Duarte turned back to me, a slight pull of amusement on his lips. "He didn't do a very good job."

"My job isn't done yet," I snapped. "And I'm going to get her out of here so you might want to hold your tongue."

He arched an eyebrow, glancing between Milena and I. His hand lifted to rub against his chin and he laughed as he turned back to João. "Did you know your daughter was sleeping with her bodyguard?"

João's eyes darted to me as I glanced at Milena who was already looking at me. "We weren-," she started to say but Duarte waved his hands, cutting her off. "Please, Milena, there's no need to lie now. Anyone with eyes can see there is something between the two of you."

I glanced between Duarte and Milena. He was eyeing us, clearly trying to figure out the nature of our relationship. Yes, we slept together but that wasn't all it was. It was the most real thing I had ever experienced but I didn't feel like having a fucking heart to heart with the man trying to kill her.

"That's obviously why you came here, isn't it?" he asked me. "You thought you could save your damsel in distress."

"Milena has never been and never will be a damsel in distress," I replied. "Anyone with half a brain can see she's perfectly capable of handling herself."

"Maybe, but it's safe to say she's not doing too well right now."

"Duarte, *por favor, l*eave my daughter out of this," João begged, lifting his hands to rest against each other. "Whatever has happened has been between you and I. Milena had nothing to do with this."

Duarte walked towards João who was cowering away from him like an animal shying away from danger. Eduardo stood behind me which meant I had to wait for a gap before reaching for the gun that was hidden underneath my shirt. They thought they had disarmed me which was exactly what I wanted them to believe. I just needed to figure out a mo-

The sound of skin hitting skin rang through the empty warehouse as Duarte backhanded João. Milena screamed for her dad and begged for him to be left alone. I stepped forward but Eduardo grabbed my shoulder and pulled me back. I shoved his hand off of me.

"Everyone shut the fuck up!" Duarte shouted and reached for his gun, pointing it at Milena. The fear worked its way through my body causing me to freeze. Seeing her like this and not knowing how to get her out of this was driving me fucking insane. I felt helpless and I needed a plan. Quick.

"I had only planned on killing two people today but then you-..." Duarte pointed at me. "Stumbled in here and now I have to add another one to my list."

"Or you could kill none of us and we could call it a day," I suggested.

Duarte let out a breath of amusement and glanced back at Milena. "Funny guy over here. Is that why you like him?"

She glared at him. "He's a good man, which is more than can be said for you."

I shouldn't be surprised that Milena wouldn't cower in the presence of someone so dangerous. That was who she was. She never backed down.

Duarte turned back to me. "She's got quite a mouth there but you know all about that."

"Don't talk about her like that," I snapped.

"Ohhh there is so much more between you two, isn't there?" Duarte was amused by the puzzle pieces he was putting together of our relationship. He walked in my direction, stopping in front of me. "So what's the deal, Vincenzo, you fancy that one over there?" He gestured in Milena's direction.

"I'm not doing this with you, Duarte," I muttered.

"Oh, I think you are," he chuckled. "You're going to tell that man..." He pointed at João. "That you've been fucking his daughter."

I clenched my jaw and averted my eyes. "You know nothing about the nature of our relationship."

"But there is a relationship, isn't there?"

My silence answered his question. He laughed, finding this far too amusing for someone like him. He was getting under my skin, distracting me from trying to figure out a way out of here.

"Well as fun as this is," Duarte shifted the conversation. "I have a new plan. Milena," he turned to face her, "you're going to watch me kill your boyfriend. João, you're going to watch me kill your daughter, and then I'm going to kill you." He turned to face João who was now trembling in fear.

"Now, *Senhor Neves,* there's no need for the theatrics." He shook his head. "At least this way you'll be able to see your other daughter."

"Damn, Duarte, you're quite a sick fuck," I muttered. "Making comments about his dead daughter - way below the belt there."

Duarte eyed me. "You have a lot to say for a man who is about to lose his life."

"Would you rather I cower away in fear? That's not really my style."

He eyed me with a glimmer of something more in them. "Fearless. I like it. Maybe there is a use for you after all." Duarte walked over to me, "New plan - Vincenzo, you can get out of this right now. Come work for me."

"I would rather drop dead."

Duarte shrugged. "Your choice."

As he went to reach for his own gun, I took the opportunity to grab the two guns I had hidden beneath my t-shirt. I pulled a gun out in each hand, stepping back to point one at Eduardo and the other at Duarte. Milena's cries filled the room and João shouted at me to back down. I would blow the head off every single man here if it meant I would save Milena.

"Vincenzo, you're never going to win," Duarte said, his voice full of warning, "So save us all the trouble an-..."

I pulled the trigger and a bullet went flying, landing in Eduardo's chest.

His eyes widened in surprise as he glanced down at the blood spilling onto his shirt. I was sick to death of people underestimating me. Was I wearing my 'no need to take me seriously' shirt? What the fuck?

I turned to pull both guns on Duarte. The henchman that was holding João let go of him and rushed over to Duarte who lifted his hand to stop him. He shook his head, clearly thinking he didn't need any backup here.

"Eduardo had worked for me for almost ten years." Duarte flicked his eyes over to the, now, dead body.

"Does it look like I give a fuck?" I muttered. "Let them go."

"You and I both know I can't do that. He's going to pay for what he has done - they're both going to pay for what they've robbed me of." For a split second, Duarte showed a flicker of vulnerability in his eyes over his reference to his son.

"Milena didn't do anything wrong."

"Her father took my son from me!" His voice boomed through the warehouse, echoing off the walls. "He deserves to watch the life drain from her and suffer before I send him straight to hell."

"At least he can say hi to Antonio for you."

He gaped at me, the anger radiating off of him. "I'll fucking kill you!"

I ignored his threat. "Either we do this the easy way or my way which ends with me putting a bullet in your head," I warned. "So let's try this again, Duarte - let them go."

"I have a better idea." He pulled his gun and pointed it directly at Milena who broke out in a cry at the sight of the gun. My stomach dropped at just the sight of her staring down the barrel of a gun.

"You put your guns down or I will shoot her right now," Duarte threatened.

"You put your gun down first," I threw back.

He shook his head and clicked his tongue. "That's not how this works."

I looked at Milena, her teary eyes full of emotion. Fear, sadness, anger - it all swam in those deep brown eyes and I fucking hated to see her like that. My sweet Milena. So deserving of much more than the world had given her and now I had a decision to make.

She shook her head. "Don't do it, Vincenzo. Fucking kill him!" She shouted, causing Duarte to whip his head around to her.

"Milena! No!" Her father begged but it was too late. Duarte pulled the trigger and the sound of a gunshot echoed through the warehouse.

CHAPTER 35:

Milena

The bullet pierced my skin and I screamed as the pain started to spread down my arm. He fucking shot me. I turned to my shoulder that now had the bullet nestled inside of it and the tears streamed down my face.

"You're a terrible shot," I spat at Duarte, clenching my jaw to try and ignore the intense throbbing. My mouth had immediately gone dry and I didn't know if I had it in me to ignore the torturous pain of my bullet wound.

"Oh trust me, Milena, when I'm ready to kill you, this bullet will go straight into your head," Duarte said, turning back to Vincenzo. "Are you taking me seriously now?

Vincenzo tried to rush over to me, but Duarte stood in front of him, stopping him dead in his tracks. Instead, my father rushed over to me, lowering himself in front of me as he reached for my arm.

"Milena, *desculpe-me,*" he cried, the tears streaming down his face as he tried to stop the bleeding.

"*No, pai,*" I reassured him. "You don't need to apologize."

He pulled the jersey that was tied around my waist and used the sleeves to tie it tightly around my arm, trying to apply pressure to the wound. I tried not to cry out in pain but it was no use. It fucking burned. My tolerance for pain was usually quite high but even this was too much for me. My father leaned around, reaching for the ropes around my wrist.

Duarte noticed him. "Uh uh, João. I didn't give you permission to untie your daughter."

My father turned around, dropping to his knees. "Duarte, please. I am begging you to let her go. You can kill me. You can do whatever you want but my daughter deserves to live!"

"*Pai, no. D*on't say that," I cried.

The sound of cars against the gravel road caught our attention. Duarte had ordered Eduardo to call for backup earlier and by the sounds of things, they had just arrived. There was no light at the end of this tunnel and I was starting to accept my fate. There was no way I was going to get out of here alive. It was now or never.

"Vincenzo, I'm sorry I made your job so difficult," I cried. "I should have listened to you. I am sorry for eve-"

He interrupted me. "*Tesorina,* no. You have nothing to apologize for." He tried to step forward again but Duarte leaned the end of his gun against his chest, stopping him again. He flicked his gaze to meet Duarte and I could see he was seething.

"*Tesorina h*uh? Little treasure," Duarte translated, turning to me. "That's quite a pet name he's given you. Clearly there is much more to the two of you than we realize."

Duarte kept his gun pointed at Vincenzo but his attention was on me. He seemed amused - it was sickening. "You're in love with him, aren't you?"

I clenched my jaw and kept my eyes firmly on Duarte, refusing to give into his little game. My silence gave away what was already obvious between us. Turning to face Vincenzo again, Duarte laughed. "And you're in love with her. Your little *tesorina.*" Duarte lifted his other hand and slapped Vincenzo playfully against the cheek causing him to lift his hand up and block him from trying again. Even from here I could see Duarte had struck a chord. I should revel in the fact that Vincenzo didn't deny what Duarte said but the circumstances were anything but romantic.

"You still haven't given me your guns, Vincenzo," he reminded him, eyeing the gun in his hand.

"And I'm not going to," he said before he grabbed Duarte by the shoulders and headbutt him, catching him completely by surprise. Duarte dropped his gun and stumbled back. I watched as my father got to his feet, rushing for the gun now on the floor as Vincenzo ran straight to me. The henchman threw himself forward but Vincenzo noticed him from the corner of his eye and pulled the trigger, stopping him dead in his tracks.

"Vincenzo, get her out of here!" My father shouted as he grabbed the gun off the ground, lifting it to point at Duarte who had his hands against his forehead. "I'll hold them off."

Vincenzo cut the ropes around my wrist with the pocket knife he had on hand and I pulled my arms forward, feeling the freedom of free movement again. I reached down and used my good hand for the ropes around my legs and quickly kicked them off.

"We need to help my father," I shouted as we heard a rush from outside. The men were just about to storm the place and we needed to get the fuck out of here.

"I need to get you out of here, your father was very clear," he said, reaching for my hand. I turned back to face my dad who had walked closer to Duarte.

"I had never intended to kill your son," my father started to explain. "I stuck to our agreement the best I could but you went back on your word."

"You fucking owed me!" Duarte's voice boomed through the warehouse. "I gave you the money you needed and all you had to do was sit back and mind your own fucking business."

"I couldn't allow you to do what you were doing. You were a lot of things Duarte but you were never a drug dealer."

"My business had nothing to fucking do with you," Duarte stalked forward.

"*Pai*, let's go!" I shouted, needing this nightmare to be over.

"*Senhor Neves,*" Vincenzo shouted, "We need to get out of here now. They're getting close."

My father shook his head, "Vincenzo, get my daughter out of here!" He shouted back, not breaking eye contact with Duarte who had the gun pointed directly at his chest. "I started this and now I need to finish it."

"No *papa*, *I*'m not leaving you!" The emotion caused my voice to crack.

Vincenzo's arms came around my waist as he started pulling me to the emergency exit in the far corner. Men started to fill the warehouse and our window of opportunity was quickly disappearing. I watched as my father turned towards the men, firing the gun in every direction.

"Get out now!" my father's voice boomed through the warehouse.

I was desperate to get us all out alive and that included my father.

"*Pai,* no! Come with me!" I screamed, trying to wiggle myself out of Vincenzo's grip but he wouldn't budge. "Vincenzo, let me go!" He ignored me and continued to pull me further.

"They're getting away!" Duarte shouted and bullets started flying. We were far enough to dodge them but my father was in the firing line. He met my gaze long enough for me to realize what was happening here. He had no intention of leaving here alive - that was what he wanted for me.

"*Te amo,* Milena," he said as the men started to flood around him. "Take care of your mother."

"*Te amo também, papa,*" I cried, the emotion causing me to choke on my words as Vincenzo dragged me further and further from my father. "I'm not leaving you here!" I tried to continue to shout but it was no use. The world around me came crashing down as I watched the bullets flying, hitting my father in the back as the Nazario men came to Duarte's defense. A blood-curdling scream echoed through the warehouse and I hadn't realized it had come from me until I felt the pain in my throat. My vision was blurred by the tears that filled my eyes and I became dead-weight in Vincenzo's arm as the pain consumed me. Before I knew it, I was being pulled through the door and we were running. I didn't know how I was moving but my body knew we had a short window of opportunity to get out of here. My father knew they needed to be held off and the way to save me was to sacrifice himself. I was so consumed by the pain that I could hardly breathe. Vincenzo stopped by a black SUV and pulled the door open, yelling at me to get in. I went into auto-pilot and followed his instruction, shutting the door behind me. Within seconds he was putting the car into gear and speeding down the gravel road, leaving a hail of bullets in our wake. Some of them hit the outside of the car but I was so consumed by my own grief that there was nothing I could do but drown in the realization that my father had just been killed. Right in front of me. I watched them shoot him and there was nothing I could do to stop it.

I felt Vincenzo's hand on my leg but I couldn't bring myself to open my eyes. The tears wouldn't stop streaming down my face and the ache in my chest was a deep pain I had only ever experienced once before - when I lost Carina.

"Milena, hey, I'm here."

I shook my head. "He's dead. He can't be. Oh my God, he,-" I was heaving now, my breath getting caught in my throat each time I tried to take a deep breath in. There was nothing I could do to stop the pain from consuming every part of me and I had no idea how I was going to survive this grief.

I felt his hand on the outside of my wound, causing my attention to refocus onto the physical pain. I opened my eyes to look over at him. His apologetic eyes met mine. "I'm sorry. I'm not trying to hurt you but I need you to apply more pressure to the wound." He pulled the one sleeve tighter and handed it to me. "Wrap this around your arm again as tight as you can."

I did as I was told and wrapped it around my arm, squeezing it tight against my arm. The pain was unbearable - at least it should have been but it didn't compare to the pain of my broken heart.

"I told you we needed to save him," I cried. "We were supposed to help him."

"Milena, I needed to get you out of there. That was the only chance we had."

I shook my head, the tears streaming down my face. "We could have found another way. We could have done something but we left him. We left him to die all by himself. We didn't ev-..." My airways tightened from the pain in my throat as I cried. I was in shock and I couldn't even fathom how I was supposed to process this. How was I supposed to tell my mom? *Oh my God, my mother.*

"Where's my mother?" I shouted. "Why wasn't she with him?"

"I don't know." Vincenzo reached for my hand but kept one on the steering wheel as he bolted down the road. "Your parents' bodyguard Carlos betrayed them. He betrayed us all."

"What?" My jaw dropped slightly.

"He's the reason they knew where you were. He gave away our location and then he took your father there. I'm guessing it was Duarte who ordered him too."

"He was working for them this whole time?" I didn't even bother to hide my contempt.

"I don't know. I never expected this from him." The emotion in Vincenzo's voice was unmistakable. Carlos' betrayal was a bitter pill to swallow.

"We need to find my mom." My lip trembled but I caught it between my bottom teeth.

"We need to get that wound sorted out first." He eyed me. "I have to take the bullet out."

"No fucking way!" I shook my head.

"Milena, it's not going to stop bleeding if we don't get it out. It won't be able to heal until we do that."

"And since when did you become a fucking doctor?" I shouted.

"I'm the best chance you have right now. We can't afford to take you to a hospital. The hit ordered on you didn't disappear because your father is dead - I need to keep you safe."

I swallowed, attempting to keep my emotions at bay. Vincenzo had gone straight into bodyguard mode which meant his every decision was made on logic and not emotion, including his choice of words.

"I don't need *bodyguard Vincenzo* right now. I need the human one who realizes that I don't need you to throw it in my face that my father is dead as if it's nothing," I snapped.

He was silent for a moment before I heard him sigh and tighten his grip on my hand. "You're right. I'm sorry. That's not what you need right now."

The softer version of him only made me cry harder. I didn't know what I needed right now but I wished the pain would stop. My chest was burning and the hollow pit in my stomach was making me feel as if I was going to throw up at any moment now. I was sweating and my body was heating up. Emotionally and physically, I was fucked.

My eyes started to close but Vincenzo's voice pulled me back. "Milena, hey - look at me. I need you to keep your eyes open, *tesorina*. Can you do that for me?"

I tried to reply, but all I could manage was a slight nod as my eyes fell shut again. I forced them open in an abrupt motion which only made me feel worse. The pain from my wound was burning worse than before and I couldn't even move my arm now.

"Milena, you need to fight through this!" Carina shouted.

"I can't, Carina. You're gone, pai is dead. I've had enough."

"Yes you can! Mãe needs you. You have to push through - you've always

been stronger than you've given yourself credit for."

Was I? I had always felt like the world constantly chewed me up and spat me back out. It was a cruel one that I wasn't sure I could survive in.

Mãe needs you.

My eyes flung open again at that thought. I couldn't leave my mother alone in this world. She had already lost so much, I had to fight through - for her.

And for him.

Vincenzo.

I slowly moved my other hand over to my knee where his hand was resting on. Leaning my head to the side, I managed to open my eyes and look over at him. He was glancing between the road and me, his eyes full of apprehension and fear. I hadn't seen him like this.

"Vincenzo," I murmured, my voice barely a whisper. I tried to call for him again but my words got lost to the darkness as I fell unconscious.

CHAPTER 36:

Vincenzo

"Milena!" I shouted, trying to shake her awake while still focusing on the road. Thankfully there were only a few cars passing every now and then but I couldn't let my guard down. Anything could happen at any point and I would be foolish to think otherwise. We may have managed a narrow escape but that didn't put her in the clear.

She dropped out of consciousness. Between the amount of blood she was losing and the emotional trauma of watching her father being killed in front of her, I couldn't be surprised but I fucking hated it. I felt helpless and I couldn't ignore the hovering fear that she could slip through my fingers at any point. I couldn't lose her. Not after everything. I was sick to my stomach with fear. I had only ever experienced this deep kind of fear once before and that was when my parents died but there was something different about this time. When I learned of my parent's death, it was already too late. Now, I still had a chance to save her but there was no guarantee that I would. I had never experienced a fear this intense before. The fear of losing someone you're in love with.

Love.

"You're in love with her."

Duarte hit the nail on the head with that one and it took watching her life in the hands of a man like that for me to finally admit it to myself. I was completely in love with Milena Neves. She found a way into my heart and she had consumed every part of me ever since. My whole life I kept myself guarded from anything even remotely resembling feelings but with Milena, there was no escaping it. She broke down my walls and for the first time I longed to love and be loved. Seeing her in the state she was in now evoked an empathy inside of me that had been otherwise dormant. I never thought I was capable of it.

"Milena," I repeated. "Can you hear me?"

No reply.

"Damn it!" I shouted and banged my hand against the steering wheel. I stepped on the accelerator and watched the speedometer read an illegal speed as I raced down the open road. A light drizzle had started, the droplets scattering across the windscreen. I needed to sort her wound out - or at least remove the bullet because the longer it stayed in there, the worse it would be for her. I had removed a bullet before but never from the woman I love. God, I didn't even have the stomach to think about the amount of pain she must be in right now.

As if by some miracle, the sign for a gas station flashed in the distance.

"Meno male!" I muttered to myself.

Pulling the car towards it, I sped down the road leading towards the entrance, getting closer and closer to the small convenience store that stood on the property. I slammed on breaks, bringing the car to a halt across the open parking spots and jumped out of the car. Rushing over to Milena's side, I yanked the door open and reached for her face, cupping her cheeks with my hands.

"Milena, hey." She was hot against my hands. Was she getting a fever? Fuck. Her eyes fluttered ever so slightly giving me enough hope that she was still with me.

"We're going to sort that wound out now," I told her before I scooped her into my arms, pulling her outside the car. An older gentleman stepped outside of the store, his eyes widening at the sight of the two of us. I couldn't blame him. Between the blood stains on my clothes and the blood that had soaked Milena's jacket wrapped around her wound, anyone would have gone pale at the sight.

"Oh Dios! ¿Necesitas que llame a la policía?" he asked and I shook my head. The last thing I needed right now was the police to show up. There would be no way to explain our way out of this. The Nazarios were

untouchable which meant law enforcement was not an option.

I switched to Spanish to reply, *"¿Dónde está el baño?"*

His shaking finger pointed towards the sign and I darted in that direction. I headed towards the bathroom with the family sign on it. I turned and used my back to push it open. I kicked the door closed behind us as I heard Milena whimper in my arms.

"I've got you," I reassured her. "We're going to sort that out."

I gently placed her on the toilet seat. Her body was limp but she was able to hold herself up again. I quickly turned and locked the door before turning back to her. I went down on my haunches in front of her, resting my hand on her knee.

"Milena, can you hear me?"

She let out a small groan in response and her eyes slowly fluttered open. The color had drained from her face and she looked as if she was going to be sick.

"You're okay," I reassured her, cupping her cheek with my hand.

"It hurts," she cried.

My eyes darted to the material that was tightened around her arm. The once light gray jersey was now soaked in dark red. Taking a deep breath in, I reached for the material and slowly started to unwind it from her arm. She whimpered, no matter how gentle I was trying to be and the tears were streaming down her face again. She refused to look at the wound and I couldn't blame her. I dropped the jersey to the floor and the sight of the hole in her arm even sent a rush of brief nausea over me.

Pull yourself together.

I kept my eyes firmly on her wound, remembering what I was doing here. I needed to remove the bullet. If I didn't, who knew what was going to become of her arm. I slowly did a closer inspection - by the looks of things, nothing vital was hit but there was a big risk of infection if the bullet stayed in any longer. A deep rage burned inside of me towards Duarte who was responsible for her pain.

"I swear to you Milena, I'm not going to rest until I've killed him. Duarte is a dead man," I said through gritted teeth.

I felt her hand on my arm causing me to turn towards her. Her head had fallen to the side and she was trying to keep her eyes open as she looked at me but she was weak.

"Let's just focus on trying to make it out of here alive then we can talk about your revenge fantasy." Even in a situation like this, here she was with her attempt at humor. I lifted my hand to cup her cheek again and her eyes landed on mine.

"I-I thought I had lost you," I admitted, my voice barely a whisper. "He pulled the trigger and I swear, Milena, my world stopped."

"Vincenzo…" She breathed and opened her mouth to say something further but she couldn't form the words.

"Save your strength," I told her. "Let me be the one to do the talking this time."

She managed a small smile and I just clung to that. I wanted to spend the rest of my life making sure I saw that smile of hers. The kind of smile that had the ability to brighten even the darkest parts of your soul.

"I never want to feel that again. You deserve to live in a world that is safe for you and I swear to God, I am going to do everything in my power to make sure that happens." I took her hand in mine. "It won't be like this forever."

"I believe you," she whispered.

I lifted her hand to my lips, resting them against her soft skin. Tears burned in my eyes and my throat tightened from the pain of holding them back. Expressing my own emotions had never been something I was very good at. Milena was my weakness. She was the closest way to my heart and it was becoming more and more difficult to separate my feelings from this situation. It was all too real.

I took a deep breath in and placed her hand down. I glanced over to her wound again, blood was spilling down her arm and dropping onto a puddle that had formed on the floor.

"I need you to be strong now, okay?" I started to say. "I have to get that bullet out. The good news is that it doesn't look like it hit anything vital but we can't leave that in there. I...I have to remove it."

"How?" she asked.

What were my options here? I definitely couldn't shove my fingers in the wound - it was too narrow. A really big pair of tweezers would probably do the trick but I did not have that at my disposal. I patted down my pockets, trying to see what my next option was. My hand landed against my pocket knife. I slowly pulled it out and Milena's gaze fell on it.

"Oh, fuck no!" She shook her head, tears already spilling from her eyes.

I couldn't believe I was asking this of her now but I didn't have another choice. I needed to flick it out and right now, the knife was the best option. My mouth went dry at the thought of the pain I was about to put her in.

"Milena…" I started but she shook her head continuously, interrupting me.

"You ca-can't." She begged, "Please, Vincenzo."

"I don't want to hurt you, baby," I murmured. "But if I don't do this now, it's going to end up worse. I promise we'll get you to a doctor but until then, I can't leave the bullet in there. You understand that, right?"

I could see in her eyes that she did but she hated it. I hated it too. The last thing I wanted to do was put her through anymore pain and this was probably the worst thing I would have to do. I glanced around the bathroom.

"What are you looking for?"

"Something for you to bite down on."

A small cry escaped from her and my heart broke at the sound of it. This was such a fuck up. I used to believe I was strong enough to face anything. That was part of why I chose the career I did - nothing could break me but I was wrong. If you wanted to get to me, she was the way to do it.

There was nothing hygienic enough in this shit hole for Milena so my only option was my shirt. I pulled it over my head and turned it inside out, rolling it up, making sure to give her a piece that wasn't stained with blood. I lifted it to her. "When I start getting the bullet out, you need to bite on this. You're going to want to scream but we can't bring any attention to ourselves. I'm sorry, Milena. Th-this is the last thing I want to do to you but I have to." I couldn't hide the defeat in my voice and she knew we were at a crossroads here. I brought the shirt closer to her mouth and she used her other hand to hold onto it. She slowly opened her mouth and placed the material between her teeth. I grabbed my lighter from my pocket and lit it up, bringing the flame to the tip of the blade of the knife. Milena's eyes widened in fear.

"I-I have to disinfect the blade. I don't want you to get an infection and this is my only option," I explained.

Her eyes closed as she mentally prepared for what was headed her way. There was no time for me to do the same - I knew what was needed of me now. I put the lighter back in my pocket and gently blew against the blade, attempting to cool it down. I lifted my hand and rested it as gently as I could on the outside of her wound. Her skin slowly separated as I used my thumb and index finger to open it up further. She whimpered at that already and I didn't know how I was going to stomach cutting the bullet out of her. I took a deep breath in and slowly lifted the pocket knife up, the blade hovering close to the wound. Her blood had already soaked my fingers and I knew that the longer I waited, the more blood she was going to lose. She was already slipping away from me. I brought the blade closer to her skin, skimming the outside of the wound. Her cries deepened into a muffled sound against the material as I started to slowly push the tip of the blade deeper.

"I'm so sorry," I murmured, trying my best to keep my own emotions intact as I heard her muffled cries turn to screams. Pushing through this emotional hell I was in, I focused on the bullet. I could see it and I was thankful it wasn't as deep as it could have been. I needed to get the tip of the blade to push underneath the bullet so I'd be able to flick it out. It was lodged between muscle and skin and the blood continued to pool, making it difficult to find the right way to get around the bullet.

Milena's cries continued, the pain from what I was doing was only getting worse and I quickened my pace, wanting to end this as soon as I could. This was fucking torture for me.

"Almost there, *tesorina,*" I said softly. "You can do this."

The blade tapped against the bullet. *Finally.* I opened the wound further and used all my strength to push the blade underneath the bullet. Milena cried and cried, but I was too close to stop now. I started to push the bullet towards the entrance of the wound and with one swift movement, it pushed through and dropped to the ground. The pocket knife fell next, the blade clinking against the floor as I rushed to cup Milena's cheek.

"It's done. You did it, Milena. You did it." I repeated over and over as she released the material from between her teeth and let out a deep cry, her head falling against my chest as I held her for a moment. She needed so much more from me but I needed to close up her wound. At least until I could get her to a doctor. I pulled away and reached for my shirt, unwinding it so I could use it on her arm. I wrapped it around her wound, tightening it to apply pressure.

"Push down on that," I instructed her. "I need to grab something to clean the wound and then we're going to get out of here."

She nodded, her eyes all swollen from the tears. I stole a selfish moment with her as I leaned down and rested my lips against hers. She kissed me back and for that moment, it was just the two of us in an alternate space. One where none of this was our reality and I promised myself that I wouldn't stop until we got what we deserved.

"I'll be right back," I murmured, kissing her forehead before turning towards the door.

CHAPTER 37:

Milena

I had never considered myself to be very religious. I often had too many questions that were frowned upon by my mother who was led by her blind faith. Her beliefs were strong enough to carry her through life as she trusted that the man upstairs had a plan but looking at all that had happened now, how could this have been part of the plan? Why would this have been allowed to happen to us? Why were we being put through complete and utter hell here? I tried to rack my brain, trying to find a bigger picture that I could focus on to distract from the immense pain I found myself in. Physically and emotionally. The more I thought back to everything that had happened, the more I wanted to cry but I had no more tears left. I had been so consumed by the pain that it was starting to numb me. Maybe I was going into shock? Or denial? How was I supposed to accept that my father was dead? And yet, the memory of watching the bullets flying at him was so fresh that I was finding it difficult to focus on anything else.

I felt a hand on my knee, forcing my eyes open to land on Vincenzo. The sky had darkened since I had last opened my eyes and he had brought the car to a stop just outside an apartment building. I had no idea where we were or how long we had been on the road. After he cleaned my wound, we got straight back into the car and headed to our next destination. He tried to explain what the plan was but truthfully, I hadn't paid attention. I was so wrapped up in my own thoughts that I couldn't focus on anything else.

"Milena, we're here," he said.

"Where is *'here'*?" I asked, ducking to try and make out the building in front of us through the windscreen. I quickly counted the floors and the building stacked up eight of them. The moon had disappeared behind the building and the only sounds surrounding us, other than the engine from the car, were the crickets in the distance.

"Afonso - the guy you met at the motel - his sister is a nurse," he started to explain, "She's going to look at your wound and we're going to spend the night here."

"She's just okay with letting strangers stay at her place?"

"Afonso has places all over and this is one of them. Lu has been staying here for a while and I've met her a few times."

We were parked on the curb across the road from the apartment building and there was a small entrance just across. Vincenzo turned the car off and jumped out, closing the door behind him before rushing over to my side. I was drained. My body lacked any of the strength it needed right now and I knew I was going to have to rely on him for assistance. I had never been very good at accepting help from anyone. I was always the one who made sure she could do things for herself - no matter what it was but with Vincenzo, I didn't mind relinquishing control. He opened my door and slowly reached for me, helping me out of the car. I used my other arm to support the one that was wounded. A whole fucking gunshot wound. Never once in my life did I ever fear being shot. The chances of that had always been pretty non-existent but clearly, I had underestimated how quickly things can change. My feet landed on the ground and my legs almost gave in but Vincenzo caught me.

"I got you," he murmured, slipping his hand around my waist. He used his other hand to shut my door and started guiding me towards the entrance. Glancing up and down the empty street, there was no one else in sight but that didn't stop him from being on high alert. I could see it in his eyes, he wasn't about to let his guard down. We stopped at the keypad by the gate and he quickly put in the correct code. The gate buzzed open and he pulled it open, guiding me through it before letting it close behind us.

"How are you feeling?" he asked.

I snorted. "I don't know how to answer that question."

"I know. It was probably a stupid thing to ask but I'm trying to be here for you. I am here for you, Milena so please, lean on me whenever you need to. And I don't just mean physically like you're doing right now."

I almost smiled at his attempt at making a joke. I wanted to smile but I didn't have the energy for that. I didn't even have the energy to be walking right now but my legs carried me through the entrance of the building.

"Thank you," I replied. "Ask me tomorrow."

He leaned down and left a kiss against my temple. My heart warmed at that small gesture and I was thankful there was some kind of flicker of feelings inside of me. Even if it was short-lived before the ache of loss returned. After calling on the elevator and making it up to the fifth floor, we stopped outside the second door along the corridor. Vincenzo knocked lightly, glancing around us to make sure no one else was around. A few moments later, the door was yanked open.

"Vincenzo!" The woman exclaimed and stepped back, gesturing for us to come inside.

"Hi, Lu." He replied and stepped inside, guiding me with him as she shut the door behind us. "Lu, this is Milena."

A warm light spilled across the room as we were welcomed into the apartment. I tried to glance around and see what I could notice but I couldn't bring myself to even move my head. I had never felt so weak before. Lu walked around to stop in front of me, pulling a chair from the dining room table. I noticed her kind eyes. They revealed a clear fatigue but they still managed to be some-what comforting. They were the complete opposite of her brother's dark ones when I first met him but there were enough similarities between them for there to be no question about whether they were siblings or not. From their particularly high-cheek bones covered in the same brown complexion to their full lips. Different from Afonso though, Lu's features were more delicate and a youthful sweetness came in the form of the small crease in her left cheek. Lu was a fresh-faced natural beauty. "It's nice to meet you, Milena - I do wish the circumstances had been better." There was a flicker of a Spanish accent when she spoke. I was placed down on the chair and I dropped my weight against it. "Nice to me..." My words trailed off as the strength to finish the sentence washed through me, leaving me with nothing but a hovering nausea. My eyes were starting to force themselves shut as my world started to spin. I wanted to stay conscious. I fought to open my eyes but there was nothing I could do to fight the darkness as it consumed me.

CHAPTER 38:

Vincenzo

I closed the door behind me slowly, careful not to wake her. I took a moment and released the breath that I had been holding in. Taking a deep breath in, I filled my lungs with air but it was never quite enough. The deeper I breathed, the more I felt like I was fighting for more air. The pressure in my chest had yet to alleviate itself and seeing her pass out again didn't help.

"She's going to be fine, Vincenzo," Lu's voice brought me out of my own thoughts. I turned and she was leaning against the wall of the corridor. I turned to lean my back against the wall next to the door, my eyes closing as I tried to reassure myself that she was right. After Milena collapsed, I helped Lu get her onto the table where she was able to still sort out her wound. Not once did Milena stir as Lu stitched her up but the small rising of her chest reassured me that she was alive. She had gone through so much in the last twenty-four hours that I couldn't blame her body for finally giving in. Once she was all stitched up, I took her to the guest room and tucked her in. She needed all the rest she could get right now.

"Thanks for helping us out," I said, opening my eyes to meet Lu's gaze.

She was still in her navy-colored uniform from the hospital that she worked at. Exhaustion was clear in her eyes but she still managed to force a comforting smile. Lu was beautiful in a natural way. Not a sliver of makeup sat on her face. I hadn't known her for very long but she always had this wonderful way of welcoming you, no matter the situation.

"You're welcome," she said. "It's a good thing you got here when you did. That wound was a nasty one but she's going to make a full recovery.

She'll be in pain for a while but you can give her those pain meds I left next to her bed."

I nodded. We stood in the dimly lit corridor, neither one of us making any move to suggest we would be leaving our positions anytime soon. I didn't want to leave Milena alone but I also needed a moment to try and pull myself together. I had never needed to do anything like that. I usually prided myself on being able to handle anything but the universe had finally found my weakness.

"You're in love with her, aren't you?" Lu asked softly.

I glanced down at the ground, emotion suddenly getting caught in my throat. I was completely in love with Milena. I had never given a piece of myself to anyone - I had never even allowed myself the chance to but she didn't give me much of a choice.

"I don't know how it happened," I admitted.

Lu let out a small breath of amusement. "No one ever knows how it happens. Loving someone isn't something we have any control over. If we did, I'm sure a lot of us would choose differently."

She was right. If there was any way for me to have controlled falling for Milena, I would have done it - *right?* But that's the thing about love - it creeps up on you when you least expect it, showing you all that you didn't know you were missing. You believe that you're whole on your own until you meet the missing part of you that just makes everything feel right. You finally feel like you belong in this world and suddenly, everything else makes sense. I never truly felt like this world had a place for me but now I know there is no doubt that it's with her.

"Have you ever been in love?" I asked her.

"Once. A long time ago."

"What happened?"

"He died," her voice was hollow as she shared. "Heart attack. He was only thirty-eight."

My mouth went dry as I, unwillingly, empathized with her pain. *What have you done to me, Milena?* She awakened the part of me that was able to experience emotions and now the floodgates to it had no way of closing themselves back up.

"I...I'm sorry," I said.

She gave me a small smile and shook her head. "It's okay. It was a long time ago."

Lu was much older than Afonso and had clearly lived through the cruelty that the world had a tendency to show people. I couldn't even allow myself to stomach the thought of losing Milena. It filled me with a burning rage and I refused to let that happen.

"Would you have chosen differently?" I asked. She looked confused and I continued to explain. "If you had known that he was going to be taken from you so young and you had the chance, would you choose differently?"

She didn't even hesitate before shaking her head. "If I had, I wouldn't have allowed myself to experience some of the happiest years of my life. *Better to have loved and lost than to never have loved at all.*" A yawn escaped from her mouth and she lifted her hand in front of it before continuing. "Someone said that to me once. A quote from some famous dead person. At the time, I completely disagreed. The pain was just too much to handle that I found myself wishing I had never loved him at all but death is the only thing we are guaranteed in this life. It's how we choose to spend the time until then that really matters."

A chuckle escaped from her, causing me to meet her eyes. "I know I sound like some silly motivational speaker or something -" I let out a small laugh in response. "But it's true, Vincenzo, and I think you know that too. Would you really stop loving her if you had the chance?"

Without hesitation, I knew the answer was no. I had spent most of my life as nothing more than a hollow shell of a man. I kept myself so shut off from the world that I deprived myself of anything good in it. How could there be anything good if all I had ever known was loss? But then she came along. Milena seeped life back into me and for the first time, I started to notice the beauty that this world had to offer. There was no denying that this world was a complete fuck up. Even the circumstances surrounding how Milena and I had even come to cross paths just proved that but the beauty that she had to offer the world was enough to forget all the cruelty.

"No," I finally said out loud and Lu smiled a knowing smile at me before another yawn escaped from her.

"Okay, that's my cue," she announced. "If you need anything, I'll be in my room but otherwise, *mi casa es tu casa.*"

"Thanks, Lu."

She nodded and disappeared down the corridor to her room. I was left with nothing but the sound of a slight buzzing from the light above me and my thoughts. Thankfully, my mind had started to calm itself down thanks to the exhaustion and the thoughts were few and far between. Only one thing kept repeating over and over in my mind.

I would do everything in my power to make this world safe for Milena again. I wouldn't stop until every single person who dared threaten her existence was taken out. You come for the woman I love, I end you. Simple as that.

I slowly opened the door to the guest bedroom again, stepping inside before shutting it behind me. A small lamp sat on the bedside table that I had turned on earlier. The pain medication and water sat next to it. She was sleeping peacefully, her chest softly rising and falling as her small breaths were all that could be heard. I walked over to the empty side of the bed. She was facing it and her arm was bandaged up with her hand resting against her stomach. There was still so much for me to learn about her and in an ideal world, I would spend as much time as I could doing just that. Every quirk. Every habit. Every facial expression and what they meant. All there was to know about her life before I knew her. Those details were important in shaping the woman she is today. A strong, courageous, stubbornly-brilliant woman.

Bringing myself onto the bed, I shifted to lean against the headboard. I felt her stir next to me and her eyes slowly fluttered open. She glanced up at me and a small smile formed on her lips. "Hi."

I reached out and slowly pushed back the strands of hair that had fallen in front of her eyes. "Hi."

"What happened?" she asked.

"You passed out. Lu still managed to stitch you up though so you're going to be just fine. No need to amputate that arm today." I attempted a joke and was rewarded with a small chuckle.

"Good."

Her eyes closed again before she forced them open. I caressed her cheek with my thumb. "Rest, *tesorina*. You need it."

"Mm-hmm." She was quiet for a moment. "Will you stay with me?"

"Of course."

She shifted herself closer to me, her leg brushing up against mine. Her eyes closed again and it wasn't long before she found sleep again. I wish I could do the same. No matter how badly my body was fighting for rest, my mind wouldn't allow it.

"Milena," I said softly, knowing she was too deep in her sleep and wouldn't be able to hear me anyway. I had so much I wanted to say to her - so much she deserved to know, but I couldn't be selfish with her. I couldn't tell her all that I wanted to without the inevitable hurt and disappointment that would follow.

"I promised I wouldn't say this to you unless I knew I would be able to remind you of it every single day after that but I need you to know." I slowly ran my fingers through her soft hair. "I'm in love with you, *tesorina.*"

I took a deep breath in before the words continued to fall from my lips. "I don't know how it happened. Somehow you managed to weasel yourself into my heart - even when I tried so hard to keep you out but that's just a testimony to who you are. Brave. Tenacious. Defiant. Stubborn as hell." If she were awake right now, I knew that would earn me a playful eye roll. That's her go-to reaction. "I've never met anyone like you before. Someone who challenges me. You refuse to take things lying down and truthfully, I wondered if you ever really needed protection because knowing you, you'd probably be able to take care of yourself. You've been doing it for the longest time now and I wish I could tell you that you don't need to do it anymore. I want to be the one who is here for you - who protects you and allows you a moment of weakness when you need it. You don't have to be strong all the time."

Hearing how she spoke about how things have been for her since her sister died, I knew that Milena had been living a lonely existence. You can be surrounded by plenty of people and still feel completely alone. I knew that because I had been living the same way. Distant. Guarded in an attempt to shelter myself from anything that could cause me pain again.

"I refuse to allow you to continue to live in fear so I promise you now that I am going to take care of it. I'm going to make this world safe for you again. You deserve a chance at the life you've always wanted - whatever that is. It won't always be like this - I promise."

And I would keep that promise. No matter what I had to do.

CHAPTER 39:

Milena

"Please don't tell me you're sneaking out again," Carina muttered in a hushed tone, glancing back at the door to our bedroom that was already closed. Her paranoia of our parent's barging in at any moment had yet to waver.

"Of course I am," I replied, pulling my hair up into a high ponytail as I admired myself one last time in front of the mirror.

"Milena, you're already on thin ice with papa. I don't think he's fully gotten over having to pick you up drunk from that party you went to for that annoying friend of yours."

"Rosanna isn't annoying."

"Yes she is. Have you heard that voice?" Carina pulled a face. "I'd rather listen to nails on a chalkboard."

I chuckled as I applied the last of my lipgloss. "It's not her fault she sounds like that. She didn't choose her voice."

"No, but you chose her as a friend."

"She's a good friend."

Carina snorted. "No, she's not. She's condescending and a bad influence. She's probably the same one convincing you to go out tonight, isn't she?"

I turned to face my sister who was seated on her bed. It was mind-blowing how we managed to be similar in every way humanly possible except for our personalities - and in our friend choices it would appear. A book lay on her open bed. Typical Carina. Curled up in bed with a book on a Saturday night. I wished I could be like her. I wished I could find enjoyment in the little *things like that but for some reason, I craved more. I craved the need for attention and excitement. I wasn't sure what I lacked in my life but there was something missing that pushed me to continue to want more.*

"Are you going to cover for me or not?" I crossed my arms, eyeing her. We held each other's gaze before she sighed and rolled her eyes.

"You know I will." She said as she lifted her duvet and tucked herself back into her bed. "I just wish you wouldn't poke the bear - the bear being our parents - you never give them time to get over your last transgression before finding another way to piss them off."

Transgression. What kind of sixteen year old used a word like that?

"What they don't know, won't hurt them," I pointed out.

She sighed and lifted her book. "Will you at least let me know when you get wherever you're going?" She placed her book back down. "Actually, where are you going? You haven't even told me."

"Marcio's house party."

This earned me the same judgemental look I had seen from her a million times before. I rolled my eyes. "Don't even start, Carina. I really like him, okay?"

"He's not good for you, Milena."

"You don't even know him."

"I know that he treats you like shit."

I shook my head. "I'm not getting into this with you now." I grabbed my sling bag off the chair it was hanging on by my desk and walked over to the window of our room. "I'll be back before midnight."

"I'm not trying to fight with you, Lena," Carina said, stopping me as I opened the window up, getting ready to climb out of it. "You just deserve better than someone like Marcio. You deserve someone who treats you right and will do everything he can to make you happy. You understand where I'm coming from, right?"

I avoided looking at her. She was always right. Deep down I knew that I would constantly be making the wrong decisions but she would always be there as the voice of reason in my life, reminding me of the things that I tended to avoid. Whenever I was close to making a bad decision, somehow she was there to pull me away from it before it was too late.

I sighed and closed the window.

My eyes flung open. The memory had materialized itself as a dream and I didn't realize I had been crying until I was brought back to consciousness. I lifted my hand to wipe away the tears that had stained my cheeks. *Carina.* There wasn't a day that passed where I didn't miss her and when I was reminded of memories such as that one, it hurt even worse than usual. Darkness surrounded me as I tried to gather my bearings, trying to figure out where the hell I was. Okay, I was in a bed - someone's bed - this evident by the mattress beneath me and the soft pillow my head lay against. I remembered Vincenzo lying with me. *Or was that a dream? My* thoughts were all in disarray and I couldn't distinguish reality from what was happening in my mind. I rolled over and extended my arm, immediately regretting my movement as I was reminded of the bullet wound.

"Fuck," I muttered in pain as the door to the room opened, allowing the light from outside to illuminate the room just enough for me to make out Vincenzo entering.

"Milena?" He closed the door behind him, shutting the light off. I heard him rush over to where I lay and a lamp was turned on. The warm light spilled over, finally showing me exactly where I was. I didn't recognize the room but it definitely seemed like a guest room. There were no personal touches and nothing but the double bed stood in the room, with two bedside tables on either side of it.

"How are you feeling?" He reached for my hand gently as he sat down on the edge of the bed.

"Sore. Tired," I admitted. "What happened?"

"You passed out as we arrived. Scared the fucking shit out of me but Lu assured me that you needed your rest after everything you went through."

Spot on. I could have slept forever if my own memories hadn't betrayed me like that.

He lifted his hand towards my injured arm and I followed his gaze. A white bandage had been wrapped around it. "Lu left you some pain medication over there." He gestured towards the bedside table.

"I like her already."

A small smile played on his lips but it never quite reached his eyes. He looked exhausted in more ways than one. I squeezed his hand. "How are you feeling?"

He glanced up and met my gaze. "Better now that we got that sorted out." He eyed my injured arm. "I'm sorry about the pain I put you through back at that rest stop. I just-I needed to get the bullet out. I was so terrified..." He was rambling on now. He had always managed to hold himself together but there was a new vulnerability to him.

"Enzo, hey." I squeezed his hand again. "You don't need to apologize. I should be thanking you for doing what you did."

He let go of my hand as he stood up, walking over to the empty side of the bed. I watched as he brought himself onto the bed, shifting closer to me. "I need to know that you're okay, Milena. So much has happened and I don't want you thinking you have to go through this alone. I'm here."

The tears swelled in my eyes again as I was bombarded with the flashes of all that had happened in the last twenty-four hours. I had never been on such an emotional rollercoaster before and I didn't even know where to begin to start dealing with any of it.

"I don't think I'm ever going to be okay again," I whispered.

He slipped his hand into mine, intertwining our fingers. "You won't feel like this forever," he said softly. "But I don't need to tell you about loss. You've already experienced way too much and I'm so sorry for that."

Grief consumed me when Carina died and I often thought I was going to suffocate because of it. The world I had known had changed and it would never be what it once was. The absence of her was everywhere. In every interaction, every thought, every moment - I felt her loss. Over time, I had never gotten over it and I never would - I had just learned to live with the pain. It became a part of who I was and now I was going to have to do it all over again. The loss of my father was like a fresh wound and it was going to take very long before that healed. Even when it did, the scar would remain and I would be reminded of this feeling.

The tears had started to fill my eyes again but I ignored them, not wanting to allow them out right now. "What's going to happen now?" I asked.

"Once you're up and ready to go, I'm going to take you to your mother. She's safe with Afonso right now."

My mother. *Mãe*. She's all I have left.

"Does..." I paused for a moment, my voice cracking with emotion.

"Does she know what happened?"

Translation - does she know her husband is dead?

"Afonso told her."

I closed my eyes, this time not being able to stop a few tears from spilling over at the thought of my mother going through this alone. My heart ached at just the thought.

"She's all alone," I said, my voice barely a whisper.

"Which is why we need to get you two reunited. That way we can also plan the next step."

"Which is?"

"Getting you both safely out of the country."

My bottom lip trembled and I quickly caught it between my teeth to stop the emotion from consuming me. I couldn't believe what my life had become and I already longed for the one I used to know.

"But then you wouldn't have met Vincenzo."

She was right. Everything that had happened led up to having him in my life now and I didn't want to think of one without him. He was my comfort and my strength when I needed it. And right now, I could use all the strength I could get. I felt his thumb gently caress my hand and I glanced down at our hands together. Just the sight allowed a flicker of warmth inside my otherwise desolate heart.

"As soon as you're out of here, you'll be safer but I don't trust that Duarte is going to just leave you guys alone," he said, causing me to turn to face him.

He was already looking at me and for a moment, I just soaked him in. His dark eyes were swimming with exhaustion. I reached out and rested my hand against his rough beard. He leaned into my touch and I managed a small smile, even if it was fleeting. I was in love with this man. Everything that happened in the last twenty-four hours was too much to think about all at once but a new wave of emotion washed over me as I thought back to the sound of the gunshot echoing around me.

"I thought they had killed you," I murmured, my hand dropping. "Whe-when they dragged me to the car, I heard a gunshot and I-I didn't know if you were okay."

I relived that moment in my mind. The fear was overwhelming and the not knowing if he was okay or not after that had started to destroy me. He reached for my hand again. "Hey, I'm right here. I'm okay."

"I know," I whispered and tightened my grip on his hand. "I was so scared that I had lost you."

He gently took my chin between his fingers and turned me to face him. His hand slid into my hair, cupping my cheek. "You're not going to lose me, *tesorina*. I'm right here."

I didn't have it in me to lose anyone else. I wanted- no, I needed him in my life. With him by my side, I believed I could survive this pain. It would hurt like hell but knowing I had him to turn to brought me a comfort I had never experienced with anyone else. He made me feel like I belonged.

But I couldn't ignore the looming question in my mind - was he going to come with me?

"When I leave, are you coming with me?" I asked.

The way his face dropped already told me the answer I didn't want to hear. I closed my eyes, not being able to hold back the tears.

"Milena, hey, look at me." He cupped my face with both hands. I opened my tear-filled eyes to meet his. "I need to make this world safe for you again. There are a few things I have to take care of before we can be together."

Hope flickered inside of me for a brief moment. "You want us to be together?"

"More than I've wanted anything else," he answered, his voice full of surety. "But I can't sit by while there is still a threat out there. You have to trust me."

"I do."

There was no changing his mind once he had made it up. He was painfully stubborn - just like I was and I couldn't be angry at the fact that he wanted to protect me. He had laid his life on the line for me more than once and as much as I wanted him to keep himself safe, I knew he would never budge when it came to my protection.

He leaned down and pressed his lips against my forehead, holding the moment for both of us to appreciate. "You're going to get the life you deserve, *tesorina.*"

"My sister told me once that I deserved someone good in my life. Someone that would do all he could to make me happy." I pulled away to meet his eyes. "If she was here right now, she'd tell me that I finally found that."

Carina would have approved of Vincenzo. The kind of man that - quite literally - put his life on the line to save mine. A soft-hearted soul with a hard exterior. There was so much more to Vincenzo than what meets the eye. He was selfless, kind - a little bossy at times but it was only because he was so dedicated to his job that he wouldn't let anyone get in the way of that. Including me. He was protective and he made me feel safe. And calm. For the first time in my life, I felt like I belonged. I had completely fallen for him and there was no going back now. He had infiltrated every part of my body, soul and heart.

I wanted us to have a life together. In an ideal world, that's what we would get but I knew him well enough now that when he says he is going to do something, there is no shaking him.

"I could sit here and beg you to come with me but I know you've already made up your mind," I said. "And I can't be mad at the fact you want to keep me safe."

"That's all I want, *tesorina.*"

My heart leaped whenever he called me that and to know that it came from a place of love had awakened a happiness that was otherwise locked away. My head rested against his chest, my eyes begging to be rested again. I felt his hand against my hair, slowly caressing it as I soaked in his touch. I didn't have the energy to move or even continue speaking.

"You should rest a little longer," he murmured.

"Will you stay with me?"

"Of course. I'm not leaving your side until I have to."

The looming reality of us parting ways surrounded us but I refused to even acknowledge it. I didn't have it in me to emotionally deal with everything that was happening inside so instead, I focused on one thing at a time. Vincenzo was with me. He was holding me and I felt comforted. Safe. Loved. My heart would never be the same again now that I had lost my sister and my father but what was left of it, it was all Vincenzo's. Maybe in another life, things could have turned out differently for us but what would have been the chances of our lives ever crossing any other way? Everything always happens for a reason.

He shifted us down so he had his head against the pillow. He hooked his one arm underneath his head and tightened his other one around me, keeping me close to his chest. My arm continued to throb but I tried my best to ignore it.

"Does this mean I get to pick a new name?" I asked. If my mother and I were going to flee, there was no way we'd be able to keep our current identities. The Neves family was no more.

"Yes. You'll both have to get new identities. Afonso is working on it."

"He better choose a good name for me," I warned playfully.

"I think he said something about you looking like a 'Lilith'."

I snorted. "As in the demon?"

His chest lifted as he let out his laughter at my reaction. It felt normal. I wanted to cling to this moment.

"I'm just messing with you. You're a real-life angel in my life so we're going to find a name more fitting."

God, I was so in love with this man. And he loved me too. Right?

"I'm in love with you, tesorina."

Wait - had I dreamed that? Or did he really say that? I could have sworn that I had heard him say that. But when? My thoughts were in complete tatters right now.

"Di-did you come to lie with me earlier?" I asked.

"Yes until I got a call from Afonso but then I came right back here."

He said it. He *had* to have said it. There was no way I could have dreamed that. His voice, I heard it so clearly in my mind. I wanted to bring it up but I would wait. If he wanted to tell me that again, he would. Right now, I was just thankful to be holding him.

"Will you wake me when we need to go?"

"Of course, but don't worry about that now. You can take a little longer to get some more sleep in." I felt his lips against my hair and I fell asleep to his words repeating in my mind.

CHAPTER 40:

Milena

A re goodbyes better when you're able to prepare for them? I had always thought they would be. You'd have the time to say everything you would have wanted to say but as we pulled into the underground parking of the airport, I couldn't think of what to say to Vincenzo. I was at a loss for words because the truth was, I didn't want to say goodbye to him. I didn't want this to be the end for us. After everything that had happened and all the loss I had already experienced, I didn't want to lose him too. He made me feel like I belonged. For the longest time I walked this earth as an empty soul until I met him. He challenged me. He pushed me to deal with things I would have otherwise just ignored. He cared for me and listened when I shared things with him without a flicker of judgment. We mirrored each other in many ways and I had never met someone like that before. He comforted me and when he was around, I felt protected. Not just in the physical sense but emotionally. He allowed me to explore my vulnerability and show me that I no longer had to be guarded - not with him.

And now it was time to say goodbye.

We hadn't shared many words since we left Lu's apartment. After thanking her for all her help, we were back on the road headed to meet my mother and Afonso. We sat in silence - a comfortable silence this time - with our hands intertwined the entire time. Even now, his hand rested on my thigh and my hand was in his. I slowly caressed his hand with my thumb as I glanced down at them as one. I had always believed I was too difficult to make a connection with someone. I was too outspoken. Too stubborn. Too independent. But with Vincenzo, I didn't feel like that. He embraced every part of me and he loved me for it. Loved. *Love*. I swear he said that to me. His words repeated over and over in my mind but I was swaying between what was real and what was a dream.

"How's your arm?" he asked, breaking the silence.

"Tender."

"It will heal in no time." He lifted my hand to meet his lips and left a small kiss against it.

It was gentle. Soft. Everything you wouldn't think Vincenzo would be capable of but I knew that side of him now and I felt lucky to be on the receiving end of his kindness. I glanced down at my arm that was now in a material sling. Lu cleaned the wound one last time before we left and after bandaging it up, she placed the sling on as a precaution. The wound still throbbed - reminding me that it seemed to have it's own heartbeat. The pain I experienced from Vincenzo removing the bullet would be forever ingrained in my mind. Besides the physical pain, I was in emotional turmoil. It was crazy to think that all this had happened just over twenty-four hours ago. Time moves differently when you're in a highly-emotional situation. Besides the continued throbbing in my arm, the dull ache in my chest was still present and always would be. At least until I had learned to live with this new wave of grief.

He pulled into an empty parking space and cut the engine. Deep disappointment smothered me as we were approaching the end. I dropped my head as the tears filled my eyes.

"Milena," he said softly, reminding me that I would never hear my name sound so sweet ever again. With his accent and deep voice, there was something hypnotic about the way he called me.

He rested a finger under my chin, gently turning me to face him. "Are you ready?"

"Not in the slightest." I shook my head. "I don't want to say goodbye to you."

Before he could reply, his phone started to ring. He dropped his hand and answered the call. "You here?" There was silence for a second before he continued. "Okay. On our way up."

He ended the call and turned back to me. I took a mental snapshot of this moment. Remembering every detail of his face that I could. His dark beard that had grown out and the way it would feel when I would cup his face. Rough against my skin but I would continue to slowly scratch against it. I would remember the way he would soak in my touch and the way his dark eyes would say more than his words needed to. I reached for him, cupping his cheek as my fingers sunk into the back of his hair.

"It's time, isn't it?" I asked, already knowing the answer.

"Yes, *tesorina*, it's time."

***

The airport was swarming with people as Vincenzo led us through them, his hand still in mine. Neither of us had managed to put into words what we wanted to say and with the way I was feeling, I didn't think I would be able to anyway. The deep grief had settled itself around my heart over the loss I was still reeling from. It was reminiscent of how I felt when they told me Carina had died but this was still worse. I would never be able to get the mental image out of my head of watching those bullets pierce through my father as if it was nothing. He sacrificed himself for me and I would have to live with that for the rest of my life.

"He's given you a second chance, Lena," Carina's voice whispered. *"You've got this."*

What I would give to be able to give my sister one last hug right now. Somehow, she was always there - even if it was an illusion. It was what I needed and as long as I could hear her voice, I was never truly alone. Up until now, I was using all the strength I had left to hold back my tears but when my mother's grief-stricken face came into view, I lost it. Letting go of Vincenzo's hand, I ran to my mother and wrapped my good arm around her as we both allowed the tears to flow. My wound was throbbing now from the contact against her chest but I didn't care.

"Oh Milena," my mother cried. "You're here!"

"I'm here, *Mãe.*" I squeezed tighter, my eyes shutting as a new wave of emotion hit me. Sadness. Anger. Relief. Regret. Everything was hitting me all at once but for that moment I became a child again, wanting nothing more than the comfort that my mother could give.

"He's gone..." Her cries turned to wailing and I realized that I was going to be her comfort now. For the longest time, I viewed my parents as just that - parents. Not human beings but in this moment, I was reminded that my mother was just like I was. She hurt the same. Cried the same. Needed comfort the same. And I was all she had left. I caressed the back of her hair, trying my best to console her but knowing there was nothing I could do to take the pain away. I pulled away and cupped her face, her light eyes swimming with tears.

"You and I are still here, *Mãe*. We're going to protect each other and we're going to get through this."

She nodded, the tears continuing to flow down her cheeks. Afonso stepped from behind my mother and nodded to me in a greeting. I gave him a small smile. "Thank you for letting us stay with your sister."

"You're welcome." He looked at Vincenzo and nodded, as if the two of them exchanged words without opening their mouths. He turned back to me. "How's your arm?"

"Still attached," I shrugged, earning me a small smile from Vincenzo.

My mother's hand went up to my bandaged arm. "*Meu deus,* you're hurt."

I shook my head. "No, *Mãe, I*'m okay. Don't worry about that."

Before she could say anything, Afonso spoke up. "*Senhora Neves, d*o you have the passports?"

She nodded and pulled away from me, turning to the small sling bag she had across her body. She grabbed a passport and handed it to me along with a plane ticket inside of it. "Afonso organized us with new identities and I was able to drain our accounts."

I took the passport and opened it up, glancing down at the destination. "Cape Town?"

"Your sister always wanted to go there." She sniffed, trying to get a handle on her tears but the gesture made me emotional. Carina had always wanted to explore the world and while there were many destinations she spoke of, Cape Town was one that kept popping up.

"Do you think we'll be safe there?" I asked, turning to Vincenzo who remained silent behind me. "From the Nazarios?"

He nodded. "They're not going to hurt you, Milena. As far as they're concerned, Milena and Francisca Neves are no more."

I looked back down, sliding the ticket between the pages of my passport as I learned of my new identity.

"Gia Aurelia," I read out loud, looking up at Vincenzo who had stepped closer to me. "At least it wasn't Lilith."

He let out a breath of amusement, his lips pulling slightly into a smile. "I had to help him out with that one." He looked up to Afonso and my mother who were watching us. "Do you think you could give us a moment?"

I looked back at them, my mother's eyebrow raising in suspicion and Afonso just nodded. "Two minutes, Enzo. They need to get to their gate."

The two of them put enough distance between us that they gave us the privacy that Vincenzo asked for. I turned back to him as he reached for my hands, cupping them and bringing them to his lips.

"In Italian, Gia, means 'a gracious gift' which was only fitting for the woman who is, quite literally, a gift to this earth," he murmured, pressing his lips against my fingers as he flicked his gaze to meet mine. Between his beautiful words and the looming reality, I wasn't doing well at keeping it together.

"Vincenzo," my voice cracked with emotion at his words. "This isn't what I want."

"I know, *tesorina, b*ut right now, your safety is the most important thing to me."

"Then come with me. There's no one who can protect me better than you can." I couldn't hold back the tears that started to spill over.

He cupped my face and forced me to look up at him. "I'm doing this because I'm trying to protect you. I meant what I said - I am going to make this world safe for you again. And once I do, I am going to come and find you."

For a second, a flicker of hope presented itself. His hand dropped to my chest, his finger slipping underneath the necklace he gave me. "This is my way of being close to you. Promise me that you'll never take this off?"

"I promise."

He pulled me into his arms, my head resting against his chest as his hand cupped the back of my head. I cried into his chest as my heart shattered. I had experienced heartbreak over the years but this was different. I had fallen in love with Vincenzo and now I had to live without him.

I wasn't ready for that.

CHAPTER 41:

Vincenzo

"I can't do this without you," she cried into my chest.

I hated this. I hated to hear her like this and know that there was nothing I could do to make this better. This was how it had to be for now.

"Yes, you can." I leaned down and planted a kiss against her hair. "You're the strongest person I know. You can do anything you set your mind to."

If anyone was going to survive the cruel circumstances of the world, it was my Milena. She was strong, tenacious, independent - a Godly kind of beautiful and so much more. I had never been religious but I knew that she was a gift from a higher power because there was no way I would have just stumbled upon someone like her. It was all calculated. A cruel fate but the only one that brought us to where we were meant to be. Together. Even if it was short lived. Being with Milena was like taking a cold shot of tequila. It hurt to let her in but once I did, she consumed every part of me and there was no way to escape her. She had opened me up to a world I didn't know was possible - one where I could love and be loved in return.

I pulled away and cupped her face. "Look at me," I said softly, her eyes flicking up to meet mine. With the light coming through the windows, her eyes had brightened to a golden light brown. They were swimming with so many emotions and I wished for nothing more but the ability to calm her storm.

"Two minutes is not enough for me to tell you everything you deserve to hear but I promise, this isn't how our story ends." I leaned my forehead against hers. "We're going to make it, Milena. "

She shut her eyes, trying to stop the tears before opening them up again. "I love you, Vincenzo."

I love you. Those three words that had the ability to awaken the deepest part of my soul. Any defense I had, they slipped away for good at hearing those words from her. My existence suddenly had meaning. She was everything. I loved her more than my own existence. Without realizing, she became the center of my universe which is why I have to do this. I *have to* give her a world where she belongs. Where she can be safe and never have to worry about a looming threat.

I brought my lips down to hers, not caring that Afonso and her mother were watching. I didn't care about any of that anymore. She was all that mattered.

I pulled away slightly. "I love you, Milena."

It didn't matter that I had promised myself to not tell her those words until I could guarantee that I'd be able to remind her of it every day. She needed to know. After everything, I had fallen in love with her and that was the most exhilarating experience of my life. Nothing would compare to the way she made me feel. I would fight for her future - *our future* - because we deserve it.

"Vincenzo!" Afonso shouted.

"Lo so, " I replied, never once taking my eyes off her. "Time to go now, baby."

The moment I had dreaded had arrived. I needed to let her go because I had a mission to complete. I was going to take out anyone who was a threat to her. No matter how long it took and I didn't care if it killed me. She deserved to live in a world that was safe.

She shook her head. "I'm not ready to be Gia Aurelia."

I pulled her into my arms again, my lips finding her hair. "You'll always be Milena Neves to me."

CHAPTER 42:

Milena

I stared outside the plane's window and thought about how bittersweet this moment was. Somehow, after everything, I was still alive. I had a chance at a new life away from the chaos. So much had been lost and I would never be able to live without the constant reminders of that. *Papa and Carina* had taken up permanent residence inside of my heart and as fresh as the wounds were right now, they would eventually heal. That's what time does. The cliche of *time heals all wounds h*as truth to it. Not only would the wound of losing them need to heal but the fresh loss I was sitting with now over having to say goodbye to Vincenzo. I had no more tears left to shed - my body having seemed to have dried out for the day - so now all that was left was the remnants of emotion. He told me he loved me and that was all I needed to hear to believe in our future. It fuelled me with the strength to believe that there was going to be more for us. This wasn't the end - I refused to believe that. We deserved this and as uncertain as my future was right now, I knew that one day I would see him again. I clung to that. It was all I had to keep me going right now.

I felt my mother's hand in mind, turning my attention back to her. "Are we going to talk about the fact you kissed your bodyguard?"

"Are you mad?"

She shook her head. "Just confused. That certainly wasn't what we hired him for."

I laughed. For the first time in days, I managed to laugh and it felt good. "Trust me, we didn't expect this to happen. I didn't even like him in the beginning."

"Your father had a feeling you wouldn't. *'My Milena isn't going to enjoy being told what to do'*, my mother mimicked him playfully, a soft laugh falling from her lips. "But we were just trying to keep you safe."

"I know." I squeezed her hand. After a moment, I turned back to her. "Did you know that *pai had* taken money from them?" I didn't need to say their name for her to know who I was referring to.

She shook her head. "I didn't ask too many questions. You know how your father liked to keep business dealings to himself but he assured me that he had it under control."

She was silent for a moment before continuing. "I want to be angry at him - part of me is - but he was doing this for Carina." She lifted the tissue in her hand to wipe her newly formed tears. "All we had ever wanted to do was save her."

My throat tightened as the emotion tried to force new tears out. I caressed her hand with my thumb. "You guys did all you could but when it's your time to go, there's nothing you can do about that."

"It's all part of God's plan," she said.

I wasn't sure that I believed that but I didn't tell my mother that. Now wasn't the time to question what was completely out of our control. A part of me knew that there had to be some kind of plan in play - some reason that all of this had to happen. Maybe I just needed to start believing that.

"I know things have been difficult these last few years but it's going to get better now. It has to," she murmured, saying it as if she was trying to believe it herself.

"It will."

The vibrations of the engine from the plane started to make its way through the plane as I continued. "We're lucky to still have each other. After everything that has happened, we have a chance."

She squeezed my hand and smiled. "Thank God. You're all I have left. I just wish they were here, you know?"

"Me too."

"Good afternoon passengers. This is your captain speaking. The cabin crew and I would like to welcome you on the Blueair flight 1207 to Cape Town, South Africa." The captain's voice announced over the speakers. I turned my attention back outside the window, taking one last look at the place I had called home my whole life. Nostalgia was at the forefront of my feelings right now with hope coming in at a close second. This was our chance to start over. To figure out what it is that we want out of life.

"You're going to get the life you deserve, Milena," Carina's voice *whispered in my mind.*

Maybe I was.

CHAPTER 43:

Vincenzo

I watched as the airplane took off, soaring into the air taking my heart with it. I stared outside the window, watching as it got further and further from my view. I wasn't used to allowing this many emotions in but Milena had opened me up to a world of experiences in more ways than one. But with her slipping through my fingers, I was solidifying myself once more. It was what I was used to and the only way I would get through this was through sticking to my new plan.

Take out Duarte Nazario.

The head honcho. The untouchable one. At least that's what they made us believe but after coming face to face with him, he was just as vulnerable as anyone else. I should have taken him out when I had the chance but with Milena's safety hanging in the balance, I wasn't going to take a risk.

Afonso stepped next to me, finally pulling my gaze from the, now, empty sky. I turned to him as he slipped his hands in his pockets and stared out in the distance.

"So what are you going to do now?" he asked.

"Maybe take a vacation. I think we've earned it, don't you?"

He scoffed, an amused smile forming. "You know that's not what I was referring to."

"How do you know I'm going to do anything at all?" I side-eyed him.

"I saw the way you looked at her. There's no way you're going to just let her go that easily."

"It's that obvious, huh?"

"Well, that and the fact you kissed her. You clearly didn't listen to my advice of ending whatever it is between the two of you."

"Nope, but points for trying."

He nudged me as he rolled his eyes. "You can count me in for whatever you have planned."

"No way." I shook my head and turned to him. "You're done, Afonso. Now's your time to get away from all th-"

"Enzo- " he tried to speak but I interrupted him.

"I'm serious. Look, you and I have had our differences but I'm not putting your life in danger, too."

"That's not up to you. You're my friend and if you're going to go storming the castle - metaphorically, of course - then count me in."

I opened my mouth to reject his offer but he put his hand up. "Remember when you called me a coward?" I nodded ever so slightly but it was enough to acknowledge that memory. "Turns out you were right. I was afraid - always living in the shadows while you and Carlos did all the heavy lifting…" A bitter taste spread on my tongue at the mention of Carlos and his betrayal. "I'm done doing that so why don't you just tell me what we're going to do next?"

I thought for a moment, thinking about what his words meant to me. I appreciated his sudden need to help out and his unexpected declaration of friendship. Sure, we had worked together in the past but were we *friends?* I had never really thought that but there was something comforting about knowing someone had your back. He waited patiently for my response. I rolled my eyes and sighed, finally caving.

"Fine. I'm going to go after Duarte."

His expression didn't even falter. "*Joder,* straight for the top dog, huh?"

I shrugged, turning my attention back outside the window. I wasn't delusional - I knew how idiotic and risky this was going to be but I didn't care. My mind was made up and I was focused on my new task at hand.

"I can't have them going after her," I explained. "She may be protected now, but you know as well as I do that it's not going to stay this way unless I finish him off."

Afonso lifted his hand, rubbing his chin with his finger as he processed my words. I would never ask this of anyone. I was well-aware of the danger we were charging into but Afonso wasn't taking no for an answer and I could use all the help I could get.

He clapped his hands together and turned to me. "So, where to then?"

"I have to go back to Italy for a couple days. There's a few things I need to sort out but then we're going to go back to Algarve. That's where we'll start looking for him."

We started to head towards the exit, zipping through the crowds of people. Indistinct chatter surrounded us but I couldn't focus on anything but what we were heading into. Every part of my being missed her already. We had been practically attached at the hip for all this time but now knowing that her safety was no longer under my control, I was completely unsettled.

"You tell me when you're ready and we'll go," Afonso said as we stepped into an empty elevator, heading down towards the basement parking lot.

I was surprised by his determination to my cause. It's not that I didn't think Afonso had it in him, I had just never seen him like this. I didn't know if the sudden change was due to him believing he had something to prove but he wasn't backing down. The elevator came to a sudden stop and we stepped outside, side-stepping the people trying to get on. The dim lights illuminated the parking lot as I led him to where I had parked.

"I never asked how you felt about Carlos' betrayal," Afonso said, surprising me yet again but this time with his choice of topic.

"What? Is this a therapy session now?" I unlocked the car and slipped into the driver's seat with Afonso heading to the passenger seat. The smell of her fresh scent still lingered, reminding me of the ever-present memories that I would now cling to until I saw her again. We shut the doors and brought the seatbelts over, clipping them in place. I turned the car on, the engine roaring to life.

He shrugged. "Might as well be. You and I are the only ones that worked closely with him - you more than me anyway. And then he just tossed Milena to the enemy like a piece of meat. That's got to have struck a chord."

I had forgotten how much of a *"Chatty-Cathy"* Afonso was. I pulled out of the parking spot, headed towards the exit. My hands tightened on the steering wheel as I thought back to Carlos stepping out of the warehouse. At first I felt relief at his presence until that guilty look on his face revealed there was something more going on here. I never would have expected it. He was the closest thing I had to a companion. I almost trusted him - I did trust him but he tore that down quicker than it was built. There was no room for redemption with me. He had earned that bullet in his chest.

"Carlos got what he deserved," I muttered, not wishing to comment more on the topic.

Afonso picked up on my hostility and reluctance around the conversation and didn't push further. We pulled out of the airport parking and onto the busy street, heading back in the direction I had originally come from.

"Are you going to stay with Lu?" I asked.

He nodded. "Just until you're ready."

"I'm sure she hates what you do."

"What makes you say that?"

"She told me about her boyfriend," I said. "The one who passed away."

"She doesn't talk about Martin much. I'm surprised she mentioned him to you."

I shrugged. "It just sort of came up."

He clicked the button on the window, opening it up and allowing the fresh air to surround us as we hit the highway. "She worries about me but she's surrounded by death every day with her job. Doesn't stop her from trying though - my mother, too, but this is my choice. There's nothing either of them can say to change my mind."

"Stubborn," I commented.

"You're one to talk."

I chuckled. That trait seemed to be quite obvious to everyone I came into contact with. I definitely got that from my father. He was dead-set in his ways - not in a 'closed-of' kind of way - but he stuck to his guns. Swaying him was nearly impossible which is why he was so good at his job. Once he decided he was going to take each case seriously, that's exactly what he did. I was glad I got that trait from him.

"This isn't going to be easy, you know?" Afonso said after a moment of silence.

"I know but I have to try."

"We can't do this alone."

I nodded, agreeing with his words. "That's why we need to find those who hate the Nazarios just as much as we do. I doubt we're going to be in short supply."

"A man with a plan, I see."

I didn't quite have it all figured out but I knew I would. If I kept my main goal in mind, I would make this work. I had to.

"All this for one woman?" he murmured, forming the phrase as more of a question.

"She's pretty fucking special."

EPILOGUE:

ONE YEAR LATER

Milena

I strolled along the promenade, the wind blowing my hair all around my face. I stopped and pulled it into a bun. I would never get used to the wind here but with the way it was blowing the fresh sea breeze into my airways, I couldn't be too mad. The sun was starting to set in the distance, the deep reds and oranges glistening against the water. I was calm. It took months but I was finally at a place where I knew what it felt like to feel calm again. No continued fear. No more glancing over my shoulder. No more running. We had managed to set up a life for ourselves here and I was happy to continue this under-the-radar kind of living if it meant we got to do just that - live.

My hand reached up to the necklace that has lived around my neck since I got it. I would never not feel the dull ache in my chest whenever I thought of Vincenzo De Rossi. All this time had passed and yet, my feelings had yet to falter. They never would. I clung to this desperate belief that one day, just one day, I would see him again. I hadn't heard from him since we said goodbye over a year ago. It wasn't safe. The Nazarios were well-aware of who he was and what he meant to me. If they wanted to lure me back, Vincenzo would be the perfect way to do so.

But there was nothing. No threats. No flicker of life from that side of the world. Just a few headlines that I couldn't escape every now and then of how more and more of the Nazario men had been taken out. Murdered with no answers as to who was behind these attacks. For months, no one could understand how it was possible for this organization to be taken out from the inside out. Conspiracy theories were floating around but I knew. I knew it was Vincenzo.

"I'm going to make this world safe for you again."

*H*is words repeated over and over again in my mind. I had put all my faith in him and I believed he would. Maybe one day, the world would be safe and fate would bring us back together. Or we would never see each other again. I didn't care to entertain the latter.

I stopped by a bench along the promenade that had the perfect view of the sunset. People were walking up and down, indistinct chatter surrounding me. Some were alone with their music. Others were with their families. The fitness people were getting their daily run in - some with their dogs, some without. I had immersed myself in the lifestyle here and over time, it started to feel like home. A different kind of home. One that would never quite be full like what I once knew but it would do. I was safe - we were safe and we would be happy.

Eventually.

My phone started to ring and I glanced down at my mother's name on the screen. I brought the phone to my ear. *"Olá Mãe."*

"Olá amor," *s*he said. "Are you at the promenade? You didn't let me know."

"Desculpe Mãe. I forgot but I am here. I'll be home soon."

"Okay, you know how worried I get." She sighed as I heard her increase the volume of whatever she was watching. *"Meu deus, M*ilena, have you seen the news lately?"

The news? "No, *Mãe, w*hy woul-"

She interrupted me before I could get my sentence out. "Duarte Nazario was killed."

I froze, allowing myself a moment to process what she had just said.

"Wait, are you being serious?"

*"Si, si. T*hey say he was shot at his home in Lisbon last weekend. Good riddance." She clicked her tongue. "He got what was coming to him."

It has been over a week since he was killed. but this was the first I was hearing of it. Clearly the story wasn't that big of a deal here. "Yes, *Mãe, he did.*"

We didn't need to say the words for both of us to know that our anger and resentment was well-justified in the death of my father at the hands of Duarte's men. A memory that I chose to avoid at all cost but the pain had turned to nothing more than a dull ache that I could live with. It would never truly be gone but I knew that already.

"Well, now I think we have more to celebrate than just my promotion."

I smiled. "Definitely. I'll get us a bottle of wine for the occasion."

"*Perfeita!*"

"See you soon."

We said our goodbyes and I placed my phone back into my pocket. Adjusting to life here was a challenge at first. Neither of us had many skills to offer. I never finished studying and my mother had spent most of her life as a housewife - with the occasional assistance at the hotel but that proved to be our saving grace. My mother was the first to get a job at one of the hotels here and managed to work her way up to manager in just shy of a year. I took on a few jobs here and there. Some at the hotel. Some at restaurants. All while I tried to figure out what it was that I wanted out of life. I was still grappling with that but I stopped putting pressure on myself. I'd figure it out. Eventually.

I couldn't quite put into words what I was feeling after hearing the news about Duarte. I refused to have anything disturb my peace and instead, I turned and focused on the breathtaking sunset in front of me. I appreciated more knowing that the one man I truly feared in the world was no longer something I had to be concerned about. I would never have to worry about Duarte Nazario again.

"Milena?" A deep voice said, causing me to freeze.

My name. My real name. And that voice. *It couldn't be.* I turned to face the figure that had joined me and I was unable to move. Unable to fathom what was happening.

He was here.

"Vincenzo?" My voice was barely a whisper. He smiled and obliterated my heart into a million little pieces. I didn't believe it. I reached out, needing to make sure this wasn't just in my head but when it landed on a solid arm, I knew this was really happening. My hand flew up to my mouth. It was him.

He was still just the same as I remember except he had allowed his hair to grow out a bit more, sharing a bit of curliness on the top. His dark beard was thick and well-kept and his eyes - oh God - those dark eyes were still a weakness to me.

"Hello, *tesorina.*"

I dragged myself across the bench and threw myself into his arms. Feeling every part of him. His back - yes that's his back and his neck and his hair. I couldn't believe it. I pulled away and cupped his face. "You're here. I-I can't believe this."

"I told you that I would find you."

"But how?" I shook my head. "I haven't heard from you. We haven't made contact. I don-...." My sentence trailed off as I failed to form a coherent sentence.

He chuckled. "So many questions to answer. Which one do you want to start with?" "How are you here right now?" I managed to ask.

"Well, I got on a plane in Italy and it brought me here."

I rolled my eyes and smiled. Good to see his sarcasm hasn't changed. "You know what I mean."

He turned to me, leaning his arm over the back of the bench. "I told you that I would come and find you once the world was safe for you again." He reached for my hand with his other hand. "That's what I'm here for. You're safe, Milena. You don't have to worry about the Nazarios ever again."

I tried to process everything he was telling me but I was still in shock that he was here. Sitting across from me. Holding my hand. Looking as sexy as ever.

"It was you, wasn't it?" I asked. "All those headlines about them being taken out. Duarte being killed, you were behind that?"

"It wasn't all me. Turns out there were enough people who were sick of that family to work on getting rid of them."

"I can't believe it," I gaped. "And how did you find me?"

He tapped the necklace against my chest with his finger. "That."

I glanced down at my necklace before flicking my gaze up to meet his again. "Serious answers only."

"I am being serious." He smiled and it almost sent me flying off the bench. It was beautiful. He was beautiful. He shifted closer to me and lifted his hands towards my neck, "May I?"

I was confused but I nodded, waiting to see what he would do next. He reached around my neck, his fingers gently brushing against my neck as he unclasped it, bringing it to rest against his hand. He shifted to make space on the bench and turned his hand around, slamming my locket against the bench.

"What the hell are you doing?" I asked, the confusion causing my voice to rise. He removed his hand and revealed the pieces of my locket. I leaned closer to his hand as he picked up a small black square that looked like a chip.

"Is that-"

"A tracker? Yes."

My jaw dropped slightly. "This whole time, you've had a tracker around my neck?"

He nodded. "Told you that as long as you were wearing that, I'd be able to find you."

I was shocked. All this time, he was watching me. Making sure that I was constantly on his radar. I had always felt safer when I had my necklace on and now I knew why. Vincenzo was always there. Always watching. And now, he found me because of it.

"You can come home now, Milena." He reached for my hand. "Or if you want to stay here, we can do that too but I hope you know that wherever you go, I'm going to be right beside you because our time is now."

He lifted my hand to his lips. "If you'll still have me."

"Vincenzo," was all I said before slipping my hands into his hair and brushing my lips against his. Everything came rushing back. All the time we spent together. Every lingering look. Every touch. Every kiss. Everything overwhelmed me in that one kiss and I felt as if my heart was going to explode. After all this time, it was still him. It always would be.

I pulled away from him with enough space to look up at him. "I can't believe you're here."

"I'm here, *tesorina.*" His lips pressed gently against my forehead. "And I'm not going anywhere."

My heart warmed at his words and I couldn't hold back the smile that formed. I had never felt happiness quite like this before. Everything in my life had seemed to align again and we were finally going to get the future we deserved, whatever that may be. At least we would be together.

"So, are you going to show me around?" he asked playfully. "You can be my tour guide."

I chuckled. "Sounds good but fair warning, you're not allowed to sleep with your tour guide. It's very unprofessional."

"You're fired then."

I threw my head back in laughter as he stood up, extending his hand to me. I stood up, turning to face his broad chest as I always did. I looked up and he was already smiling down at me.

"Shall we?"

"Lead the way." He nodded. "You're in charge now."

THE END

ACKNOWLEDGEMENTS:

I never know where to start with these because I don't think I will ever be able to find the words to truly express my gratitude. Thank you for reading this book. I hope that you enjoyed it as much as I enjoyed writing it. It was different from what I've done in the past but that's what I enjoyed about it. I got to delve into different kinds of characters and different tropes I hadn't explored before. I loved sharing Milena and Vincenzo's story with you.

Thank you to Traci Hohenstein for her ongoing mentorship and continued assistance with the editing of my books. I couldn't do any of this without you and I am really thankful for your support.

Thank you to Bob for always being so willing to assist me with the formatting of my books.

Thank you to my wonderful supportive beta readers. You are all so special to me and your feedback helped make this book what it was. You are so appreciated and I want you to know how much I value you.

Thank you to Miguel for constantly listening to me explaining every detail of this story before even giving you a chance to read it. Your support and enthusiasm to what I do just makes it a million times better. You're my best friend and you make everything better.

To my parents and sisters - thanks for putting up with me when all I want to do is share every little detail about how exciting all this is. I love you all so much.

To the women in my family, thank you for teaching me what it means to be a badass bitch. I have grown up surrounded by all of you and you have instilled the independent nature in me that makes me who I am today and helped influence the character of Milena.

To the #BookTok and #Bookstagram community - you have changed my life. The support I have received not only for my books but for me as an author has been surreal. You support me more than some friends and family out there and it has changed my life. You continue to push me to want to do better and to continue to share these stories with you. I feel like I have so much more to share with you guys and knowing I have you in my corner means the absolute world to me. You are everything.

Onto the next one!

Love,
Dominique x

FIND ME ON SOCIAL MEDIA:

- Join my Facebook group: Wolf's Den
  (https://www.facebook.com/groups/wolfsdenbydominiquewolf/)
- Follow me on Instagram and TikTok: @itsdominiquewolf

OTHER TITLES BY DOMINIQUE WOLF INCLUDE:

- More Than Once (Book #1 in the "More Than" series)
- More Than This (Book #2 in the "More Than" series)
- More Than Us (Book #3 in the "More Than"series)

www.ingramcontent.com/pod-product-compliance
Lightning Source LLC
Chambersburg PA
CBHW030426180626
46812CB00005B/2204